A PLACE TO CALL HOME

FAY KEENAN

Boldwood

First published in Great Britain in 2019 by Boldwood Books Ltd.

This paperback edition first published in 2020.

2

Every effort has been made to obtain the necessary permissions with reference to copyright material, both illustrative and quoted. We apologise for any omissions in this respect and will be pleased to make the appropriate acknowledgements in any future edition.

A CIP catalogue record for this book is available from the British Library.

Paperback ISBN: 978-1-83889-841-0

Ebook ISBN: 978-1-83889-209-8

Kindle ISBN: 978-1-83889-208-1

Audio CD ISBN: 978-1-83889-223-4

Digital audio download ISBN: 978-1-83889-206-7

Large Print ISBN: 978-1-83889-419-1

Boldwood Books Ltd.

23 Bowerdean Street, London, SW6 3TN

www.boldwoodbooks.com

To the Mums' Hotline Bling Ring

1

'White sage is all very well,' Holly Renton reflected, 'but the ashes are a bugger to get out of the carpet.' Earlier that morning, before the shop had opened, Holly had carried out a ritual called smudging, which was meant to purify the energy in a building, promote positivity and remove negative energies. Picking up the dustpan and brush, she emptied the pungent remains of the dried herb bundle she'd ignited and then wafted around the windows and doors of the shop into the bin.

'I know you recommend this all the time for other people's houses, but why are you so bloody obsessed with doing it in the shop?' Rachel, Holly's sister, glanced down at where Holly was still brushing the rug under the mullioned front window of ComIncense, the shop specialising in herbal remedies and well-being aids that Holly ran in the sleepy but nonetheless New Age small town of Willowbury and smiled. Just beyond the shop's counter, the door that led to Holly's small back yard was open and Harry, Rachel's three-year-old son and Holly's nephew, was playing happily with a set of wooden animal-shaped blocks in their own lorry, which had come from a box of assorted toys that Holly kept specifically for the younger customers. Holly didn't believe, unlike some of her business-owning neighbours, that children should be banned from places like hers, and since the early-spring weather was warm and pleasant, Harry had trundled out into the sunlight to play.

'You've got to refresh places from time to time,' Holly replied. 'Especially when there's been a lot of negative energy about, and since all of the scandal with Hugo Fitzgerald, I really felt like this place needed a spiritual cleanse!'

'You can say that again,' Rachel reached under the wooden apothecary's dresser that displayed countless jars and pots of dried herbs and flowers, all purporting to be of some spiritual or physical benefit, to retrieve one of the toy llamas that Harry had thrown under it. 'What a way to go...'

'Oh, I don't know,' Holly replied, still sweeping. 'At least, having had a massive coronary, he wouldn't have known much about it.'

'But what a waste of a good plate of scones and jam!' Rachel grinned. 'Mum told me that his constituency agent found him face down in them at his desk.'

'I wouldn't have fancied digging him out of them,' Holly said. 'But from the size of him, the heart attack was an accident waiting to happen. And gossip has it, he had his finger in a lot of pies, not just the odd plate of scones.'

'Oh, you know how the rumour mill goes into overdrive when something like this happens.' Rachel, who had more of a tendency to see the good in people than her sister did, dismissed Holly's comments with a wave of her hand. 'I mean, I'm not saying he wasn't a prat, but nothing was ever proven about his financial misdemeanours. Although, I have to admit, since he couldn't have given a stuff about Harry's condition, and getting access to these new drugs, I'm hoping the new guy will be more receptive to the cause.'

'It's still bloody unfair that he gets to swan in here and take the seat after only the quietest by-election,' Holly grumbled as she replaced the dustpan and brush on the shelf behind the counter. 'I mean, the guy's only a year older than me and he's been parachuted into one of the safest seats in the country. Even if we have a change of government, he's unlikely ever to lose his seat. What if he's just as crap as Fitzgerald and couldn't care less about us here in his constituency? We're stuck with him until he chooses to retire.'

'Give him a chance,' Rachel said reasonably. 'He might be good for this place.'

'Have you made an appointment to see him yet?' Holly asked, glancing down to where Harry was now building a tower of exotic wooden animals that was getting more and more precarious the higher it got.

From the outside, Harry looked like any other energetic three-year-old, but on the inside, it was a different story. Weeks after he'd been born, Rachel had been launched into a perpetually revolving carousel of physiotherapy, medications and experimental trials in an attempt to alleviate the chronic condition, cystic fibrosis, that would, in all likelihood, limit Harry's life. The latest medication, which might make a huge difference to Harry's life expectancy, was currently being held up because the government was still negotiating with the pharmaceutical company involved over a reasonable price to supply it to the National Health Service. How it was possible to put a cost on a life such as Harry's was a source of increasing frustration and heartbreak for Rachel and the family.

'Not yet,' Rachel sighed. 'If Hugo Fitzgerald couldn't be arsed to do anything other than toe the party line, then why should this new guy be any better? Especially if he is a total rookie. I doubt he'll stick his neck out for Harry.'

Noticing Rachel was, unusually for her, close to tears, Holly hurried around from behind the counter and gave her sister a hug. 'Don't let it get you down,' she murmured. 'I'll always be right there with you, campaigning to get this little munchkin the treatment he deserves.'

'I know,' Rachel replied, giving Holly a shaky smile. 'I'm fine, really. It's just when he has a bad day, it reminds me of the challenges he's facing, which will only get worse as he gets older. And knowing that the new medications could potentially make those challenges so much easier to face...'

'We'll get there,' Holly said. 'I'll be with you every step of the way, like I always have been. And I still think it's worth a punt with this new guy, you never know.'

'I'll try and get in to see him over the summer,' Rachel replied, breaking the embrace from her sister and grabbing the last of the wooden animals to add to Harry's tower of jungle wildlife. 'Can I make a drink?'

'Of course,' Holly said. 'I've got some organic fair-trade matcha tea in the kitchen.'

'Is that the super-energising stuff?' Rachel asked. 'After being up with Harry last night, I could certainly do with a lift.'

'Honestly, it'll keep you going until midnight!' Holly said. 'Go on... you know you want to.'

'All right,' Rachel replied. 'But if I end up buzzing around Willowbury like a wasp for the rest of the day, I'm blaming you.'

'Fair enough. And make me a cup, too,' Holly called as Rachel disappeared up the stairs to Holly's flat above the shop. Popping the dustpan and brush behind the counter again, she continued the conversation, since Rachel had left the door to the flat open. 'Perhaps I should give this new guy the benefit of the doubt,' she said, adjusting the labels on the jars of dried herbs and plants on the dresser so they all pointed uniformly outwards. 'After all, new blood could be a good thing.'

'Perhaps we should be fair and reserve judgement until he's been in the job a few months,' Rachel said over the bubble of the kettle. 'You never know, he could be just the tonic this place needs, politically.'

'You always try to look on the bright side, don't you?'

Holly was preoccupied for a moment with the Bluetooth speaker that usually piped relaxing, locally composed and produced music through the shop during business hours. The thing was a touch temperamental, but she'd just managed to reconnect it to her phone. Scrolling through her Spotify playlists, she thought she'd better try it out with something a little more lively, so she selected one of her current favourite film soundtracks, an all-singing, all-dancing number that was sure to blast out any gremlins from the Bluetooth connection. As the singer's voice boomed through the shop, Rachel's response to her somewhat rhetorical question was lost in the pleasant din of the soundtrack.

Determined to stop talking about a subject that was clearly getting more under her skin than she'd anticipated, Holly raised her voice above the music, calling up the stairs to her sister, and, unable to help herself, lifting her arms to sway to the beat of the song. 'Well, he'll have to do a whole lot more for this constituency than Fingers-in-the-till Fitzgerald did to get my vote. And, to be honest, I don't really hold out much hope for some career politician who's just been parachuted in, do you?'

Holly, caught in the rhythm of the song, completely failed to notice the appearance of a figure at her open shop door, who paused, motionless, unsure now of what his approach should be. To be fair, though, even if she had been aware, she probably wouldn't have been too concerned; Holly wasn't one to worry too much about what people thought. Having lived the life she had, and owning the business that she did, public opinion was the least of her worries. What she didn't realise, though, was that the encounter with this particular customer would change her life forever.

_____

The voice, clear as a bell, cut over the top of the cheesy tunes of _The Greatest Showman_ as Charlie Thorpe walked in through the open door of ComIncense. Although somewhat stung by the stridency in the speaker's voice, he reflected, perhaps he shouldn't have been surprised. Surveying the shop floor, he'd been assailed by hanging crystals, his nostrils filled with the scent of burning herbs, his eyes assaulted by the myriad rainbow-coloured New Age books on the shelves, and his mind overwhelmed by the shelves of apothecary jars of weird-looking dried plants, all labelled, he admitted grudgingly, with exquisitely handwritten names. He wondered how many of them were strictly legal, despite what the labels said.

'Er, Miss Renton?' he asked, closing the shop door behind him, which elicited an alarming jangle from the bells tied to the top of it.

The dancing figure froze with her arms above her head; slim arms, Charlie noticed, with the hint of a tattoo peeking out from one shoulder, revealed by her vest top. Charlie felt even more like an intruder on some strange planet. He'd known Willowbury was the home of all things alternative when he applied to stand as the replacement Member of Parliament, but the last time he'd been inside this shop, admittedly some years before, and long before he'd considered becoming an MP, this place had been a toyshop. He'd bought a cuddly toy dog for his newborn nephew, which the baby had promptly vomited on. The only touch of normality, to his eyes, was the sight of an adorable, curly-haired toddler sitting on the floor by the open back door, playing with a selection of exotic wooden animals.

As the dancer turned around, Charlie noticed her clear-blue eyes, the pale skin and the long, messily tied-back auburn hair, tendrils escaping to soften the high cheekbones and the slightly pointed nose. A large, generous mouth, probably captivating when it smiled fully, was curled up slightly at the edges as she looked him briefly up and down.

'It's Holly,' the woman replied, seemingly not embarrassed in the slightest by the fact she'd been sprung swaying to some highly suspect soundtrack during business hours, not to mention slagging off the local MP to his face. Well, almost. Not that she knew that, of course. 'And you are?' She glanced down to her phone and slid the volume control down a notch or three, to a more sociable level, before putting it back on the shop counter.

'Charlie Thorpe.' He extended a hand and tried not to look too closely at the one she offered in return, which appeared to have traces of nicotine staining on the fingertips. 'I'm just doing a quick tour of the local, er, businesses to introduce myself.'

'Why? Are you the new manager of the pub?' Holly asked, having clocked his looking-but-not-looking glance at her fingertips and the way he dropped his hand immediately after he'd shaken hers. She was surprised he didn't wipe his hand on his jeans, he seemed so put off. She thought about explaining that she'd been hand-dyeing some fabric out the back in a strong turmeric solution but didn't bother. He probably wouldn't have got it anyway; from the looks of his clothes, he was more of a designer guy. The crisp white shirt, open at the neck and the dark blue, slim but not skinny jeans with a tan belt looked suspiciously expensive. As did the boots he was wearing. Somehow, she doubted that they were vegan leather...

'Not exactly,' Charlie smiled what he hoped was a winning smile. 'I'm the new Member of Parliament for the area.'

Charlie felt a stab of satisfaction as Holly's cheeks flushed slightly, clashing with her hair. Clearly she hadn't expected to be overheard in her vocal criticisms of him and his new job.

'So, you're the one taking over from Fingers-in-the-till Fitzgerald, are you? Good luck with that.'

'Thanks,' Charlie said gruffly. He wondered if he should leap to the defence of his predecessor but conceded that actually Holly was probably right about the fiddling, and not just with cash, but also with interns, if local gossip was to be believed, so he decided not to. 'It's going to take a while to get my bearings, so I wanted to come and say hello while Parliament's in recess for the Easter holiday. Since I'm new to the area, I want to make the most of the time to settle in.' Among his plans was a visit to every local business in his constituency, which included several cider farms, as well as quite a few smaller concerns like Holly's shop. While he was looking forward to sampling some of the produce at the cider farm if he got the chance, he wasn't entirely sure if anything from ComIncense really took his fancy.

'Oh, I see,' said Holly. 'Doing the rounds, checking out your patch, then?'

'So how long have you had the shop?' Charlie asked, ignoring the veiled jibe. *Press the flesh, Charlie... form a rapport with everyone you can. You never know when you might need their support.*

'About four years,' Holly replied. 'I was left some money by my grandfather, and after wondering what on earth to do with it other than blowing it on fast cars and drugs, I decided to invest in this place.' She grinned. 'I'm joking about the drugs, by the way.'

Charlie found himself smiling back, and trying not to glance again at the weird dried herbs and plants that had caught his attention as he'd walked in. 'I'm glad to hear it.' He glanced around the shop. 'So, what are your, er, best-selling items?'

'Oh, you know,' Holly replied. 'Everyone who moves house wants a stash of white sage to burn to chase away the bad vibes, and I get a lot of tourists in who love the fact we're in the shadow of Willowbury Hill here, which, I'm sure you know, is a hugely important spiritual and archaeological site.' She pulled an odd-looking doll off the shelf behind her. 'And people fed up with their jobs tend to like these.' She pressed it into his hands.

Charlie looked alarmed, until he took a closer look and found it was a jokey representation of a voodoo doll, split into sections marked with things like 'talked over me at the meeting', 'stole my ideas' and 'denied me a pay rise'. He laughed gamely. 'I can see why they're popular. Perhaps I'll buy a few to take back to the House!'

'Have this one on the house,' Holly said. 'Or would that constitute a bribe?'

'I think I can put it on the declaration of members' interests,' Charlie said.

There was a barely perceptible pause between them.

Charlie cleared his throat. 'Well, thank you for this,' he tucked the doll into his pocket. 'And it was nice to meet you. As a local business owner, I hope we'll be able to discuss your concerns in more detail.'

'Oh, you can save me the political spiel,' Holly's eyes sparkled. 'I'm afraid you shouldn't count on my vote. I'm rather more in the Green Party camp these days.'

Charlie grinned at her, oddly charmed by her forthrightness.

'Then I hope between now and the next general election, I might be able to change your mind!'

Holly smiled back. 'Been there, done that, did some student conferences!' she countered. 'I found I wasn't too keen on the company, after a while.'

Charlie felt a sudden rush of recognition at her words. Now that she'd dropped her guard, and he'd spent a little time talking to her, he couldn't help thinking that she looked like someone he'd known a long time ago... for one night only. But it couldn't be her. The girl he knew had been sensibly dressed in an on-the-knee, neutral suit; *party colours and party line,* he thought wryly. Nineteen years old, with subtle lipstick and strawberry-blonde hair cut in a sensible bob. But then, he supposed, it was a decade and a half ago. Anything more adventurous would have been unexpected, especially in that context. He was sure, looking back on it, that his sartorial choices would have been just as suspect.

'I can't say I blame you,' Charlie replied gamely, trying to shrug off the sense of déjà vu that Holly had suddenly evoked. 'I intend to spend as much time in the constituency as I can. Westminster can be a bit of a bubble, if you know what I mean.'

'I suppose that's what you all say when you get appointed,' Holly said, with a slight edge to her voice. 'I bet even Hugo Fitzgerald was an idealist twenty-five years ago. Shame he never really got anything done around here!'

'We're not all lazy fat cats, you know,' Charlie replied, a little more sharply than he'd intended. 'Some of us go into politics for the right reasons.'

'I'm sure,' Holly replied. 'But you'll forgive me if I say time will tell on that.'

'I hope I'll be able to show you,' Charlie said. There was a pause, which he took as his cue to leave. 'Take care, Holly.'

'You too,' Holly said brightly, gesturing to the door. 'I look forward to you proving me otherwise.'

Charlie, feeling more unsettled with the encounter than he had so far with any of the other shop owners, walked to the door. He suspected that he'd have a long way to go to demonstrate his worth as an MP to Holly; strangely, however, he found himself wanting to do so, if only to prove her wrong.

3

'Who was that?' Rachel came carefully down the steep stairs from Holly's flat to the shop floor carrying two mugs and a teapot on a wooden tray. 'Looked fit from behind, whoever he was.'

Holly shook her head. 'You should get out more.' Taking the mug from the tray once Rachel had poured some tea into it, she sipped the strong, re-energising tea.

'So, who was it?'

Holly felt her cheeks warm a little as she recalled the slightly awkward encounter. 'That was Charlie Thorpe, the new MP for Willowbury and Stavenham.'

'Wow, really? I hope he didn't hear you slagging him off,' Rachel grinned. 'I mean, that would have been... awkward.' She paused, catching sight of her sister's expression. 'He heard you, didn't he?'

Holly grinned. 'From the way he couldn't wait to get out of here, I assume he did!' She took another gulp of her tea. 'I don't care. He needs to know that some of us aren't just going to give him the easy ride that Hugo Fitzgerald had. He's going to have to work to represent us.'

'Oh, hark at you!' Rachel teased. 'Sounds like he's bringing out your militant side already. Not that it needs any encouragement, of course.' Holly had taken part in several high-profile Green Party demonstrations over the years, and was known as a bit of a rabble-rouser, as well as a keen supporter of local Green initiatives. She'd organised several litter picks and recycling runs in the town since taking on the shop and was known to wince every time she saw a discarded plastic bag or bottle blowing in the breeze. An ethical eater, her love of a good bacon sandwich meant she couldn't quite become fully vegetarian, but she tried to source her food as locally and organically as possible. Outside, in the small courtyard behind the shop, she had a raised bed that was packed full of aromatics and herbs, which she cooked fresh when she could and dried and stored in jars for the winter months.

'I just don't like seeing someone getting something for nothing,' Holly muttered.

'What, you mean like we did?' Rachel reminded Holly gently. They'd been the joint beneficiaries of their paternal grandfather's will; the money had been in trust until they both reached adulthood. While their father had initially raised an eyebrow about Holly's business venture, he couldn't dispute the fact that the shop made money, however improbably, and he was justifiably proud of the path she'd taken. Rachel, the more conventional sister, had put most of hers into buying a home for herself and Harry after her divorce.

'That was different,' Holly said. 'Grandfather made a weird decision, but one we've really tried to make the best of. After all, I don't think you'll find Mum and Dad complaining that we're not running to them every five seconds for money!'

'Absolutely,' Rachel agreed. 'Although, for all of my looking on the bright side, as you call it, there's not enough money in the world to get Harry new lungs, or in the trust to fund the drugs he needs privately.' She shook her head.

'We'll get there,' Holly said softly, looking over at where Harry was now playing. 'The government and the drug companies will see sense eventually, the way the issue keeps being highlighted by campaigners and the media. You have to keep believing it, sis.'

'I know.' Rachel drank the rest of her tea. 'I've got to go. Harry's got a check-up at the hospital. We're going to make an afternoon of it and grab an early dinner in Bristol if it all runs to time.' Gesturing to Harry, she took the toddler's hand and, after kissing her sister goodbye, she headed out of the door of the shop.

Holly's heart ached as they left. She wished there was something else she could do, but even if she sold the shop and the two sisters pooled their resources, it still wouldn't be enough. Since Rachel had got divorced a couple of years ago, the main responsibility for caring for Harry had become hers alone, with her ex-husband having moved to Singapore for his career. Rachel and Harry were financially provided for well enough by him, but that wasn't the same as having someone to share the ups and downs of having a child with a serious illness day to day. Thus, the two sisters had grown closer, to the extent that they saw each other most days now they both lived in Willowbury.

Reluctantly, Holly's thoughts wandered back to the visitor she'd just had; perhaps Charlie Thorpe would be able to help, after all. Then again, after he'd heard her opinion about him jumping into his dead colleague's seat, she wondered if he'd be willing to listen to her anyway.

Sighing, she changed the background music and settled in for an afternoon of retail. She'd recently taken a massage course, which she was considering offering to customers, but she hadn't yet been brave enough to advertise it in the shop. Perhaps it was time to take the plunge.

Taking a deep breath, she logged into ComIncense's website and created a new page, titled 'Holistic Massage Therapy' and filled out a few details. Printing out a copy to put in the window of the shop, she wondered if anyone in Willowbury would let her loose on their back, shoulders or even feet. She could think of a few people who she wouldn't want to touch with a barge-pole, and it would be just her luck to be lumbered with some of Willowbury's less savoury residents as clients. But who knew, perhaps some would give it a go.

As she was finishing the page, she couldn't help wondering what Charlie Thorpe would look like with his shirt off on her massage table but quickly squashed that idea; after the way he'd reacted to her and her shop, she couldn't imagine him crossing the threshold anytime soon.

4

Charlie had been under no illusions that he was going to have a tricky time when he took on the Willowbury and Stavenham parliamentary seat. It wasn't just that Hugo Fitzgerald had been cordially loathed by his constituents (although enough of them had kept voting him in, year after year, to give him a very comfortable majority), but also, in comparison, he'd be seen initially as nothing more than a wet-behind-the-ears career politician. He was resigned to the fact that it would take at least five years to gain their trust – a Westminster parliamentary term, in fact – and probably twenty before he was regarded as a local in this most Somerset of Somerset villages. Yet again, he wondered why he'd said yes. He was a Yorkshireman by birth, and felt like a fish out of water down in the West Country, even though he'd often visited when he'd had a girlfriend who lived in the area. The Mendip Hills were no substitute for the York-shire Moors, he felt; too smooth, too green, not angular enough for his tastes.

Exiting Holly Renton's ridiculously named shop, still smarting from her casual dismissal of his effectiveness, or lack thereof, he'd wandered back up Willowbury High Street, noticing, properly, for the first time, just what kind of stock in trade this place had. When he'd been offered the seat after Hugo's death, he'd imagined Willowbury to be a kind of tea shops and gourmet ploughman's' lunches patch; wealthy, middle-class and churchgoing constituents, whose main concerns were where the new motorway junction was going to be built and whose view was going to be ruined by the next new housing development.

While Willowbury wasn't exactly inner-city Leeds, where he'd cut his teeth campaigning as a candidate in a seat that hadn't been held by his party in nearly forty years, it wasn't what he'd been expecting either. For a start, the preponderance of what might be called New Age establishments (although he'd been warned that this was not a moniker that the traders themselves much cared for) was rather more akin to Totnes, the place in Devon where he'd spent holidays as a child.

There was no getting away from it, he thought as he wandered back up the rather steep High Street. Everywhere you looked in Willowbury was a crystal, a mural or a shop selling spiritual how-to guides. And this was one of the major towns in his constituency. While not himself a religious man, Charlie had grown up as a kind of fair-weather Christian; church on Christmas and Easter Days, a carol service every year and a Remembrance Parade as a Scout. This kind of earth-based, alternative spirituality took some getting used to. And get used to it, he must, he supposed. He looked down at the toy voodoo doll Holly had given him and grimaced.

'Morning, m'lord!' A broad, rather mocking voice, rich with the vowels of the county, broke into his thoughts. 'And how are you on this very fine day?'

Charlie's head snapped up and he came face to face with Miles Fairbrother, who considered himself a local wit, as well as the owner of the town's bakery.

'Charlie'll do fine,' Charlie replied, smiling gamely at the master baker. 'I'm not in the House of Lords just yet.'

'Only a matter of time, I'm sure,' Miles winked.

'So, how's business, Miles?' Charlie asked, keen to practise his small talk. *Press the flesh, Charlie, no matter how unattractive or annoying it is.*

'Not bad, not bad,' Miles said. ''Course, I'm not sellin' quite so many scones as I used to, given what happened to your predecessor, but at least the gluten-free bread's starting to shift. That's a fad that seems to be sticking.'

'Glad to hear it,' Charlie replied. 'I must pop in and try some when I'm a bit more settled in.' He was slightly surprised at how easily the platitudes could come when talking to someone like Miles. Privately, he thought that he'd rather get gluten-free bread from anyone other than Miles, even if he was a local businessman.

'On the house for the local MP,' Miles said. 'At least, your first one will be. Never know when I might need a favour.'

Charlie suppressed a grimace. He had no idea what Hugo's dealings with the baker had been, but instinctively he knew he probably shouldn't go too far to find out. 'That's very kind of you, Miles, but I like to support the businesses in my constituency.'

Miles held up a hand. 'I'm joking, of course. Me, personally, I'm glad you've taken over, but there are some round here who'll be harder to please.'

'I think I've already encountered one of them,' Charlie said, glancing unthinkingly back towards ComIncense.

'Oh, don't you worry about *her,*' Miles said. 'She and her sister are always on their high horse about something. Doesn't know how good she's got it, living here, with that shop smack in the middle of the High Street.'

Charlie, kicking himself mentally for speaking carelessly to Miles, of all people, smiled. 'Oh, it was nothing like that, honestly. Anyway, I'd best get on. It was nice to see you, Miles.'

'Nice to see you too, m'lord,' Miles winked again and strode off back to the bakery, which was at the bottom of the High Street. The Fairbrothers had been the town bakers for five generations, and Charlie already knew that Miles held sway on the town council and the Chamber of Commerce. He was also a significant donor to Charlie's local party funds. Much as he'd instinctively disliked the man, he was one that he definitely had to keep on side if he was to get anywhere politically.

Looking at his watch, Charlie cursed as he realised he was going to be late for the first of several appointments at his constituency office. He was due to start at twelve, and he'd not read through the briefing notes his ever-efficient agent had emailed him the night before. Pulling out his phone, he scrolled through his appointments list and, with a stab of dismay, concluded he was going to be holed up in the office until well after six o'clock that evening. The life of a rural MP, he thought, was not exactly a sleepy one. Resolving to grab a quick takeaway coffee from the Costa machine at the newsagents, he hurried towards his office.

As he let himself back in through the door, he couldn't help reflecting once again on his meeting with Holly Renton in her shop. Something was niggling at him; something about her he just couldn't place. He couldn't help thinking he'd met her somewhere before.

Holly closed the shop after a relatively successful day's trading and headed up the stairs to the flat she lived in above the shop. Having bought the freehold of the building with her inheritance, she had taken time to make both the shop and her home exactly as she wanted them to be, and she even had the benefit of a small, enclosed garden at the back of the property, where she would sit out sometimes, and, in good weather, lead the odd meditation or yoga session. A haven of peace and serenity, the garden was footed by a large, ancient horse chestnut tree, which Holly occasionally called in the local tree surgeon to prune, and under whose boughs she could conduct her meditations and sit and read in the warmer months.

Tonight, though, she needed to get inside and feed the mewing ball of ginger fur that was weaving in and out of her ankles on the way up the stairs.

'Arthur!' She chided as the cat skittered in front of her again. 'If I break my neck on these steps, you'll only have me to eat, and I'm not sure you'll enjoy that.'

Arthur turned at the sound of her voice, gave her a withering look and then bounded ahead to the kitchen, to where his bowls resided in the corner. Giving a hungry yowl, he sprung up on his hind legs and dug his claws playfully into the back of Holly's knees as she pulled down the cat food from the cupboard.

'Is it any wonder I can't wear short skirts, with you lacerating my legs at every opportunity?' Holly reached down and gave the cat a playful tap on the nose. She filled his bowl with food and then, mission accomplished, Arthur turned his back and began to devour his dinner.

Turning her mind to her encounter with Charlie Thorpe as she prepared her own food, Holly was irritated to feel another blush creeping up her cheeks. It hadn't exactly been her finest hour, she conceded, although she'd never been one to hide her true feelings. Her father always said that she and Rachel would have made the perfect child if combined; Rachel was diplomatic, and perhaps a little *too* self-effacing, whereas Holly spoke her mind at every available opportunity, and had done since she was knee high to a grasshopper. Her mouth had got her into hot water more than once in her youth, and while she'd learned to think before she spoke most of the time these days, she was still prone to being more honest than was good for her when she was rattled or irritated.

And Charlie Thorpe had rattled her before she'd even met him. Perhaps it had been a little unfair to write him off before he'd had the chance to settle into Willowbury, but she trusted her gut, and her gut was telling her that having a new MP wouldn't make a scrap of difference to her, or, more importantly, to Harry.

But what if she was wrong? What if Charlie was being sincere in his desire to make a positive difference in Willowbury? Or was is possible that Holly was just being distracted by the fact he was rather good-looking, in that classic tall, dark and handsome kind of way.

'Stop it,' Holly said.

Arthur looked up from his bowl, where he was making short work of his Whiskas.

'Not you, gorgeous,' Holly added hastily.

The cat gave her another look and got back to his food.

Holly sighed as she grabbed the jar of linguine from the back of her kitchen counter and slapped some into her pasta pan. There was no point in continuing to think about Charlie Thorpe. She'd probably never cross paths with him again. After all, she couldn't remember Hugo Fitzgerald ever bothering to visit her shop when he'd been alive, and he'd been the MP for over twenty years. Why should Charlie be any different? Willowbury and Stavenham was a cushy number, and all he really had to do was show his face a bit and kiss a few babies and he'd be guaranteed the seat until he retired.

A few minutes later, having sautéed the contents of her vegetable drawer and thrown in a few of the herbs she'd gathered fresh from the raised bed in her garden, Holly grated some of the Cheddar Gorge Cheese Company's finest mature Cheddar over her dinner and settled down on the balcony overlooking her garden, where she'd placed a small bistro table and two chairs: one for her, she'd joked to Rachel when she'd bought it, and one for Arthur. Now she was over thirty, she wondered how much of a joke that actually was, these days. Was she doomed to grow older and more eccentric, until she became the tie-dyed kaftan-wearing, wild-haired stereotype of a Willowbury alternative-health business owner? Just her and Arthur, for ever more?

As if he could read her thoughts, having demolished his own food, Arthur came padding out to the balcony and sprang up onto the other bistro chair, settling down on the cushion to take in the early-evening sun's rays.

While not a compulsive phone checker, Holly had her mobile at the side of her dinner plate to hear from Rachel about Harry's afternoon check-up. On cue, her phone pinged. Heart thumping, Holly swiped the screen, hoping that the news from the hospital would be good. Harry seemed to be having a settled few months and was remarkably stoical about the huge amount of medications he had to take every day, but she still breathed a sigh of relief when she read Rachel's update. Harry's lung function had been as expected, and his meds hadn't been increased, so that was a definite win. Texting back a quick reply, Holly relaxed into her chair and finished her dinner. If nothing else, Harry's condition had taught her to take each day and count each blessing as they came. Who knew what tomorrow, or the next day, might bring?

While she had her phone open, Holly decided to check to see if anyone had signed up for a massage, now that the online booking had gone live on ComIncense's website. Since she'd have to offer the massages after ComIncense had closed for business, given that most of the time she was on her own at work, she didn't intend to take more than one or two bookings a week. Tapping through to the admin pages on her site, she smiled to see that there had been a fair bit of interest. But, just as quickly, her heart sank when she saw the name of the person who'd made the first booking. Of all the people she wouldn't have wanted to get her hands on, *she* had to be the worst. *Oh well,* Holly thought, *at least I'll have the chance to practise on her, and she'll certainly tell me if I'm no good.*

Swiping the screen to confirm the booking for tomorrow and send an automatic confirmation email, Holly stood up again and took her plate back through to the kitchen. She'd better spend the evening mugging up on some of the techniques she'd learned on her massage course, to make sure she did the best job she could on her first paying client. What a shame, though, that it had to be Rachel's irritating next-door neighbour, Harriet Meadows. With more bark than a Jack Russell, the woman barely kept quiet long enough to relax and enjoy anything, let alone a massage.

If nothing else, having her on the table might help Rachel's stress levels a little, since Harriet had a tendency to complain about everything, from the height of the fence in Rachel's back garden to the sound of Harry playing out with his little friends in the summer.

Holly grinned to herself as she put her mind to the kind of massage that would best suit Harriet the Harridan and found she was quite looking forward to trying out some of her firmer techniques.

6

At around eleven o'clock the next day, Charlie decided he'd had
enough of unpacking, both in his new home, which was a
charming town house a stone's throw from the High Street, and
in his new office, which he'd virtually had to gut to make it more
to his tastes. When he'd walked into the door of what had been
Hugo Fitzgerald's erstwhile office, he'd imagined, for one
terrible moment, that he'd be confronted with the corpse of the
MP, still face down in the scones. Cursing himself for his child-
ishness, he'd been only slightly less horrified when he'd realised
the MP and his constituency agent, who'd retired when his boss
had died, hadn't exactly been experts at filing. He'd spent the
next eight hours sorting out the box files and papers on subjects
as diverse as the much-disputed Willowbury bypass (thirty-five
years at least in the discussion) and a complaint from a resident
of the High Street that one of the shop owners was sunbathing
nude on the flat roof of their establishment during their lunch
hour. Given Willowbury's long tradition of embracing all things
alternative in terms of lifestyle, religion, spirituality and music,
Charlie wasn't as surprised by this complaint as he could have
been.

When nine-tenths of the paperwork had gone the way of his brand new office shredder, and he'd relocated the rest into relabelled box files, he decided it was time for a break before his constituency agent came in for a meeting. Assured by the chairman of his local branch of the party when he gained the seat that Tom Fielding would be an excellent candidate to fill the role of party liaison and constituency agent, especially for a rookie MP, Charlie hoped that Tom would be able to brief him on what the really important issues were in Willowbury and Stavenham. He'd met Tom briefly after he'd moved in and had already established a good working relationship with the man, who, being in his late fifties, was the kind of authority figure it was useful to have on your team.

Charlie could have made a coffee from the jar of instant he'd found stashed away in the kitchen area of the office, but when he'd opened the lid, a moth had flown out, so he decided to get some fresh air before his morning meeting with Tom and head over to one of the cafes on the High Street he'd spotted when he'd dropped in on ComIncense. Locking the door, he pocketed the key and headed up the road.

As he wandered back along the row of the weird, wonderful and decidedly wacky shops that lined Willowbury High Street, the variety made him smile, as it did every time he walked this way. There was a bookshop called Vale Volumes most of whose titles in the window seemed to focus on either spiritual healing or the search for King Arthur; a musical instrument shop, which, from the looks of it, didn't stock anything that was instantly recognisable to Charlie as anything that might be found in an orchestra; a shop front full of crystals of various sizes all glinting in the sunshine; and an artisan handmade candle shop with wax creations of all kinds. Added to that, was a brightly painted shop front emblazoned with 'Fae Floristry' and bedecked with all kinds of blooms, local and more exotic.

Charlie's back stiffened as he found his footsteps drawing

closer to ComIncense Health and Well-being, where he'd encountered Holly Renton yesterday. A prickle of embarrassment and irritation prodded at the back of his neck as he recalled her casual dismissal of him – both before she'd been aware of his presence in the shop and, even if she had blushed a bit, after. He wasn't sure what was worse, really: indifference to politics or firm opinions, forcefully held. He was sure he'd come across plenty of both in this new job.

Drawing level with the door of ComIncense, he found himself pausing to look at the window display. A mixture of tall altar candles, sparkling crystals of all colours and hues that caught the light and the odd sprig of dried herbs, it looked exotic and inviting, and Charlie had to admit that Holly had an eye for the enticing. If he had the slightest clue what any of the items in her shop window actually did, he was sure he'd be sold on them. As it was, he couldn't imagine having use for any of them in his life, even if the comedy voodoo doll was funny.

Suddenly aware he might be seen to be loitering, and definitely not wanting to be caught, Charlie quickened his pace again, but not before he caught sight of Holly again, with her back to the window, hair in the same unruly updo that was escaping in tendrils down her shoulder blades almost to her waist, atop a ladder and pulling down one of the large apothecary's jars that resided behind the counter in a tall dresser. She had the kind of hair he longed to touch, and he was astonished to feel that prickle of irritation he'd felt turning to something else altogether as he allowed himself another moment to watch her. There was something so familiar about the curve of her shoulders, the gentle sweep of that long back into her waist... why did he feel as though he'd encountered her before?

Shaking his head, he tore his eyes back to the High Street, in search of the coffee shop he knew was up the top of the town somewhere.

Picking up his pace, he was tickled to find, on entering

Willowbury's number-one coffee establishment (as dictated by the sign in the window, at least), that even the hot beverages in this place had a twist of the alternative about them. Among the Americanos, lattes and flat whites that could be found anywhere was a smattering of exotic twists from all around the world, from Turkish to Egyptian to Vietnamese blends and varieties. Charlie wondered wryly whether air miles were factored into the costs.

'Morning, sir!' A cheery voice greeted him as he walked up to the counter. The owner of the voice, a man who Charlie judged to be in his late thirties, and from his name badge was called Jack, gestured to the menu behind him. 'What can I get you?'

Charlie glanced up at the menu boards and then back at the barista. 'Just a flat white, thanks.'

'We've got a promotion on the fair-trade South-west Guatemalan beans this week if you'd like to give them a go,' Jack responded. 'A hint of chocolate and almond. Goes down beautifully with one of our amaretto croissants, if you'd like one.'

'Sounds great, thank you,' Charlie replied.

Five minutes later he was chowing down on a flaky, amaretto-soaked croissant and trying to identify the alleged flavour notes in the coffee. He'd taken a seat by the window, so he could gaze out at the High Street, which was showing more signs of life now than when he'd headed to his office earlier that morning.

Even on a workaday Tuesday, he was surprised to see the more unusual inhabitants of Willowbury out in force. He was jolted to see a woman in nun's robes standing by a cool box of what appeared to be wrapped sandwiches, which had a sign propped against it reading 'Free lunch for the homeless'. There were one or two people taking advantage of this gentle charity and being handed a sandwich and a bottle of water with a calm and gentle smile by the nun. He had no idea that Willowbury had an issue with the homeless, although, he figured, perhaps with its proximity to both the Strawberry Line cycle track and the more major towns of Wells and Taunton, both tourist traps, it became more of a magnet during the summer months. He made a note on his phone to add that to his list of enquiries for Tom Fielding when they met later on. Some members of his party were positively medieval when it came to their attitudes to the homeless; Charlie wasn't one of them. He believed in supporting people until they no longer needed to be supported, and if homelessness was an issue here, he needed to know about it.

'How are you settling in?' The barista's voice broke into Charlie's thoughts, bringing him back into the moment. Jack was wiping a recently vacated table near to where Charlie was sitting in the window, and Charlie turned his head slightly to reply.

'Well, thank you. I'm sorry I haven't popped in more officially yet, but I've been up to my ears in paperwork.'

'I can imagine,' Jack grinned. 'Your predecessor didn't strike me as the most organised of folks. Spent more time in the bars in Westminster than in the chamber, by all accounts!'

'I couldn't possibly comment,' Charlie said wryly. 'Although his filing did leave a lot to be desired.'

'Happen to come across any paperwork concerning that proposed new motorway junction?' Jack asked, ultra-casually, as he continued to clear up the table. 'Rumour has it that Hugo Fitzgerald took rather a large cut of the profits from the farmer who sold the land it's being built on in return for pushing it through under the new, more relaxed planning laws.' Jack shook his head. 'Although it's on hold now, of course.'

Ignoring Jack's obvious fishing for grubby specifics, Charlie raised an eyebrow. 'On hold?'

'Yup.' Jack's eyes twinkled. 'Apparently, when the archaeological dig was scheduled, it turned up artefacts of specific historical interest to the town. Until the site can be fully excavated, there won't be a new junction going through there.'

Charlie raised his eyes skywards. He was rapidly finding out that Willowbury was full of oddities – some good and some rather less so. 'That seems quite a coincidence,' he said.

'Well, you know how it is,' Jack said, flinging his damp towel over his shoulder. 'It's amazing what turns up when you least expect it. I mean, who knew there was an old Roman encampment right where the proposed junction was going to go? Not to mention possible proof that King Arthur really might have existed.' His eyes twinkled again.

'King Arthur as well?' Charlie smiled into his coffee. 'This place is full of surprises.' Finishing up his croissant and his coffee, he glanced at his watch and realised that Tom would be waiting at the office in a few minutes. 'Thanks for that,' he said as he took his plate and mug back to the counter.

'No problem. See you again soon,' Jack replied. 'This place is a hub for local gossip, so if you need the low-down on any of the local rumblings, feel free to ask. I'm the soul of indiscretion, as is my Twitter feed!'

Charlie laughed. 'I'll bear that in mind.'

Strolling back out of the coffee shop, he shook his head. Small-town living was going to take some getting used to, he thought, especially in a town as out there as Willowbury. But something told him he was going to like it.

7

That same afternoon, Holly was taking a lunch break while Rachel kept an eye on the shop for half an hour, when their mother came through the back door of the flat with something large and bulky in her hands. As she waved off Holly's offer of help, she headed into the living room and placed the object, which was a little dusty, on Holly's coffee table in front of the sofa.

'Your dad and I were having a bit of a clear-out of the eaves cupboards, and we thought you might like to have this.' She gestured to the coffee table. 'We took a quick look inside and it seemed to be most of your university stuff.'

Holly laughed as she flipped the catches on the old-fashioned blue suitcase. 'I hope you didn't find anything too incriminating in there!' The suitcase smelt a little musty from well over a decade in her parents' attic cupboards, but as she turned it over and flipped the rusting silver catches, opening the lid, she gasped. There, inside the case, was the contents of her university bedroom, complete with essays, posters and even the old college handbook from her first year.

'Bloody hell,' Holly said. 'I had no idea you'd kept this stuff.'

Pulling out a blue cardboard document wallet, she scanned through one of her English Literature essays and shuddered. 'I can't believe I ever got my degree with work like this.' Holly had graduated with a more than respectable upper second-class honours degree in English and Politics from the University of York, and as she riffled through the papers and pictures that were still neatly packed into folders and envelopes after thirteen years in her parents' attic, she was assailed by memories of people, places and experiences she'd not thought about in years. Alongside the posters of classic films – *Star Wars*, Zeffirelli's *Romeo and Juliet* and *Bladerunner*, was a copy of the college handbook, a programme from a play she'd acted in during her first year and a stack of photocopied journal articles on the Romantic poets.

As she opened a large, manila envelope, an equally large stack of photographs was revealed. Some of the snaps took her back instantly; the photograph of her dearest friends from university, taken after they'd laughed themselves weak watching an episode of *Desperate Housewives* late one night while drinking sangria mixed in a storage box from The Works, reawakened a lot of good memories. Pictures of a couple of boyfriends from uni evoked some slightly different feelings.

Nights out, nights in, famous sights, all were captured on disposable cameras and sent to actual film processing places to develop. Somehow, that seemed to make the memories more precious, despite the poor quality of the images. While Facebook meant that she'd reconnected with quite a lot of her university friends, it was still nice to see pictures of them all as they once were. One particular shot that made her smile was their recreation of an iconic scene from *Friends*, with each of them looking around the door frame of one of their hall's bedrooms.

Reaching for another pile of photographs, she furrowed her brow, trying to remember when they were taken. They were mostly of London landmarks, and many were blurry and out of focus. She couldn't remember ever going to London when she was at university, as it was quite a trek from York, and for a moment she was confused. Were these her photographs or had she picked up someone else's when she'd cleared out her room for the last time? Goodness knows things were very hectic at the end of that last summer term, and she and her friends were always leaving stuff in each other's rooms. But as she flipped through them, she was brought up short by a very familiar face and her heart started to flutter as the spreading brushstrokes of recognition filtered across the blank page of her memory. Something she'd forgotten about. Some*one* she'd forgotten about. For nearly a decade and a half. As the brushstrokes joined together, her heart started to hammer. It couldn't be... could it?

'Oh my God...' she muttered. There, standing by the sign for Great Portland Street Underground station, dressed in a badly fitting maroon blazer and a pair of fawn chinos, tie askew and looking as though he'd had a drink or two, either that or the photo had been taken after a very late night, was someone with a very familiar smile. Very familiar indeed.

Vivian Renton looked over her daughter's shoulder and grinned. 'That must have been taken when you went to that student conference,' she said. 'I remember you talking about some bloke you'd met there. What was his name?'

As Holly gazed at the picture, it all came back to her. Fifteen years ago, in her first year at university, she'd been a student delegate at a political conference in the capital. She'd been of a slightly different political persuasion back then than she was now, and far less sure of herself and her beliefs. Feeling like a fish out of water, she'd been flattered and charmed when a lanky, slightly geeky young man from Leeds University had started to talk to her and had shown her around, sticking by her side for the day's conference and then into the evening event, which was being held at a Leicester Square nightclub. Happy to have someone to talk to, she'd been too shy to kiss him for more than a moment on the dance floor, but when he had rather haltingly asked to hold her hand as he walked her back to her hotel at the end of the night, she'd accepted. She remembered taking the picture of him at Great Portland Street, and smiling herself at his huge, attractive smile. He'd seen her back to the hotel, kissed her on the cheek and they'd swapped home phone numbers. Jolted rather more by him than she'd realised, Holly had been surprised when he'd called her at home during the Christmas holidays, but by then she was seeing someone else, so she'd drawn a line and not seen him again.

Vivian was still looking at the photograph in Holly's hand, but she glanced at her face when she realised how stock-still her daughter had gone. 'What is it, Hols?'

'Can't you see it?' Holly replied. 'I can't believe I'd forgotten all about him until now. I mean, it's been thirteen years since I graduated, and I haven't given him a second thought until now.'

'So?' Vivian replied. 'He was just some bloke you met in London, wasn't he? I remember you talking about him after he rang you at Christmas. Nice, gentle Yorkshire accent, if I remember correctly. Very polite on the phone.'

'Very polite in person, too,' Holly murmured, remembering the sparkling brown eyes, the slightly sweaty palm held by her own and the chaste goodnight kiss. 'And still is,' she added unguardedly.

'What do you mean? I thought you just said you'd forgotten about him. You never mentioned him again. Not to me, anyway.'

'Er, Mum,' Holly cursed as she felt her cheeks flaming. 'The boy in the photograph... he grew up to be Charlie Thorpe.'

Vivian looked quizzical. 'As in Charlie Thorpe, the new MP? Are you sure?'

Holly traced Charlie's face in the photograph with a turmeric-stained fingertip. 'Yup. I didn't twig before when he came into the shop, but now I've seen this photo again it's all coming back to me.' To be fair, Charlie's hairstyle had changed and he'd filled out a bit so that he wasn't lanky any more, and he'd obviously ditched the glasses, too, but the sparkle in his eyes and that smile were instantly recognisable now she'd seen the photo again. 'Charlie Thorpe is Lovely Charlie, who looked after me when I had no one to talk to at that conference.'

'Well then,' Vivian said. 'Perhaps that's something to mention to him if you bump into him again.'

Holly had said to her mother, in passing, that Charlie had come into the shop but not told her the exact nature of their conversation, as she was still a little embarrassed by it all. 'I doubt he'll have remembered me anyway,' she laughed, putting the photograph back into the envelope. 'After all, it wasn't until I saw this photo that I realised we'd met before. And he's probably met loads of women, er, people since then. It's not even worth bringing it up. I'll just look like an idiot.'

'If you say so,' Vivian raised an eyebrow. 'But you never know... he might have thought of you all these years as Lovely Holly, just as you thought about him.'

Holly really did laugh, then. 'Mum, there's no way I'm ever owning up to that, especially now. And if you breathe a word of this to Dad or Rachel, I'll burn the whole bloody suitcase!'

Vivian laughed too, well aware of her daughter's legendary impulsiveness, and in no doubt that she was serious. 'Fair enough. But perhaps it's worth keeping that photo somewhere safe. After all, if he ever gets into the Cabinet, you could flog your story to the *Daily Mail*.'

'Nothing happened, Mum,' Holly said. 'We held hands and he kissed me goodnight. Hardly grounds for an actual kiss-and-tell story, is it?'

'Oh, the media can make a story out of anything these days,' Vivian replied. 'And you never know, it might pay the lease on your shop for a month or two.'

'I own the place, remember?' Holly replied. 'Bricks, mortar, concept and execution, thanks to Grandfather. I don't think I'll ever need to sell *that* story.'

'Still worth keeping hold of it,' Vivian said. 'But I must get back to Dad, anyway. He's having one of his *days.*'

'Is everything all right, Mum?' Holly was aware that her mother had to deal with her father's occasional bouts of anxiety and had done a lot to support them both over the years.

'Oh, you know how he is,' Vivian replied. 'He'll be out the other side by tomorrow morning. It's just the anniversary of your grandfather's death that set him off last night. He'll be back on an even keel soon. He's worrying about Harry's latest check-up too, no matter how much Rachel tries to reassure him.'

'Let me know if there's anything I can do,' Holly said.

Like many men of his age, Edward Renton internalised most things, resulting in darkish spells, but these were improving with every passing year now that his father, Holly's grandfather, had passed away. Holly knew there were some things she'd never know about her father's relationship with his own dad, had resigned herself to that years ago, but it didn't make her mother's life any easier.

Rachel was prone to the odd bout of anxiety herself, and Holly kept the encroaching demons at bay with a rigorous routine of yoga and meditation; she knew her mother did her best to keep her father afloat, too.

'I will.' Vivian hugged her daughter and then headed back out of the back door. 'See you soon.'

As her mother left, Holly closed the lid on the suitcase and dragged it into her bedroom. There would be plenty of time later to go through its contents and see what else she'd stashed from her university days.

Placing the photograph of Charlie firmly to the back of her mind, she flipped on the kettle and made a cup of coffee to take back down to the shop to Rachel. She'd get the photo of her friends out later, scan it and upload it to Facebook. Not for the first time, she was thankful that smartphones didn't exist when she was at university; there were plenty of memories, especially those concerning the sangria, that were best consigned to memory rather than the internet. And as for that sweet remembrance of the tall, awkward boy in London... that was definitely better consigned to the past.

8

After their initial encounter in the shop, Holly's path didn't cross with Charlie's for a few weeks. She'd heard through the grapevine that, like a lot of Members of Parliament, he was spending Monday to Thursday in Westminster every week, with Friday as his constituency day, although she'd spent enough time learning about politics in her teens to know that this was often a moveable feast. She wasn't surprised he hadn't sought her out on his constituency days, really – she realised he must be absolutely up to his neck in work, establishing himself and setting out his stall as the new MP. All the same, now she'd remembered their one brief evening of history all those years ago, she was curious to encounter him again. Would she be able to talk to him and not mention their previous meeting? He probably wouldn't even remember her if she did bring it up.

On a sunny Friday afternoon, after a successful day's sales and a meditation class, Holly was just about to flip the sign on the shop's door when she was jolted to see Charlie ambling up the High Street. Taking a moment to observe him from the vantage point behind a display of altar candles in her shop window, she noticed that he was rubbing his neck, slipping a hand underneath the collar of his white shirt, which he'd unbuttoned a notch when he'd loosened his tie. His waistcoat was also unbuttoned. Holly smiled to herself. Since Gareth Southgate had worn waistcoats all through the last World Cup tournament, they were having a bit of a resurgence. Obviously Charlie thought he should tap into this. She did have to admit, he wore them rather well. Presumably straight off the train, his laptop bag was slung across his body and his hair was dishevelled. With a start, Holly realised her eyes had followed him all the way down the street, and any minute now he'd pass her shop, then turn off the High Street and into Wells Close, where he lived. The location of his house had become common knowledge since he'd moved in, so she didn't feel like too much of a stalker by mentally plotting his route home.

As if she had no control over them, Holly found her feet stepping out of the front door of the shop and her eyes inspecting the terracotta pots of rosemary and thyme that adorned the doorway, testing the soil for dryness and rubbing the spiny leaves of the rosemary between her fingers, that suddenly itched for something to do. As if it was the most natural thing in the world, when she sensed Charlie was close enough to talk to, she raised her eyes from the plants and smiled.

'Hi,' Charlie said, pausing as he reached Holly, who straightened up and turned around just at the right moment. 'How are you?'

'Not bad, thanks,' Holly replied, carefully and neutrally, as if this was just any other exchange with any other passing local.

Charlie's eyes were friendly, and he was smiling, which was definitely a good sign. He obviously didn't hold grudges.

'Have you had a good week?' he said, glancing towards the open shop door as if checking out if there were any other customers still browsing and buying.

'Oh, same old, same old,' Holly smiled, flattered that he'd

stopped and not just said hello and moved on. 'I've sold a lot of Himalayan salt crystals this week – I think it's the spring-cleaning vibe that everyone gets this time of year – people are determined to do a bit of polishing of their auras as well as their houses!'

'And an aura is...?' Charlie tried, and failed, not to look amused.

'The light that surrounds you,' Holly replied. 'Skilled readers can work out a lot from the colour of your aura – your thoughts, your emotions and your preoccupations.'

'Really?' Charlie tried, and once more failed, to affect a more serious expression, and Holly knew he was taking what she said with a rather large pinch of salt, Himalayan or otherwise.

'Oh yeah,' she continued, remembering what Mariad O'Fla-herty, who owned the shop a couple of doors down from hers and made a living from reading and cleansing auras, had told her the last time they'd had a conversation. 'A dark one might indicate health issues, or things on your mind, an inability to let go of something, for instance. It's a good idea to spring-clean it once in a while.'

'I'm not sure I want to know how you spring-clean an aura!' Charlie laughed. 'Although I'm sure the inhabitants of the Palace of Westminster could provide all kinds of shapes and colours that a reader of such things would have a very interesting time with.'

Holly laughed as well. 'I can't see them, personally, but if you were ever interested in having yours read, I can refer you to our local practitioner, Mariad.' She fingered the sprig of rosemary she'd picked from the pot by the shop door. 'But enough of that. How are you settling in to life as an MP?'

'Pretty well, thanks,' Charlie replied, 'although the weather's making us all very sleepy. I dread to think what we've agreed to this week in the chamber, and all for lack of air conditioning!'

'If Willowbury gets a new retail park slap in the middle of it, we know who to blame!' Holly joked. Then she paused, looking at Charlie properly for the first time since he'd stopped. He still had a hand up to his neck, and now he was up close, Holly noticed his shoulders were tensed. 'Are you OK? Is your neck sore?'

'Just a little bit,' he admitted. 'I've not been sleeping too well, and the train was busy on the way back tonight, so three hours from London Paddington crammed against the door did nothing for my neck. I really should get a new desk chair for what passes for an office in London, too.'

'You should take better care of your back and neck,' Holly chided. 'If you hang on a minute, I've got some fantastic rose-mary and peppermint essential oil. Just get someone to massage it in. It'll help you sleep, too. Although it sounds like you're doing enough of that at work!'

'Er, OK,' Charlie said.

Holly noted with amusement Charlie's sudden look of discomfiture that didn't seem to have anything to do with his professed neck pain. Grinning, she opened the door to her shop. 'Come in while I dig that oil out.'

As she pushed open the shop door, Holly realised that, much like a lot of her customers, ComIncense seemed to both fasci-nate and unnerve Charlie. She'd seen it a lot since she'd opened the shop; people were drawn to ComIncense because of its outlandish range of dried herbs, sights and scents, but also terri-fied that they would do, say or buy something that was wrong or inappropriate, or even break something. Most of the time, she tried to quell these worries with her own friendly presence (it was useful to be approachable to make sales, after all, despite what some of her fellow business owners believed), but for a moment, devilry won with Charlie as she saw him looking around.

'Of course, the latest thing in relaxation is Shamanic Dolphin Choir music,' she said as they wandered back through the shop. 'I've sold a lot of CDs of that lately. People find the sixteen-part delphinidae harmonies do wonders for stress.' She glanced back over her shoulder and was inwardly tickled to see Charlie's face registering that familiar look of intrigue, discomfort and incomprehension that tended to happen when some of the more reserved clients looked too closely at her stock. 'Perhaps I can lend you a couple of CDs to try out?' She paused and pushed her advantage a little, staring into his eyes intently, as if selling Shamanic Dolphin Choir music was her complete raison d'être.

'Um... yeah, thanks,' Charlie stammered. 'Sounds, er, great.'

At his look of stammering incomprehension, Holly burst out laughing, unable to keep up the charade any longer. 'It would be,' she smirked. 'If I hadn't totally just made it up.'

Charlie, obviously relieved, grinned back. 'Thank Christ for that. Honestly, you wouldn't believe the things I've had foisted on me to try out since I took this job. I think I can live without the singing dolphins.'

'Fair enough,' Holly kept smiling. Turning towards the rack of shelves where she kept her essential oils, she picked up the bottle of rosemary and peppermint infusion. 'I can mix this with some base oil if you don't want to faff about with warming up olive oil at home.'

'That would be great, thanks,' Charlie replied.

As Holly decanted some of her neutral-scented base oil into a fresh glass bottle and added several drops of the rosemary and peppermint, she was aware of Charlie watching her hands intently. She'd made up this mixture a hundred times, and with cool efficiency she mixed the oils, filled the bottle to the top and then finished it off with a cork stopper. Then, she grabbed her calligraphy pen, wrote the contents and the date on one of her pre-printed ComIncense labels and handed it over to Charlie.

'Just massage a bit into your neck and shoulders tonight, or, even better, get someone to do it for you, and you will really feel the benefit.' Was she imagining things, or was Charlie Thorpe actually starting to blush? 'Did I say something wrong?' she asked.

'No, not at all,' Charlie laughed nervously. 'It's just that I don't really know anyone well enough in Willowbury yet to ask them to get their hands on me!' Trying to make a joke of it, his laugh faltered.

There was a pause between them, while Charlie stared fixedly at the bottle Holly had just given him and Holly debated within herself.

Eventually, she smiled. 'I'll do it for you if you like.'

Charlie's head snapped back up. 'Oh, it's all right, that wasn't a hint. I'm sure I can see to myself. Oh, Christ...' At the clearly unintentional innuendo, Charlie really did laugh.

Holly, tickled, joined in. 'Honestly, I don't mind. I'll just close the shop and then we won't get interrupted. It's closing time anyway.' She gestured to the room off the back of the shop. 'That's my treatment room. Don't worry, it's not as clinical as it sounds. Why don't you go in and get yourself comfortable and I'll be with you in a sec. Just slip the top half of your clothes and your shoes off and lie down on the massage bed.'

'If you're sure you don't mind,' Charlie replied. 'I thought you needed to take bookings for these sorts of things.'

'Usually, yes, but for you I'll make an exception,' Holly smiled. 'I'd only be worrying about you if I let you go home with that sore neck.' She did wonder why she was making a sudden exception and letting Charlie onto her massage table without an appointment, but, she figured, she'd dissect her own reasoning later. She was nothing if not spontaneous.

Charlie smiled. 'OK, sounds great.' He ambled towards the small room at the back of the shop while Holly locked the front door.

Turning off the shop floor lights, she went to the counter and scrolled through her phone for some suitably relaxing music to pipe through to the treatment room. Selecting some middle-of-the-road Celtic relaxation music, not wanting to totally freak Charlie out with something more out there, she lit a lavender incense stick and slotted it into the holder just inset into the doorway of the treatment room.

Opening the door, she couldn't help a sharp intake of breath as she saw Charlie stretched out on her massage table. Naked to the waist, his white shirt, waistcoat and tie slung over the chair in the corner of the room, his dark, slightly dishevelled hair contrasted with the pale skin of his back. Legs encased in his suit trousers stretched tantalisingly down the table, and his muscular arms were stretched out at his sides. He was turned away from the door, but as she came in, he turned his head and just for a moment, his deep, brown eyes looked sleepily in her direction before he remembered himself. He already looked far more relaxed than when he'd entered the shop, and she hadn't laid a hand on him yet.

'Are you comfortable?' Holly asked, once she'd remembered to breathe again. She'd had a few clients since she'd started the massage part of her business a few weeks back, but none of them had affected her in this way, no matter how gorgeous they were. Harriet Meadows, certainly, hadn't made her catch her breath when she'd given her a massage. She needed to get a grip. An uncomfortable reminder of how attracted she'd been to him all those years ago worried at her memory, until she resolutely pushed it to one side. *That was then, this is now*, she thought.

'Really comfortable,' Charlie said. 'It feels so good to lie down after three hours crammed in the corridor of the train.'

'Good,' Holly said, focusing on the techniques she was about to employ on Charlie's back in an attempt to keep the professional distance. 'Well, hopefully after this massage you'll feel even better. So, I'm going to start off with medium pressure on your neck and shoulder blades. If it feels too hard, or too soft, just let me know and I'll change it up a bit.' She rubbed her hands together and then uncorked the freshly prepared massage oil. 'Likewise, if you think my hands are too cold, let me know and I'll warm them up a bit.' She dribbled a little bit of the oil onto her palms and then rubbed them together again. Then, taking a deep breath, she put her hands onto Charlie's broad, muscular back. Feeling the tension in his neck and shoulders, she began to press and squeeze, working her fingertips into the knots and kinks of his shoulders and neck. 'Some people like me to talk to them while I do this, but others prefer to be quiet, so let me know if you want me to shut up,' Holly said. She felt the smooth warmth of Charlie's skin, in contrast to the tension in his back, and she pressed her fingers deeper into the junctions of his shoulder blades, easing out the very worst of the stiffness she found there.

Charlie groaned as she switched tack and dug her elbow into a particularly stubborn knot between his shoulders.

'Too hard?' Holly asked. She was leaning over Charlie's back and felt a sharp, pinpricking tingle deep within herself as she smelt the remnants of his musky aftershave, underpinned by his own scented warmth, combined with the deeper, more peppery scent of the massage oil. In response to her nearness, she saw her breath lift the hair on the back of his neck when she spoke. She was compelled to pause the movement of her hands for a moment, and drew another deep breath.

'No...' Charlie murmured. He was face down, resting his head on the circle of the massage table, so Holly couldn't see his expression. 'It feels amazing. I don't know why I haven't had one of these before.'

'You feel quite knotted,' Holly said, focusing on the vertebrae in his neck. 'I really would think about getting a new office chair. And booking a seat on the train home.'

'It's been a busy few weeks,' Charlie's voice, muffled from the position he was in, sounded more relaxed. 'But this is definitely... helping.'

Holly, who was again using her elbows as well as her hands, felt the warmth of Charlie's back against her own skin as she pushed deeper into his shoulder blades, feeling him breathing in and out, his chest rising and falling, and then hitching slightly, as she hit another tender spot.

'Did you want me to work on your lower back a little bit, too?' Holly asked as she straightened up.

'If you've got time,' Charlie replied. He sounded as though he was almost dropping off to sleep. Holly took that as a compliment.

'No problem.' Shifting down the bed, Holly drizzled some more massage oil onto her palms and began to manipulate Charlie's lower back. 'You've got a really good, long, straight back,' she said as she focused on his spine, trying not to notice how attractive it was as it swept into the curve of a very delectable bottom. 'You should take better care of it.'

'If it means getting more massages like this, then I definitely will.'

They lapsed into a more comfortable silence as Holly continued to work, to the gentle beat of the relaxation music and the scent of the incense in the air as it burned slowly down. After a few more minutes, Charlie's breathing seemed to slow, and Holly felt his back muscles relax under her hands, and she knew he was starting to drop off to sleep. This wasn't unusual with her clients; she'd been told when she took the massage course that this was definitely a sign that she'd been doing her job right.

With a feeling of slight regret that the massage had come to its natural end, Holly wiped the oily residue off her palms with a fluffy white towel and then spread a larger one over Charlie's back to keep him warm while he lay there. Giving him one last, long, lingering glance, she padded from the treatment room.

9

Charlie woke with a start. Heart thumping as he breathed unfamiliar scents and heard exotic music, it took him a good few seconds to realise that he'd dropped off to sleep on Holly's massage table. Feeling slightly embarrassed, and hoping against hope that he hadn't been snoring, he sat up slowly, grabbing the tumbler of water that was on the unit beside the massage table, because he felt incredibly thirsty. As the cool water hit his throat, he realised that his neck and shoulders, while feeling as though they'd had a workout, felt a million times looser and more relaxed than they had before he'd entered the world of ComIncense. Holly had worked wonders with her hands and elbows.

Squashing the hugely erotic thoughts about where else Holly's hands might feel good on him, he stood up and grabbed his shirt from the chair in the corner of the room, buttoning it up hastily in case he'd been asleep for hours and Holly was waiting to call it a night. He was glad he'd been face down during the massage so that Holly had been unable to see the look of pleasure on his face, as he wasn't sure how appropriate that would have been, under the circumstances. Glancing at his watch, he was relieved to see that he'd only been asleep for half an hour or so. Hopefully he hadn't put Holly out too much.

As he exited the treatment room, he noticed the lights were out in the shop, and that the only illumination was coming from a couple of thick altar candles that had been placed in dishes on the shop counter. The music had changed from the Celtic-sounding melodies to something that sounded a little more Eastern mystical, and as Charlie cast his eyes around for Holly, it took him a moment to realise that she was curled up with her legs folded under her in a yoga position; child's pose, he seemed to remember it being called, courtesy of an ex-girlfriend who was a yoga convert.

Charlie padded out across the shop floor, not wanting to disturb Holly in the middle of her routine. As he drew closer to her, she straightened up to a sitting position and raised her long, shapely arms in the air, palms flat and together, before bringing her hands down in front of her. From where he was, behind her, Charlie was struck once again by the beautiful contrast of brilliant red hair, somewhat subdued in the candlelight, roughly plaited and tumbling over her back to just below her bra line, which he could see through her vest top when she stretched her arms. He felt a sharp sting of longing spiralling downwards into his abdomen as he saw the sweeping curve of her waist and hips, and the outline of one full, rounded breast as she turned slightly to one side. She was utterly, completely gorgeous; not just in this light but in any light.

Clearing his throat, as much as to dislodge the sudden dryness that seeing Holly like this had created as to announce his presence, he spoke, hoping that his voice wouldn't betray the sudden sting of arousal that he felt. 'Um... I'm sorry if I've kept you waiting.'

Holly took a moment to complete her yoga pose, bowing her head to her chest, which again made Charlie's heart skip a beat as her plait flopped forward to reveal an elegant, swanlike neck, strangely vulnerable against the red hair. She then swung her legs around and stood up, turning around to face him.

'Don't worry,' she said softly. 'I was going to do some yoga tonight anyway. How are you feeling?'

'Great,' Charlie replied, caught off guard by the light reflecting in her hazel eyes. 'Thirsty, though. Is that normal?'

'Yes, completely,' Holly replied. She gestured to the jug of water on the shop counter. 'Help yourself to some if you like.'

Charlie grabbed the glass by the jug and poured himself some more. Downing it swiftly, he relished the coolness, hoping it would help to cool the unbidden thoughts about Holly herself.

'Well, you should sleep well tonight,' Holly said. 'Although, don't go running any marathons for a couple of days; the toxins will be working their way out of you for forty-eight hours or so. And drink plenty more water.'

'I will,' Charlie replied, thinking that Holly's hands must truly be magic if they were able to relax him so much. He hoped he didn't end up dreaming about her tonight, though. That might make things awkward between them again. He felt as though their relationship was a little easier now than it had been when he'd introduced himself to her in the shop a few weeks ago, and he wanted to keep it that way. 'So how much do I owe you for the oil and the massage?' he asked, aware that time was marching on and he should leave Holly to the rest of her evening.

'If you'd like to book in for another one, then this one's on the house,' Holly said.

'Are you sure?' Charlie asked. 'I mean, I don't want to leave you out of pocket.'

'It's something I offer my customers if I think they might give me the repeat business,' Holly said. 'And, from the feel of your shoulders and neck, it would be a great idea to schedule a massage at least once a month or so.'

'I'll bear that in mind,' Charlie replied. 'That's if you're sure you don't want anything for this one?'

Holly shook her head. 'Once I get you hooked, you'll be booking in a session every week!'

'I don't doubt that,' Charlie said, although inwardly he wondered if he'd cope with Holly putting her magical hands on him that regularly without wanting to pull her down on the massage table and kiss the life out of her. But that was probably the oil and the massage talking. If he couldn't even get a massage from someone without thinking sexy thoughts about them, he was clearly far more buttoned-up than he realised. 'Thanks again, Holly.'

'Any time.'

Holly walked over to the front door of the shop and unlocked it, allowing him to step through.

What would the Prime Minister, the leader of his party, think if they could see him stepping out of a shop like ComIncense with an untucked shirt and a relaxed grin on his face? Or, worse, his own mother? Kathleen Thorpe wasn't exactly what you'd call progressive in her attitudes – political or otherwise. An old-school conservative, she viewed Charlie's more liberal views with genteel disdain.

Grinning even more widely, he said goodnight to Holly and set his mind to the rather more mundane task of what he was going to eat tonight. Sadly, he thought, after all of the talk about releasing toxins from his body, he'd probably end up with some sort of takeaway, as he felt far too chilled to bother cooking. His new job had taken him to some interesting places so far, but Holly's massage table was definitely one of the nicest. Resolving to book in another massage that he was actually going to pay for, he headed home.

10

_____

'So, I had that Charlie Thorpe on my massage table last night,' Holly said playfully as she handed Rachel the folded-up T-shirts she'd been taking off the washing line in Rachel's neat back garden. Rachel was housebound with Harry for a few days, as his stomach was playing up. Tummy troubles were a symptom of his condition, and while he was, on the whole, a healthy, happy little boy, apart from the obvious, when he did have a health wobble, it tended to put the brakes on family fun. As a result, Rachel was going slightly stir-crazy in her house in one of Willowbury's modern new-build cul-de-sacs, so Holly had shut up shop and headed over to the house, picking up an easy dinner for her and Rachel on the way.

'Oh really?' Rachel raised a wry eyebrow. 'Isn't there some sort of practitioner-client confidentiality involved in massage? Should you really be telling me that?'

Holly grinned. 'I trust your absolute discretion, of course!'

'So, what you're telling me is that he's only been in the area a few weeks and you've already got his kit off? You're a fast mover these days, sis.'

Holly flung one of Harry's vests at her sister. 'It wasn't like that,' she said. 'Besides, it's weird enough seeing him around, let alone actually seeing him with his shirt off.' Realising she might have said too much, she grabbed some more washing off the line and concentrated on folding.

'Why's it weird?' Rachel's brow furrowed. 'I mean, apart from him being the new MP, of course. But you met enough of them in your days as a student party member not to be freaked out by that.'

Holly paused. She'd made it clear to her mother that she didn't want the information that she'd met Charlie before being shared, but she trusted Rachel, and apart from a little good-natured ribbing, her sister could be relied upon not to broadcast it to all and sundry. Rachel had teased her, often, about how much the previously strait-laced Holly had loosened her stays over the years, and perhaps she should know that there was a small, missing puzzle piece now that Charlie Thorpe had rocked up in Willowbury.

'So, Mum gave me back a suitcase from their loft the other day,' Holly said, trying to inject a casual tone into her speech. 'And it turns out that, according to some very old photos, and you'll never believe this, me and Charlie have actually met before.'

'Really?' Rachel paused in her own folding. Glancing to where Harry was playing contentedly with the toys in his tabletop sandpit, making sure he wasn't up to no good, she looked questioningly at Holly. 'When? And I'm hoping you don't mean in a past life or something, because that's not something I, personally, can buy into!'

'Oh, ha-ha,' Holly threw a line-dried flannel at her sister, who caught it, folded it and popped it on her own pile of washing. 'You remember that conference I went to in my first year at university? When I was still really into party politics.'

Rachel snorted. 'Party line doesn't even begin to cover it! That old boyfriend of yours from school has a lot to answer for.'

'OK, OK,' Holly said. 'Let's not go down *that* road.' She placed the clothes she had folded into Rachel's washing basket. 'Anyway, it turns out that I met Charlie at that conference... and I, er, well... that's to say *we...*'

'Oh my God, you didn't shag him?' Rachel's jaw hit the floor. 'But you were in the no-sex-before-marriage brigade back then, too! That's basically why Simon dumped you during your A Levels!'

Holly rolled her eyes. 'Chill out, sis. I didn't shag him.' And, stung, even after all these years, she couldn't help adding, 'And Simon didn't dump me because of that. We made each other bloody miserable for a whole bunch of other, teenage-angst-related reasons, not sex!'

'So why did he end up going out with Chantelle the village slapper straight after you, then?' Rachel teased.

'Ask him,' Holly replied tartly. 'But the fact is, Charlie and I have met before. And we kissed a little bit back then. And, to be honest, I'm feeling a bit weird about it.'

'Does he remember you?' Rachel asked, as, washing all off the line, she slumped down into one of her garden lounge chairs.

Holly shook her head. 'I don't think so. I mean, he'd have said something by now if he did, surely.'

'Perhaps he just feels a bit awkward bringing it up,' Rachel said. 'I mean, you haven't said anything to him yet, have you?'

Holly shook her head. 'I feel pretty awkward, too, to be honest. I mean, I'd completely forgotten about him until I found a photo of him in that suitcase.' She didn't add that she wasn't that keen to revisit the dorkier elements of her teenage years – she was definitely a different person then to the one she was now.

'So, are you going to say anything?' Rachel asked.

'Oh, I don't know.' Holly put her head back on the sun lounger she'd sat down on, lifting her ponytail to get some air to her suddenly sweaty neck. 'It was such a brief encounter, it hardly seems worth it. And yet, it's making me feel a bit weird that I remember it and I don't know if he does.'

'Just ask him, then!' Rachel said. She smiled as Harry came trotting up to her carrying a small, castle-shaped bucket full of play sand. 'One thing being mother to this munchkin has taught me is that you need to seize the day whenever you can. No point hiding behind things that are worrying you.' She took the plastic spoon that Harry was offering her and pretended to take a big mouthful of the sand. 'Mmm, that's lovely. Is it chocolate?'

Harry giggled. 'No, Mummy!' He toddled around to Holly. 'Aunty Holly want some?'

'Thanks, gorgeous,' Holly said, taking the spoon and doing the same. Looking at Harry's sweet, open face, she realised exactly where Rachel's carpe diem advice was coming from. Not a day was wasted in Harry's life; they were all too precious. 'Perhaps I will,' Holly mused. 'But, in the meantime, don't mention it to him, if you see him, will you? I'll do it in my own time.'

'I'll be the soul of discretion,' Rachel assured her. 'So long as you give me all the gory details when you do tell him!'

'He'll probably just laugh in my face,' Holly said. 'After all, it was fifteen years ago, and only a couple of hours of our lives. Not exactly the love affair of the century!'

'You never know,' Rachel said. 'He seems nothing if not polite, from what I've seen of him in the media. I'm sure he'll be tickled to be reminded.' She gave Holly a mischievous look. 'And since you've already got your hands on him on your massage bed, it seems only fair to mention your prior connection!'

Holly felt her face flushing, and it wasn't entirely because of the warmth of the afternoon. 'If the moment arises, I'll drop it into conversation,' she said. 'But for the moment, I'd better head off. I've got Harriet Meadows coming in for another massage this afternoon.'

'Lucky you,' Rachel snorted. 'Tell me, does she stop moaning long enough to enjoy it?'

'Only when she falls asleep but then she doesn't stop snoring – though, of course, you haven't heard that from me!' Holly laughed. She pulled Harry up onto her knee and gave him a cuddle. 'Look after Mum for me until next time,' she said into his thick blond hair.

'I will,' Harry said solemnly.

Holly smiled. She was still thinking about Rachel's advice to seize the day as she walked back to her flat. Perhaps she had been a little cautious and land-locked lately. Maybe it was time to live a little dangerously.

11

Much to her surprise, when Holly checked her online bookings for massages the following week, she found that Charlie had booked himself in for one on Thursday evening. *He's probably going to claim it on expenses,* she thought, then chided herself for her cynicism. Despite Charlie's political party affiliations, she was sure not everything came down to money.

She cashed up quickly that afternoon, and about ten minutes before Charlie was due to arrive she found herself upstairs applying a little more deodorant (a freebie from an organic fragrance company that was trying to court her business) and running a brush through her hair. Ruefully, she realised she wouldn't be doing this if she had any other client coming. She didn't want to question her motivations too closely, though.

Just as she was about to head back down to the shop and light the candle in the massage room, she heard a muffled meow from behind her.

'Hey, Arthur,' she said fondly as she turned around. 'Are you hungry? Oh, I see you've brought your own food tonight.'

There, in the ginger cat's jaws was a large field mouse. Holly was generally unfazed by Arthur's tendency to hunt and bring her home some of his catches, reasoning that it was par for the course when you owned, or were indeed owned by, a cat, although she would have preferred it if he finished them off beforehand – she'd had to rescue rodents and even small rabbits from the dark corners of her flat on a few occasions and it was quite tedious and time-consuming.

Unfortunately, this time Arthur's catch was large, vocal and very much alive. And as she strolled towards Arthur to try to shoo him back down the stairs and out of his cat flap, he dropped the mouse and shot into her bedroom.

'Great. Thanks so much, Arthur!'

Holly glanced at the clock and realised Charlie was due any minute. Swearing under her breath, she debated the options. Her living room was very open, but there were enough crevices for a rodent to hide, and while she wasn't squeamish, the thought of a mouse running over her feet at an unwary moment made her skin crawl. She could close the door to the flat temporarily, but there were gaps under her doors that a mouse might easily slip under. The last thing she needed was it loose in ComIncense. There were far too many tasty things for it to nibble on down there, not least the expensive artisan beeswax candles she stocked from a local supplier near Wells. Nor would a free-ranging mouse be the most inviting sight for her customers.

The bell over the front door of the shop tinkled and Holly's heart quickened.

'Charlie, is that you?' Holly called.

'Yes, it's me,' a voice returned her enquiry. 'Are you OK?'

'Can you drop the latch on the front door, and flip the sign then come up here for a sec?' Holly replied. Charlie was a few minutes early, after all, and four hands would be better than two for catching the recalcitrant rodent.

'Sure, OK.' Charlie sounded intrigued, but the clunk of the catch of the front door showed he'd done what she'd asked.

Holly heard his footsteps coming up the back stairs to her flat and felt even more irritated by the loose mouse. In a few moments, Charlie was at her door.

'What *are* you doing?' Charlie's voice was laced with amusement as it wafted from the open door of the flat.

'Close the door, quickly!' Holly hissed from over by the sofa, from which she'd removed the colourful throws so that she could see underneath it. She was holding the dustpan from the shop and was peering under the sofa, watching intently.

Doing as he was told, Charlie pushed the door shut and padded over to the sofa.

'Can I help?' he asked. 'Are you looking for something?'

'Arthur brought in a mouse just now,' Holly muttered. 'And, being the considerate soul that he is, he decided to show it to me before he polished it off, but because he's so old, and his teeth are a bit crap, he dropped it and it escaped before he could catch it again. And I've cornered it to this part of the room, but the last thing I want is to let it loose downstairs – there's too much for it to feast on down there.'

'I'm sure I've got a spare mousetrap at home,' Charlie offered. 'The town house was riddled with the buggers when I moved in, but a colleague suggested peanut butter in a trap; worked every time.'

'No way,' Holly snapped. 'It's one thing Arthur bringing them in for his dinner, but I don't want to kill it unnecessarily if I can help it. Arthur's curled up on my bed, asleep, of course.'

'Shall I go and get him?' Charlie asked, feeling at a bit of a loss.

'No point,' Holly sighed. 'He'd just look at you like you're mad. Bloody cats!'

Charlie dropped down to his knees and peered under the

sofa. 'Are you sure it's under here? I can't see any— Oh, Christ!' Grabbing his ankle, he let out a yelp.

'What is it?' Holly dropped the dustpan and looked up to see Charlie, whose hands had suddenly moved up to the back of his right knee and were gripping on for dear life. 'Have you got cramp?'

'I think I've found your bloody mouse,' Charlie spoke through gritted teeth.

Holly glanced down to Charlie's knee, then she burst out laughing. 'Are you serious?' There, below the fabric of Charlie's suit trousers, was a small, frantically wriggling ball, that was only being prevented from shooting further up Charlie's trouser leg by his furiously gripping hands.

'Can you stop laughing and help me?' Charlie's face was torn between abject terror and ticklish laughter.

Holly thought, for a moment, how funny but lovely that looked, before common sense returned.

'You'll have to drop your trousers,' she said, choking back another gale of laughter. 'And try not to let the thing get away when you do.'

'Sod it getting away,' Charlie howled, 'I need it out of my trouser leg!' With both hands still clutching either side of the mouse bulge down his leg, Charlie looked helplessly at Holly.

'What?' she said, still finding it extremely difficult to keep a straight face.

'I can't move my hands,' Charlie said, his panic rising. 'If I do, the bloody thing's going to shoot straight upwards.'

'And they've got seriously sharp teeth,' Holly said. 'I remember getting bitten by one when I was a kid. Drew blood and everything.'

'That's not helpful,' Charlie winced.

'Sorry,' Holly smirked, realising exactly now why Charlie didn't want the mouse travelling any further up his leg. 'What do you want me to do?'

'Well, isn't it obvious?'

Suddenly, Holly twigged. If Charlie couldn't move his hands, then there was only one thing to do; she'd have to undo his flies. And she had to do it while ignoring the urge to make any jokes about honourable members. 'Are you serious?' Laughter won again.

'Just bloody well get on with it, will you,' Charlie snapped, hands still firmly glued to his knee.

'This is going to be a bit tricky from the position you're in,' Holly said, trying her hardest to keep a straight face.

'Hurry up.'

Kneeling down in front of him, smothering the thought that in another context this would be extremely erotic, Holly found herself nose to groin with Charlie. 'Are you ready?'

'Yes,' Charlie hissed. 'Never more so.'

Hands trembling slightly, suddenly nervous, Holly reached out and gently unbuckled Charlie's tan leather belt, before fumbling a little with the button of his trousers. Finally managing to release it, she unzipped his flies, trying not to notice Charlie's figure-hugging grey boxer shorts, or, to be truthful, to stare at what they contained. From this angle, had she dared to look for longer than a second, the view was *very* interesting.

'Do you want me to, er, take your trousers down?' Holly asked, glancing upwards at Charlie. Because he was bent over, his face was quite close to hers, and she felt a stab of sympathy as she realised just how embarrassed he was by this whole situation.

'If you wouldn't mind,' Charlie said stiffly, his face rather flushed.

'OK. Here goes. Try not to let go of the mouse while I do it.'

'Bugger the mouse,' Charlie muttered, but his hands stayed put either side of it.

Carefully, mindful of the strange angle and not wanting

Charlie to be mortified any more than he was already, Holly eased down Charlie's trousers until they were around his knees. 'I think you can let go now,' she said as they both paused.

'I'm not sure I can,' Charlie said.

'Of course you can,' Holly said, stifling the urge to laugh again. Charlie's constituents would have a field day with this if they ever found out. The MP and the mouse would be a story to dine out on. If she ever went to dinner parties, that was.

'Shit. You'd better undo my shoes, too, before I take off my trousers or it'll get stuck if it goes down.'

Holly lost the battle against the giggles this time, but, not daring to look Charlie in the eye, she quickly untied his shoes and helped him to step out of them.

'OK, we're good,' she said. 'If you take your top hand away, I'll pull your trousers right down and hopefully I'll be able to catch the little bugger on the way out. Three... two... one...'

In a split second, Holly found herself crushed under Charlie's weight as he caught his right foot in the hem of his trousers and fell forward. From the corner of her eye, she saw the small, brown field mouse, the cause of so much aggravation, scuttle out from the top of Charlie's left trouser leg and dash underneath her sideboard, but what was more pressing was the warm, slightly trembling body that had ended up on top of hers, and the stirring of something even more alive than the mouse inside a certain pair of grey boxer shorts.

'Did you see where it went?' Holly asked, once she'd tried to draw air back into her slightly winded lungs.

'Not really,' Charlie murmured from his position on top of her. 'I was more interested in trying not to crush you to death.'

'I'm not sure if you managed it,' Holly said, realising that Charlie seemed disinclined to move. Their lips were very close as he hovered above her, and she felt another distinct stirring from where their hips were touching, which turned her insides into fluttering, flapping madness. It was certainly proving even more difficult to breathe.

'Are you OK?' Charlie said, a husky note in his voice.

'I think so,' Holly replied. 'But I think the mouse got away again.'

'Sorry about that.' He really didn't sound sorry.

The pause stretched for a delicious, aching moment as their lips hovered just a breath away. Holly craved that final step and desperately wanted to wrap a thigh around Charlie where he was lying between her legs. Heart hammering, she shifted slightly so that their lips were millimetres apart. She could feel his breath hitching in his throat as he looked down at her, and she was willing it to be down to more than just the adrenaline rush from the mouse up his trouser leg. Closer... closer...

'Are we interrupting something?' A deeply amused voice came from the same door that Charlie had entered a few minutes ago, followed by the pattering of toddler's footsteps.

'Rachel, Harry!' Holly gasped as two pairs of feet, one small, one larger, came into her sight line.

'Next time you fancy getting jiggy with the local MP, perhaps it would be wise to lock your back door before you start,' Rachel said wryly, her face, once it came into view as Holly shifted, asking a thousand questions that Holly didn't think she'd ever be able to answer. Holly, for once struck dumb, wondered how she was going to explain this one to her sister.

Harry, round-eyed with wonder at seeing his aunt pinned beneath a strange man with his trousers around his ankles, suddenly pointed in excitement. 'Look, Mummy, look, Aunty Holly!' Turning her head to see where he was pointing, Holly saw the brown field mouse, the reason for this ridiculous situation, scuttling nonchalantly past her nose and under her Welsh dresser.

12

After the mouse debacle, Holly wasn't quite sure how she or Charlie got through his booked massage, especially since Rachel took her time to leave with Harry, having just popped in to collect a couple of toys Harry had suddenly decided he couldn't live without, which he had left in the flat during his last visit. Once she'd dispatched her sister and nephew, Rachel's amused gaze lingering long after they'd left, Holly decided to just ignore what had gone on. She was mortified, and from the way Charlie readily agreed to head back down to the shop to keep the appointment, she sensed he was, too. There was certainly something a little different in the air than the first time, and she felt a mixed sense of disappointment and relief when it was over.

As he emerged from the treatment room, looking more relaxed than when he'd entered it (although, to be fair, he couldn't have been much more tense in the wake of the mouse incident), Holly looked up from her yoga mat. She hadn't been able to let go of the tumult of emotions that the whole thing had unleashed, and coupled with that was the nagging, unnerving, unresolved issue of the photo in the suitcase. Although now was hardly the time to bring *that* up in conversation.

'How are you feeling?' she asked him softly as he closed the treatment room door behind him.

'Pretty good,' he replied. 'All things considered!'

Holly smiled. 'I'm glad.'

There was an almost imperceptible pause between them.

'So, er, how much do I owe you?' Charlie asked. He fumbled in the inside pocket of his jacket for his wallet.

'I sort of feel like I should be paying you compensation for what you went through earlier!' Holly said.

'Oh, I don't know,' Charlie grinned, 'worse things happen in Parliament. But, seriously, I can't keep snagging freebies off you. You have a business to run, after all.'

'Fair enough.' Holly smiled back. She got to her feet and ambled over to her counter where the till was. 'It's twenty-five pounds please.'

'Reasonable at twice the price,' Charlie said, handing over his debit card.

As their hands touched, Holly felt a jolt of electricity. She glanced up at Charlie and noticed his eyes widening. There was definitely something between them; something more than the artificial intimacy that the massage had provided. But perhaps he still felt weird about landing on top of her in the way he had.

Holly rang through the sale and then presented him with a receipt, 'Just in case you *can* claim it on your expenses!'

Charlie laughed. 'I'm sure stranger things have been claimed. Not that it was strange at all,' he added hastily. 'In fact, it was lovely.'

Holly cast around for something, anything, to keep this moment going a little longer. 'Look, er, about what happened earlier... I feel really bad about you being in that situation.'

'Don't worry about it,' Charlie said. 'It wasn't your fault. Although Arthur might not be getting any catnip from me for a while!'

'I don't blame you!' Holly laughed. 'So, I'm cooking dinner for Mum and Dad at their place on Sunday. Their kitchen's a million times bigger than mine, and I do it about once a month. Rachel and Harry usually come over too. Would you, er, like to come over and have lunch with us? By way of an apology for Arthur's poor behaviour?'

The minute she'd said it, she felt herself blushing at the absolute dorkiness of the invitation. Asking him for a drink at the local pub on the High Street would have been a far more sophisticated and grown-up option. Why the hell had she invited him to lunch with her parents? He looked surprised by the proposition, to say the least.

'You know what, don't worry, it's a stupid idea. You've probably got loads to do anyway, and we should maybe just forget this whole thing happened—' She hated it when she babbled.

'Holly,' Charlie cut over her monologue calmly, 'I'd love to. It's been ages since I've had a proper Sunday lunch. In fact, I don't think I have had one since I got this new job. It would be a pleasure.'

'Oh, OK. Well if you're sure,' Holly said. 'And I do cook a mean roast lamb!'

'Really?' Charlie asked. 'I was expecting some kind of vegan nut roast.'

Holly grinned, realising immediately that he was teasing. 'And why would you think that?' she asked, pretending to rise to the bait.

'Well, I mean this place... I just kind of assumed that being vegan was all part of the package.' Charlie shook his head. 'Shows what I know.'

'Sometimes you can't put everyone into neat little boxes,' Holly chided. 'Much as I'm sure you'd like to as a politician. Things aren't always that clear-cut.'

'Tell me about it,' Charlie replied. 'The more I find out about this place, the more it confounds me.' He was warming to the subject, she could tell. 'I mean, you couldn't get two more different towns than Willowbury and Stavenham on the face of it, and yet they expect their MP to navigate between them effort-lessly.' He shook his head. 'There's more to this place than meets the eye.'

'And there you were, thinking it was going to be all crystals, hippies and ley lines!' Holly teased. 'It's a bit harder than you thought, is it?'

'Like you wouldn't believe.' Charlie admitted. 'In fact, I find myself having sympathy for Hugo Fitzgerald at times.'

'I wouldn't go that far,' Holly said darkly. 'Rumour has it, he was more interested in feathering his own nest than helping other people build their own.'

'I'd heard that, too,' Charlie said. 'But from my point of view it's better not to know too much. I don't want to get dragged backwards into whatever his affairs were, or weren't. I just want to do the best by Willowbury and its residents as I can.'

'I'm happy to hear that,' Holly answered. 'After all, everyone's sick of politicians who have their own self-interest at heart. If you do mean what you say, it'll be a relief.' She wondered if this would be the right time to talk to Charlie about Rachel's campaign to get the new drugs for Harry but decided to leave it for now. Rachel would raise it with him officially, in her own time.

'So, can you give me your mum and dad's address?' Charlie was saying as Holly hurriedly zoned back into their conversation.

'Sure, sorry,' she said, giving herself a mental shake. She scribbled the details down on the block pad near the till. 'Come round for about one o'clock.'

'I look forward to it,' Charlie smiled. 'I'm not much of a cook, so I tend to make the wrong choices at the weekends. In London it's a bit easier because of the canteen at work, but I really must get my act together.'

'You make it sound a lot cosier and less exclusive than I bet it really is!' Holly said wryly. 'I've read Edwina Currie; I know the food's great and there's wine on tap.'

'Not so much any more,' Charlie countered. 'At least, not for those of us who take the job seriously. Things have changed a bit since she wrote those novels.'

'I'm sure,' Holly's tone was still teasing. 'But that's what you *would* say to a constituent.' Aware that she was probably being a little too snippy for someone who was just, at this stage, a good acquaintance rather than a friend, she smiled apologetically. 'Sorry. I'm just used to doubting everything politicians say these days.'

'I understand that,' Charlie said quietly. He looked at her intently. 'But I do mean it, Holly. I didn't take this job for an easy ride, no matter how safe I was told the seat was. I want to make a difference here. And I really think I can, too.'

'I hope so, Charlie,' Holly said softly. 'There's a lot you can do here, in your position.' She again dithered on whether to tell him about Harry, but thought better of it. There would be another occasion, she was sure of it.

His serious brown eyes were still locked on hers, and she found herself looking from them to his mouth and back again. God, he was attractive.

Suddenly awkwardly aware of their intensity, Holly shook her head and looked across to the door of the shop. 'Well, I'd better lock up properly and barricade myself in upstairs with Arthur until one or other of us finds this mouse!'

Charlie took the hint. 'Good luck with it. You'll understand if I don't offer to help.'

'Sure,' Holly laughed. 'See you on Sunday.'

'I look forward to it.' Giving her another smile, during which

Holly quite perceptibly felt her insides flutter, Charlie headed for the door. 'See you soon.'

'See you,' Holly said, still rooted to the spot behind the counter. She watched him walk through the door and close it quietly behind him. Somewhere, buried deep within that man, was the teenager she'd met all those years ago. Holly was shocked at how much she wanted to find him again.

13

After another sound night's sleep, albeit interspersed with the odd mouse-infested dream, Charlie woke to a full day of appointments at his constituency office. Tom was going to open up, as usual, and his new case worker, Helen Groves, was proving to be calm and efficient, and just what he needed as he was navigating the tricky waters of the issues of his constituents. Glancing at his diary as he grabbed a quick slice of toast and some coffee to take with him in his (not yet Instagrammed) travel mug, he was pleased to see he had a wide variety of people, and issues, to deal with that morning. Sooner or later, he knew he'd greet the information with a little more weariness, but for the moment he was pleased that so many people were seeking him out for help and advice. Working for his constituency was one of the main reasons he wanted this job, and so the more he could do while he was here, the better.

It was another lovely day in Willowbury as he walked down the path from his front door and onto the road that led to the High Street. He noticed that Fairbrothers was doing a roaring trade, as usual, and waved to Miles as he caught his eye through the bakery window. Jack, too, in his coffee shop, seemed to be trading briskly. The taxidermist on the corner of the High Street was polishing his front window, and Charlie found his gaze drawn to the sinister-looking stuffed crow on a tree branch that took pride of place. Every time he passed it, it seemed to have its beady eye on him, as if it was reminding him to behave himself. Years ago, when he was at school, he remembered the science department having a similar piece in its office, that some joker had made a miniature mortarboard for.

From the High Street, he could see the silhouette of Willow-bury Hill a few miles further on, backlit by the sun and majestic in its dominant presence, even from this distance. Tourists flocked from miles around to climb the hill and experience the breathtaking views from the top. Willowbury also had its own ruined religious building, too – a priory that was destroyed during the Reformation, which was an increasing draw to tourists now the National Trust had acquired it.

Musing on this, he passed ComIncense, but clearly Holly hadn't opened up yet as the shop front lights weren't on. He glanced at his watch and realised it was only half past eight, and most of the shops that didn't sell food and drink didn't open until nine o'clock anyway. He tried not to imagine Holly padding around upstairs in her flat, perhaps making a coffee and going through her tasks for the day. An image flashed into his mind of Holly in a skimpy cotton nightgown, with her vivid red hair in a bed-tousled plait over one shoulder, the other fully revealed as a strap slipped down... He swallowed hard, chiding himself for letting his imagination get the better of him.

Letting himself into the office a few minutes later, he put his travel mug down on his desk and went through the diary for the day on his iPad. Tom had access to it, as did Helen, and both were proving adept at managing his constituency days beauti-fully. So long as he kept himself briefed on who was coming to visit, the logistics of the appointments were out of his hands.

This suited Charlie perfectly as it allowed him to concentrate on the actual issues at hand.

Glancing down his list for the morning, he didn't see anything too controversial or odd – a bit of noise pollution, a Rachel Jamieson coming in to discuss a health issue, and a meeting with the head of the local Chambers of Commerce about boosting tourism in the area. So far, so safe.

* * *

'So if you could just see fit to have a word with him, I'd be ever so grateful,' the little old lady in front of Charlie's desk continued. 'Only I don't know how as I can go on like this with the blessed music blasting out night after night. My husband's deaf, so it doesn't bother him, but my hearing's still as sharp as ever, and I really can't get any sleep.'

Charlie felt a pang of sympathy for her. Mrs Garner lived in the middle of a row of local authority houses in Willowbury, which had a high turnover of tenants, except for her and her elderly husband, and the current tenants on one side were clearly being more than a little antisocial.

'I'll see what I can do, Mrs Garner,' Charlie said. 'But perhaps you'd be better off phoning the local council offices? They tend to deal with environmental health issues, rather than me in this office.' This wasn't the first Willowbury resident who'd come to him with matters better suited to the council, but Charlie was loath to turn them away out of hand. He relented a little. 'Are you online at home at all? It's quite easy to email them, too.'

Mrs Garner laughed. 'You're pulling my leg, love. It was hard enough getting my husband to use a push-button phone.'

'Well, perhaps my assistant can email the council for you,' Charlie said. He picked up his phone and spoke briefly to Helen, who occupied the front office. Smiling as he put the phone down, he turned back to his constituent. 'Helen's going to send them an email, and when they respond, we'll drop you a line and let you know. Or you might get a letter from them.'

'Thank you, my love,' Mrs Garner's rheumy eyes brimmed. 'It wouldn't be so bad if my husband didn't have dementia, but facing this on my own is a bit difficult these days.'

Charlie felt a lurch of sympathy. He could well imagine the trials of the woman in front of him. 'Does your husband have a carer to come in at all?' he asked gently. He knew he had another appointment in a few minutes, but he was reluctant to let Mrs Garner go just like that.

'Oh, they come in, these lovely foreign girls, twice a day, but they don't get paid enough, and they're always so pushed for time,' Mrs Garner sighed. 'It's not their fault, but it does mean long stretches where we're on our own.'

'I see.' Charlie's mind was whirling. 'What about respite care? Is your husband eligible for that?'

'He goes into the local nursing home for a couple of nights a month,' Mrs Garner replied. 'Which would help, but with the noise from next door, it doesn't make a great deal of difference.'

'I see.' Charlie was determined now to try to help. He stood up from behind his desk and came round it to help Mrs Garner to her feet. 'If we can help with the noise issue, I promise we will.'

'Thank you so much,' Mrs Garner smiled up at him. 'Now I'd best be off. You've got other people to see, I'd imagine.' She walked with a surprisingly brisk step to the door of the office.

'Take care now,' Charlie said as she left. He hoped he would be able to help her. It was the work of a few minutes, time-wise, but it might make a big difference to her. Walking back to his desk, he made a note in his diary to check on her case again in a week or two, and, if necessary, hassle the council himself.

When he looked up again, he saw a woman in his doorway.

She was clutching a folder to her chest and looked a little nervous, but very familiar.

'Hello,' Charlie said, rising from his desk and holding out a hand. 'I'm Charlie Thorpe. How can I help you?'

The woman smiled, and then it clicked.

'Of course,' Charlie said. 'You're Rachel, aren't you? We, er, *met* last night at your sister's place.' Unsurprisingly, he'd been more concerned about getting his trousers back on than paying attention to the woman and child who'd appeared at that highly embarrassing moment in Holly's home.

Rachel smiled, blushing slightly. 'Yes, that's right.'

'So, what can I do for you?' Charlie hadn't made the connection when he'd seen Rachel's name on his appointments list, but, of course, she had been married, so her name was different now to Holly's.

'It's about my son, Harry,' Rachel replied, still smiling. 'You, er, met him last night, too.' She took a seat in front of the desk.

Charlie made a mental note to get some comfortable chairs to put in the bay window of the room as he, sat back down behind his desk, although it felt a little formal. But then, he figured, given the position he was in when he'd met Rachel last night, perhaps a little formal distance was just what was needed.

'How can I help?' Charlie smiled, trying to forget that the last time Rachel had seen him, he'd been spreadeagled on top of her sister with his trousers round his ankles.

'I don't know if Holly's told you about Harry's condition, but he was born with cystic fibrosis.' Rachel paused and shuffled the folder she'd brought in with her. 'There's a new generation of drugs coming from a large pharmaceutical company, but there's a hold-up because the company can't strike an agreement with the government to supply them on the NHS. So far, they're in a stalemate.' Rachel handed over some documentation to Charlie that outlined the issue in more detail. 'I did speak to Mr Fitzgerald about it back when Harry was a baby, but he was unable, or unwilling, to progress the case, so it kind of stalled here, as well.'

Charlie 's heart went out to the woman sitting on the other side of the desk. He remembered seeing little Harry, first in Holly's shop and then, he winced inwardly, when the loose mouse had caused such an embarrassing stir. The little boy looked just like any other child; who would have imagined that he had such a heartbreaking condition? He didn't know a lot about cystic fibrosis, but his sense of responsibility to those in need in his constituency, as well as his own, very human emotions at Rachel's revelation made him want to find out more. He scanned through the précis that Rachel had given him. On paper it all seemed clear enough, though, understandably, frustrating for Rachel and her family.

'It's a conflict because of the cost issue, I see,' he murmured. It wasn't an unfamiliar story; the NHS was stretched and often it was a question of economics. That in no way made decisions easier, but they had to be made, nonetheless.

'That's true, but there may be grounds for reassessment,' Rachel said. 'So far, there have been a couple of MPs who've got behind the campaign, but as the new MP here, I wondered if you might give it some thought, too.'

Charlie nodded. 'Leave it with me. I'll need to look into it, get some more facts and figures and find out exactly what's involved, but I promise I'll come back to you when I've had the chance to do a bit of homework.' Charlie felt a tingle of excitement; the Ministry of Health was his ultimate aim, in a few years, and taking on Rachel and Harry's case might be as useful for him politically as it was for them. That wasn't as venal as it sounded; as one of his constituents, it was equally important to give them the attention and service they needed, too. Perhaps there was a way to help them both.

'Thank you,' Rachel said. 'Being the parent of a child with CF feels like being on borrowed time.'

Charlie nodded. 'I can't imagine, but I can try to help.'

There was a pause, which seemed to signal the end of the formal part of the appointment.

Rachel stood up and Charlie went to hand her back the folder, but Rachel shook her head. 'Keep it – I made copies for you for reference.'

'Thanks.' Charlie rose to his feet when Rachel did, and she grinned.

'It's good to see you with your trousers on this time.'

Charlie laughed out loud. 'I have no idea what you must have thought.'

Rachel smiled wryly. 'With Holly, I've learned not to read too much into anything – for all I know it could have been some kind of alternative therapy!' She paused. 'She did text me and say she and Arthur flushed out the mouse in the end, though, if that's any comfort.'

'I'd like to say it was,' Charlie joined in the laughter, 'but I'm still having flashbacks!'

'Well, thank you for seeing me,' Rachel said. 'Holly's been nagging me to make an official appointment with you since you moved in, but I've been so tied up with the campaigning, and Harry's been on some new medication recently, that I haven't had the chance. There have been a lot of demonstrations by the families of CF patients in your neck of the woods at Westminster lately. You've probably come across them. The campaign's colour is yellow.'

'Yes, I've seen one or two,' Charlie acknowledged. 'It always amazes me how well attended these things are, and how much support they have.'

'We like to be vocal about it when we can,' Rachel replied. 'People with the condition themselves can't be too close physically, because there's a danger that they might make each other ill, so friends and families choose to campaign on their behalf.'

Charlie was shocked, and he felt his heart, again, go out to the woman opposite him. How incredibly isolating that must be for those with the condition, never able to interact with each other in person for fear of getting ill. 'I can't imagine how difficult that must be for you, and for Harry,' he said. 'If I can do anything to help, I will.' He paused. 'And do keep in touch if there's anything else I should know. I want to help.'

'Thank you,' Rachel stood up. 'It's a step forward just to be here in this office; Hugo Fitzgerald used to send out a letter in response to me every so often, but that was about as far as it went.'

Charlie tried not to grimace. He'd been hearing far too much about the actions, or lack thereof, of the previous incumbent, and while respect for the dead and for the holder of the seat before him counted for some things, it was getting more and more difficult to remain diplomatic, the more he found out. 'I'll be in touch,' he assured Rachel.

Wandering to the door to escort her out a moment later, Charlie turned back to Helen when Rachel was gone.

'Can you get all the info you can on the re-evaluation of the next generation of cystic fibrosis drugs and email anything useful you find?' he said.

'Sure thing, boss,' answered Helen, coolly efficient as ever and already working through Charlie's burgeoning pile of email and paper correspondence. 'Do you want me to update the office Twitter feed as well? I've got the photos from your visit to Willowbury Primary last week that still need to go on.'

'Yes, that would be great, thanks,' Charlie replied. He tried to get a visit in to a school or other community concern as often as he could, both to raise his own profile and to shine a light on their achievements or needs, and he'd particularly enjoyed visiting the primary school; the children were so unguarded in their attitudes towards him, it made a refreshing change. He still couldn't quite get used to being asked by five-year-olds if he had a girlfriend, but he'd definitely enjoyed seeing what schools were like since the last time he'd been at one himself.

He was also a keen Instagrammer and had already amassed nearly five thousand followers since his election to the Willowbury and Stavenham seat, but he still had yet to get to grips with Twitter, and relied on Helen, who was ten years younger, and far more in tune with social media, to handle that and the official Facebook pages. Social media had its advantages, and its disadvantages, as he knew from being one of the first students to adopt it at university. He was part of a generation that had some of their memories on actual, printed photographs and a lot more stored in the ethereal world of online and digital. Everything he did, now more than ever, would be under scrutiny. If he'd been more reckless in his university days, he felt sure he'd have been more concerned, but he was fairly certain there weren't going to be any skeletons leaping out of closets at an inconvenient moment.

Certain numbers of his colleagues had not fared so well at the hands of social media, though. He still felt a pang of sympathy for one former party leader, whose apology for a poor policy decision had been memed, autotuned and posted on YouTube for all to see. It was an occupational hazard these days.

Wandering back into his office, he picked up the paper file that Rachel had left him to take a closer look. Leafing through the press cuttings, the leaflets and the copies of letters that she'd sent to Hugo Fitzgerald and other MPs, it was clear she didn't just have a mother's knowledge about her son's condition; she, by necessity, had become a bit of an expert on drug funding, policy and procedure. She could probably teach him a thing or two.

Sitting down at his desk to read, he became engrossed in the file, and was only distracted by his email notification ping some time later. Helen had collected as much information as she could, including links to the most relevant debates in Parliament. Hansard, which was the official record of debates of the UK Parliament, had an open-access digital archive stretching back a hundred years, making searching it for incidences where the issue had been raised in the House an easy matter. Charlie was shocked to see that the funding of the new drug had been raised numerous times over the years. Cystic fibrosis was a condition that affected seventy thousand patients worldwide, ten thousand in the United Kingdom alone, and one which seemed in desperate need of more publicity, understanding and, most of all, effective treatment. Given the inevitable stints in hospital that patients had to endure, anything that prevented costs escalating in that way had to be a bonus, surely?

A number of MPs had taken up the cause, according to the records of debate in Hansard, but Rachel was right, it had stalled over the past year or so. Could he – should he – take it on? It was at times like these he wished he'd been in the House a little longer. While he was a nodding acquaintance to some of the more local MPs, the job was often an isolating one, and he hadn't yet formed an effective network in London. The party helped, of course, but even within that, there were always shifting loyalties and alliances. Someone who supported you one week could change their mind the next. It was like being in a huge class, back at school, at times, and Charlie was acutely aware that as a rookie MP, in his first term of office, he was vulnerable, even with a so-called safe majority in his constituency.

But wasn't it his duty to put his constituents first? Surely, that should override all other concerns. And Rachel was a voter, after all. Jotting down a couple of things to check out, he then glanced at his iCal diary and, with a jolt of pleasure, realised he had a free couple of hours. He should be cracking on with some more paperwork, but since it was such a glorious day, he decided to get out and stretch his legs. He knew that free time was precious, as constituency work and work in the House could get extremely intense, especially in the run-up to the summer recess. Time where he could just get out and soak up the atmosphere of his new home would be scarce, so he was determined to make the most of his free time.

As he wandered out of his office, he called to Helen. 'I'm off for an early lunch. I'll be back in a bit.'

'Okey-dokey,' Helen said, not glancing up from her computer. 'Have you got your phone on you in case I need to get hold of you urgently?'

'Yup,' Charlie replied.

Helen might be a lot younger than him, but she still sounded like his mother at times. It was only fair that she reminded him, though. He'd already left his phone in Jack Winter's coffee shop on the High Street once, and been roundly bollocked by Tom Fielding for it. Although it was fingerprint-locked, he used it to check his emails, and so there was a fair bit of sensitive material on there. Things must have been simpler back in the old days, he thought, when all you had to worry about was the paper contents of your briefcase or ministerial red box and documents actually crinkled when you folded them, instead of flying off into the ether electronically.

Walking along Willowbury High Street, though, almost timeless in its abundance of weird and wonderful shop fronts, Charlie felt as though he had, at least, come to the right place to live. There was definitely something in the air, and not just the medicinal herbs.

'You know when you say something in the heat of the moment and then spend the next fifteen hours regretting it?' Holly said as she passed Rachel a glass of wine from the bottle she'd brought over to her sister's house that evening.

'Not really,' Rachel teased. 'Since Callum and I got divorced my only real conversation is with Harry most of the time, and he's pretty immune to me putting my foot in it!'

'Fair enough,' Holly replied. 'But, your lack of actual adult conversation aside, I'm sure you must sort of know what I'm saying.'

'What have you done?' Rachel raised an eyebrow. 'I thought you'd managed to curb your foot-in-mouth tendencies since you became a respectable business owner?'

'Most of the time, yes, but these were, er, slightly unusual circumstances.'

'Are you talking about Charlie Thorpe and his lack of trousers by any chance?'

Holly laughed, in spite of herself. 'How did you guess?'

'So, what have you said to him?'

Holly shook her head. 'Something *really* stupid.'

'Spill.'

'I might have, er, invited him to Sunday lunch at Mum and Dad's place this weekend.'

Rachel nearly spat her wine out in amusement. 'You did what? How bloody square are you?' She put her wine glass down on the coffee table in front of her, since it was dangerously close to spilling. 'I mean, ask him out for a drink or a coffee, or even a walk up Willowbury Hill, but to Mum and Dad's for lunch?'

'I know.' Holly felt her face start to burn. 'Maybe it's because, for some reason, he makes me feel as though I'm that nineteen-year-old kid again, but it just came out. And now we've both got to sit around the table on Sunday with Mum and Dad, and you and Harry, of course, and make polite conversation after he fell on top of me in his pants.'

'Well, when you put it like that...' Rachel collapsed into giggles back into the cushions of her sofa. 'And he actually said yes?'

'Yup,' Holly groaned. 'Do you think I should call him and cancel it?'

'Wouldn't be very polite of you,' Rachel said reasonably. 'And the fact that he's agreed to it suggests he wants to come. Unless, of course, he looked too terrified to say no?'

'It was after I'd given him a back massage, so he might not have been in his right mind,' Holly sipped her wine and tried to quell the butterflies in her stomach. 'Perhaps he'll do us a favour and cry off when he's come to his senses.'

'Or perhaps you'll have to suck it up and just make sure you ply him with enough booze round Mum and Dad's dinner table that he forgets what a closet nerd you are!'

'Thanks for the moral support, sis,' Holly replied. 'And remember, not a word about the photo-in-the-suitcase business, or you'll be wearing the trifle rather than eating it.'

'I'll be the soul of discretion,' Rachel said. 'But don't you think it's about time you told him, just to get it out in the open?'

'Probably,' agreed Holly, 'but it just seems so random. I mean, we've chatted a lot, but I still haven't found the right time to mention it. It's hardly like, when he's on my massage table, I can just casually drop it into conversation, is it? "Oh, by the way, it seems like you clearly don't remember one night fifteen years ago when we had a bit of a kiss and you held my hand."' She shook her head in exasperation. 'Maybe I'm overthinking it.'

'You think?' Rachel rolled her eyes. 'But I promise I won't say anything. Better remind Mum not to, as well, though. You know what she's like after a glass of wine!'

'I threatened to burn the whole case if she said anything,' Holly replied. 'And I would, too.'

'Fair enough.' There was a pause as the two sisters sipped their wine. It had been a busy week for them both. Rachel had enrolled Harry into the local nursery school, and she was preparing herself for handing over his care to them for sixteen hours a week. 'How did Harry get on at his orientation morning at nursery?'

'Really well,' Rachel replied. 'He loved the staff, and all the new toys were definitely a good reason to go back, he said.'

'Sounds encouraging,' Holly said carefully. She knew that, underneath her quiet, capable and calm facade, Rachel was likely to be more than a bit nervous about handing over Harry to anyone else, if only for a short time each week. 'And you're OK with it?'

Rachel paused. 'Yes, I *think* so.' She sighed. 'I know I should be preparing myself to take a step back, with him starting school this year, but it's been just me and Harry for so long, since Callum and I went our separate ways, that I'm struggling to let go of the reins. And there's the risks of illness and infection, of course.'

'The nursery's got a great reputation,' Holly said. 'And they're small enough to be able to give him all of the support he needs. I'm sure he'll be fine.'

'Oh, so am I, really,' Rachel said. 'It's just that I worry about him picking up a bug. I mean, I know all kids do, but it puts him back for days, if not weeks, at a time.'

Holly's heart ached for Rachel. As Harry's aunt, she knew to a certain extent how tricky managing his condition could be, but it was Rachel who coped, largely alone, with the day-to-day issues. And Rachel who had to contend with the fact that her beloved son could gain valuable years of his life if given access to the next generation of medications. In the three years since Harry had come into her life, she'd become almost as much as an expert on cystic fibrosis as Rachel had, but it still frustrated and saddened her that the government couldn't come to an agreement about the funding of the new drugs.

'But today I did get to see your Sunday lunch guest in his official capacity,' Rachel continued. 'I thought I'd book an appointment since Harry had his session at nursery, and I've given him all of the information to look at, so who knows?'

'I hope he can help,' Holly said carefully. As an MP, she still couldn't quite trust that Charlie would help, but from what she was beginning to get to know about him as a person, he seemed sincere in his desire to change things and engage with his constituents. 'Let me know what happens.'

'Oh, I will,' Rachel said. 'And you keep me posted, too. I can't wait to hear how he reacts when you do eventually come clean to him about your scandalous past!'

Holly picked up the cushion that was in her lap and chucked it at her sister. 'Scandalous, my arse! You were just taking the piss about how boring and square I still am.'

'Even so, I bet he'll be surprised,' Rachel said. 'And you might end up underneath him for non-mouse related reasons, if you play your cards right!'

Holly snorted. 'One step at a time. Besides, who says I *want* that to happen?'

'Really?' Rachel raised an eyebrow. 'I think you and I have

both been single for entirely too long, and I'm pretty convinced that, if he's said yes to Sunday lunch with our folks, he must be keen on you. You could do worse, you know.'

'I'm perfectly happy as I am, thanks,' Holly said primly, although, even as she said it, she thought back to the flapping butterflies she'd experienced when Charlie had landed on top of her. And perhaps if she managed Sunday lunch without a hitch, she'd be a little more relaxed the next time he came in for a massage. Finishing her wine glass, she stood up. 'I'd better go. Weekends have been busy in the shop since the weather got warmer, so I'll have to open up on time tomorrow.'

'See you on Sunday, if not before,' Rachel said, rising and seeing her to the door. 'And don't forget to include an aphrodisiac or two on the Sunday lunch menu if you really want to get Charlie's trousers off again! I'm sure you've got a few in the jars in the shop.'

'No comment.' Holly grinned as she left. Her sister, when she allowed herself to let go of some of her ever-present worries about Harry, really was incorrigible.

15

Charlie wasn't quite sure what he'd imagined when he'd thought about Holly's parents, but something along the lines of *Meet the Fockers* had sprung to mind pretty soon after he'd met Holly. Surely someone with her passionate belief in all things alternative, spiritual and green could only have sprung from the loins of two hippies, probably full of sixties zeal for free love, peace and the odd spliff?

It came as quite a surprise, then, and not a little relief, that when he came face to face with Mr and Mrs Renton for Sunday lunch, they were conventionally dressed, lived in a spacious four-bedroom bungalow in the suburbs of Willowbury and there wasn't a dreamcatcher in sight at any of their large, double-glazed windows. He was doubly relieved that he hadn't brought along a bottle of Monk's Mead from the independent alcohol retailer on the High Street but had opted instead for a regular bottle of Sancerre, albeit an organic one, just to be on the safe side.

'So, how are you finding Willowbury life?' Vivian Renton asked as she handed him a glass of lager, cool from the fridge in the spacious kitchen.

'It's been interesting so far,' Charlie replied, smiling. 'But in a lot of good ways, of course,' he added hastily.

Vivian smiled back. 'Don't worry – we're incomers to the town ourselves, in a way. We lived closer to Bristol before we moved down here, which is where the girls grew up, but when Harry was diagnosed with his condition we wanted to be more on the doorstep.'

Charlie felt a lurch of sympathy. Vivian was a relatively young grandmother; did she fear outliving her much adored grandson?

'Holly decided to come back from working in Manchester at around the same time, so she's not exactly a native to these parts, either,' Vivian continued. 'So it's nice to all be in one place together.'

'Holly seems so at home here,' Charlie replied. 'I mean, with the shop and everything. I just assumed she'd lived here for ages.'

'A town like Willowbury is a welcoming place,' Vivian replied kindly. 'Before you know it, you're so settled you can't ever imagine living anywhere else.'

'I'm sure that's just the weed in the air, Mum!' Holly teased as she came through to the kitchen. 'I know I probably shouldn't say it in front of you, Charlie, but quite a few of the town's residents swear by its medicinal properties!'

'I'm sure,' Charlie replied wryly. He was relieved he hadn't been imagining it when he'd smelt it last week; although he was intending to turn a blind eye as much as he could. There were bigger battles to fight in Willowbury than a few middle-aged dope smokers.

He took a sip of his beer and glanced around the neat, tidy, cream-coloured kitchen. Charlie was amused to see that there was a child's paintings on the fridge, presumably created by Harry, and some adorable photographic fridge magnets of the two now grown-up sisters. He couldn't imagine his own parents displaying photos and memories on the fridge, or even thinking to make magnets out of them. They were much more the official-school-photos-in-brass-frames-on-side-tables types. Continuing to peruse the fridge, he was brought up short by a picture of Holly in her mid-teens, hair a reddish blonde, certainly a lighter colour than it was now, cut in a very sensible late-nineties style. She was wearing a long, button-down summer dress in a ditsy blue floral pattern that subtly complimented her creamy white skin and serious Bristol-blue eyes. She was smiling rather guardedly at the camera, and didn't seem to have the self-confidence she had all these years later. As he stared at the photo, lost in his own world for a moment, that prickle of recognition caught at the back of his mind once again; why did she look so familiar?

'Earth to Charlie,' the Holly of today, with longer, darker red hair cascading over her shoulders and a look of amusement on her face, chimed into his thoughts, and he started slightly, realising he'd been spending entirely too long staring at the fridge. Her hand, placed lightly on the crook of his arm, just on the bare skin underneath the sleeve of his T-shirt, sent a shock of electricity through him. It was a playful gesture, but Holly's eyes widened a little as they met his gaze, which snapped him back to reality. Why did he feel as though they were on the cusp of something?

'You've changed a lot since that photo was taken,' Charlie injected a note of lightness into his tone to hide how jolted he was by her touch.

Did he imagine it, or did Holly's face colour slightly at his comment?

'A lot can change in fifteen years!' Holly replied, seemingly equally lightly. 'Come on, the first course is already on the table.'

She still had her hand on Charlie's arm, and as he turned to follow her, his heart skipped several beats as her hand slipped down his arm to nestle in his own. He felt a rush of blood to his head, and other regions, and mentally told himself to get a grip. It was almost as if he was a teenager again, reacting so strongly to the slightest of physical stimuli. It took all of his self-control not to pull her to him and kiss her.

* * *

Lunch passed amiably, with Charlie answering the questions from Holly's parents politely and with a rather adorable dose of humour that Holly found herself beginning to really like. After the dishes had been cleared away, with Charlie helping her parents and on his best behaviour, they sat round the dinner table finishing off the wine. Unnerved as she was by Charlie's sudden interest in the old photos on the fridge, the fact he hadn't identified their previous connection came as a relief. After all, the past was the past. She'd learned that there was no point in looking back, in thinking of what might have been. When all was said and done, it was more important to be present in the moment, to take every day as it came.

'...And when I woke up, I realised I was about seventeen stops past my home town, and spent the next three hours on a platform in the middle of nowhere to get the next train back!' Charlie's voice zoned back into her consciousness and, with a pang, Holly registered that she wasn't actually living in the moment right now, however lovely that moment was.

She glanced at Charlie as she reached for the white-wine bottle and topped up his glass as well as her own. His face was slightly flushed from the wine, and he was leaning back in his dining chair. As he picked up his glass to take a sip, her eyes were drawn to his throat and his gorgeous hand holding the wine glass. She nearly choked on her own wine.

'Are you OK?' Charlie immediately put his glass down and turned to her in concern.

'Fine,' Holly gasped. 'Thanks.'

'Have some water,' Edward Renton passed his daughter a tumbler. 'Honestly, we can't take you anywhere!'

'Thanks, Dad,' Holly muttered.

When her breathing had returned to normal, she turned back to Charlie. 'Shall we go and sit outside? Mum and Dad's patio is a real suntrap.' She glanced at Rachel and Harry; the little boy had done remarkably well at sitting quietly at the table, and she smiled. 'Do you want to come outside with me and Charlie and show him the chickens?'

'Yeah!' Harry shouted, slithering down from his chair. Rushing round to Charlie, he grabbed his hand. Holly felt a glow of pleasure at how easily the two had taken to each other.

Charlie, smiling, allowed himself to be pulled to his feet by the little boy and led towards the patio doors that opened out into the Rentons' large back garden.

'I'll put the kettle on,' Rachel said. 'Tea or coffee, Charlie?'

'Coffee, please,' Charlie replied. 'I've got a train to catch back to London later, so I'd better try to stay awake after that amazing lunch.' He turned back to Harry, who was dragging him towards the patio.

Holly, smiling, got up from her chair and followed, but not before her mother had shot her a he's-pretty-nice look from under her lashes. Holly pretended not to notice.

Sliding open the doors that filled the entire wall of her parents' lounge diner, Holly felt the sun on her face and automatically turned her gaze upwards. She loved the early summer sun and was glad to be out in it. She glanced back at Charlie, who, attention momentarily diverted from Harry, was watching her. 'What?' she said teasingly.

'The sunlight really suits you,' Charlie said softly. 'Catches the light in your hair. It's like you were born to live in this season.'

'That's quite poetic for a politician!' Holly laughed nervously. 'Are you sure you've not been passive-smoking marijuana?'

Charlie laughed too, as he stepped out of the patio door, still being led by Harry. 'I hope not. I still don't know if the rumour that we get tested for drugs occasionally is actually true!'

'Come on, Aunty Holly!' Harry's little voice piped up, now fed up of the lingering adults as he took off down to the bottom of the garden where the chicken coop resided.

'We've been told,' Holly laughed as she fell into step beside Charlie and followed in the toddler's wake. They wandered down the garden, and as they drew closer, Holly was jolted to feel Charlie's warm hand slipping into hers. It felt so right there that she just enjoyed the sensation, in this beautiful garden, out of sight of her parents for a moment. She turned back to face him. 'I'm glad you came today,' she said softly. 'It might feel a bit juvenile, inviting you to Sunday lunch, but I wanted Mum and Dad, and Rachel and Harry to properly meet you. As well as apologise for, well, you know.'

'I'm really glad you did,' Charlie said.

A slight breeze rustled the leaves of the apple tree that they were standing under and loosened a strand of Holly's hair from the toggle at the base of her neck. She felt a tingle of desire as Charlie reached up his free hand and brushed it away from her mouth. Holly's stomach started to flutter. Charlie dipped his head slightly and they were within a breath of each other.

'Come and see the chickens!' Little Harry's voice broke into the moment and Holly jumped away from Charlie as if she'd been up to something naughty.

'OK, munchkin.' To break the tension, Holly bent down and placed a kiss on Harry's forehead, blowing away a lock of unruly blonde hair as she did so. 'I'll race you to the chicken house,' she said. She glanced up at Charlie, who was, thankfully, smiling. 'Come on, Charlie, you too.'

'How can I refuse?' Charlie grinned. 'Come on, Aunty Holly!'

Holly smiled. 'You're on.' Both of them took one of Harry's hands and scampered towards the chickens, who, somewhat surprised to be the focus of so much sudden attention, clucked disapprovingly.

Holly's heart thumped as she saw Charlie smiling down at Harry as her nephew pointed out all of the different-coloured chickens in the coop. They'd come close to something just now. The question was, was it something that either of them would pursue again?

16

The next morning, Holly grinned as she read the message that had just arrived on her phone. She briefly considered setting Charlie his own notification sound but dismissed the idea as far too ridiculous. They hadn't even kissed yet, after all. Although, for a long moment while she was reading his message, she did think about the kind of sound that would be appropriate for his messages. Justin Timberlake's 'SexyBack', perhaps, or, more wittily, 'Moves Like Jagger', which she was sure he'd be flattered by.

Say thanks again to your folks when you see them, he'd written. I'm stuck on the train just outside Reading, as usual, and I wish you were here with me! C x

Holly's heart thumped as she saw the kiss at the end of the text. They'd been so close yesterday, so achingly close, and yet they'd both paused. Perhaps, even fifteen years on, they were still the same reticent, geeky teenagers underneath it all. Holly was stunned that, even having seen the picture of herself as a teenager on the fridge, Charlie still hadn't made the connection that they'd met all those years ago. It wasn't a great indicator for a politician, she thought wryly, if he couldn't remember a face. Or perhaps she just hadn't made as much of an impression on him as he had on her. Having said that, she thought, she'd forgotten all about him until her mother had passed on her university stuff, so it wasn't as if he was the great, lost love of her life or anything. It was all just a rather pleasurable coincidence.

Thanks, she replied. But I think I've got the better deal. It's a gorgeous day in your new home town, and I'm looking forward to a nice long walk later.

She paused before adding her own X, after deciding that it was juvenile to worry about it. He'd used it first, after all. Who knew text communication could be so confusing?

They'd parted last night once again without kissing, as Rachel had offered to give Holly a lift back home, and Charlie had chosen to walk. Frustrated somewhat by her sister's, as ever, perfectly imperfect timing, she and Charlie had said goodbye on her parents' doorstep, and she knew, since he was getting an early train in the morning, she wouldn't get another opportunity to be alone with him until the end of the week when he came home from London. Why hadn't she just taken the initiative and kissed him in her parents' garden? What was holding her back?

It wasn't until she was at the end of a deep-vision meditation session with a small group of clients the following morning that it hit her like a bolt from the blue. Curled in child's pose at the end of the session, she suddenly knew *exactly* why she hadn't taken the lead. It was so obvious. She was, deep down, miffed that he hadn't recognised her. She was, basically, suffering from a case of bruised ego!

Putting those thoughts to one side abruptly as the bell above her shop door tinkled, she glanced up from the book she'd been flipping through on deep meditation techniques. She'd been trying to develop her practice lately, with a view to branching out and holding more regular sessions in the outdoors. She always felt so much more in touch with the elements when she meditated outside, but she'd only ever really held sessions in the shop. Perhaps outside was the next step. Placing the book down, she smiled at a small group of people, obviously tourists, who were glancing around the shop in trepidation. Realising that often people just came in to gawp, she smiled again, and left them to it. Sales of anything other than novelty crystals were rare in this instance.

Once they'd bought a couple of trinkets, and she'd filled them in on where the best places to get a coffee and a snack were (namely Jack Winter's coffee shop a few doors further along), Holly decided to take the bull by the horns. Flipping the sign on the shop's door to 'Closed' for a few minutes, she padded up the stairs to her bedroom, where she'd stashed the blue suitcase under her bed and released the mottled catches and lifted the lid on it again. Finding the old manila envelope that contained the photographs, she shook them out onto the bed and picked up the one of Charlie that had triggered her memory. Her heart thumped as she saw his smiling, open face, framed by those thick, black glasses. He looked so young, so different, and yet there he was, Charlie Thorpe, the glimmer of the man he was to become hidden in those deep brown eyes. She'd made the connection; why hadn't he? Was she really *that* unmemorable? No, that wasn't fair on Charlie. So why was she letting it hold her back? Why hadn't she just kissed him in the garden and moved on, whichever direction it would have gone?

She shook her head in exasperation. This was getting her nowhere. Then she had an idea. She could just tell him, of course. Smile, laugh, drop it into conversation the next time they happened to meet. The air would be clear, and things would move on naturally. But where was the fun in that? No, this deserved a little more fanfare. He'd caught her off guard in the shop when they'd first met; now it was her turn to do the same to him. After all, she reasoned, a politician had to be able to think on his feet; let's see what happens when she springs the reveal on him.

Now grinning, she grabbed her phone and texted him. The instructions were simple; turn up to the flat on Friday night and bring a bottle. The rest was up to her.

17

Friday evening seemed to come around swiftly. Holly, who'd
been mercifully busy enough in ComIncense all day to put her
date with Charlie mostly to the back of her mind, opened the
door of her flat and smiled when he arrived. Charlie, who'd
obviously come more or less straight from work having spent a
rare Friday in Westminster rather than in Willowbury, was still
in his suit. His tie was a little askew, but he'd clearly not wasted
any time in getting to her, as she'd told him to. He'd swapped his
bag for a bottle of Sancerre, which still had the mist of conden-
sation from whichever fridge he'd removed it from, his own or
that of the off-licence on the High Street. She could even smell a
tantalising scent of the last of his aftershave mixed with that
enticing smell of London: slightly smoky, a little bit stressed and
sublimely sexy.

'Hi,' she said softly. She was tickled to see him hesitating on
the doorstep – perhaps still a little embarrassed by the mouse-
up-the-trouser-leg incident, which was the last time he'd crossed
the threshold. 'Come on in.'

'There aren't any loose mice around are there?' he asked, as if
he'd read her mind.

Holly laughed. 'Not as far as I'm aware, but Arthur's not come back from his evening constitutional yet, so you can always tuck your trousers into your socks if you want to!'

Charlie laughed too. 'That would be a great look, wouldn't it?'

Despite his apparent rodent-related reservations, Charlie needed no further invitation and stepped into the flat, blinking a little at the dim lighting.

Holly had lit a candle in the hall, which rested in a glass bowl on the narrow console table under the mirror, and as they wandered back through to the living area off the hall, which incorporated Holly's kitchen and lounge space, more candles could be seen burning around the edges of the room. Some of them were on the worktops and sideboard, but, and Charlie seemed a little unnerved by this, some were just lit at random and placed carefully on the floor.

'Don't you worry about Arthur singeing his tail with all these naked flames around? Or knocking one over and setting fire to the place?'

'He's not particularly interested in them, to be honest,' Holly said as Charlie passed the bottle of wine to her. Wandering over to the kitchen area, she swiftly found the corkscrew and poured them both a chilled glass. 'Thanks for this. Just what I need on a Friday evening after a busy week.'

'Ley lines giving you grief?' Charlie teased. 'Chakras not aligning properly?'

'Oh, I know it's not like I'm running the country or anything,' Holly replied, a twinkle in her eye. 'But believe it or not, being a small business owner comes with its own stresses. Not that you'd know anything about that, of course, in your Westminster bubble for most of the week.'

'On the contrary,' Charlie said, taking a sip of his wine. 'I've spent most of this week reading emails from business owners in Willowbury bemoaning the lack of progress on the new motorway junction.' He smiled ruefully. 'Your local baker, Miles Fairbrother, has a thing or two to say about the delays, as I've been finding out.'

'I wouldn't worry about him,' Holly snorted. 'He's taken so many backhanders about that bloody junction over the years, he can afford to wait a bit longer. They can't do anything while the site's being investigated, anyway, and that's even before the local wildlife trust have fully examined the area. There's still the toads and bats to consider.'

'You seem remarkably knowledgeable about it all,' Charlie said. He glanced at the cosy sofa that was covered with a patchwork rug. 'May I?'

'Wait a second,' Holly said. She had her own reasons for keeping him standing at the moment. She felt a flutter in her stomach, a prickle of indecision about what she was going to do. What if, after all, Charlie just looked blankly at her, denied ever having met her and the whole thing was just a massive embarrassment? Perhaps she should just sit down with him and forget it.

But still, this was the reason she'd been holding back from him. He'd landed on top of her in her own living room, for goodness' sake! And the way his eyes were widening in the (admittedly dim) light had to be a sign. That walk in her parents' garden, underneath the apple trees, where they'd come so close to a kiss, had to mean something. And the fact he'd come virtually straight from the train to her home. She needed to get over this hurdle, get over her own hang-ups about that night in London fifteen years ago and move forward. But, first of all, she had to know if he really had forgotten all about her.

'What is it?' Charlie said, his voice betraying a little concern. 'Is everything OK?'

Holly smiled again, as much to reassure herself as him. 'It's fine, honestly. But will you trust me for a moment?'

Charlie raised an eyebrow. 'Of course. But you're not going to

make me do any twilight rebirthing or transcendental meditation? I've had quite a long week!'

'No meditation, I promise.' Taking a deep breath, Holly
prepared to level with him. She took the wine glass out of his
hand. 'Give me a minute, OK?'

'Sure,' Charlie said.

He looked as nervous and uncertain as he had all those years
ago, Holly thought. Somewhere, in this very grown-up man,
were the vestiges of the boy she'd met; the boy with the smiling
eyes. She turned away from him and prepared to let him in on
the secret she'd been keeping to herself.

* * *

Charlie felt distinctly unsettled. He'd had a long week, and he
still felt befuddled by the low candlelight and the rather odd
expression Holly had had on her face before she'd turned away
and headed to the bedroom of her flat. Charlie prided himself
on his efficiency, on his ability to put all aspects of his life into
the correct mental pigeonholes and deal with everything in the
most effective way possible. And now, here was Holly Renton
suggesting that he'd made an error; an error that he should have
remembered.

'You really don't remember, do you?' Holly's voice was
teasing as it floated through from the other room.

'Remember what?' he asked. His voice was a little more
brittle than it should have been. 'Did I do something stupid after
you gave me that first massage? Did I leave here stark bollock
naked or something?'

Holly laughed. 'Don't you think that would have been all
over the local paper if you had? "Willowbury MP in flashing
scandal"?'

'Round here, I doubt it would have been much of a scandal,'
Charlie replied, remembering the notes about the nude

sunbathing shop owners that he'd found in one of Hugo Fitzgerald's box files.

Still none the wiser, he heard what sounded like the flip of a briefcase catch and the rustle of some papers. Taking a sip of his wine, he willed the chilled, bone-dry liquid to calm him down. There were too many mixed signals here, standing in this house, with this woman, waiting for the big reveal. Charlie was about as risk-averse as he could be, even more so now he was an MP, and being here made his stomach flutter and his hands shake in a way they hadn't for years. In fact, the last time he could remember feeling so unnerved was... was... He reached for the memory, for the tantalising truth that had been eluding him since his arrival in Willowbury, but once again it danced from his fingertips, away from his mind. And then, before he could try to grasp it fully, Holly returned, clutching a couple of what looked like photographs to her chest.

'Christ,' Charlie muttered, heart beating faster. This was worse than he'd thought. 'What are those?' It was a politician's worst nightmare, he thought; photographs were more likely to be digital and pop up all over Instagram these days, but the thought of being caught on camera doing something that looked incriminating was an unnerving one.

'Oh, calm down,' Holly replied. 'They're nothing that would drag you into a scandal. But before I show you them, will you let me do something?'

'That depends.' But, intrigued as he was, Charlie couldn't refuse. He'd crossed the threshold after all, and the wine and the candles were working their magic on him. 'Oh, all right then.'

'Just stay there for a sec.'

Charlie did as he was told, and before he could catch a glimpse of the pictures, Holly had tucked them into the back pocket of her jeans. Grabbing her phone, she swiped to Spotify and selected a song. As the song began to play through the Bluetooth speaker, Charlie raised an eyebrow. 'Getting a bit retro tonight, aren't we?' The song was one from a few years into the millennium, possibly even old before then, with a sultry beat and a smoky-voiced singer. Charlie's spine began to tingle. 'This takes me back...'

'Ssh.' Holly swayed a little to the beat. 'Think...' She took the glass from his hand and placed it down on the side table, where it glinted in the candlelight. Straightening back up, she drew a little closer to Charlie. He could see the flecks of light from the candles reflecting off her tousled hair and, just for a moment, a slight hesitation in her expression as she put a hand on his chest.

Charlie, entranced, but mind still whirling from the strangeness of the situation and the elusiveness of his own memory, slipped his hands around Holly's waist. They began to sway to the beat as the rhythm throbbed in the air. Charlie felt Holly slip her hand upwards until it rested on the back of his neck, causing his skin to tingle and a shiver to run down his spine. He drew her closer to him until their hips were almost touching and his hand was resting in the small of her back.

He looked down and saw the top of Holly's head, and as she lay her cheek on his shoulder, nestling closer and closer, he was assailed by a memory, long lost and almost forgotten, of two people on the cusp of adulthood. On the cusp of... something. Of swaying together in a nightclub in Leicester Square as other people danced and pressed in around them until they were far closer together than they'd intended to be. Of a throbbing R&B beat and a drink or two to lower the inhibitions, a face upturned to his, and a gentle, feather-light kiss on the lips that promised so much but never had the opportunity to be delivered. The shiver down his spine, the breath that he'd unconsciously been holding, the sudden, sharp pinprick of desire. And then he knew.

'It's *you*...' he breathed, as the memories of a strawberry-blonde bob, a sexy yet conventional black velvet evening dress and a smattering of freckles across the bridge of a longish nose came back to him. And the feeling of a pair of demurely painted pink lips brushing his in a kiss that was more nerves than passion.

'It's me...' Holly replied softly as she drew closer to Charlie. 'And it's you. Lovely Charlie from Leeds University, who made me feel safe in London.'

Although his eyes had closed in anticipation of the kiss, Charlie could sense how close Holly's lips were to his, and he felt his body responding immediately, as it had done fifteen years ago when she'd been in his arms in the nightclub. Back then, he'd been achingly self-conscious about his near instant hard-on; he'd sensed how reticent she was, how both of them weren't ready for anything other than a kiss and a moonlit walk, despite what his body was screaming at him. Now, as the blood surged to his cock and he felt that familiar ache of lust and long- ing, all he had to do was dip his head for his mouth to reach hers. Time and experience had taught him that to betray a response wasn't always a bad thing; that it could, in fact, be a very good thing. And something was telling him that this time Holly wouldn't be the nervous girl he remembered. It *was* her, then. The one who wasn't even there long enough to get away. Life, and coincidence, had thrown her into his path and taken her away. But now they were here, together again. How had he not realised before? He was determined that nothing would get in the way now.

The kiss, fifteen years in the making, was as sweet for the waiting as he'd wished it could have been back then. Back then he'd wanted so desperately to find the words to get to know her better, to kiss her again, for longer, but there was no time. As the pressure of their lips gave way to open mouths and exploring tongues, Charlie ached.

Eventually, they broke apart.

'You were going to show me something?' Charlie asked, when his brain had begun to engage again.

Holly laughed breathlessly. 'You'll never believe how dorky we looked back then.' She pulled the photographs from the pocket of her jeans with a smirk. 'I mean, it's no wonder we both didn't recognise each other, really.'

Charlie glanced at the first photograph and gave a snort of laughter. 'Thank God I ditched those glasses and got contact lenses. I don't know why I ever thought they suited me.' His brow furrowed. 'And that side parting is hell. Not to mention that godawful blazer and tie.' Embarrassed at just how gangly and awkward he looked in the candid snap, taken a decade and a half ago, he felt his stomach clenching and his cheeks burning, a complete antidote to the fiery passion that had been building a moment ago. 'I honestly don't remember you taking that picture at the Tube station though. We must have been really drunk – or really tired!'

'Give yourself a break,' Holly said. 'You haven't seen the one of me, yet.' She passed him the other photo and Charlie had to suppress another grin. 'You looked very, er, lovely.'

'Give it a rest,' Holly murmured. 'That skirt length was about ten years too old for me and bobs went out in the early nineties, unless you suited a Rachel cut. I was about the most sensible girl in the world. Hence my interest in party politics, I suppose.'

'Well, I remember you now,' Charlie said, a husky note in his voice. 'And, if it's all the same to you, I'd like to make up for lost time. Fifteen years of lost time, in fact. So, will you dance with me, and kiss me again, and maybe allow me to do a little more than just hold your hand?'

Holly smiled. 'I'd like that. I'd like that very, very much, Lovely Charlie.'

As their lips met again, Charlie felt his defences begin to come down. He spent so much of his life taking steps to be seen to be doing the right thing, saying the right thing, that to be alone, in this room, with Holly now was a feeling so powerful, he felt himself losing his breath. Fifteen years ago, their paths had crossed so briefly that it hadn't warranted further exploration, even though he'd never really forgotten that night, that girl. Despite not having recognised her again until now, he did have some sense that he'd kept the memory with him. Who knows what would have happened if the two of them hadn't been those awkward teenagers in that terribly conventional setting, part of a world that was too old for them, wearing clothes that were too old for them. But now, they'd rediscovered each other, and Charlie wanted to seize the moment.

The kisses grew deeper, and as Charlie felt Holly's warm hand raking through his hair, the back of his neck been to tingle. Drawing her closer to him, feeling that quick, white heat of arousal, her body against his felt instinctively right. There was so much he wanted to say, so much he wanted to do. Her lips were warm, and soft, her mouth sweet-tasting. Charlie had the sensation, right then, that he'd come home.

The insistent ring of Holly's mobile on the kitchen counter brought them both out of the moment. Holly, regretfully, broke free from Charlie and, with an apologetic smile, wandered on unsteady legs to answer it.

'Sorry,' she said. 'I keep the phone on because Harry's having a bit of a tricky spell at the moment.'

'No problem,' Charlie said. He finally sat down on the sofa, but, realising that his suit trousers left very little about his arousal to the imagination (not that Holly could have failed to notice when she was in his arms and pressed against him), he grabbed his wine glass again and rested it in his lap. The cool glass took the edge off things a little bit.

'OK... No, that's fine... I'll drop it over to you as soon as I can... No, don't worry.' Holly threw an apologetic glance in Charlie's direction. 'I'll see you in a bit.' Tapping to end the call, Holly wandered back to the sofa. 'I'm really sorry,' she began. 'I've got to dash out and pick up some Creon granules from the late-night chemist in Stavenham for Harry. Mum and Dad are away visiting friends in Bristol tonight and Harry's been quite poorly.' She smiled regretfully. 'He needs it to help him digest his food properly, so it's kind of an essential. I'm not sure what time I'll be back here. Can we, you know, pick this up another time?'

Charlie, stung with disappointment, but knowing there was little else to be done, smiled back. 'Of course.' He drew her to him as they both stood up. 'You've given me a lot to think about, Holly Renton.'

Holly laughed nervously. 'In a good way, I hope!'

'Definitely.' Charlie dipped his head and kissed Holly lingeringly on the lips. 'This is the kind of kiss I desperately wanted to give you, all those years ago on that dance floor. But I was so scared you'd run away. You looked absolutely terrified when we did actually kiss.'

'I was,' Holly admitted. 'I'd only had one serious boyfriend when I met you, and I guess that's why I was so nervous that night.'

'You looked so gorgeous. I can't believe I didn't realise it was you.'

'I look a whole lot different now,' Holly smiled as they broke apart. 'And so do you, Lovely Charlie.'

'Still gorgeous, though,' Charlie stroked a stray tendril of hair back from Holly's face. 'I've got a hectic weekend coming up,' he said. 'A couple of events and a whole pile of paperwork to get my head around. But we need to continue this conversation. Will you text me if you get a moment? Perhaps we can meet before I head off to Westminster again.'

'I'd like that,' Holly murmured. 'And I'm sorry it can't be now.'

'Me too.' Charlie pulled her close again and felt another surge of heat. 'But we will find the time, I promise.'

Kissing her deeply, one last time, he headed towards her

front door. Although his body was tingling from their contact, his mind felt free of the niggling, nagging feeling he'd had since he'd met her again. His discomfiture suddenly all made sense. With a surge of excitement that his adolescent self would have been proud of, he headed off home, determined to see Holly again before the weekend was out.

18

'I'm sorry to drag you over here on a Friday night,' Rachel said as she flipped the kettle on in the kitchen. 'I honestly thought I had all bases covered, but then I realised I was completely out of Creon, and Harry's been so low lately, I just didn't dare risk not giving it to him, even for one night.'

Holly felt a stab of sympathy for her sister. Rachel looked preternaturally tired, more than the usual tiredness that came from looking after a young child, especially one with Harry's condition. Although she worked in Holly's shop a couple of shifts a week, the added stress of looking after Harry when he had one of his wobbles was obviously taking its toll on her. Despite the fact that her sister had got into a brilliant routine over the years, ensuring Harry took his medication like clockwork, like any parent, she had her good and bad days. Being a lone parent was an added strain, although she dealt with it in the same calm, efficient way she handled everything in her life. Holly was constantly in awe.

'It's fine, sis, don't worry about it. I wasn't, er, busy.' Holly felt her cheeks start to burn as she remembered just what she'd been doing about an hour ago, before Rachel's call.

'Are you sure I didn't drag you away from anything?' Rachel said. 'Weren't you supposed to be seeing the Honourable Charlie tonight?'

'Well, yeah,' Holly admitted. 'In fact, you caught us in the middle of, well, not exactly *that,* but...'

Rachel, tired as she appeared, perked up instantly. 'Oh yes? Do tell!'

'Nothing to tell,' Holly said quickly. 'Except...'

'What? Spill!'

Holly giggled in a most un-Holly-like way. 'He's rather a good kisser.'

Rachel squealed, then, remembering that Harry had only just got off to sleep, clapped a hand over her mouth. 'Well, it's about time.' She gave Holly a playful nudge on the arm. 'Let me make this tea and you can tell me all about it.'

Holly found herself giggling again. 'What are we, fifteen? Do I have to give you all the gory details?'

'Absolutely,' Rachel said firmly. 'It's just a shame I dragged you away from him before things got really interesting.'

Holly rolled her eyes. 'Well, I was right about one thing,' she said. 'He can kiss like no one I've ever kissed before. Makes me kind of wish I'd been braver back when we'd first met.' She sighed. 'Who knows what might have happened.'

'Oh, come on!' Rachel said. 'You were so flipping square back then; you'd have been terrified if he'd put any moves on you. Probably best nothing more serious than kissing happened.'

She passed Holly her mug of tea and they wandered through to the living room, which was still scattered with Harry's favourite toys. What a contrast, Holly thought, to the nursery medical cabinet upstairs with its wide variety of suspensions, nebulisers and medicines that Harry was, even at age three, so proficient at taking. The little red tractor and its toy farmer that Holly had bought him for his third birthday took pride of place in the middle of the living room floor and Holly stepped around it carefully.

'I wasn't *that* much of a nerd,' Holly insisted, but she knew that Rachel was probably right. All the years she'd spent studying English Literature at university, all the passionate poems, plays and novels she'd read, and it wasn't until quite a while later she'd let herself feel the heat she'd spent so much time reading about.

'You totally were,' Rachel settled herself on the sofa. 'But that's ancient history. What did he say, once he twigged that the sexy owner of the local well-being shop was *that girl* from all those years ago? Did he remember you?'

Holly drew a deep breath. 'Well, he reckons he does,' she said. 'Although I did rather ambush him in the end with the music, and then the photos, so he probably thinks I'm some madwoman, too.' She furrowed her brow. 'Perhaps it was a bit of overkill really. What if he thinks I've been holding out for him all this time and I'm some kind of weird stalker?' Suddenly, dashing away from Charlie before they'd had a chance to talk seemed like a really daft idea. It was like London all over again. Back then, they'd only had a few hours, and afterwards they'd never seen each other again. What if they were destined never to really connect? To be ships that just passed in the night?

'Oh chill out, sis!' Rachel countered, sipping her tea. 'You're both grown adults. Charlie only has to look at you to see you haven't spent the last fifteen years pining for him, and if he really needs more proof, you can always whip out the pictures of you and Andrew that are on your Facebook page as proof you're not some heartbroken damsel. That ought to show him you've gone out and got a life in the meantime.'

'Do you think I'm overthinking things again?' Holly asked, although she already knew the answer.

'Of course you are!' Rachel said. 'And that was the whole reason you opened up the shop, wasn't it? To give yourself some quality time and a chance to fulfil your ambitions. To give yourself the thinking space you needed in a proper, legitimate way. We both know what happens when the darkness takes over; the damage it can do.' Both had seen their father's anxiety affect his life and theirs over the years, and both had felt it encroaching on them, too, from time to time. The secret was finding the right coping strategy to make life liveable. Holly had her shop, and Rachel now had the goal of getting the right treatment for Harry. It was ironic that, for Rachel, her coping mechanism had come out of the thing that caused her the most anxiety.

'I think we've got a bit more talking to do, anyway,' Holly mused.

'*Talking*, yeah right! Snogging more like.' Rachel snorted. 'And a fair bit of catching up to do. "Oh, Charlie, show me your honourable member!"'

'Oh, bog off,' Holly laughed. 'We just kissed.'

'Yeah, no thanks to me and Harry,' Rachel said. 'That's twice you've been cock-blocked by your own nephew. Hopefully it'll be third time lucky.'

'I'll keep you posted,' Holly smiled. 'If *you're* lucky.'

'Oh, come on, you have to fuel the fantasies of a knackered single mother somehow,' Rachel said. She fell silent as the baby monitor crackled into life, but it was only Harry turning over in his sleep. Visibly relaxing, she smiled. 'Thanks for getting the Creon for me, though. I would have called Mum, but they're not back home until tomorrow.'

'It's fine, honestly,' Holly replied. 'And perhaps it'll give Charlie time to process everything. After all, I've had a few weeks to get my head around it!'

'It's not like you had some great love affair,' Rachel said. 'It was a few hours in a club in London. Not that much to have to process.'

'True, in one sense,' Holly acknowledged. 'But the coincidence of it? Him rocking up as the local MP? A believer in fate, destiny and a greater power might say it was written in the stars.'

Rachel grinned. 'You might be a believer in all that mystical rubbish, but I'm rather more pragmatic, as you know. But if it makes you feel better about snogging the local MP, who isn't exactly your soulmate, politically speaking, then you go for it.'

Holly groaned. 'I was wondering when you were going to get to that. I can't imagine the kind of discussions we're likely to have around the dinner table. If we ever get as far as dinner, that is!'

'You both behaved yourselves at Sunday lunch last weekend,' Rachel said. 'Although, since you hadn't snogged each other at that point, perhaps neither of you wanted to argue about politics.'

'Ha-ha!' Holly said mutinously. She glanced at her watch. 'It's getting late – I'd better head off.'

'Thanks again for tonight.' Rachel shook her head. 'I'm usually so on it with Harry's meds, but I've really been off my game lately. I'm just crap.'

'You are *not* crap!' Holly replied hotly. 'You're doing the best you can under very tricky circumstances. And I don't know how you manage it. Especially since Harry's miserable excuse for a father has bogged off to the other side of the world. You do an amazing job and you give Harry everything he needs.'

'Thanks, sis,' Rachel replied. 'It's just hard, you know, knowing that there's a drug out there that could make all the difference for Harry, give him, and us, a new lease of life, and yet he can't have it.'

'You need to nudge Charlie,' Holly said. 'Forget about what's going on with him and me. Make another appointment to see him and get him to help. He's the MP, for goodness' sake. That's his flipping job.'

'I will,' Rachel sighed. 'As soon as Harry's settled into nursery, I'll book in to one of Charlie's surgeries again. Who knows,

Charlie might be able to do some good where Hugo Fitzgerald couldn't.'

'I'm sure he will,' Holly said softly. 'He seems like a good bloke. And I'm not just saying that because I snogged him tonight.' She hugged her sister. 'Call me if you need anything, OK?'

'I will.' Rachel smiled. 'And hopefully I won't interrupt your next session with Charlie!'

"Night, sis,' Holly said as she walked to the front door.

As she left Rachel's place and got in the car to head home, Holly mused on what she and Rachel had discussed. It was still early days with Charlie; should she be the one to broach the subject of Harry's medication needs with him, or should she leave it to Rachel? She was Harry's aunt, after all. She was too fuzzy-headed with the stress of tonight, and the earlier excitement of kissing Charlie, to think straight. He'd said he was busy all weekend, and perhaps that was a good thing. They both needed some space to breathe.

19

Charlie wasn't joking when he said he had a busy weekend ahead. As he'd feared, Westminster business was taking up more time than he'd anticipated and so he found himself catching up with constituency work in the evenings and at weekends. He also had the Summer Fayre to open in one of the smaller villages on his patch on Saturday afternoon, a Youth Speaks debating competition to judge on the Saturday evening and then, on Sunday, a few hours' work on all of the papers he'd brought back with him. The life of an MP was certainly a busy one, but this was why he'd got into politics in the first place: to feel as though he was making a difference. And he'd got fed up of shouting at the TV and radio about it – he wanted to be part of the change.

Ruefully, he looked at his phone on Saturday morning. He so desperately wanted to reconnect with Holly, but he just wasn't going to get the time. A few text messages would have to do until he came back again on Friday. Or would it?

Glancing at his iCal diary, which synched with the MacBook, his phone and his e-reader, he saw he had an evening out in

Stavenham, the larger town in his constituency, on Wednesday night, so he'd have to make a midweek trip back to attend.

Stavenham was the sensible older sibling to Willowbury's wayward prodigal child. The major source of his comfortable majority, it boasted red-brick buildings, an ageing population and an abundance of wealth. The local party was holding a dinner dance. Events like this, Charlie had assumed, had died out years ago, but not in this part of the world, it seemed, where trial by canapé was still very much in vogue. He, as the new Member of Parliament, was the guest of honour. Charlie suspected that Hugo Fitzgerald would have relished the opportunity to drink good claret and press the flesh of his wealthier constituents, but he was rather more concerned with when he was going to find the time to complete the ever-growing pile of paperwork that seemed to be permanently in his in tray. Remembering the advice that Tom Fielding had given him on their first meeting, though, he realised he couldn't cry off the dinner. The kudos of having an MP at an event in person was worth its weight in gold, Tom had said, no matter what your own views on the matter.

Looking at the invitation, that Tom Fielding had popped into his paper diary, Charlie gave a lurch. *Charlie Thorpe MP and Guest*, it read. Great. He barely knew anyone round here well enough to invite as a plus-one to a starchy evening with a bunch of the blue-rinse brigade, and it was too short notice to ask one of his London mates to go with him – they'd all be caught up in their lives in the capital. But if he didn't take someone, he'd spend the evening fending off interrogations from grannies wanting to marry off their granddaughters to him. He sighed. Now he really did wish he'd spent more time with Holly on Friday night, but he could hardly just text her and ask her to be his date for this thing.

Or could he?

Remembering the big reveal of their previous connection on

Friday night, he grinned. She'd obviously been to a fair few of these events in her time, being a former student member of the same political world. Although time had moved on, and, from what she'd said, her own political beliefs, he wondered if she'd be willing to grin and bear it and accompany him to the dinner. After all, it would be packed full of small business owners and might be an opportunity for her to do some networking for ComIncense, do a little promotion perhaps. He wondered if, and how, he could sell it to her. Deciding a text message might be the safest option (she could only say no, right?), he quickly composed something and, before he could change his mind, pinged it to her.

I've got a dinner dance to go to next Weds and would love you to be my plus-one! Could you bear to hang out with party members for a couple of hours? I think you owe me after that big reveal on Friday ;) x

Heart thumping, he put his phone down and tried not to admit he'd be waiting with bated breath for a response. He turned to his in tray and began reading through the latest minutes of the Health and Social Care Committee. Although he was very much at the start of his career, he wanted to stay informed of as many of the developments as he could. Well briefed is well armed, which was another of Tom Fielding's maxims. He had the feeling that Tom would end up teaching him a lot.

He noticed that one of the issues on the discussion list for the committee was the funding of several new drugs by the National Health Service, and one of them caught his eye. It had been a long-term battle between the NHS and the pharmaceutical company to find a price for the drug that was mutually acceptable, and it seemed that the committee was still wrangling. Momentum was building, though, for this particular drug, through a combination of social media campaigning and public action. However, the two parties had been at stalemate for some time, despite legislation being agreed across Europe and the wider world. It was the drug that Rachel Jamieson, Holly's sister, had come to see him about. With a lurch, he realised that a week had gone by and he'd almost completely forgotten to look into it. The folder of paperwork that Rachel had handed him was still sitting unattended in his in tray.

It was one of those dreadful predicaments, Charlie thought as he grabbed it and started to skim the contents. There was only so much money, to go only so far. When it came to people's health, though, like so much of his new career, it was almost impossible to separate the emotional costs from the financial ones. How could you explain to the family of a seriously ill child that the drug that might save or prolong their life was too expensive to be funded? How could you look someone in the eye and basically admit that their child's life wasn't worth saving? But the sad truth was that decisions had to be made: close the maternity wing of the hospital or fund a lifesaving drug for ten cancer patients; advance research into dementia or take the same money and fund a campaign to mitigate obesity? These decisions were heartbreaking, but ultimately the government was at the behest of the drug companies, who had their own research and interests to fund. These questions had dogged and fascinated Charlie for a long time, as the child of two practising GPs, and now he was actually part of the legislature, he desperately wanted to find the answers. The problem was, as with all things political, answers were often more difficult to give than the questions were to ask.

Lost in his musings, his heart thumped when his phone bleeped. With a slightly shaky hand, he swiped the screen.

Not sure I owe you THAT much! Can you promise a roll of gaffer tape if I need it to keep my subversive opinions to myself? X

Charlie grinned, and swiftly texted back.

Is that a yes? X

The response came back quicker than he'd thought it would.

Only because it's you. I wouldn't have said yes to Hugo. X

Letting out a sigh of relief, Charlie texted back a quick thank you, and then dropped in that the event was, *naturally,* black tie. Having imparted that information, he was relieved that Holly didn't reply back with a snarky response. Judging by her current look, she may well have an ideological disagreement with the dress code as well as the event. Then he chided himself for thinking that way. What did it matter what she wore? This was the twenty-first century, and these dinners were a complete anachronism anyway. She could rock up wearing a hemp over-coat, Doc Martens and a tutu and he wouldn't care. And, living in Willowbury as she did, he had to be prepared for the possi-bility that she might. The important thing was, she'd said yes.

Oh God. She'd said yes!

Charlie's stomach fluttered. An actual, formal date. And one where he'd have to be on his best behaviour because the constituency would be watching. But then, weren't they always? And he didn't have the faintest idea where his dinner suit was, either. Somewhere in the bottom of one of the boxes he hadn't yet unpacked, he guessed. Suddenly, this dinner seemed a while lot more complicated than he'd initially thought.

Another text message came through, but this time it had a link to the dinner dance in its body, as well. It was from Tom Fielding, who was already developing the uncanny ability to tap into whatever Charlie was thinking about without having actu-ally spoken to him.

Have you written your speech for the dinner on Wednesday? Do we need to meet before you head back to London? Am free on Sunday night if you need me.

Shit. The speech. Charlie had forgotten that that was also part of the deal. Ah well, he thought, there was no such thing as a free lunch, or dinner in this case.

Texting back an affirmative to Tom (that put paid to his sudden, mad notion of actually spending some time with Holly before Westminster beckoned on Monday morning), he put his mind to the speech. He was a good public speaker, and it shouldn't have presented any problems for him, but the thought that Holly would be sitting by his side as he spoke suddenly made him feel like the cripplingly self-conscious teenager he'd been the night they'd met all those years ago. He'd chosen politics as a way of exploring his own opinions, constructing a persona back then, being involved in something that felt worthwhile. He supposed, actually, that his reasons, fifteen years on, hadn't changed that much.

'Come on, Charlie, get a grip,' he said, realising too late that it was out loud.

The week ahead had suddenly got a whole lot more challenging. He hoped he'd be up to it.

20

Holly, having accepted Charlie's invitation to the dinner dance, had spent a considerable time wondering what the heck had possessed her. She hadn't been to a black-tie event since her graduation, and certainly didn't have anything decent to wear. Mutinously, she considered just showing up in skinny jeans and her black satin corset, but the corset was rather eye-popping (and distinctly uncomfortable when you tried to eat or dance in it) and she couldn't, in all honestly, have looked Charlie in the eye if she'd rocked up in jeans.

As a staunch believer in sustainability, she'd baulked at buying something brand new from one of the many fast-fashion online retailers, and she simply didn't have the time to trail up the A38 into Bristol, or across to Taunton, to check out the high-street stores. But there was, actually, very little she owned that she could wear. There were, of course, many clothes shops on Willowbury High Street, but they were of the New Age and alternative variety, and while she secretly wanted to buy a mock Pre-Raphaelite crushed-velvet maxi dress, she didn't think it would strike quite the right note with Charlie's local party members. Her last hope, therefore, in the brief breaks she had when Rachel was minding ComIncense, was to check out the rails of the two charity shops that bookended the top and bottom of the High Street. Holly hoped that one or other of them would come up with something she could wear for this night out that would be a happy compromise.

Miraculously, she spotted the absolute perfect dress in the St Peter's Hospice shop, albeit in a rather subversive colour, and snapped it up for a fraction of the price it would have cost when it was new. Sustainable box ticked, and feeling distinctly happier, she headed back to her shop.

* * *

On Wednesday evening, Rachel came over, having left Harry at his grandparents' for an hour, to help Holly get ready. Holly hadn't really needed any help, but Rachel, sensing that Holly was more nervous than she was letting on, had insisted.

'I feel as trussed up as a turkey the night before Christmas!' Holly grumbled as Rachel put the finishing touches to her hair.

'Well, you look stunning, so suck it up, sis,' Rachel replied. 'That colour really suits you, although it shouldn't, with the shade your hair is at the moment.'

'Thanks,' Holly said dryly. She stood up from the stool at her dressing table and smoothed down the velvet bodice of the long, fishtailed dress she was wearing. It was a vintage piece and, much to her surprise and Rachel's approval, it fitted her as though it had been made for her. Of an early 1990s pedigree, it looked astonishingly like the dress Julia Roberts wore to eat snails in *Pretty Woman* and, with her long red hair piled on top of her head and her late grandmother's pearls at her throat, Holly did bear more than a passing resemblance to the heroine of the iconic film. The butterfly tattoo on one shoulder blade that just peeked out from the high back of the dress gave the look a bit more of her signature individual twist, and as she turned to face her sister, Rachel smiled in approval.

'I know this isn't usually your thing,' Rachel said as she tucked a stray strand of unruly hair behind Holly's ear, 'but when you get dressed up, you look absolutely amazing.'

'Thanks,' Holly muttered. 'Although, to be honest, I don't know why I'm bothering. I had enough of these stupid political dinners when I was involved in local politics as a teenager, and I'm about as far from all that now as I could possibly be. Why the hell did I agree to be Charlie's plus-one tonight?'

'Because he asked you, and you fancy him rotten?' Rachel teased.

'Well, there is that,' Holly conceded reluctantly. 'But I never thought I'd end up sucking up my politics and hanging off his arm all night.'

'It won't be like that,' Rachel said soothingly. 'He did say that there would be lots of small business owners there, like you. You might be able to do some networking.'

'I doubt the Stavenham business owners would want to consort with the likes of me!' Holly snorted. 'It's all artisan cheeseries and high-end boutiques there. Not exactly my target market. I doubt we'd have a lot of customers in common.'

'You never know,' Rachel soothed. She went to the tote bag she'd brought with her and pulled out a black cashmere wrap. She slipped it around Holly's shoulders. 'And before you grumble, it's from that brilliant place that sells recycled cashmere accessories online, so you can wear it with a clear conscience,' she said.

'You know me too well,' Holly smiled at her sister in the mirror.

'Charlie won't be able to take his eyes off you,' Rachel said softly. 'And rightly so.'

Holly's eyes filled with tears and she blinked furiously. 'You're too much.'

Rachel smiled. 'Sorry. I didn't mean to make you risk your mascara!'

'Sure you didn't,' Holly grumbled, to hide how touched she really felt. 'Now, where did I put my handbag?'

'It's on the bed. Don't forget your phone, just in case you need picking up or something.'

'And in case you need me.'

'Don't worry about that – Mum and Dad are around if I suddenly have a brain freeze and Harry needs anything. You can relax for the night.'

'Relaxing is the last thing it'll be,' Holly sniffed. 'But at least it's a free dinner.'

As if on cue, there was a knock at her door. Holly's stomach fluttered. 'I don't know about this.'

'Too late to back out now,' Rachel said briskly. 'You have a wee and do whatever you need to, I'll let him in.' She leaned forward and gave Holly a brief hug. 'You look amazing. He'll be blown away.'

As Rachel went downstairs to open the door to Charlie, Holly took a deep breath. They hadn't seen each other since she'd dashed away on Friday evening and suddenly her stomach was awhirl with the memory of those kisses, and what they'd nearly led to. She wished that, for the first time since then, they'd arranged to just go for a drink or something. Being on show at a constituency dinner was just too much pressure, too soon. After Sunday lunch with her parents, and now this, it wasn't as if their dates had been any way conventional so far.

'Oh, for fuck's sake! You're not nineteen any more, and you've kissed him. Get over yourself.' She reflected, as she said this out loud, that her inner voice was far more critical than Rachel's more diplomatic forms of reassurance. But it was too late to back out now. Grabbing her beaded black handbag and checking her hair and face in the mirror one last time, she headed out of her bedroom and towards the steps that led to her front door.

Just as she was about to descend the steep staircase, she paused. There, chatting amiably to Rachel as if they'd known each other for years, was Charlie. But this was a Charlie that took her breath away. Hair slicked back from his face, in an impeccably cut dinner jacket and a bow tie that looked as if he'd actually tied it himself, he looked every inch a superstar.

As he glanced upwards, she caught a flash of the dark crimson lining of his dinner jacket, and suddenly all the pithy lines she'd rehearsed in her head, all the ironic snark she'd wanted to hit him with went up in smoke. She felt her body responding to him in ways that it hadn't responded to anyone since she and Andrew had gone their separate ways, and she was totally blindsided. The moment was complete when, as she paused at the top of the stairs, Charlie's jaw dropped at the sight of her.

'Wow...' he said, visibly jolted. 'You look absolutely amazing.'

Holly's eyes met Rachel's, and her sister gave an almost imperceptible wink.

'Thanks, so do you.' The unexpectedly breathy and high pitch of her own voice made Holly wince.

Thankfully, Rachel came to the rescue.

'Well, I've done my bit by way of being the doorman, so I'll make myself scarce,' she said.

Shooting Holly a tell-me-all-about-it-tomorrow-and-I-mean-everything glance as she left, Holly and Charlie were suddenly alone. And the hallway of Holly's flat seemed incredibly intimate.

'Are you ready for tonight?' Holly asked as she drew a little closer to Charlie, who was still standing, looking ever so slightly dazed at the sight of her. 'Did you manage to get your speech written?' She continued, trying to steer the conversation away from her thumping heart and onto safe ground.

At the mention of the speech, Charlie seemed to snap back

to reality. 'The speech. Yes. Yes, I did. It's all fine. And did I mention you look amazing?'

Holly laughed. 'You might have stammered something, yes. And thank you.' She moved a little closer to him. 'You scrub up pretty well yourself.'

'Thanks,' Charlie's voice had a husky undertone. 'Although I should take issue with the colour of the dress, it really, really suits you.'

He dipped his head and Holly gasped as his lips met hers. All of a sudden, as the kiss deepened and he pulled her close towards him, she wanted to forget all about this starchy dinner and drag him upstairs to her bedroom. But, once again, time was against them.

'Steady on,' Charlie breathed. 'It's going to be a long night if you keep reminding me of all the kissing we could be doing instead!' He broke away from her, and she could see his eyes were dark with desire. 'And we really should get going.'

Holly smiled. She felt about a million miles away now from the shy, hesitant girl she had been all those years ago in London, and although the dress was also miles away from what she would normally wear these days, she had to admit that she liked the effect it was having on Charlie. 'OK. But I'm warning you, I can only keep a lid on my subversive opinions for so long. You might have to drag me away if I end up getting too outspoken.'

'So long as I can drag you away and be alone with you, that's fine with me,' Charlie said, that husky note still very much in his voice. 'But for now, let's go and mingle, shall we?'

Heart thumping almost painfully under the bones of the bodice of the dress, Holly wondered what would happen after the mingling; was tonight the night that she and Charlie would take a step further in their relationship? Her body, already beginning to ache for his touch, was sending signals that it, at least, really hoped it was.

21

Holly felt a fresh flutter of nerves in her stomach as Charlie pulled into the car park of the Swanley Hotel. A triumph of Victorian industrialist architecture, its austere windows peered suspiciously out across the town centre, seeming to glare at all newcomers.

Holly shook her head. 'I thought this kind of gig had died out along with Nokia phones!'

'Sadly not,' Charlie said wryly. 'But then, most party members are twice your age, and probably still using that kind of mobile.' He turned off the engine and looked at her. 'Thank you for coming with me tonight,' he said softly. 'I know this isn't exactly your cup of tea, but I'm glad you agreed to it.'

'Don't thank me until later,' Holly joked. 'It's been so long since I've been to a function like this, I've forgotten how to behave myself!'

'I'm sure that's not true,' Charlie replied, although he did look a little unnerved. He hopped out of the car, and before Holly could open her own door, he'd hurried round to her side and opened it for her.

Stepping out of the BMW in such a tight dress was a bit of an issue, and she was grateful for his hand as he offered it to her.

'Did I tell you how amazing you look?' he whispered into her ear, sending a shiver down her spine.

'Yes, you did,' Holly replied playfully, 'so stop trying to butter me up.'

'As if I would!' Charlie said. 'Come on, let's go and do this.' And with that, they headed into the foyer of the hotel.

* * *

A little time later, and Holly was beginning to relax a bit. She knew, from Charlie's slightly set jaw, that he was still feeling tense; he had his speech to come when coffee had been served after the meal. But the food was decent, and she was sitting next to the mild-mannered husband of the town's mayor, who was doing a good job of lightening her mood. Aged around sixty, he had the slightly resigned air of a man who was used to being in the shadow of a politically powerful spouse, and he'd been pointing out people to her in a calm undertone for most of the evening.

'On that table to your left are most of the members of the Stavenham Chambers of Commerce and their spouses,' he was saying. 'Perhaps you should have a word after dinner – get your name into the mix as a local business owner.'

'I'm not sure they'll have much to say to me,' Holly's eyes glinted. 'I'm hardly their typical member.'

'Still worth a chat,' he replied. 'All contacts are good contacts.'

The mayor was still chatting animatedly to Charlie, who was nodding and smiling, although Holly noticed he did seem a bit distracted.

'Have you known him long?' the mayor's husband asked, catching the direction of her gaze.

'Not very,' Holly admitted. 'And have you been married long?'

'Forty years next year,' he said. 'Three sons and a daughter, and six grandchildren to show for it. And, for the past few years, quite a lot of these kinds of dinners.' He patted a slightly paunchy belly. 'Price you pay, among other things.'

Holly was intrigued. 'Such as?'

'Oh, you know,' he smiled at her. 'Being under scrutiny all the time, on display a lot, but also in the background. Keeping your opinions to yourself, in public, at least. I often wonder how the other halves of the really prominent politicians cope with it.'

Holly glanced back at Charlie, feeling the slightest sense of unease. 'I don't think he'd be hugely worried about my disagreeing with him.'

'You'd be surprised,' he said. 'So long as it's in private, you're all right. But express an alternative view in public and things might get tricky.'

Holly felt a bigger shiver of disquiet at the man's words. She and Charlie, potentially, could have a lot to disagree on. Would growing attraction and affection be enough to counteract that?

'But don't you worry too much,' he broke into her thoughts again. 'Perhaps it's a bit different now to what it was.'

Holly smiled but said nothing. Something told her that things weren't as different as all that.

'Everything OK?' Charlie asked as he turned towards her. He slipped a hand into hers, where the one not occupied with her wine glass was resting in her lap. His hand was warm and dry and did not betray for a moment any nervousness about having to make a speech in front of all these people.

Holly again wondered if that confidence came from conviction that he was right, or if he'd trained himself to project it. What if they truly were at opposite ends of the political spectrum these days? She felt a frisson of nerves that wasn't just to do with Charlie's hand in hers.

'Fine,' she smiled tightly. 'You'll knock them dead with your speech.'

'Not literally, I hope,' Charlie said dryly. 'One or two of them look like they're halfway there already.'

As the coffees were served, Holly's sense of disquiet was growing. She sat quietly beside Charlie as he took a sip of his coffee, before the leader of the Chamber of Commerce tapped his wineglass with a spoon to get everyone's attention. Gradually, the buzz of chatter diminished and, as it did, Charlie got up to speak. He glanced briefly down at Holly as he rose, and she tried to summon up an encouraging smile.

'Good evening, ladies and gentleman,' he began, looking around the function room at the assembled diners, who, replete with three courses, coffee and wine, were in a mellow, responsive mood. 'It's such a pleasure to be here among you tonight...'

As Charlie launched into his speech, acknowledging the hard work of the Chamber of Commerce and the local party faithful, singling out particular business owners and local bigwigs for dutiful praise, Holly felt increasingly conflicted. Charlie was a charismatic speaker, who struck the perfect balance between deference, knowledge and personality. He was rubbing all the right tummies, making these fat cats purr with pleasure, and it was easy to write him off as just another one of those self-serving politicos on the make. However, just as Holly's mind was starting to wander, Charlie changed tack. What had, up to this point, been an anodyne, palatable speech became something a little different.

'I want to make some changes, both here and in Westminster, to really improve the lives of those in the constituency who need it the most. Hugo Fitzgerald might have been a long-serving MP, but his voting record left a lot to be desired at times. I welcome feedback from each and every one of you, and I look forward to taking Willowbury and Stavenham further into the twenty-first century. There are things to be improved, even in this leafy, wealthy part of the countryside, and I will make it my business to make it happen.'

'What side is he meant to be on, again?' the mayor's husband whispered to Holly, with a twinkle in his eye.

Holly shook her head. She hadn't expected such a blunt dismissal of Hugo Fitzgerald from Charlie, and she suddenly felt a lot less conflicted. If he really could make positive changes, if it wasn't all just bluster and posturing, then perhaps she could give him a break, politically speaking, after all.

Charlie sat down to happy applause; the audience were prepared to be forgiving for his first official dinner it seemed. Holly wondered, though, how forgiving they'd be if Charlie did make some radical decisions.

'Well done,' she whispered, while the applause was still ringing around the hall.

'Impressed?' Charlie said, a glint in his eye.

'Perhaps,' Holly replied.

'Good.' Charlie glanced at Tom. 'He, on the other hand, is going to bollock me for going off script.'

'Really?' Holly asked. 'I would have thought he'd welcome a little independent spirit.'

'Only so far as it doesn't put me out of favour with the donors!' Charlie replied. 'And anyway, actions speak louder than words, don't you think?' He held her gaze for a fraction longer than necessary, and Holly felt her stomach flip with a combination of nerves and desire.

She opened her mouth to respond, but then the disco began. As a familiar tune from the early noughties came over the speakers, Holly was grateful for the distraction.

'I can't believe they're starting off with this one,' she laughed. 'But perhaps you should show willing and start the dancing.'

'You are joking, aren't you?' Charlie grimaced. 'I haven't been on a dance floor since... well, for a very long time, anyway.'

'Oh, come on, stick-in-the-mud!' Holly said, eyes glinting

with amusement. 'Don't you remember dancing to this one at school discos?'

'I do,' Charlie replied. 'And I've got absolutely no desire to relive that experience!'

'Please yourself,' Holly said. Turning to the wife of Charlie's constituency agent, who'd come over with Tom to discuss the speech, she gestured, 'Do you fancy it, Claudia?'

'Oh, why not?' Claudia said, rising from the table like a rather rotund Greek goddess, resplendent in a one-shouldered, peppermint-green sheath dress. She raised an eyebrow at her husband and Charlie, who remained resolutely seated.

As the familiar, cheesy strains of 'La Macarena' took hold, echoing across the dance floor, Holly and Claudia took to the parquet.

Glancing back at Charlie, Holly couldn't tell if he looked pleased or mortified. Then, as she picked up the familiar moves of the song, she saw Tom whispering something in his ear. Without missing a beat, Charlie stood up and strode to the dance floor, taking his place alongside Holly. Holly nearly lost her step as Charlie joined in the dance.

'I didn't think this was your thing,' she said wryly as he showed a surprising aptitude for the moves.

'Tom thought it'd make a good photo opportunity,' Charlie grinned back. 'And who am I to refuse?'

Holly slapped his arm playfully. 'You're such a media whore!'

'Yup,' Charlie agreed, 'but there are at least four people filming me doing this blooming dance, and you never know, it might make me more down with the kids.'

'I doubt it,' Holly murmured. 'If you were dabbing or flossing, perhaps, but the Macarena was old when we were kids!'

Charlie looked baffled. 'Dabbing and what? The only thing I've flossed lately is my teeth. Are you telling me I'm that out of touch?'

'I'd organise a trip to the local secondary school if you want to connect with da youth,' Holly teased. 'They'll set you right about what's new and current.'

'In the meantime, you'd better remind me how this flipping dance goes,' Charlie said. He looked down at her moving hands, and then appreciatively at her as she put them behind her head, shimmied and jumped to the beat.

Holly felt her stomach flipping with desire. They'd got close to something the other day, and it seemed they were edging ever closer with every minute they spent together. Was tonight going to be the night?

Then she chided herself; did anyone else get horny when they saw their date doing the Macarena?

Throwing herself into the dance, and putting all thoughts of shagging Charlie out of her mind, she concentrated on remembering the moves. Eventually, the song ended and transitioned into something a little more sedate. Holly, breathing a little more quickly due to the tightness of the dress and the energy she'd thrown into the Macarena, again felt her heart flip as Charlie slipped his hand around her waist. The song that had come on was again rather an old one but definitely written for a different kind of dancing.

As Charlie pulled her in a little more closely, she could feel his warm breath on her cheek. They swayed together, as did all the other couples on the dance floor, and Holly started to relax.

'That was exciting,' Charlie murmured. 'But not quite as exciting as this.' He slid a hand tantalisingly lower on her back, but not too far down as to cause a scandal among this particular crowd.

'I can't quite believe I'm saying this, but it's nice to be here. Right here,' Holly clarified. 'Although I'm still a bit under duress.'

'I know,' Charlie's eyes were twinkling. 'But you're really impressing the hell out of everyone here, despite yourself.'

Holly shook her head. 'Night's not over yet.' She turned her head slightly and caught sight of Miles Fairbrother propping up the bar in the corner of the function room. She could barely suppress a shudder. 'That man makes my skin crawl,' she muttered into Charlie's shoulder. 'How do you manage to be so bloody polite to everyone? Even when you might not be able to stand the sight of them?'

'Desire to keep hold of my seat, and a lot of massages from a very good local practitioner,' Charlie said playfully, although Holly noticed an intensity in his eyes.

'I've heard she's good with her hands,' Holly murmured, and then gasped as Charlie pulled her closer, leaving her in absolutely no doubt as to where his thoughts were going.

'Steady on,' he whispered. 'An MP with an erection would not go down well on this dance floor, with this crowd.'

'You might well finish off some of your more elderly voters,' Holly said wryly.

'Shall we get out of here, then?' Charlie suggested, his eyes growing darker with desire. 'I think I've done my duty. And you've certainly gone above and beyond yours.'

'Sure,' Holly said. 'I could do with getting out of these heels.' She smiled mischievously. 'And I'll need a hand with the zip on this dress – Rachel had to shoehorn me into it.'

'It would be my pleasure,' Charlie replied. 'But can you stop making me imagine unzipping your dress? I'll never manage to say goodbye coherently to all these people otherwise!' He smiled down at her. 'Speaking of which, I should let Tom and Claudia and the organisers know we're off. Shall I meet you in the foyer?'

'Sounds good,' Holly said. 'I'll just go and grab my stuff and meet you out there.'

With palpable regret, they broke apart.

Charlie strode off to make his excuses and Holly cast around for Rachel's pashmina and her handbag. Seeing them on one of the chairs at the dinner tables, she wandered over to collect them. As she did so, she was irritated to see Miles Fairbrother and his fellow business owner passing the other way.

'Bit of a turn-up to see you here, missy,' Miles said, distaste evident in his tone. 'Wouldn't have thought this was your kind of scene, with all of these filthy capitalists.'

'Well, it was a favour to a friend,' Holly replied, trying to inject a note of brightness into her voice.

'Yes, I can see that,' Miles leered. 'Really *friendly*, aren't you?'

'Excuse me.' Holly tried to push past Miles, in pursuit of her borrowed pashmina, but he refused to budge.

'Don't you think it's just a little bit rich of you, coming here tonight to schmooze the local business owners, when you're so uppity about those of us who don't conform to your so-called eco principles?'

'Not really, Miles,' Holly's temper was starting to fray, but, mindful that this was Charlie's patch, and Charlie's night, she tried to keep her voice neutral. 'Now I must be going.'

'Not so fast, girly,' Miles hissed. 'I'm not finished yet.' His face was puce with drink, his purple nose an unattractive, clashing shade. 'You'd better not get any ideas about bending Charlie Thorpe's ear to your Green-freak ideas. We don't need any more of that rubbish in Willowbury.'

'Well, you would say that, Miles,' Holly's voice was louder than she'd have liked, but she couldn't help it. She wouldn't let herself be walked over by Miles, especially after such a civilised night. 'So long as you're turning a profit, you couldn't care less what, or who you damage, could you?' Rumours were rife about the reasons why Fairbrothers had such a high turnover of staff and exactly how they disposed of their waste products.

'Just remember, missy, it's people like me who bankroll the campaigns of your new boyfriend. Without us, he wouldn't have half the influence he has. You'd do well to bear that in mind.'

'Are you threatening me? Because that's what it sounds like.' Holly lost what was left of her temper. 'I might have known twats like you couldn't help muscling in on nights like this. Well, you can leave me out of it.' She pushed past Miles and retrieved her pashmina and handbag.

Miles put up a hand, in a patronising gesture that infuriated Holly even further. 'No need to start calling me names, Miss Renton. I was merely having a chat.'

'Oh, fuck off,' Holly said mutinously. 'You've been trying to get me thrown out of my shop ever since I bought it.'

Miles affected innocence, and for a moment, Holly wondered why. Then it clicked. Like a sixth sense, she knew that someone was standing right behind her.

'Charlie's waiting for you in the foyer, Holly,' Tom Fielding's voice, smooth and soothing, took the tension off the exchange. 'Miles, can I buy you another drink?'

Miles glared one last time at Holly

'Shall we, Holly?' another voice said softly. It was Charlie, who'd obviously clocked what was happening and had hotfooted it back from the foyer to Tom's side.

'Yes, let's.' Holly pushed past him, her fury bubbling over as Charlie clasped Miles' hand and shook it. She could hear him murmuring platitudes as she walked out of the ballroom, probably trying to smooth over the scene she'd just been a part of. She felt an ugly, red, heated flush creeping up her neck to her face in her anger and frustration. So much for principles, she thought. Charlie was obviously more interested in keeping his voters and benefactors sweet. Debating about whether or not to call a taxi, she figured she'd better wait for him and have it out.

Sure enough, he exited the ballroom a minute or two later, a look of undisguised irritation on his face. Taking her arm, he led her out of the building. 'Let's get out of here, shall we?' he said. 'I think you and I need to talk.'

22

Charlie, to his credit, maintained a polite silence until they'd both got into the car. He even opened her car door for her, but Holly knew something was coming. She felt hot with mortification again as she recalled just how much she'd let Miles wind her up. But that didn't stop her from being angry with Charlie, too, for not coming to her defence. Charlie had just stepped in and placated that slimy bastard without so much as an enquiry as to what had riled Holly in the first place.

'That man's a tosser!' she said furiously. 'He just won't leave me alone.'

Charlie said nothing; just kept his eyes on the road ahead. It had started to rain, and he flipped the wipers on to clear the screen. With his left hand, he reached over to turn on the demister, and Holly felt a jolt as his palm brushed her knee, which was close to the gearstick. She wasn't going to give into that right now, though; she was still too angry.

'He thinks he's got the right to tell me what to do about everything. It's so frigging patronising.'

She glanced at Charlie, but in the darkness of the country

lanes between Stavenham and Willowbury, all she could see was his profile, jaw set as tightly as it had been before his speech.

'Aren't you going to say anything?' Holly, frustrated by Charlie's silence, raised her voice again.

'I think you've said enough for the both of us tonight,' Charlie said quietly. 'I really don't think there's much more I can add.'

'And what's that supposed to mean?'

'I think you know.' He kept his eyes steadfastly on the road.

'Oh, I see,' Holly snapped. 'I've said something I shouldn't, to someone I shouldn't, and now I get the passive-aggressive treatment? Very grown-up, Charlie. Is this how you treat everyone who disagrees with you?'

Still silence. Charlie reached over and changed gear as they turned one of the many sharp corners on the road, and Holly scooted her knees defiantly out of the way.

'Aren't you going to say anything?' she tried again, softening her tone.

This, finally, seemed to get through to him. 'Holly, I've got a job to do! I can't get into an ideological debate every time someone says something I don't agree with. I've got to generate enough goodwill to make these very wealthy people part with their cash to support the party. That way, I get to make the changes I want to make. Changes that are good for the whole community, not just a few. What don't you understand about that?' Charlie raked a hand impatiently through his hair and swerved to narrowly avoid a cat that had strayed out onto the country lane, obviously mid-hunt.

'I'm not stupid, Charlie, I get that you've got to smile and pretend to agree for the sake of the party line, but do you have to be quite so nice to those money-grabbing tossers who'd happily see your new home town cut in half by having the M5 slapped straight through the middle of it?' Holly, aware she was raising her voice, tried to curb herself. Frustration, and irritation that she could still fancy Charlie quite so much in the midst of a row was making her rash. Not to mention a few glasses of cheap Prosecco. Had she been in a better mood, she'd have made a joke about the affluent party members not being able to run to some decent fizz for their fundraising gig.

'Well, if you know that, then why the hell did you have to rile up one of the biggest party donors this side of Wells? If Tom hadn't stepped in and smoothed the waters, he'd have pulled the plug on it.'

'There's more to life than money, Charlie, or have you forgotten that?'

'Not when you're trying to actually change what matters.' Charlie was pulling up outside Holly's home, now, and the phrase hung in the air between them. 'You can pick up all the plastic bottles and bags you can carry, but, ultimately, I rely on people like Miles Fairbrother to help me to fund the real changes, and you mouthing off to him about his business is the absolute last thing I need.'

Holly, stung, shook her head. 'Well, I guess that's told me, then. I mean, what's the point of doing anything if it achieves nothing?'

Charlie, sensing he might have gone too far, tried to grab her hand. 'Look, I'm sorry. Of course what you do matters. I'm just frustrated. Can I come in? We can talk about this.'

She couldn't see his eyes in the darkness of the car.

'I think you've said all you need to say, and you're obviously not going to listen to me. Goodnight, Charlie.'

She picked up her evening bag from the footwell of the car and was out of the passenger door before he could respond further. Slamming the car door behind her, she felt his eyes on her back, until, evidently exasperated, he started the engine of his BMW and drove off.

As she walked up the path to her door, she felt at once deflated and angry. She couldn't wait to get out of the dress, and although she'd entertained notions of Charlie being the one to unzip it, she was too cross now to fantasise. She'd known this dinner was a bad idea from the start, and it had shown her quite clearly that she and Charlie would never see eye to eye, no matter how sexy she found him.

Thrusting open her heavy wooden front door, she did her best to slam it behind her, to let out some of the irritation, nearly decapitating Arthur in the process, who was attempting to sneak in and find a warm place to sleep.

'Sorry, my lovely,' Holly said, picking him up and cuddling him to her. 'Looks like you'll be the only male sharing my bed tonight, and for a while yet.'

Slinging her bag down on the hall table and stepping out of her deeply vertiginous heels, she wandered off to bed.

* * *

Charlie, still seething, reached his house and drove swiftly into the parking space outside it. Pulling the key from the ignition, he slammed his car door shut and hurried up the path to his front door. He was twitching with irritation, laced with a deeper desire for Holly that, even though they'd parted acrimoniously, still throbbed inside him.

How could she have been so tactless? Honestly, the woman was like an unexploded bomb at times. A smaller voice whispered that he'd been an idiot to have put her in that position in the first place – after all, he knew how far apart they were ideologically, but he'd just assumed that she'd suck up her principles for his sake. That was clearly his first mistake; he had no right to assume anything of her. Why should she have to stay silent just because airing her opinion might make his life tricky? That was not the right way to conduct any relationship.

Pushing open his front door, he pulled out his phone in the lame expectation that in the two minutes it had taken him to drive from her place to his, Holly might have texted him. Even though he knew she wouldn't have, it still struck him in the gut when that was confirmed by a distinct lack of messages.

Sighing, he grabbed a glass of water and headed upstairs. He should probably email Tom and touch base before he went to bed, but he just wanted to black out and forget the evening. As debut dinners in the constituency went, this one had been memorable – in the end, for all the wrong reasons.

Loosening his bow tie and shrugging off his dinner jacket, he placed both over the chair in his bedroom and then shed the rest of his clothes. His body was buzzing as much as his mind was, and when he glanced in the mirror to take out his contact lenses, he was struck by how flushed his face was – and he'd not even been drinking. Holly had really got under his skin. Should he text her? Or should he let things calm down between them and try to speak to her when they'd both had a bit of breathing space? Perhaps *he* should calm down too.

Sighing, he decided on a cold shower and a good night's sleep. Perhaps then he'd be able to face Holly tomorrow.

23

'I can't believe you let that twat wind you up,' Rachel chided the next morning when she popped round for a post-mortem of the grisly night before. 'Miles has always had it in for you, ever since you bought this place. Why on earth would you let him get to you so badly last night?'

'I suppose I was wound up already at the thought of going to the thing, and I'd held my tongue so much all night, that Miles just pushed me over the edge.' Holly shook her head. The remnants of a Prosecco-induced hangover were pounding at her temples and the matcha tea was making her feel nauseated rather than improving things. She cast around the shop for her supply of milk thistle leaves, which made the best hangover cure, since the matcha wasn't cutting it.

'Why don't you get your head down for an hour?' Rachel said. 'I can mind this place for a bit longer – I don't have to pick Harry up from nursery until twelve thirty.'

'How's he settling in?' Holly asked.

'Loving it,' Rachel said. 'Can't wait to get there in the mornings. Makes me feel quite redundant, actually!'

'As if,' Holly snorted. 'But I'm glad he's getting on well.'

Harry was a lively and outgoing little boy, who seemed to take everything in his stride, and the nursery school had been more than reassuring about making sure he took his Creon at snack times, and alerting Rachel if any of the other children had particularly bad coughs or colds. A simple cold, if Harry was to catch it, could rapidly turn into an infection, which meant, at the very least, a round of antibiotics, or, worse, a hospital stay.

'Fingers crossed it stays that way,' Rachel replied. 'But stop changing the subject. Are you going to lie down or what?'

Holly shook her head, then wished she hadn't as it gave a resounding thump. 'I'm fine.'

'You're stubborn,' Rachel chided but fell silent as the shop door opened with a tinkle of the bell.

Holly, who had her eyes on her coffee mug, caught a familiar scent in the air that made her senses tingle and, stomach fluttering not just from the hangover, she slowly raised her eyes and cursed inwardly. There, in the doorway, looking as delicious as he had last night, even dressed down in jeans and a casual shirt and, because he'd been driving, not hungover in the slightest, was Charlie.

'Hello, you!' Rachel said brightly. 'What can we do for you on this fine day?'

'Hi,' Charlie smiled. 'I was just wondering if you had anything I could burn to relax me? I had a bit of a night of it last night.' He glanced at Holly, who was busying herself with removing the coffee cups.

'So I hear,' Rachel said wryly. She turned to Holly. 'Why don't you and Charlie escape into the sunshine for a bit? I'll keep an eye on things here.'

Holly grimaced; sunlight would do nothing for her headache, but she realised she wasn't going to get out of this one. 'OK,' she said ungraciously. 'Let me just grab my sunglasses from upstairs.'

'Here, have mine,' Rachel rummaged in her handbag.

'Wouldn't want you making a break for it out of your own back door,' she muttered.

'Thanks, sis,' Holly said dryly. Taking a sip of the glass of water she'd also brought down to the shop counter, she stepped out from behind it and looked up at Charlie. 'Shall we go then?'

As she turned towards the door, she was sure she saw Rachel and Charlie exchanging a significant look, which did precisely nothing for her already embattled mood.

'I'm surprised to see you,' she said as they headed up the High Street and away from ComIncense. She was glad of Rachel's oversized shades, as the sun was warm on her face and she could feel herself breaking out into a not entirely sunshine-induced sweat.

'Well, I thought I'd better come over and clear the air, as we didn't part on the best of terms last night.'

Charlie had a long stride and Holly found herself struggling to keep up. They were heading towards Willowbury Priory, a glamorous-looking ruin that the National Trust was restoring and saving for future generations. On a sunny day like this, the stonework glinted in the light, and it was easy to fill in the visual gaps to see, in your mind's eye, the dreaming arches of the complete building. Jokes and stories had endured through the ages about nuns and monks commuting between Willowbury and Buckfast to share worship and mead recipes, and the aching romanticism of the Priory seemed at odds with the devout purpose of the building. It seemed a bit incongruous to have such a high church icon smack in the middle of such a spiritually diverse town as Willowbury, too, but perhaps that was just another example of its all-welcoming ethos.

'That's very gallant of you,' Holly's mood was not improving as she remembered the exchange with Miles last night, and Charlie's subsequent dismissal of it. 'Were you worried I was going to trash your reputation even further?'

'Holly, stop.' They'd reached the Priory gardens now, and

Charlie paused in his walk. He reached out a hand to her, and reluctantly Holly allowed hers to be taken in his warm, dry grip.

They were standing under one of the few intact archways on the site, the drop of the chapel nave, shielded by a glass wall, strikingly close. Holly swallowed as the sight of it made her dizzy. She stared steadfastly at her feet.

'I came to say I'm sorry. About Miles, about putting you in that situation, expecting you to just suck up your own opinions for my sake, everything. It was wrong of me to expect you to do that.' He glanced up at the archway above his head. 'When we were on that dance floor, surrounded by all the party faithful, all I could think about was being alone with you. None of that stuff mattered. And yet when I saw you and Miles arguing, the politician in me kicked in.' He ran his free hand through his hair. 'I have to be a diplomat with people like Miles. I don't like it, but he's part of the backbone of the local party, and the local economy.'

'What, do they teach you that stuff in politician school?' Holly's tone was rather more withering than even she'd intended, and Charlie looked stung. 'I mean, do you have to suck up to everyone for the sake of the party?'

'Well, I'd draw the line at bolshy well-being shop owners,' Charlie teased. 'It seems they're unsuckupable to.'

'Touché,' Holly said. She looked up at him and couldn't help smiling. 'And I'm sorry I let him get to me. I'm so cross that I allowed him to get under my skin in such a public place.'

'What is it with you two?' Charlie asked. 'This is more than just opposing politics, isn't it?'

Holly sighed. 'You could say that. When my grandfather was alive, he and Miles had a kind of feud, all stemming back to them being in school. That extended through their lives, and, unbeknown to me, when I put in an offer for the freehold of what was to become ComIncense, Miles already had plans to turn the building into a second site for his bakery. He never really got over that I'd bought the place, and with my inheritance from grandfather, too. Ever since, he's been trying to discredit me and my shop but has never managed to do so. I suppose he now thinks that because you and I are, well, whatever we are, he's going to lose an ally.' She sighed. 'He and Hugo Fitzgerald were big mates, going back years, and he clearly wants to maintain that connection with the new guy. I figure Miles dislikes the fact that you and I are getting closer and that he can't count on you, like he did Hugo, to support him if he starts making trouble again.'

'So that's what you were arguing about?' Charlie said. 'He's been putting pressure on you?'

'Not exactly pressure,' Holly said hurriedly. 'I mean, he's not been physically intimidating or anything, more a kind of word-of-mouth campaign to slag me and the shop off whenever he can.'

'Well, if he carries on, let me know and I'll do something about it,' Charlie said.

'With your MP's hat on or your, er, friendship hat on?' Holly smiled.

Charlie drew Holly closer, so they were both standing underneath the archway. 'With the hat that says I want to be a little bit more than friends,' he said gruffly.

Despite the rising warmth of the day, Holly shivered as their bodies drew closer. She wanted him so much, despite their being worlds apart ideologically these days. Who knows what would have happened if they'd taken things further all those years ago? Perhaps she'd have become the perfect politician's wife, with the perfect family, all Boden dresses and sending the children to small, fee-paying schools? However, that was then, and this was most definitely now. Things were different; *they* were different. But try telling that to her raging emotions. She couldn't fight her attraction to Charlie any more than she could stop the sun moving round Willowbury Hill.

Charlie's hand snaked around her waist, closing the final gap between them, and with his other hand, he reached up and gently removed the dark glasses she'd borrowed from her sister. 'It's OK,' he murmured. 'We're in the shade enough to hopefully not aggravate your hangover!'

'I'm not hungover,' Holly said mutinously but couldn't help herself smiling. 'Well, OK, maybe I am a little bit. But I had to get through last night somehow.'

Slowly, gently, Charlie dipped his head until his lips were within a breath of Holly's own. She felt relieved that, as a consequence of last night's excess of booze, she'd cleaned her teeth a few times when she'd got up. Their lips met in the gentlest of kisses that again took her back to when they'd first met, but as those kisses became deeper, more passionate, she realised they were heading in a much more grown-up direction.

Sliding a hand around the back of Charlie's neck, she encountered the waves of hair that curled on his collar. Her knees grew week, and it wasn't just from lack of breakfast.

'Is that an apology then?' Charlie asked as they broke apart.

'For what?' Holly asked, trying to catch her breath.

'For having a public barney with one of my wealthiest but most obnoxious constituents!'

Holly laughed shakily. 'I guess so.'

'When can I see you again?' Charlie asked. His arms were still tightly around her. 'I've got to head back to London from here, I'm afraid, but I should be back tomorrow evening, if you're free.'

Holly shook her head. 'I'm going to be tied up tomorrow and all weekend stocktaking, in between opening hours. And getting ready for Willowfest, which is happening the weekend after, of course.'

'Willowfest?' Charlie looked blank. 'Oh yes. What with spending so much time on that speech for the dinner dance last weekend, I'd forgotten that was coming up.' He furrowed his brow. 'Remind me exactly what it is, again?'

'The Folk and Fey festival that takes place here every year,' Holly replied. 'Did your amazing agent not brief you?'

'Folk and *what*?' Charlie replied.

Holly pulled away slightly but kept her hand firmly clasped in Charlie's as they began to walk back to ComIncense.

'It's evolved over the years,' she explained as they headed out of the Priory grounds, 'but it's basically a weekend of folk music, fancy dress and celebrations of all things fey.'

'Again, Holly, I'm none the wiser.'

Holly laughed. 'Why does that not surprise me?' She turned and gestured across to the ruined Priory buildings. 'All this, believe it or not, is thought to have been erected on a cross-section of some of the strongest ley lines in the country. It forms one point of a spiritual triangle, with Stonehenge and Avebury stone circle at the other points. If you do happen to believe in such things, it means there's a huge amount of spiritual energy in this place, centred on the Priory grounds but radiating outwards through the town.'

'*If* you believe in such things,' Charlie echoed.

'Well, plenty of people do, around here,' Holly replied. 'Otherwise I'd be out of business. Anyway, Willowbury decided about thirty or so years ago, when the town was a bit more run-down and a bit less wealthy, to try to cash in on this huge amount of spiritual energy. Hence, Willowfest was born.'

'Is it anything like the Reading Festival?' Charlie asked, shuddering at the prospect of mud-soaked tents and acres of lost wellies.

Holly laughed. 'Well, there's music, but it's on a much smaller scale. Although the guy who first came up with the idea, Alan Somerville, aspires to make it big enough to rival festivals like that one day.'

'Alan Somerville? Wasn't he the lead singer of that seventies prog rock band?' Charlie wrinkled his brow.

'Yup. The very same. Wrote several of his biggest hit albums while living in Willowbury, in fact. Claims the ley lines allow him to tap into a deep and abiding spirituality that gets somewhat, er, diluted by the more commercial aims of the music business these days.'

'He's never been asked to headline the O2 Arena, then?' Charlie asked playfully.

Holly laughed. 'Not so far as I know. But he lives in hope. Although I think he quite likes being a big fish in this small Willowbury pond, anyway.'

'So, what am I to expect of Willowfest?' Charlie asked.

'Why don't you let me show you,' Holly murmured. 'Come and be my date for it.' She drew in closer to him. 'It starts on the Saturday morning and winds down on Sunday afternoon.'

Charlie smiled. 'That sounds great, and just what I'll need after a few days back in London.' He paused momentarily. 'I know I've got something constituency-based happening on that Friday night in Stavenham, but how about I come over first thing Saturday morning and we can, er, catch up a bit? Then you can show me exactly what Willowfest is all about.'

'Sounds good.' They'd reached the front door of ComIncense again, and Holly paused. 'I look forward to it.'

'Me too,' Charlie replied. Then he dipped his head and kissed her again. 'I'll see you soon.'

'I can't wait,' Holly said, insides churning again.

As Charlie left, Holly, knowing that she had the most ridiculous grin plastered on her face, pushed open the shop door.

'I take it you two have made it up, then?' Rachel asked as she clocked the look on her sister's face.

'You could say that,' Holly grinned. 'Although, considering Charlie's just agreed to be my date for Willowfest, how long for, I really don't know!'

'Does he know what he's letting himself in for?' Rachel laughed. 'It's probably a bit more, er, *alternative* than he's used to.'

'I did tell him about some of it,' Holly replied, 'but I think it's probably best he experiences it for himself.'

One thing was for certain, Holly thought, if Charlie didn't run screaming from the Folk and Fey festival, he'd certainly experience the best Willowbury had to offer that weekend.

24

Charlie wasn't joking when he'd said he had a busy time between then and his date with Holly for Willowfest. The House was in full swing, and, because of his interest in becoming more involved in the Department of Health and Social Care, he'd also earmarked some time on Tuesday to observe the next meeting of the Health and Social Care Committee. Although membership of the committee was out of the question at this early stage in his career, he hoped to listen, learn and get his face known by the Chair, with a view to joining it later on in his tenure. Sometimes, the route to advancement was about who you connected with, rather than what you knew. And nowhere more so, it seemed, than in Westminster.

Charlie was well used to networking from his days as a House of Commons researcher, and having worked in the Palace of Westminster before he got his parliamentary seat, he knew his way around fairly well. He wasn't a natural 'operator', as so many politicians seemed to be; he struggled to make the seemingly inconsequential small talk that might lead someone into further confidences that he could use to his advantage, preferring to connect with people on a more personal and sincere level

where he could. He knew that there were plenty like him in the
House; it was just that those who knew how to play the game
instinctively were the ones who tended to rise the fastest.
However, a fair number of them fell quickly, too, he consoled
himself.

He glanced through the briefing notes that were available to
those who might be interested in attending the session and felt
his heart start to beat a bit faster. The committee was in the
process of discussing the issues around funding the next generation of cystic fibrosis drugs, and their next session was going to
be focused on it. Reading through the document swiftly, he then
did a quick search of the Hansard records to find out if anyone
had spoken on the issue lately. It appeared he may be in luck, as
seconds later, he'd established that the last debate in the House
was well over a year ago. This seemed to be because talks with
the governing bodies and the drug companies had ground to a
halt. Was now the time to bring the issue to light again?

It wasn't as if he didn't have reason to raise this issue; indeed,
it directly affected at least one family in his own constituency,
and he was fairly sure he'd be able to find out quickly if there
were any more people whose lives were touched by it in his area.
And he already had a clutch of paperwork and research materials that had been given to him as a starting point.

And, a small voice, which he quietly hushed inside his head,
added, *it will really impress Holly if you do this.*

That, of course, wasn't his reason for thinking this way, at all.
But, he thought, with a flush of excitement, it couldn't hurt.

But he needed to sit in on the committee first; after all, if
there were already developments there, it might render tabling
an Adjournment Debate on the issue redundant and make him
look behind the curve. Or like some overenthusiastic idiot who
didn't know what he was talking about. This early on in his
parliamentary career, he couldn't afford to make that kind of
mistake.

Plenty of time for that later, he thought wryly. Several of the more infamous soundbites from his colleagues on both benches sprang to mind.

* * *

When Tuesday dawned, Charlie ensured he got to the committee room early, bagged a good seat and prepared to absorb some information. If things worked out as he hoped, he'd be well briefed by the end of the afternoon.

After two hours of listening to the testimony of doctors, an adult cystic fibrosis patient and various representatives of charities and research organisations, Charlie felt both hugely moved and far better informed. There seemed little doubt that the drug Rachel and Holly had been campaigning so hard for would, hopefully, make a huge difference to many CF patients' lives, hopefully including little Harry. So why wasn't this being taken forward by the NHS?

Charlie returned to his office and thought carefully. After a little while, he drafted an email to his agent back in Willowbury. Tom was a fount of information about how best to proceed, and Charlie was confident that he'd know the best approach to take.

A short time later, Tom duly replied, and Charlie raised his eyebrows in surprise. Tom had suggested that, instead of tabling an Adjournment Debate, which Charlie would have to wait to do until he'd delivered his maiden speech in the House, Charlie put his name and question forward to go into the ballot for none other than Prime Minister's Questions. The response wasn't quite what he'd expected, but he trusted the man's judgement and decided to go with it. After all, there were few more visible platforms than the one he had suggested, and, if nothing else, it would get his face out there to the public, and his voice known to those who tuned in on the radio. The wording, of course, would have to be checked with Tom, too, but Charlie suddenly felt a frisson of excitement. If he was selected to ask his question, not only would he get his voice heard, but it would garner much-needed publicity for Harry and the other CF patients across the country. Of course, it all depended on the ballot; his question might well not be picked, but it was definitely worth a go to get his name, and the cause, out there. Also, he thought, with some sense of relief, being picked for PMQs was an acceptable substitute for a maiden speech: he'd be free to table an Adjournment Debate later on if he wanted to, having popped his parliamentary cherry.

Charlie paused. As a politician, he needed a healthy dose of pragmatism; it wasn't always possible to make the decisions people wanted. As a human being, and, more specifically in this case, a close friend (and hopefully, so much more) of the aunt of a CF patient, his heart was telling him he should be shouting his support for the cause for new medication from the rooftops of the House.

Grabbing the notepad from his desk drawer, he began to draft a series of versions of the question he wanted to ask. The wording had to be spot on; neither accusatory that the government had stalled, nor piling blame on the pharmaceutical companies, whom the Health Executive had to work with if the deal for this drug was going to be negotiated successfully. It was harder than he thought to strike the right tone, but this platform was the biggest he was likely to get. And time was short; the deadline was fast approaching. He'd better get a move on.

Back in the old days, it would have been unheard of for a new Member of Parliament to be in a position to ask a question in this form, but thanks to the electronic ballot system, known as the 'shuffle', he had as good a chance as any. Or as bad a chance, he thought ruefully. One thing was for sure, if he did get picked for Prime Minister's Questions, it would be a nerve-wracking, adrenaline-fuelled experience.

Should he text Holly and tell her? No, better not until he

knew for sure if he was going to be called. He didn't want to get her hopes up.

Finally, happy with the wording he'd scribbled out and crossed through a million times, he typed it up and pinged it over to Tom. As soon as Tom gave him the go-ahead, he'd send it off via the Commons intranet. And then cross everything he'd get picked.

It didn't take long for Tom to come back to him, and, taking a deep breath, Charlie filled out the online form and submitted his question. It would now be a nail-biting wait before the results of the shuffle was announced.

Feeling in need of some human interaction, he decided to head off to lunch.

'All right?' The chirpy tones of Stephen Brabham, Opposition MP for a constituency a couple along from Charlie's own, broke into his thoughts. Stephen had entered Parliament at the last general election as a new MP and, a few months more familiar with the place and the processes than Charlie, could often be found tucking into the all-day breakfast in the House of Commons Members' Tea Room. A man who'd been described by many as far too amenable to be a serious politician, in the short time he'd been working in the Commons, he'd proved surprisingly effective at networking and seemed to be in all places most of the time.

'Hi, Steve,' Charlie replied. 'Early lunch?'

Stephen glanced at his watch. 'Not exactly. Late breakfast, more like. Was up until all hours sorting out the wording for my speech to the local branch of the National Union of Students.'

'I'm sure they'll love it,' Charlie replied. 'Government-bashing, I suppose?' he added wryly.

'Oh, you know,' Stephen said airily. 'Chances are they'll be more interested in their smartphones than anything I have to say, but you've got to take the opportunities where you can, haven't you? Especially since not all of us have the comfort of a huge, safe majority in our seats.'

'Touché,' Charlie grinned. He knew Stephen was only teasing but in some cliques in Westminster, the same accusation could be a lot more vitriolic. 'Although it's not something I take for granted, I can assure you.'

'Not at the moment, perhaps,' Stephen took another bite of his sausage. 'But give it a few years and you'll get complacent like the rest of them on your side.'

'Nah,' Charlie knew, from a lot of conversations with the other man (perhaps a few too many in the opinion of some of his fellow party members, who weren't such believers in collaboration), when Stephen was pulling his leg. 'I'm well aware of the precariousness of this business.'

'Perhaps calling it a business is your first mistake,' Stephen said between bites of toast. 'I thought your lot were thinking about expanding your compassionate side after the last few years?'

Charlie shook his head. 'Sorry, Steve, I'm not on the right form for an ideological discussion today. Got things to sort out in the real world.'

Stephen smiled. 'Don't tell me your leafy constituency's working you too hard already? Isn't it all stockbrokers one end, hippies the other?'

'Not exactly,' Charlie said. 'But they keep me busy.'

'Well, don't let me keep you,' Stephen said. 'Drink later next week?'

'I'd like that,' Charlie replied. 'Might need one to commiserate or celebrate after next Wednesday if I get picked for PMQs.'

'Bold move,' Stephen raised a speculative eyebrow. 'Especially this early. Perhaps I'll give the lottery a spin myself.'

'No harm in trying,' Charlie replied, heading to the counter to get some food of his own. 'You've got as good a chance as any.'

'Best of luck in the ballot,' Stephen said. 'I know I'm supposed to hope you fuck it up, but I hope, if you do get through, it goes well.'

'Thanks,' Charlie smiled wryly. 'Fingers crossed.'

As he grabbed a drink and a bacon roll from the counter, he felt a sudden, unaccustomed flutter of nerves and the thought came into his head that, well-meaning colleagues or no, the only thing worse than not getting picked to speak was, most definitely, getting picked. Something told him that if he did end up winning in the shuffle, he wasn't going to get a whole lot of sleep between now and then.

25

At around 2.31 on Thursday afternoon, the results of the PMQs shuffle were posted online and all respondents received an email letting them know whether or not they'd been successful. Charlie, who'd been compulsively checking his phone like a teenager expecting a saucy SnapChat message, felt his heart leap into his mouth as his phone pinged. This was it. This was the moment he'd been waiting for.

Swiping the screen, he scrolled down the message and felt his stomach disappear and his hands, suddenly sweaty, struggled to keep hold of the phone. As he digested the information on his screen, he let out a long breath. Reading it again, just to be sure he wasn't making any mistakes, he closed his mail client and swiftly found Tom Fielding's mobile number.

'Tom? Charlie... Yes, fine, thanks. Anything I need to know about back home?... OK. Well, guess what?... Yup, that's right.' He took a deep breath, aware he was babbling, a deeply unattractive trait in a politician, even an excited one. 'Sorry, yes, we're on. Question six of fifteen... Honestly? Crapping myself... No, don't worry, I'll be calm enough by next Wednesday... No, I'm going to call her next.' Charlie's face flushed slightly at the mention of Holly's name. 'And I'll give Rachel a ring, too – after all, Harry's her son and she should know before Holly does, really.'

Heartbeat starting to return to normal, Charlie bade his agent goodbye and then rang Rachel, who was, predictably, very pleased. Then, feeling suddenly teenagerish and nervous again, he dialled Holly's number.

'Hey,' he said, voice softening a little as he heard her voice on the other end of the line. 'I'm hoping you'll be pleased when I tell you what I've just heard.' He smiled. 'No, I've not made it to Prime Minister just yet!' As he told Holly, his heart sped up and he had to take a deep breath to calm the sudden rush of adrenaline that surged through his veins. 'Thanks,' he breathed as she congratulated him. 'I'll fill you in on the details when I see you on Saturday morning. OK. Bye.'

Sitting back in his office chair, Charlie finally allowed himself a moment to digest the news. Next Wednesday he'd be speaking for the first time in the House of Commons, at Prime Minister's Questions no less, and he'd no longer be anonymous. As far as putting his name and face out there went, he couldn't be doing it any more publicly. He hoped he was up to the job.

* * *

Back in Willowbury, Holly put her own phone down on the shop counter and breathed out. For the first time since she'd met Charlie, since he'd come back into her life, she dared to hope that he might actually be one of the politicians who meant what he said. By raising the CF medication issue at PMQs, by setting it out in front of Parliament for the whole country to hear, he'd not only be raising the profile of the campaign but also setting out his own stall in support of it. That had to mean something, she was sure. It was more than Hugo Fitzgerald had done on the matter in his whole tenure.

'Hey,' Rachel said as she wandered through the shop door, Harry in tow. He'd been off nursery for a couple of days because he'd contracted a cold, but Holly knew how much Rachel wanted to keep things normal for Harry, so she was pleased to see them both. 'Have you had a call from Charlie?'

'Just now,' Holly replied. 'Great news, isn't it?'

'The best,' Rachel said, releasing Harry's hand so he could go to the toy box in the corner of the shop. 'Well, nearly the best, anyway,' she added, looking fondly after Harry as he began to open the box and search for his favourite toys.

'Who knows?' Holly replied. 'Maybe Charlie's question will push things on a bit more.'

'I hope so,' Rachel replied. 'But there's been so much stalling along the way, I don't think I can get my hopes up too high.'

'Why don't you go down and watch?' Holly said suddenly. 'I'm sure Mum and Dad would have Harry for the day.'

'I could,' Rachel said. 'He's nearly over his cold now, and if we don't go too nuts at Willowfest this weekend, he should be fully recovered by Wednesday.'

'I could ask Isabella and Chelsea if one of them's free to mind the shop if you want me to come down with you,' Holly said, eyes lighting up at the prospect of a jaunt to London.

'That sounds like a great idea,' Rachel said. 'Unless...'

Holly spotted the mischievous twinkle in her sister's eye. 'Unless what?'

'Well, won't I be cramping your style by tagging along? What if your new boyfriend, high on his success at PMQs, wants to take you out to dinner and then ravish you?' She raised her eyebrows suggestively.

'Then I shall tell him to keep his mind on the job, and that I'm here with my sister and he has to keep his hands to himself,' Holly said, affecting a prim expression. 'Besides, I can't leave this place for too long, so I should really get back the same day.'

'Oh, I'm sure one of the girls would be more than happy to

open up the next day, too,' Rachel said. 'Isabella loves this place and is desperate to do more hours when she's back home from uni.'

'I know,' Holly said. 'It's lucky my profit margins are up this financial year. If I keep playing hooky, I'll need all the money for staffing I can get.'

'No thanks to Miles bloody Fairbrother,' Rachel said darkly. 'I heard him slagging you off again in the coffee shop the other day. He just can't let it go that you got the building and he didn't, can he?'

Holly tossed her head impatiently. 'He can talk all he wants; he's not getting rid of me that easily. Willowbury's an oasis of spirituality and belief – I fit better here than his bloody bakery does!'

'Just be wary of him,' Rachel warned. 'After your run-in at the Swanley Hotel, he seems determined to discredit you and this place as much as he can. And you know what big mates he was with Hugo Fitzgerald. He's probably even more pissed off that you've got Charlie's ear and he hasn't.'

Holly shrugged. 'Let him talk. He's a miserable old windbag, and probably a corrupt one. He can't touch me.'

'No, but people talk, and it wouldn't take much for that profit margin you're so proud of to be eroded by a bit of local gossip.'

'You worry too much, sis,' Holly soothed. 'Let's just keep next week and the trip to London in our minds for now. Miles is just a prat with a chip on his shoulder, that's all.'

Rachel smiled. 'I love that you're so fearless now. I remember when you had no confidence in yourself at all. This place has brought out the best in you.'

'Fearless or just terminally undiplomatic!' Holly said, 'I never really know which.'

'Whichever, I'm just glad you're in this with me,' Rachel said. She glanced at her watch. 'We really should get going. Mum and Dad are coming over for tea after being banished all week because Dad's getting over a cold, but he swears he's better now, so I'd better work out what I'm giving them.'

'Send them my love,' Holly said. 'I'll book the train tickets and text you the times.'

'OK.' The two sisters hugged and went their separate ways.

After Rachel had closed the shop door, Holly allowed herself the luxury of fantasising about Charlie standing in the Commons Chamber, long legs encased in well-cut suit trousers, waistcoat buttoned over a crisp white shirt, authoritative voice ringing out across the hall as he brought all other the other members to a silence with his perceptive and insightful question to the PM. Just as she was embellishing that fantasy in her mind to include herself, running through the chamber doors and flinging herself into his arms, the shop's doorbell tinkled and she was brought back to reality by two local holistic healers popping in for their regular supplies of lavender oil and sea thistle. She really needed to get a grip.

26

After a busy Friday stocktaking in the shop, the Willowbury Folk Festival dawned on Saturday with a hazy, midsummer glow. Held on the weekend nearest the summer solstice, Willowfest attracted the weird and wonderful from all walks of life. From her window overlooking the High Street, Holly could already see her fellow business owners polishing windows, sweeping front steps and making their establishments even more beautiful in anticipation of the flood of people from near, far and wide who would descend on Willowbury for the weekend. Further up the High Street, she could see the members of the parish council coning off the thoroughfare to vehicles, as the street was going to be pedestrianised from now until Sunday morning. She'd look out of the window in a couple of hours and see stalls up and running, hear music of all kinds playing and feel that tingle of excitement that she felt every year that so many people were flocking to Willowbury for the atmosphere and the ley lines.

The main musical events and attractions would already be setting up in the grounds of the Priory, and Holly had drafted in Isabella and Chelsea, a couple of students who were home for the summer vacation, to take a shift or two in ComIncense over the weekend so that she could actually get out and enjoy it for a little while. The thought that she would be spending the time with Charlie filled her with both nerves and excitement. They'd texted a lot in the week since they'd last seen each other. Holly reflected that it was like having a long-distance relationship, since he spent half the week in Westminster and the other half at home in Willowbury. It gave their encounters in the flesh an added frisson.

She wondered what Charlie would make of the festival; it was his first year here, after all. He'd mostly got used to the more outlandish residents of Willowbury offering him everything from laughter yoga to organic quinoa cakes (not to mention the odd confection that had contained less than legal substances), but he hadn't yet experienced the heady, unconstrained nature of the festival. Although she knew for a fact he'd been googling like mad and watching a lot of YouTube videos from last year in an attempt to educate himself about it. Thankfully, it wasn't the kind of event that the local MP was required to officially open; that honour was reserved for Willowbury's local rock star, Alan Somerville, who'd made the town his home in the prog rock days of the early seventies and fronted several very successful bands, as well as having a stratospheric solo career. Now on the 'Retirement Tour' circuit, he'd cleaned up his act a lot from the heady days of the early eighties, but still invited his famous friends to his country mansion for the odd riotous weekend, when his hip wasn't playing up. Holly's parents, who, astonishingly, had known Alan in the seventies, had often spoken nostalgically about being invited to Alan's parties, but it was safe to say that they were all a bit less hedonistic these days.

Stretching her arms above her head, Holly glanced at Arthur, who was curled into a tight orange ball at the foot of her bed. She stepped onto the yoga mat that was permanently placed by the window and performed her morning poses, trying to clear her mind of the million and one things that she had to do before the festival actually started. Annoyingly, she found it easy to clear her mind of all but one thing; thoughts of kissing Charlie under the archway of the Priory kept coming back to her.

As they did, she suddenly felt like that nineteen-year-old geek on the dance floor again, brushing her pale-pink painted lips against Charlie's as they swayed to the music, pretending she hadn't felt the stiffness in his trousers as he'd pulled her a little closer. Unnerved by the idea of male desire, having not encountered that much of it up so close, she'd not known how to respond.

She cursed herself; she wasn't that girl any more; she had time, experience and a lot more of a sense of humour these days. It wasn't worth obsessing over. The teenage Holly would have done that; the grown-up Holly would just chalk it up to experience.

Dropping to the floor, she pushed up into cobra pose and then moved through into downward-facing dog, trying to push Charlie and his kisses, past and present, out of her mind and focus on her breathing. *Inhale... exhale... inhale...*

The ping of her mobile phone cut through her concentration and she sighed. It looked like she wasn't going to get the peace she needed before the Folk Festival kicked off.

* * *

A little time later, as she was serving some early arrivals in the shop, Holly glanced up to see Charlie standing hesitantly in the doorway.

'Hi,' she breathed, temporarily forgetting the customers and their chunks of Himalayan rock salt she was wrapping up.

'Hey,' he replied.

Holly's hands started to shake. Hurriedly, she finished taping up the tissue paper she was wrapping the rock salt crystals in and popped them into one of her recycled paper ComIncense carrier bags. 'Thanks very much,' she said to the young couple who'd purchased them. 'And enjoy the festival.'

'Thanks,' one half of the couple said. 'It's our first one. We're not quite sure what to expect!'

'Mine too!' offered Charlie. 'But Holly here's filled me in on some of the more, er, unusual things to experience. I hear the crystal-centred rebirthing sessions are well worth a go.'

'Did you just totally make that up?' Holly's eyes twinkled as the couple left ComIncense.

'Possibly,' Charlie replied playfully, 'but in this place, on this weekend, anything goes, I hear!' He wandered over to the counter as the shop door tinkled shut, and Holly slid out from behind it. Needing no invitation, he pulled her into his arms and gave her a long, lingering kiss. 'God, I've missed you,' he murmured as they broke apart. 'All I could think about this week was getting back here and spending the weekend with you.'

Holly, surprised by Charlie's unguarded admission, felt her heart thump. She knew, beyond a doubt, that if anything more serious was going to happen between them, this was the weekend it was going to happen. She was more than ready, and from the look in Charlie's eyes, he was, too. 'I've missed you too,' she said softly.

But there were other, more pragmatic things to do first.

'So, I've asked Chelsea and Isabella to come in to cover the morning and afternoon shifts between them,' she said. 'I'm just waiting for them to arrive, and then I'm all yours for the day, barring any emergencies.' At Charlie's raised eyebrow, she laughed. 'Believe it or not, this place does have them sometimes!'

As if on cue, a tall girl with fashionably cropped blonde hair walked in through the shop doorway. She looked surprised to see Charlie, but then smiled. 'Hi, Holly.'

'Hey, Isabella,' Holly said. 'Thanks for covering today.'

'No worries,' Isabella replied. 'The money's always handy for that first week back at uni.'

'Isabella's starting an MA in Creative Writing in September,' Holly explained. 'After doing exceptionally well in her English degree.'

Charlie smiled at the girl. 'Sounds interesting.'

'Should be,' Isabella replied. 'Of course, Mum's about as enthusiastic about me doing another year as you'd expect, but at least she's letting me live at home.'

'Well, if you need a few more shifts here to get you through, give me a shout and I'll see what I can do,' Holly replied. *It would be nice to be able to have more than the odd half-day and Sunday off from time to time*, she thought. Especially if it meant spending a few more daylight hours with Charlie. 'So, you know the drill,' Holly said. 'And I'll be at the end of my mobile if you need me.'

'No worries,' Isabella said breezily. 'Are you taking bookings for massages at the moment?'

'Yup,' Holly replied. 'The book's under the counter. But don't book anyone in for next Thursday evening. I've got a... regular client who likes that spot.' She glanced at Charlie and felt her cheeks colouring.

'Understood,' Isabella replied, giving Holly a conspiratorial smile.

'So, I'll pop in at lunchtime and make sure everything's OK,' Holly said. 'And as I said, call me if you need me.'

'Will do,' Isabella replied. 'Now, get out there and have some fun.'

'See you in a bit,' Holly replied. She turned back to Charlie. 'Are you ready for the full Willowfest experience?'

'As ready as I'll ever be,' Charlie laughed. 'Just promise me you'll rescue me if any of the more eccentric practitioners try anything odd on me? I don't think Westminster will look too kindly on it if I go back on Monday with green hair or a misplaced aura!'

27

Charlie couldn't remember a time when he'd felt happier, and in such a pleasingly strange context, too. Who'd have thought that he'd be wandering the High Street with his arm slung around the most beautiful redhead in the world, listening to crumhorns in one ear and pan pipes in the other as the residents of Willowbury celebrated their musical and spiritual origins long through the day and into the night? Everywhere he looked, there were people in fairy wings, face paint and fantastical costumes; he'd even caught a glimpse of someone dressed in a full suit of chain-mail, bearing a remarkably authentic-looking longsword, purporting to be the spirit of King Arthur reincarnated. Tellingly, he didn't seem to have a Guinevere with him, but Charlie was sure he'd find one among the many attendees. He'd already seen a couple of Lancelots, too.

Looking down at Holly, who kept breaking away from him to embrace friends who were passing, he felt utterly relaxed and strangely exhilarated. This was living, this was life, he thought. And it was as far away from the corridors of Westminster as could be imagined.

'All right?' Holly stood on tiptoe and whispered into his ear.

'You seem a little bit away with the fairies.' Her breath on the back of his neck sent a tingle down his spine and reminded him, as if he needed reminding, that, despite the fact they'd not known each other very long, they were getting closer to the next level of their relationship.

Charlie grinned as his eye was caught by two little blonde girls dressed as actual fairies. 'I'm fine,' he said, pulling her a little closer. 'I've just never seen anything quite like this before.'

'Willowbury's proud of its roots,' Holly replied. 'And, I promise you, once you've done one Folk Festival, you'll keep this weekend free every year.' She tucked a stray lock of hair back behind her ear with her free hand. Charlie was struck with erotic thoughts about just what else he wanted her hands to touch.

As the band at the top of the High Street struck up a fast-paced fiddle tune, Charlie pulled Holly closer to him so that they were face to face. 'Fancy a dance?' he teased as his arms tightened around her. She was wearing a strappy, flowing summer dress which kept catching in the breeze, and as he drew her towards him, he was instantly aware of the heat from her body pressing against his. Trying to mentally talk himself down from the effect that having Holly so close to him was having, he whirled her around in a loose approximation of a jig until she was helpless with laughter in his arms and her hair, loosely tied back in her habitual messy bun, had all but come down.

Slowing down as the music calmed, Charlie looked at Holly. Her face was flushed from the heat and the dancing, and her eyes were sparkling with amusement. As if his mouth had a mind of its own, he dipped his head, searching for her lips. They'd kissed a lot, but he was still slightly nervous of her response. Feeling her breath quicken, he met her mouth gently, tasting the sweetness of the elderflower wine, organic of course, that she'd been drinking. He closed his eyes in pure pleasure as her mouth opened to deepen the kiss, lifting a hand to run it through her hair.

'Isn't this a little too public for your liking?' Holly breathed as they broke a millimetre or two apart. 'You'll be all over Twitter before you know it.'

'I don't care,' Charlie murmured. 'We're not doing anything wrong.'

Holly smiled into the kiss. 'I'm glad you feel that way.'

As his arms tightened around her, everything else but the heat from their bodies seemed to melt away. Charlie had never felt such a sense of rightness, of coming home, as he did with Holly in his arms.

'Break it up, you two!' Rachel's voice interrupted their private world as she tapped her sister on the shoulder. 'You've both got a rep to protect, remember? And Charlie's got a speech to make after the fancy-dress competition.'

'Bugger, I'd forgotten I'd agreed to that,' murmured Charlie. 'What do I have to say again?'

'Oh, something diplomatic and bland, as usual,' Holly teased. 'I'm sure you'll manage.'

If he'd had more blood flow to his brain at that moment, rather than other areas, Charlie would have been able to think of a suitable pithy response, but as it was, he let it slide.

Slipping a hand into Holly's, he smiled back at her and Rachel. 'I'd better have a look around, then, hadn't I? Get a feel for the standard of fancy dress.' Although, he thought, it would be difficult to tell who was actually going to be entering the competition and who just dressed that way normally, as far as Willowbury was concerned. As a bearded, barefooted, purple-cloaked man strolled past them, tambourine in hand, Charlie shook his head. No matter how well he thought he'd settled into Willowbury, the place and its people never failed to surprise him. As he and Holly watched Rachel walking, or, rather, being dragged away, by Harry to see a stall that was selling a wide variety of sugary treats, especially designed, it seemed, to attract younger visitors to Willowfest, he really did feel as though he was becoming a part of this friendly but unusual place.

The bunting that flapped between the lamp posts on the High Street paled in comparison to the multitude of colours that the people of Willowbury themselves were wearing. Everywhere Charlie looked, there were jugglers, stilt walkers, people wearing jesters' hats, fairy wings, medieval costumes, and sometimes all three at once. The air was alive with the different sounds of folk music blended with more Eastern-inspired cymbals and instruments, and, rising above it all, some plainsong emanating from the ruins of the Priory behind the High Street. It was a riot of sounds, colours and activity, and Charlie, who should have been overwhelmed, felt strangely at ease.

Of course, that may have been more to do with having Holly beside him to guide him through the town. She pointed out things as they wended their way towards the grounds of the Priory, where a more structured concert was due to start in the mid-afternoon.

'You were right,' Charlie said, eyes still on stalks as they wandered. 'This really is like nothing else I've ever seen before.'

'It must give Westminster a run for its money,' Holly smiled. 'I can't remember ever seeing Hugo here.'

'He probably barricaded himself in at home with a bottle of Scotch and the weekend papers!' Charlie laughed.

'Or a batch of Miles' scones,' Holly said, smiling wryly. 'Probably wouldn't trust anything he could buy here.' She regarded him levelly. 'You seem far more suited to this place than he was, even in the short time you've been here.'

'I think he was definitely more Stavenham than Willowbury,' Charlie said. 'Although, to be fair, it's a fine line to walk between the two places, as I'm finding out.' He reached out a hand to take one of the tempting-looking chocolate brownies that a trader, armed with a ribboned tray, was handing out as she wandered up the street, but Holly grabbed his hand.

'I, er, wouldn't, if I were you.' Her eyes sparkled mischievously. 'Elsinore's Artisan Confectionary is notorious around here for including somewhat, er, alternative, ingredients in her brownies.'

Charlie was struck with a vision of the little old lady from *The Vicar of Dibley* who provided the refreshments for the parish meetings. 'As in, sardine and chilli-flavoured brownies?' he asked.

Holly grinned. 'You are so adorably naive, sometimes. Perhaps it's better if you think that, but I still wouldn't recommend risking it.'

Charlie's eyebrows shot up as he realised what Holly was getting at. 'Fair enough. But I'm not as square as all that, you know. I did inhale at university.'

'Really?'

'Well... sort of. Spent the rest of the evening throwing up, though, so I guess it was a bad batch.'

'All the more reason to be cautious of Willowbury residents offering you brownies, then!' Holly grabbed Charlie's hand again and steered him back towards ComIncense. 'I've got a picnic for us that I just need to pick up while I check back in with Isabella. And I promise there aren't any illegal substances in any of it!'

'Sounds good,' Charlie replied. 'After all, "MP eats hash brownie and streaks naked through historic religious ruins", probably won't do much for my majority.'

'Actually, in Willowbury you never know,' Holly smiled. 'But perhaps over the bridge in Stavenham they might have more of an issue with it.'

'I don't doubt it,' Charlie kept smiling. 'I'm glad I've got you by my side to guide me through all this.'

'I'm glad too,' Holly said softly. She paused in the street and tugged at Charlie's hand so that they were close together again. 'It's lovely to share this with you,' she murmured.

As they headed back to ComIncense to pick up their refreshments, Charlie felt a tingle run down his spine. It was as if the stars had all aligned over Willowbury, and he and Holly were at the centre of them. There was definitely magic in the air, this Willowfest weekend, he thought.

28

'How are you feeling?' Holly asked as she looked across at Charlie, who was lying, legs stretched out on the picnic blanket, sipping languidly at his glass of mead.

'It's all so beautiful,' Charlie breathed as he looked around at the grounds of the ruined Priory, and as his gaze alighted back on her, Holly smiled at his wonderment. Hanging from the broken lumps of the former building were strings and strings of amber-coloured lights, and atop the tallest pillars and arches were huge altar candles, burning into the darkening sky. They were sitting on a picnic blanket, sharing the last of a bottle of Monk's Mead from one of the stallholders. They'd spent the day nibbling and sampling their way around Willowfest, but they'd also walked what felt like miles, as well as danced to a variety of different bands and singers in the grounds of the Priory itself. The concert – the headline event of Willowfest – consisted of several of the UK's biggest folk acts, including a final set by Alan Somerville himself, who was now belting out his biggest hit on the makeshift stage that had been set up in the ruined nave of the Priory.

'It's like nothing else, ever,' Holly replied. 'Willowfest has its own charm, its own energy. It's like someone managed to distil all of the best bits of living here into one evening and put it on show for everyone to enjoy.'

'That's a great way to put it,' Charlie took another sip of his mead. 'It's like the air itself feels alive. Of course, that could just be the mead!'

'It's got quite a kick to it,' Holly warned. 'I wouldn't drink much more after this one, if I were you.' She drew a little closer to him. It was a warm evening, but she was at the point where she wanted there to be as little space between their bodies as possible.

As Alan Somerville approached the end of his set with a couple of acoustic guitar songs, Holly found they'd finished their bottle of mead. They'd also finished most of the picnic they'd brought with them, as the fresh air had stimulated their late-evening appetites.

'Snap for the local paper?' A cheery voice broke into her thoughts. Kyle Jones, the junior reporter for the *Willowbury and Stavenham Gazette* was standing in front of them with his smartphone and a smile.

'Sure,' Holly said. 'If you don't mind, Charlie.'

Immediately, she saw Charlie's back stiffen. 'That's fine,' he said.

Holly felt him shift slightly away from her and, as she watched him, he composed his features into an expression suitable both for the occasion and for the face of the local Member of Parliament.

Holly, amused, turned back to the reporter and gave her best, unguarded smile.

'How have you found your first Willowfest, Mr Thorpe?' Kyle asked, tapping his phone to record Charlie's answer.

'It's been a great day,' Charlie replied. 'I'm so impressed by everything that Willowbury has to offer.'

'Thanks very much,' Kyle said. 'It's good to see you

supporting a local event. Any comments on the progress of the planning for the motorway junction as yet?'

'Not yet,' Charlie replied. 'But thanks for asking. We'll keep you posted.'

'And can I just have your name?' Kyle turned his attention to Holly. 'For the caption?'

'Holly Renton, owner of ComIncense on the High Street,' Holly supplied.

'Much obliged.' The reporter smiled at them both. 'Thanks for your time.'

As Kyle headed off in search of more snapshots, Holly felt Charlie relax again.

'You still don't like being interviewed, do you?' she said softly.

Charlie shook his head. 'We had some media training as the new intake, but I'd far rather be the one asking the questions.'

'That's a first, surely, in your job,' Holly teased. 'A politician who doesn't get off on the sound of his own voice?'

'There you go again,' Charlie said, but there was amusement rather than irritation in his voice. 'Can we just forget what I do, and what you do, for one night, and focus on who you are, and who I am?' He pulled her closer to him on the picnic rug. 'Because I really want just to walk you home and spend the night with you.'

Holly's pleasurable gasp was swallowed as Charlie's mouth met hers. From a couple of metres away, neither registered the flash of the young reporter's camera phone as he snapped a couple of cheeky shots to spice up his Twitter feed.

'That sounds good to me,' Holly murmured once their lips parted again. 'Shall we go?'

'Absolutely,' Charlie murmured.

Swiftly, they packed up the picnic basket and then folded the blanket. Alan Somerville was just coming to the end of his last song, and as they wandered hand in hand back through the grounds of the Priory, an almost palpable tension seemed to radiate between them. At once Holly felt that the walk home was too long and not long enough. This was it, she could feel it. All of the yearning, all of the near misses, all of the barriers between them, were about to come tumbling down.

Neither said much as they headed up the slight incline of the road behind Willowbury High Street that led to the back entrance to Holly's shop and home. The moon was rising, giving them ample light to see by, and Charlie's hand in hers was warm and dry. Again, she was reminded of that night so many years ago when they'd walked hand in hand through Covent Garden in search of a taxi or a Tube station back to her hotel. His palm had been clammy, then, as he'd seemed as nervous as she was about what may or may not happen after they'd reached their destination. Now, there was no such doubt. Both ached for this night to continue, both yearned for it, and both knew exactly where they wanted to be.

'Can I get you a coffee?' Holly asked as she pushed open the door to her flat.

'No, thank you,' Charlie replied. 'Christ, Holly, I don't want anything else except you.'

Holly laughed. 'There I was thinking you had a problem with expressing yourself.'

'Not so far as you're concerned,' Charlie said huskily. He kissed her forehead, then her nose and then found her lips again. 'And I want you to know that I am very, very happy right now.'

'I can see that, and feel it,' Holly teased, to disguise how touched she was that he was being so open with her. This naturally guarded, instinctively rather reticent man was opening himself up to her, letting his defences down, trusting her. And she felt herself melting as she realised what a big step they were about to take. Pushing up against him so that his back was pressed against the wall of her stone tiled hallway, she groaned as she felt his arousal, and wanted there to be no more layers between them.

'Come upstairs,' Holly murmured between kisses. 'And yes, I am sure.'

'I'm glad,' Charlie replied. 'And for the record, I'm sure too.'

'Good,' Holly teased. 'I wouldn't want to be accused of doing anything without your consent.'

'Consent given,' Charlie murmured.

Breaking apart to negotiate the rather steep stairs that led upstairs, Holly felt as if every nerve ending was tingling with anticipation.

The moonlight shone through Holly's bedroom window, casting her white bed linen in a silvered, ethereal glow. She wandered over to the window and threw it open, letting in the warm night air. She raised a hand to draw the curtains but then thought better of it; she wasn't overlooked, and the light was so beautiful. Arthur, coat silvery rust in the moonlight, prowled the fence that separated Holly's back yard from next door.

Charlie was still standing in the doorway, and as she glanced back behind her, Holly caught a glimpse of that adorably shy boy he'd once been. There was something about the tilt of his head as he regarded her, as if he couldn't quite believe he was standing there, in her bedroom, that took her back again to the night they'd met. In a way, she was comforted, but in another moment, as he moved towards her, the boy had gone, to be replaced by a man with hunger in his eyes, a bucket more self-assurance and the warmest hands.

'Come here,' she whispered as she wandered over to her bed. Reaching out a hand, she pulled him down to the mattress, on top of her, his weight both comforting and energising.

'If you make any jokes about honourable members, I'm leaving,' Charlie murmured between kisses.

Holly giggled. 'Don't worry, I promise to behave.'

Charlie raised an eyebrow. 'I didn't say I wanted you to do *that.*'

And so, after weeks of dancing around each other, and more false starts than were sustained at the annual Mendip cheese rolling contest, they began to explore each other. As Holly slithered out of her dress and pulled Charlie's T-shirt over his head to reveal his finely toned chest, she felt the current spark between them as their bare skin touched. She was down to her knickers in a few moments more. She wanted to touch and explore every inch of him, and take her time in doing it, despite the haste with which she'd discarded her clothes.

Charlie gently pushed her back onto the soft, downy pillows and ran his hands down her body from her neck, over the curve of her waist, to her thighs. Leaning over her, he planted feather-light kisses from her jaw, down her neck and over her breasts, breathing warmly over a tautening nipple before taking it gently into his mouth. Holly arched her back in the sheer pleasure of it. Mouth occupied, his hands were still exploring, running over her body and up the inside of her thighs to the junction where her knickers were the last barrier to her warm nakedness.

Holly sighed in ecstasy, but, not to be outdone, she pulled Charlie down next to her, kissing his neck and working her own way down his body, kissing and caressing the tantalising line of hair that ran down from his navel and disappeared into the waistband of his tight jersey boxer shorts. Crooking a finger under the elastic, she gave a swift tug and Charlie's full, erect and ready form was on display in all its glory. She glanced upwards and felt a sharp pinprick of desire hot and insistent in her core as, legs spread and a look of absolute pleasure and abandonment on his face, Charlie groaned as one of her warm hands wrapped around his generous length.

'You are every bit as glorious as I thought you'd be,' she murmured before wrapping her lips around the head of his cock. Lapping gently, she felt her own arousal increase to almost unbearable proportions as Charlie raised his hips. He tasted divine.

'Come back up here,' Charlie murmured. His voice was husky. 'I want to feel all of you.'

Obligingly, Holly returned to the top of the bed and gasped as Charlie pulled her close, wrapping himself around her. The weight of his body was utterly divine. There was little between them now, and little else to say. As Charlie's hand slid between her parted thighs and began to caress her, sliding warm fingers inside her while finding the absolute centre of her pleasure with his thumb, Holly felt the long, rolling tingle becoming deeper, more insistent, until she was riding a long wave of climax that throbbed and beat insistently within her and made stars explode behind her eyes.

It was an easy matter to keep that feeling going as, after a moment's break to slip on a condom, Charlie bridged the last, most significant gap. His length inside her, his long, almost languid thrusts, gave way to a more intense and frenetic rhythm as he reached towards his own beating climax. As he came, he raised his head and looked her deeply in the eyes. 'I think I love you, Holly Renton,' he said in his most unguarded, most vulnerable moment.

'I think I love you too, Charlie Thorpe,' Holly replied. 'Lovely, lovely Charlie.'

They collapsed beside each other in the moonlit darkness of Holly's bedroom. Arthur, who'd waited decorously on the windowsill, slunk in through the window and settled himself at the foot of the bed with a rumbling purr.

'What a day,' Charlie murmured, pulling Holly close so that her head was resting on his chest. Idly, she played with the curls she found there as he caressed the back of her neck.

'Well, they say that Willowfest causes all kinds of energies to be heightened,' Holly said. 'And it's certainly worked wonders for you.' She propped herself up on one elbow to get another look at him. Post-climax, Charlie was a sight to behold; hair ruffled, five-o'clock shadow on his face and lazy, sleepy, liquid brown eyes, looking at her as though she was the only person in the world. She suddenly felt a great rush of love for him. She couldn't imagine, now they'd found each other, ever being without him.

She shook her head in bewilderment. No one had ever affected her like this. She felt punch-drunk with love, fuzzy with contentment. And she was pretty sure it wasn't just the utterly mind-blowing sex that was making her feel that way.

'I overheard Alan Somerville talking to some groupies about the benefits of tantric sex earlier this afternoon,' Charlie said, a sudden twinkle in his sleepy dark eyes. 'But I doubt even he's had it as good as that just was. Did you slip something in my glass of mead?'

Holly laughed. 'As if I would!' She leaned down and kissed him, a gentle, sated contact that seemed to seal things. 'This is all just you and me. Although I've got some gingko biloba downstairs if you start to flag.'

'As if!' Charlie snorted. 'I'll have you know, MPs are well known for their staying power in the chamber... and in other areas.'

'Looking at some of your colleagues, that's not exactly a very sexy image,' Holly laughed. 'Although it's nice to know you're all having, er, as much fun as we just had.'

'You'd better believe it,' Charlie said, burying his lips in Holly's neck. 'And I'm definitely up for another round, if you are.'

Holly's laugh turned into a sigh as Charlie's mouth and fingers started to work their magic again.

By the time they fell asleep, dawn was starting to creep like a cat after a mouse across the grey blue night sky, Arthur had retreated to the comfort of the cushion on Holly's bedroom chair and both Holly and Charlie felt more relaxed than they had in a very long time.

'I love you, Charlie,' Holly murmured as sleep finally overtook her.

As they both rested, the cold moon, ever the voyeur, stared through the open bedroom curtains and cast the inhabitants of the bed in a silvery light.

29

If he could dance like Justin Timberlake, he'd so be strutting his stuff right now, Charlie thought as he headed back down the street from Holly's flat and home for a shower and a change of clothes. By rights, after festivalling all day and making love all night, he should be knackered, but he felt revitalised, energised, and as if he could do it all over again. The latter, he thought, he'd certainly have no problem repeating. As often as possible. At all times of the day and night. In fact, he was only going home to finish up a few bits of paperwork and then he'd agreed to meet Holly on the Willowbury Hill for another picnic that afternoon.

How things had changed since his move to Willowbury! When he'd arrived, he'd been a rookie MP with no idea how to reconcile his day job and his actual day-to-day life in the place. Admittedly, there had been a few hiccups along the way, but now he finally felt as though he was gaining some ground, making things work.

And Holly had been a revelation. The sunshine on his back as he headed up the High Street was a warm reminder of every-thing she'd done for him; the light she had shone, and continued to shine, on his life. As he'd got to know her better, his own confidence had increased, and, although it might just be the hormones talking after a night of making love, he felt as though he could take on the world.

Wishing a good morning to a somewhat surprised Mrs Holderness, out early with her two Border collies, he walked down the garden path to his house and fumbled in his pocket for his keys. Once through the door, the coolness of the stone hallway brought him up short. The house, unlived in since Friday evening, and even then only briefly, smelt still and almost damp, in spite of the warm weather outside.

As he wandered through the hallway and into the kitchen, he realised with a start that he'd yet again left his bag on the scrubbed oak kitchen table instead of putting it safely away in the study. Smiling to himself, he remembered just how desperate he'd been to get over to Holly's place on Friday evening and how he had literally just dropped everything and dashed over there. Seeing his bag there, though, brought him back down to earth; he still had a mountain of work to do and he needed to be on the evening train back to London, too.

Resolving to bash on through what needed to be done and then get back to Holly as soon as he could, figuring he could sleep on the train later, he pulled the buff-coloured document wallet out of his bag and settled down at the kitchen table for a quick scan through before he made himself a coffee. The documents were all the usual stuff: requests from constituents for meetings, a couple of lobbyists representing various industries and, his heart turned over, a reminder about his scheduled question at Prime Minister's Question Time that coming Wednesday.

Charlie hoped his father and mother, two long-serving doctors, both of whom had worked until their retirement in the same GP practice in the village in Yorkshire where he'd been brought up, would be proud of the stand he was taking on the cystic fibrosis drug-funding issue. He'd always had a keen ear for the changes in policy of successive governments around the NHS. Although the medical side of health was a mystery to him, the funding and maintenance side was an area he was endlessly fascinated by, and one of the reasons he'd gone into politics was to get the inside track on how the NHS could be made to work more effectively, but not at the cost of its patients.

Being a pragmatist, he understood the tension between economic decisions and political ones; but his abiding political passion was to try to bring a balance to the opposing forces of public healthcare and economic reality. He was a believer in balancing the books but also had enough compassion and sense of social justice to know that sometimes human considerations had to come first. Asking this question in such a public forum, hopefully making himself known to the Department of Health and Social Care, with a view to representing his party on a committee within it, was a decent first step for someone who hadn't been in the post that long. He recalled what one of the more senior ministers had warned him and the new intake at the last orientation session, that to be seen as too assertive too quickly could be a bad thing; that there was no room in politics for *'rock stars or crusaders'*, but Charlie put that warning aside for the moment. He didn't feel as though he was overstepping his mark, yet. But after Wednesday, who knew?

* * *

Across the village, Holly contemplated the shadows of her leaded windows that were playing over her bedroom ceiling as her curtains flapped in the morning breeze. She should be fast asleep, after the day and night she'd had with Charlie, but she felt alive, buzzing with anticipation. She couldn't wait to see him again. Last night had felt so incredible; they'd unleashed something together that she imagined she'd never want to be without. The sensations of his hands and mouth on her had awakened a desire stronger than anything she'd ever experienced before, and their lovemaking had been exquisite. Who'd have thought the local MP would have so much passion in him?

The ping of her mobile phone brought her somewhat reluctantly out of this daydream, and she reached for it where it lay on her bedside table. Expecting it to be from Charlie, she was tickled to see a message from Rachel.

Hope you made a night of it! Here's that picture I took of you and C before it all got too messy. Xxx

Holly smiled as she saw a snapshot of herself and Charlie, arms around each other, grinning from ear to ear. Rachel had taken it shortly before she and Harry had called it a night, in between the folk bands and Alan Somerville's final, rather louder set. They both looked lit up from within, and Charlie looked more relaxed than she'd ever seen him. Then, peering at the background of the shot, she noticed with an even bigger smile that little Harry had photobombed, peering out from behind Charlie with a huge, cheeky grin on his face. *Typical Harry*, Holly thought. It was so easy to look at that photo and remember that Harry was still a normal three-year-old, away from all of the drugs and the uncertainties. He still loved the same things, had the same energies as any other child. And Holly loved him all the more fiercely for it. Despite everything, all of the challenges, it was moments like the one in the photo that made everything worth it.

Still grinning, Holly texted a quick reply, thanking Rachel for the photo but not wanting to reveal what else had happened after the music had stopped. There would be plenty of time for a catch up later in the week, when they were on the train to London to see Charlie in action at Prime Minister's Questions. For the moment, the blissful night was her and Charlie's alone.

30

After grabbing a quick shower and raiding her fridge for things to put in her picnic basket, Holly tied her hair back in a loose ponytail and headed down to the shop. The shop was normally closed on Sundays, but she'd made an exception for Willowfest and decided to keep it open until lunchtime. By then, most of the incomers to the festival would be making their way home.

As she unlocked the front door and wedged it open with the doorstop, she glanced out into the High Street and was pleased to see that quite a few people were out and about this Sunday morning. She waved at a couple of people she knew, and smiled to see the nun was in her usual position, bright and early, handing out sandwiches from her cool box to those who might have a real need of them.

It never ceased to amaze her how many people of different faiths and persuasions could live peacefully side by side in Willowbury. The place was a microcosm of harmony and contentment, and ever since she'd made it her home, she'd felt more and more at peace with herself. Perhaps there was something in the ley lines theory, after all, she thought.

Of course, taking Charlie to her bed last night may well have coloured her emotions in a rosier light this morning, too. They had been a revelation together, and mentally she high-fived her nineteen-year-old self for her good taste, if caution, all those years ago.

She stretched her arms above her head, and wandered to the shop counter, where she opened up the till and glanced at the notes Isabella had made yesterday. All seemed to have gone well, and as she looked at the booking log for massages, Isabella had even booked in a couple more for her for next week. That side of the business seemed to be taking off nicely. In fact, for once, all of the stars seemed to be in alignment.

Shortly before lunchtime, her mobile pinged again. Glancing at the screen, her heart lurched as she saw it was another message from Rachel, of which she could only see the first half of until she swiped it. She didn't waste any time. Heart beating faster, she digested the news that Harry had woken up late, and under the weather, and so Rachel had zipped him up to the Bristol Royal Children's Hospital.

So far, as a combination of Rachel's brilliant management of Harry's condition and an enormous stroke of serendipity, Harry had avoided an extended hospital stay. He had to go to the Children's Hospital every eight weeks for a check-up, to test his lung function and for a battery of blood tests, as well as a general health check, and he'd passed his last one with flying colours. However, he'd been a little under the weather recently since he'd picked up a cold from nursery and unfortunately that didn't seem to be shifting. Rachel, Holly knew, would have been careful to ensure Harry didn't over exert himself at Willowfest, but that, combined with the remnants of the cold, had seemingly affected him more than Rachel had anticipated. While children without CF would be poorly but recover quickly, the antibiotics hadn't quite worked soon enough this time, and the hospital wanted to keep him in for observation.

Do you need anything?

Holly texted her sister but was relieved when the reply came back in a minute or two. Rachel had enough clothes and supplies for a few days, and was apologetic she was going to miss her lunchtime shifts at ComIncense on Monday and Tuesday. Texting her a reassuring reply, Holly tried not to worry. Harry was so little, and cystic fibrosis was such an unforgiving condition; the unfairness of it all took her own breath away when things like this happened. But thinking like that would get her nowhere, and there was still today's morning trade, and the lunchtime picnic with Charlie, to think about.

'Good morning,' she said as a customer, obviously an incomer for Willowfest, came through the front door of the shop. He looked knackered, a bit grubby, as if he'd slept out under the stars instead of actually in his tent in the field behind the Priory last night, but curiously at peace.

'Blessed be,' he ventured shyly.

Holly smiled. It was no surprise, looking around at the shop, that customers often assumed she was a practising Pagan – especially with the long hair and the flowery dress, she thought. 'And to you,' she said. She wasn't really in the frame of mind to set him right. 'Is there anything I can help you with?'

'I'd love some of those beeswax candles to take back home with me for my altar,' he said as he wandered over to the corner where Holly had created a display of them, all sourced from a local hive owner just outside Cheddar.

'Sure,' Holly replied. 'Just select the ones you want and I'll wrap them for you.' She grabbed her roll of tissue paper from under the counter and, when the customer brought over his selection, she began to wrap them. She was so engrossed, she didn't notice until she looked up again that there was someone else the other side of the counter; Charlie.

'Hey,' she said. 'You're a bit early.'

'Couldn't keep myself away,' he said huskily.

The customer coughed discreetly. 'Er... how much do I owe you?'

'Oh, yes, right.' Holly rang in the figures and hurriedly took the proffered debit card for a contactless payment. 'This still feels like the real magic,' she quipped, as the payment went through with a wave of the card near the reader. Slipping the candles into one of her recycled brown paper bags, she handed them over to the customer, who bid his goodbyes and then left.

Charlie gave her a suggestive smile. 'Is it wrong to get turned on looking at you handling those candles?'

Holly laughed. 'I'd say you're flattering yourself, but I know, after last night, that you're not!'

Charlie pulled her close. 'Well, if you say it, then it must be true.'

They kissed for a moment, but, mindful she was keeping the shop open and anyone could come walking through the door, Holly broke the embrace. 'Behave. Or I'll have to spank you with one of my larger lavender and heather sprigs.'

'Promises, promises,' Charlie grinned. 'Didn't you know politicians are well known for their... interests?'

'I didn't realise S&M was one of yours,' Holly said. 'Fifty Shades of Westminster?' She pushed him away playfully. 'If you're not busy, you can go and wait in the flat if you want. I'm keeping this place open until twelve o'clock and then we can head out for our picnic.'

'I'll head off to Jack's for a coffee, if he's opened up this morning,' Charlie replied. 'Shall I come back after twelve?'

When she didn't respond immediately, Charlie took her hand. 'Is everything OK?'

Holly shook her head, as if shaking away her concerns about Harry; not that they ever truly went away. 'I'm fine, honestly. It's just that Rachel's had to take Harry up to Bristol Children's

Hospital this morning, and it's the first time he's been admitted properly. I guess I'm a bit shell-shocked.'

'He seemed so well yesterday when we bumped into them at the Priory in the afternoon,' Charlie said. 'You know, all things considered.'

'He's like any other child, mostly,' Holly replied. 'Except that he can go downhill quickly when he has an illness. Rachel thought they'd nipped the chest infection in the bud with the antibiotics, but I'm guessing being out and about for Willowfest was a bit much for him after being confined to barracks all week.'

'Will he be all right?' Charlie asked. 'I mean, how long will he have to stay in the BRHC?'

'Could be a couple of days, could be a week or more,' Holly said. 'If it's any longer than a day or two, I'll head up there in the evenings and keep Rachel company. She'll be going stir-crazy after a while.' She shook her head. 'If only those new drugs had been given the go-ahead, this kind of stuff could be sorted out quickly.' She looked at him keenly. 'Five days in hospital on an antibiotic IV drip and the costs will start racking up. Sometimes these decisions on drugs seem so short-sighted.'

'Is this Harry's aunt talking, or a constituent?' Charlie said gently.

Holly could feel her eyes brimming and she blinked the tears away impatiently. 'It's someone who's feeling very frustrated that she can't do more to help a poorly little boy.'

As Charlie pulled her close, Holly felt temporarily reassured and insulated by the warmth of his embrace and the beating of his heart.

'So, I guess that means Rachel won't be coming to watch PMQs on Wednesday, then,' Charlie murmured into her hair.

'Supposing Harry was out of hospital, I don't think she'd want to leave him to zoom down to London so soon, even if he was staying with Mum and Dad.'

'Completely understandable,' Charlie replied. He pulled back from her slightly. 'Does that mean that you, er, won't be there either?'

Holly smiled. 'It's been a while since I've bunked off for the day, apart from yesterday of course, and Isabella's already booked in to hold the fort at ComIncense, so I'm sure I can find my way to Westminster. That's if you still want me to be there?'

Charlie smiled in a way that reminded her, yet again, of the adorable teenager he once was. 'Of course I do. The thought of having you in the gallery as I make my speaking debut will make the whole thing a lot less nerve-wracking.' He kissed her gently. 'And who knows – perhaps it'll even win me back your vote!'

'I wouldn't go that far,' Holly laughed. 'Pretty speeches don't exactly convince me any more.'

'Fair enough,' Charlie replied. 'But will you allow me to buy you dinner afterwards?'

'I think I could stretch to that,' Holly said. 'Should I, er, change my train ticket and catch an early one back here on Thursday morning?'

Charlie's face lit up. 'If you want to spend the night in my minuscule London crash pad, you are more than welcome.'

'I'd love to,' Holly replied. 'Now, hadn't you better go off and have your coffee? I'm keeping the shop open a little bit longer until trade tails off.'

'OK.' Charlie leaned forward and kissed her. 'I'll see you in a bit.'

As she watched Charlie wander out through the front door of the shop, she felt an unsettling flood of emotions: worry and concern for poor Harry and Rachel, cooped up in the BRHC for the immediate future, and a real smattering of nerves for Charlie and his upcoming moment during PMQs. Both, in her mind, seemed inextricably and painfully linked.

31

'You know, as your MP, I will do everything I can to push Harry's case forward, don't you?' Charlie said as they began to climb the steep bank to the flat-topped hill that stood, proud and watchful over the Vale of Somerset. Holly had been acquainting him with some of the things she and Rachel had been doing to raise awareness of Harry's condition, and the need for new medications, as they'd wandered from where they'd parked the car near the foot of Willowbury Hill.

'I know,' Holly sighed. 'But Harry's so little, and so much time has been wasted already, it's difficult to feel hopeful. Don't get me wrong,' she added hurriedly, 'I know you'll do your best, but you and I both know the wheels of government and legislation turn so slowly that I'm afraid Harry will run out of time before he gets access to the next generation of drugs. Nearly three hundred CF patients have died in the time it's taken for the authorities and the drug companies to debate this so far. How many more will lose their fight before they come to an agreement on price?'

Charlie stopped on the stepped path they were treading towards the south side of the hill, where they intended to have their picnic. 'Holly,' he said, drawing her to him, 'I promise you that I will do everything I can to help Harry to get access to the medication he needs. And not just because you're living on my patch, but because health has always been the area I wanted to explore, should I ever have got to this point.' He stroked a tendril of hair back from her face and kept his palm pressed to her cheek. She looked so beautiful to him, and she would have done wherever she was, but set against the stunning backdrop of the counties-wide view from Willowbury Hill, she looked like some goddess, something not entirely of this world. Cursing himself for the flight of fancy, he struggled to focus on what she was saying.

'I know you mean well, Charlie,' she said. 'And I know you'll try to do as much as you can. The fact that you care is what makes you such an asset to this place.'

'I promise I'll do whatever I can,' Charlie murmured. 'Now, are we going to find a place to eat this wonderful picnic? It feels like a long time since breakfast.'

Holly smiled. 'Sure.' She gestured to a spot just to the right of where they were standing. 'If we sit over there, we shouldn't get in the way of any other walkers.' She wandered over and they threw down the picnic blanket.

Charlie set the picnic basket down and they began to unpack it.

A little time later, both were sitting companionably, sipping a glass of chilled Sancerre and looking at the breathtaking view that stretched from Brent Knoll and Steep Holm island to the west, through to Dorset in the south, and behind them, to the north, the faint outline of the Quantock Hills. With such a beautiful vista, it wasn't surprising that soon Charlie felt himself relaxing again, trying to push away the unsettling thoughts about his work, and the real world, losing himself in this scenery, and this moment, with Holly.

He put down his glass carefully on the dry, sun-cracked

ground next to the picnic blanket and turned to Holly. 'I can see why you love it up here,' he said. 'It feels, I don't know, timeless, somehow.'

'It's definitely the place to come to get away from it all,' Holly replied. She smiled. 'And I do occasionally lead a deep-vision meditation session up here, weather permitting. Perhaps you should come along some time.'

'Deep-vision meditation?' Charlie asked. 'Sounds, er, deep.'

'Oh, you're such an erudite speaker!' Holly teased. 'It's not as ridiculous as it sounds, honestly. It's all about starting with your own breath, which is the cornerstone of all meditation, and then feeling yourself as part of something bigger, something deeper. This place, with its long, mystical heritage, is the perfect setting for a session. People come away feeling rejuvenated and ready to face whatever life throws at them.'

'That's some claim,' Charlie said, shielding his eyes against the suddenly strong midday sun.

'Well, that's what they tell me,' Holly smiled. 'And I find it's a great way to get things straight in my own head, too; this notion that you're at one with the earth. It brings a certain amount of peace.'

'Perhaps you should show me some day,' Charlie suggested. 'But not right now.' He moved closer and kissed her, a long, Sancerre-infused meeting of mouths that conveyed exactly how much he didn't want peace at all right now, but a lot of pleasure instead. As the kiss deepened in intensity, Charlie leaned forward, until he had Holly beneath him, her hand running through his hair as one of his slipped down her body to her waist. The slight breeze in the air, and the scent of newly mown grass, as well as the taste and feel of Holly, made his senses reel. 'Do you reckon we could get away with, you know... up here?' He murmured between kisses.

Holly laughed breathlessly, eyes wide with warmth. 'You're joking, aren't you? You can get arrested for that.'

'It's a risk I'd be willing to take,' Charlie said, progressing downwards to kiss her neck.

'Well, I'm a local business owner and I've got a rep to protect,' Holly chided, pushing him away gently. 'And it's not like you don't have one to maintain, either.'

'Then can I suggest that we pack away this lovely lunch and head back down the hill, so I can take you to bed before I have to get back to London?' Charlie could feel the beat of his arousal starting to throb, and from the way Holly was reacting, she felt the same.

'That sounds like a great idea,' Holly murmured. 'Since we seem to be attracting a bit of attention from those people over there. I wouldn't want to get you into a scandal so early on in your political career.'

Charlie turned to look behind him and was irritated to see a party of what looked to be tourists, who, heedless of the fact that they were standing by one of the country's most glorious and beautiful landmarks, were more intent on taking snapshots on their camera phones of him and Holly. 'Bloody hell,' he grumbled. 'You try to get away from it all, and the bastards follow you.' Desire, he knew, was making him cantankerous.

'Ssh,' Holly said softly. 'They're only doing it because they've spotted a semi-famous face. And it's not like you're doing anything wrong. Well, not yet, anyway,' she raised a suggestive eyebrow.

Charlie groaned. 'Take me back to your place. Now!' he said. 'Or I really won't be responsible for my actions.'

'Your wish is my command,' Holly replied. 'But I wouldn't be surprised if you and I ended up on an Instagram feed later.'

'I've got quite adept at stalking myself online since I got this job,' Charlie admitted. 'It seems better to know what they're saying about you than not.'

'Forewarned is forearmed,' Holly said. 'Although, in your job, I'm not sure I'd want to read *everything* that was said about me on social media! I can't imagine what it's like to be under such public scrutiny the whole time,' she added. 'Sort of like being a celebrity, but without the adulation.'

'Sort of,' Charlie said. 'Although I'm up for a bit of, er, adulation for the rest of the day if you are!' He grinned at her.

'Oh, let me take you away from here and adore you!' Holly replied, laughing. 'It's not like I've got anything better to do.'

'Thanks,' Charlie said dryly.

Swiftly they packed up their picnic and began the descent back down the hill, to an afternoon of more earthly delights.

32

Slow, lazy lovemaking left them both sated but also starving hungry. Holly, who had nothing in her fridge as she hadn't managed to do any shopping since the previous weekend, suggested a bite to eat at the local pub. Called The Travellers' Rest, it was the heart of the town, and one of the most ancient buildings, to boot. Rumour had it that Elizabeth I had stayed the night on the way back to London after a trip to the South Western provinces, and had allegedly been terrified by the spirit of a long-dead prioress, who'd been beaten to death in the grounds by Elizabeth's own father, Henry VIII's troops during the dissolution of the monasteries. Chances are, it was just the wind whistling down the large chimneys and flapping at the curtains, but it all added to the sense of mystery that surrounded such a historic building.

'I've been meaning to pop into this place since I moved here, but drinking on your own isn't a great look,' Charlie said. 'I'm glad I'm going to discover it for the first time with such wonderful company.'

'Why, thank you.' Holly wandered over to the bar, 'What would you like to drink? My treat.'

'Are you sure?' Charlie asked.

'Come on, Charlie, we're well into the twenty-first century now!' Holly laughed. 'Besides, Willowfest is the most profitable weekend of the year for ComIncense, so I'm sure I can at least buy you a drink.'

'Dinner's on me, though,' Charlie said. 'I'll have a pint of Carter's Gold cider, please.'

'Getting into the West Country way of drinking, I see,' Holly remarked.

The bartender came over and she ordered the cider for Charlie and a Wicked Wolf gin and tonic for herself. Known as 'The Spirit of Exmoor', it was brewed a few miles away but embodied all of the flavours of the famous Somerset hills. Holly was a wine drinker, generally, but she felt in need of something a little stronger as an aperitif to clear her palate and chase away the lingering tiredness after a hectic weekend.

As they settled at a cosy table in the corner of the bar, tucked to one side of the huge inglenook fireplace that took up most of the side wall, Charlie perused the menu. 'I'm starving,' he announced.

'Well, you've worked off a lot of calories, with the walk up the hill and... other things,' Holly smiled.

Charlie groaned. 'I really don't want to have to go back to London tomorrow. Can't I throw a sickie and stay here with you instead?'

Holly simulated shock. 'Mr Thorpe! What would your constituents think?'

'Well, *you're* one of them; what do you think?' Charlie asked playfully, taking one of Holly's hands in his and turning it over. He tickled the pulse point in her wrist with his fingertips. Holly was reminded of where else those sensitive but expert fingers had made her tingle, and she felt her heart beating faster.

'Behave,' she murmured. 'We both need to eat or neither of us will be fit for anything.'

* * *

A little time later, they were both tucking into plates of steak and kidney pie, mash and peas (mostly locally sourced and absolutely delicious), and feeling more fortified. Charlie had ordered a bottle of red wine to go with their meal, and it was going down very nicely.

'This is exactly what I needed,' Charlie said as he put his knife and fork together, having polished off his entire plate. His eyes sparkled in the low light of the bar. 'I almost feel like I can face another week at the coalface now.'

Holly snorted. 'Don't let your opposition hear you calling it that.'

'Fair point,' Charlie replied. He glanced at his watch. 'I should be getting the train back in about an hour.' Willowbury station had been reopened around ten years previously as an experiment into reconnecting some of the smaller towns in Somerset to the mainline between Taunton and Bristol Temple Meads. It had worked wonders for the job prospects of local people, and been a boost to the local economy as well, bringing in tourists to the town and increasing the trade of businesses such as Holly's. Holly, of course, was hugely in favour of anything that got more cars off the road, and the increase in trade was a definite bonus.

'That's a shame,' Holly said, looking up at him from underneath her lashes. 'I was going to suggest you came back and spent the night with me.'

Charlie groaned. 'Don't give me choices like that.' Then, his face brightened. 'Unless...' He whipped out his phone and tapped the screen for a moment or two. 'Yes!' he said triumphantly. 'I haven't tried it before, but there's an early train from Willowbury that connects at Bristol Temple Meads and then direct to London Paddington. It means I'll have to get to the station by six o'clock tomorrow morning, but that's no big deal, it's only a ten-minute walk from either your place or mine.'

'Sounds perfect,' Holly said. 'And it means we can have another drink if we want one.' She finished her glass of red. 'Can I treat you to something to settle that food?'

'Sure,' Charlie replied. 'If you're sure you can manage it?'

Holly laughed. 'I'm a Somerset girl – I grew up drinking Scrumpy cider behind the cricket pavilion. What about you?'

'Had to keep the Yorkshire winters out of my bones some-how,' Charlie replied, affecting a slightly broader accent.

'Is that what you really sound like?' Holly teased. 'Before you were forced to iron out your accent to appeal to the electorate?'

Charlie looked affronted. 'I don't know what you mean. I don't sound all that different now, do I?'

Holly prodded him in the ribs playfully. 'I remember, back when we first met, you sounded like a cross between Matt Lewis and Geoffrey Boycott! Your vowels were so broad, I could have canoed the River Thames on them. I think it's fair to say that you've put a little bit of the Estuary into your English since then.'

Charlie shook his head. 'For someone who claims to have only the vaguest memories of that night we met, you suddenly seem to be a lot clearer on it.'

'Well, you know, it's coming back to me gradually,' Holly said. 'But it might explain why I didn't recognise you straight away when you came into the shop that first time – you're far less geeky and a lot less Yorkshire than you used to be.'

'Whereas you've gone the other way and I can hear the Somerset far more now,' Charlie replied. 'Perhaps I'll end up with a weird combination of both accents if I stay here long enough!'

'That would be funny,' Holly teased. 'You'd have to make sure you really thought about how you said bath, buns and foot-path, then!'

'Our kids would sound really interesting,' Charlie said, then coughed nervously. 'Sorry, that's jumping the gun a bit, isn't it?'

'Gun or goon?' Holly teased, but she was touched by his sudden reticence. 'I'll grab us another drink.'

Without waiting to see what he wanted, she headed to the bar, ordered and then returned with two glasses of a medium brown oaky colour liquid that looked suspiciously like doubles.

'Dare I ask what this is?' Charlie took the glass and sniffed it cautiously. 'Smells good, whatever it is.'

'It's Somerset cider brandy,' Holly said. 'Produced a few miles away from here. This is the ten-year-old version, but there's a five and a twenty, too. It was the only spirit served at Harry and Meghan's wedding breakfast, so I suspect it's good enough for us.'

'Well, if it's good enough for HRH,' Charlie said wryly.

Holly took a sip from her glass and let out an appreciative breath as the warming liquid slipped over her tongue and down her throat. Rich and complex, it had a spicy bouquet and a smooth finish. She wasn't a great brandy drinker, but she'd made an exception for Somerset cider brandy since she'd become a permanent resident in the county.

'Wow,' Charlie said as he set his glass down on the table, half of it gone already. 'That's quite something.'

'Isn't it?' Holly agreed. 'Slightly Christmas puddingy, I think.'

'Yes, that's definitely it.' Charlie drained his glass. 'Another?'

'Oh, go on then,' Holly laughed. 'But be careful – this stuff is stronger than you think.'

'It's at least eight hours until I have to catch the train,' Charlie said. 'I'm sure I can have another one.'

'If you're sure, then yes please,' Holly replied. She'd developed a tolerance for brandy over the years she'd been living in Willowbury, but something told her, from the sudden sparkle in his eyes, that Charlie had yet to build his own. It was a wonderful-tasting spirit, but, like a lot of apple brandies, the effects crept up on you. She was glad neither of them had to drive home.

As Charlie brought over the second round of doubles, Holly smiled. It had been a wonderful weekend, and even if both of them were going to feel the effects of the booze in the morning, it had definitely been worth it.

33

'Ugh... what time is it?' Holly rubbed a hand over her eyes and reached across to her phone to turn off the alarm, which she'd set last night alongside Charlie's to ensure that he would make the 6 a.m. Willowbury to Bristol Temple Meads service, and not miss his 6.45 connection from Bristol to London Paddington.

'About five o'clock,' Charlie murmured sleepily. He turned over and tapped his phone to turn off the cacophony of his own alarm and chucked it back on the bedside table. 'This seemed like such a good idea last night.'

Holly smiled, despite the thump in her temples that reminded her of the double apple brandies after their meal at The Travellers' Rest last night. They'd wandered back to her place, half-cut, and tumbled into bed, both of them rather too full of food and decent drink to do more than cuddle up. However, from the way Charlie was pulling her close now, Holly knew he'd made a pretty full recovery.

'You don't have time for any of that sort of thing,' she murmured as he wrapped one of her thighs around his. 'You've got that train to catch.'

'Surely we've got time for a quick one,' he murmured into

her ear, sending tingles down her neck with his breath. 'Lying beside you all night has got me halfway there already.'

'You're the one with the schedule,' she replied. 'I don't have to open up the shop until nine.'

Needing no further encouragement, Charlie made good on his word.

* * *

'Is it wrong to tell you that I'm going to miss you like mad between now and Wednesday?' Charlie said an hour later as they both stood on the Bristol-bound platform of Willowbury station. What it lacked in romantic charm, being a new installation only a decade old, the rising sun made up for as it shone warmly down on the only two passengers up early enough for the train to Bristol.

'No,' Holly smiled, and then nestled into his arms. 'I'm feeling a bit *Brief Encounter,* seeing you off on the platform. But I'll be down in a couple of days to watch you be amazing in the Commons.'

'Don't say it like that,' Charlie laughed nervously. 'I'm petrified enough as it is.'

'You'll smash it,' Holly said. 'Not just for Harry, but for all of the CF patients out there who need you to speak up.' Her clear gaze locked with his, and despite their tiredness after a night well spent, and an impromptu early morning, both could see love and hope reflected.

'I meant what I said, that night at Willowfest,' Charlie said softly. 'I'm in love with you, Holly. I can't imagine ever being without you.'

Holly's heart fluttered in her chest at his bare and frank admission. 'I love you too, Charlie. And, I think, even if you hadn't turned up in my life as the political animal that you are, if we'd met in another way, doing something else, I still would.'

'I'm glad,' Charlie whispered as he drew her to him again. 'I'm glad you don't just love me for the power!'

Holly laughed. 'Don't get above yourself. You're not Prime Minister yet!'

As the tinny voice of the automated train announcer spoke its presence with a mechanical ping, Charlie held Holly tighter. 'I really will miss you, you know.'

Holly gasped as the breath was, rather pleasurably, squeezed out of her. 'Me too. Travel safe.'

'I will.'

Within a minute or so, the Bristol-bound train, a mere two carriages on a small branch line like Willowbury, had drawn up to the platform. Charlie and Holly broke apart far enough to share one, last, passionate kiss, which would have to sustain them both until Wednesday when Holly joined him in London.

'Take care,' she said softly as the train drew to a halt.

There was a pause before the door buttons illuminated, and, turning to pick up his small suitcase and his satchel, Charlie smiled. 'I miss you already.' He glanced at the door and pressed the button to open it. 'Oh, fuck it!' Sweeping Holly up, he found her lips with his once more, as the train doors glided open, almost taking her off her feet on the platform.

'Go,' Holly said breathlessly. 'They won't wait for you, even if you are the MP!'

'I'll text you later,' Charlie said as he grabbed his suitcase and satchel.

'See you on Wednesday,' Holly called as the doors began to close.

In one more moment, the train had rumbled to life. As it pulled away from Willowbury station, Holly reflected that it might not have been as romantic as a steam train, but her heart was still thumping. Charlie loved her; he *loved* her. And, scarier still, she knew that she loved him. Thoughts raced through her mind as she realised that she hadn't felt this way for a long time, not since she and Andrew had first met, and even then, it seemed different somehow. Filled with hope, and feeling more than a little wobbly-footed with love, she headed back home to get herself together before another busy day at ComIncense.

As promised, when Charlie reached London a couple of hours later, Holly's phone pinged. Sending him a quick reply, as she was in full swing in the shop, she mused on what this week would bring. It may well be the turning point that she and Rachel and the rest of their family had waited so long for; could Charlie's question at PMQs really make a difference, be the catalyst for further discussions about getting the drugs to CF patients that might make a huge change to their lives? For the first time in a long time, Holly found herself putting her faith in politics, and politicians, and hoping against hope that Charlie would be someone who would make a difference.

Later that evening, she spoke to Rachel, who was hoping to bring Harry home from the BRHC on Tuesday morning. The intravenous antibiotics had managed to stabilise his chest infection, thank goodness, but Holly couldn't help wondering how many more trips to hospital the little boy was going to end up taking all the time he was waiting for medication that could really change his life.

34

Wednesday morning in Westminster dawned clear and bright, and as Charlie walked to work, ubiquitous coffee cup in hand, he felt more than a slight flutter of nerves that rivalled the flapping wings of the early-morning pigeons hoovering up bits of dropped pastry and bagel from the commuters over Westminster Bridge. The city in the morning thrummed with energy, with activity, with the sound of varied languages and accents from workers and tourists, and the scent of water, diesel fumes from the buses and freshly brewed coffee. As at home as he was in Willowbury these days, Charlie's heart still held a torch for London life. His job, at least, allowed him to appreciate both, so long may that job be his.

But this Wednesday was different. This was the day he was going to ask his question about cystic fibrosis medication to none other than the Prime Minister. For an MP who'd been in the job only a matter of months, this was a tremendous opportunity, and one he couldn't afford to cock up. And there, sitting in the gallery, witnessing either his first moment of parliamentary triumph or failure, would be the woman he'd twice told he loved; once after that heady mix of mead and magic at Willowfest and once on an early dawn platform as the train pulled in to bring him here. Both times, his words had been nothing but the truth.

Saying hello to the policeman at the entrance to Portcullis House, the modern glass building across the road from the Palace of Westminster where his office was situated, he headed straight through the connecting tunnel to the Commons, by way of the message board outside the Commons Chamber. Although most communication was done by email these days, it was worth keeping an eye on the board, as certain members of the House still liked to communicate that way. He would then have a little time to prepare himself for the weekly Punch and Judy show that was Prime Minister's Questions. Beginning at 12.30, it would be half an hour of pure Westminster theatre. He'd be lying if he didn't admit there wasn't a part of him that was absolutely terrified about being not just a spectator but an active participant in the show, today.

'Morning, Charlie,' Andrew Statham, the government's Chief Whip, was checking the message board as Charlie approached. 'I see you're on the list today.' Tall and authoritarian, Statham looked the archetypal Westminster enforcer, and Charlie, being around fifteen years younger, viewed him as a lower-school student might view the Head Boy.

'That's right,' Charlie replied. 'Any last-minute advice?'

'Try not to piss the PM off,' Statham said. 'You're new, so don't rock the boat.' He regarded Charlie levelly. 'The issue you're asking about is emotive... a good choice to get your name out there, but bear in mind these things are a constant work in progress. Don't expect the world to dance to your tune because you asked a question.'

Charlie tried to give what he hoped was a jovial smile. 'Understood. It's an issue that affects at least one family in my constituency, though, so it is of legitimate concern on a constituency level.'

'I'm sure you mean well,' Statham replied. 'But policy, as you know from your years as a researcher in this place, is an ever-shifting thing. Don't pin your hopes on pushing something through when there are multiple interests at stake, especially when it comes to Health and Social Care policy.'

'I have to try, though,' Charlie replied. 'What sort of constituency MP would I be if I didn't?'

'Are you sure this is about the cause, or the individuals?' Statham's voice dropped as another member wandered over to check his post. 'You seem to have a very... personal interest in this case, if social media is anything to go by. I'd hate to see you putting yourself out there for a cause that, politically, might come back and bite you in the arse.'

Charlie felt his heartbeat, already elevated at the prospect of raising his question later in the day, speed up even more. 'I haven't seen any adverse social media activity,' he ventured. 'Just friends having a good time in their constituency.' There had been one or two shots of him judging the Willowfest fancy-dress competition at the weekend, but, thankfully, none of the more intimate pictures that the tourists had snapped on Willowbury Hill had, as yet, emerged on any social media platform. Sure, he'd had his arm around Holly in one of the post-fancy-dress judging pictures, but it wasn't as if he'd been caught groping her or anything.

'So long as that's all that's driving this,' Statham said as he chucked a couple of flyers from his pigeonhole into the recycling bin. 'Remember, if the policy goes in a different direction to the one you like, as a member of Her Majesty's Government, you will be duty-bound to support it if it becomes a whipping issue.' The Whips were the staffers who made sure that, on issues of governmental importance, all party MPs voted with the government's position, regardless of personal opinion. It could be a tricky issue for a politician driven by principles, but it was the chance you took when you signed up to represent a political party. Those who dissented ran the risk of losing their seats and plunging into obscurity, losing what influence they had if they crossed the floor over a matter of principle.

Charlie's blood ran cold. Was Statham telling him to back off the CF medication issue for the sake of his own career, or for the sake of the government? His brain ticked quickly. 'Well, I still have to risk it,' he said more lightly than he felt. 'After all, as you say, policy is always a work in progress. Perhaps this work in progress will end up benefitting my constituent and their family.'

'Just bear in mind that, if it comes to the crunch, the Whip's Office will advise you,' Statham said, slipping the letters he'd picked up into the inside pocket of his suit jacket.

'I don't doubt that,' Charlie muttered. 'I'll keep an eye on the comms.'

'You do that,' Statham said. 'I'll see you in the chamber later.'

Feeling more nervous than ever, Charlie hurriedly pocketed a message he'd received and headed off to his office. In four hours' time he'd be standing in the hallowed hall of the Commons, putting a question to the PM, and he now had no idea whether or not it would advance his career, or kill it stone dead.

* * *

Holly's train arrived at Paddington promptly, and, since she had plenty of time and she loved to walk in London, she decided to meander over to the Houses of Parliament on foot. It was about two and a half miles, door to door, but there was plenty to see. If she went through Hyde Park, she could even skirt around through Green Park and pass Buckingham Palace on the way, before making her way to the Palace of Westminster. Keeping an eye on the time, because she needed to be at the Commons by eleven forty-five, she fingered the pass that Charlie had arranged for her and felt sad that Rachel wasn't by her side. Harry had come home yesterday afternoon, and Rachel was keeping him off nursery for a couple of days, just to be on the safe side. Rachel had sent her sister a crazy-face emoji earlier this morning to signify that Harry's energy levels appeared in no way diminished by his chest infection, and Holly couldn't help laughing when Rachel had sent her a picture of herself and Harry both pulling faces at the selfie camera a little while later.

Holly's stomach fluttered, and she wondered how Charlie was feeling right now. She contemplated phoning him, but she figured he'd be caught up in preparing for his big moment and may not want to be distracted. As if he'd sensed her thoughts, however, her phone pinged just as she was entering Hyde Park. Fumbling in her shoulder bag, she smiled to see that he'd sent her a shot of him pretending to bite his nails. The caption simply read:

It's all fine. Nothing to worry about! #terrified.

Grinning, she took a quick selfie by the Hyde Park Bandstand and sent it off to him.

On my way. Just imagine you're playing from here, and not the Chamber! #Breakaleg

She kept smiling as his reply came back almost instantly.

So glad you'll be here to witness my triumph/humiliation. See you after xx

Sending him a blowing kisses emoji, Holly checked her watch and upped her pace. If she hurried, she might have time to grab a snack before going into the House of Commons. Breakfast at home seemed an awfully long time ago, and she didn't want her tummy rumbling during Charlie's big moment. She was astonished about how nervous she felt for him.

35

Charlie paced the hallway outside the chamber and wondered if he had time to dash to the loo for another pee before he had to go in and sit down. Now, more than ever, he wondered at the Prime Minister's ability to do this week after week, standing up among the rowdy, opinionated masses of MPs from both sides and being accountable for policy decisions, good and bad.

He checked his phone once more, just to make sure he'd switched it to silent. As he did, he saw another message from Holly. Swiping the screen, he saw that she'd taken a selfie next to the glass wall that separated the Public Gallery from the Commons Chamber, and written 'Good Luck!' with a hand-drawn heart next to it. His actual heart flipped. He suddenly didn't know if it had been the right thing to invite her down to see him do this, after all. What if he really did cock it up? She'd be disappointed, and he'd be embarrassed. Then, he chided himself. There was no point in thinking like that; he had to visu-alise success. He smiled a bit at that – his father, a man of few words, most of them gruff, would put it another way – *Stand up straight and get on with it.* He wondered if his dad was watching or listening today; John Thorpe wasn't a huge fan of what he called 'the Lions' Den of PMQs', but Charlie hoped, perhaps, he'd make an exception today, since his son was going to speak.

It was time. He knew that, even though he looked at his watch just to confirm. He drew a deep breath and walked into the chamber, glancing up at the Public Gallery as he did so, and feeling his heart flip as he saw a redheaded figure sitting nearest the glass wall. He couldn't see her expression, but he smiled in her general direction, hoping she'd be watching.

'Order, order!' The Speaker's strident voice rang out across the chamber, and those present took their seats.

Charlie swallowed hard; he had five questions to wait before he could ask his, and every second that passed, the butterflies seemed to be breeding in his stomach. Trying to breathe normally, he focused his attention on the Prime Minister, attempting to tune out the rumbles of dissension that greeted the first couple of questions. He didn't dare look up at the Public Gallery in case he lost the thread of the process, but he could almost feel Holly's eyes upon him. He hoped he was going to make her proud.

* * *

Holly looked over the crowded Commons Chamber and smiled as she observed Charlie. He was sitting with his back ramrod straight, his hands loosely placed in his lap, but the gestures seemed conscious; she knew he was nervous. And no wonder. This was not only a public forum in terms of the amount of people in the chamber itself, but also those in the Public Gallery, which was packed, and it was being simultaneously broadcast on at least two national radio stations, as well as the BBC News channel, Sky News and BBC Parliament.

As a student, she'd been glued to the weekly parliamentary soap opera on the radio, the way that other students had watched *Neighbours,* and to see it unfolding live in front of her was a real treat. All of the big beasts were there, and although she knew that it was primarily a forum for public broadcasting rather than policy these days, she couldn't help but feel a frisson of excitement, seeing the Prime Minister, the Home Secretary, the Chancellor of the Exchequer and their shadow counterparts sitting opposite them on the benches.

But time after time her gaze was drawn back to Charlie, sitting patiently, waiting his turn. He probably didn't realise that when he was nervous his right foot tapped slightly. Apart from that, though, he seemed remarkably composed. She felt as though she was willing him on in a race as the third and fourth questions were asked. The fifth, on funding for Early Years Centres, generated howls of derision at the PM's response, and for a long, agonising moment, the voice of the Speaker fought to retain order in the chamber. Holly held her breath.

'Charlie Thorpe!' the Speaker cut over the top of the rabble-rousing of the chamber and Holly watched, still holding her breath, as Charlie got to his feet.

'Thank you, Mr Speaker.' Charlie took a split second to wait for the last of the chatter to die down. 'Since I moved into the beautiful West Country constituency of Willowbury and Staven-ham, I have got to know the people who have made the place their home. Among them is the family of three-year-old Harry Jamieson, born with cystic fibrosis, who currently takes a cock-tail of drugs and inhales a series of nebulisers every single day of his young life in order to stem the effects of the condition.' Charlie paused, even though the chamber, seemingly out of respect for the issue, had fallen silent. 'Does the Prime Minster agree that it is time to re-evaluate the position of the NHS in regard to the funding of next generation of cystic fibrosis drugs, and enter into further discussions with the pharmaceutical companies, so that Harry and patients like him could have the possibility of a healthier, more extended life?'

As the 'hear hears' echoed around the chamber, from both sides of the benches, Holly's heart thumped.

'I thank the Honourable Gentleman for his question,' the Prime Minister said as the noise died away. 'And I sympathise with the position of the constituents of which he speaks so eloquently. I will ensure the Department of Health and Social Care looks into the reasons for this stalemate and responds as soon as possible.'

Holly let out her breath. It was a standard response, that was for sure, but she couldn't help but hope it meant more than it appeared to. After all, raising the issue so publicly had to be good for something. She'd known full well that the Prime Minister wouldn't wave a magic wand, but she hoped, somehow, that she'd just witnessed a metaphorical one.

As the next speaker was called, Holly looked back towards Charlie. His expression was carefully composed and gave nothing away. She hoped that he'd be able to interpret the Prime Minister's response later when they met. She, certainly, was none the wiser.

36

Holly waited nervously out in the lobby, dodging journalists and MPs meeting guests and escaping for lunch. Charlie had said he'd meet her here and give her the keys to his flat, so she could freshen up before their dinner date. She felt such a combination of emotions, having seen Charlie acquit himself with grace and panache on the chamber floor. Not a trace of nerves had marred his voice as he'd risen and asked his question, and her heart nearly burst with pride. If Harry and Rachel had been in the audience, Charlie had planned to refer the House's attention to them, but since they weren't, he'd avoided drawing attention to Holly; it wouldn't have had quite the same impact, and may well have put him off his stride.

The lobby was a hive of activity, but eventually Holly saw Charlie heading out of the chamber and across the hall towards her. He was deep in conversation with a woman, who was smiling at him and obviously congratulating him on his debut, resting her hand briefly on his upper arm to make a point. Holly felt a slight prickle of jealousy before she hastily quashed it; it was daft to feel anything like that when Charlie was clearly just being professional. It was all part of the act, she knew. Perhaps it was the parliamentary setting, but just for a moment she suddenly felt like the student rep she'd been fifteen years ago when, as part of the conference she'd attended, she'd visited this place. It had felt intimidating then, and although she had a more personal connection now, that sense of her own insignificance hadn't really gone away.

'Holly!' Charlie spotted her and hurried over, with the woman he'd been talking to following in his wake. Aware that they were in public, Holly resisted the urge to fling her arms around him in congratulation and settled for giving him a kiss on the cheek.

'Well done,' she breathed into his ear. 'You were absolutely brilliant.'

Charlie smiled broadly as they broke apart. 'Thank you. And thanks so much for coming.' He turned to the woman who was standing next to him. 'Holly, this is Sally Okeden, who runs one of the bigger cystic fibrosis charities. I dropped her a line to see if she wanted to come down today as well. Given your campaigning on Harry's behalf, I thought it might be useful if you two connected.'

Holly shook the other woman's hand, suddenly feeling much warmer towards her now she knew who she was. 'It's lovely to meet you.'

'You too,' Sally replied. 'I've seen your picture on Twitter a few times – you've been making the cause really visible lately, even without Charlie's help here.'

'It's all for my nephew Harry,' Holly said. 'Although having Charlie to support us really helps. Our old MP wasn't what you'd call helpful at all.'

Sally smiled. 'Make use of him while you can,' she said, glancing in Charlie's direction. 'Allies in this game can be short-lived.'

Holly felt a strange chill down her spine. She knew that politics was an ever-shifting landscape, but she still hoped that

Charlie wouldn't just cut and run if things became unfashionable. For Harry's sake, she hoped her instincts were right, and not just clouded by emotion.

'I'll be in touch,' Sally said. Turning back to Charlie, she smiled. 'Thanks again. It was a brave move today, and it will bring us some much-needed coverage.' Smiling at them both, she headed off.

When they were alone, apart from the toing and froing of other MPs and visitors, Holly asked the question that had been bugging her since Charlie's stint at PMQs. 'What's *really* going to happen now?'

Charlie smiled briefly. 'Well, we've given the issue a really big platform, and we should expect some kind of communication from the PM's office or the Department of Health and Social Care soon. What that will be is anybody's guess, but the drug companies will, in all likelihood, take some note of the issue being raised here today. We just have to wait.'

'Waiting again,' Holly said, knowing that a trace of her frustration was betrayed in her voice. 'It seems to be the name of the game.'

'I'm sorry I can't be more definite, Holly,' Charlie murmured. 'But we've made a start.'

'I know.' Reaching up on tiptoe, she brushed her lips with his. 'And I do appreciate it.' She smiled. 'Are you a free agent now?'

Charlie shook his head. 'I've got back-to-back meetings until about six p.m., but after that, I'm all yours, if you want me.' He moved a little closer to her.

'Sounds good,' Holly replied. She took the keys to the flat and, looking around quickly, gave him another kiss. 'I'll see you later.'

'I'm not sure I'll make it back to the flat in time. Shall I meet you at the restaurant?'

'OK,' Holly replied. 'Where did you have in mind?'

'I'll text you,' Charlie said, a hint of mystery in his eyes.

'Any dress code?'

'I'm tempted to say a turn-of-the-millennium cocktail dress, since the last time we met in London, that's what you were wearing, but I'll leave it up to you!' Charlie said.

Holly giggled. 'So, I wasn't the only one thinking about it, then?'

'It had crossed my mind.' Leaning in for one last quick, snatched kiss, Charlie walked away, leaving Holly on her own in the lobby once more.

'He's a good one, that one, and definitely one to watch,' a voice nearby said in an undertone. Holly turned just as the Speaker of the House passed by and her eyes met his briefly. She smiled and hoped the Speaker was right. After all, time was the one thing Harry couldn't rely on.

37

'This takes me back,' Holly said softly. They were walking hand in hand through a moonlit cityscape. They'd had a lovely dinner in one of the many restaurants around Covent Garden, and now, as they meandered back, in no particular direction but heading vaguely towards Charlie's tiny rented flat in Farringdon, Holly was assailed by snatches of memory, as well as a feeling that she was creating her future. It was an odd sensation. She felt at once like a teenager and a grown woman; would being with Charlie always give her that slightly alarming sense of duality? she wondered.

As they approached the Royal Opera House, its stone a silvery grey in the moonlight, Holly squeezed Charlie's hand a little more tightly. 'Do you remember walking here back then? On that night? I didn't have a clue where we were, or at least, where we were in relation to the hotel I was staying in, but you seemed to know where we were going.'

'Can I let you into a secret?' Charlie pulled her closer as they paused to look up at the austere frontage of the Opera House. 'I didn't have a bloody clue, either! I was massively blagging it. On the one hand, I wanted to walk around with you all night, and on the other, I was desperately hoping a convenient taxi would pass that would be able to take us to the door of that flipping hotel.'

Holly laughed. 'You hid it so well. No wonder you grew up to be a politician!'

'I grew up in the north, as you well know,' Charlie smiled wryly. 'I didn't know London from Lisbon at that point. But I *really* wanted to stay with you as long as I could.'

'You were very sweet to see me back to the hotel,' Holly said, tilting her head up for a kiss. 'Especially since you were staying in completely the opposite direction, weren't you?'

'I think so,' Charlie replied. 'I can't honestly remember. All I remember from that night is you.'

'And yet how soon we both forgot,' Holly heaved a mock sigh of regret, then grinned. 'Probably just as well. We'd most likely have made a complete hash of it and been far too embarrassed to make eye contact the next morning!'

'Can you imagine?' Charlie laughed. 'I didn't really know one end of a girl from the other back then and you looked terrified when I kissed you on the dance floor in that club.'

'Thanks,' Holly said wryly. 'Although you're pretty much spot on, there. I'd only actually had one serious boyfriend at that point.'

'Age and experience is definitely a good thing,' Charlie replied, a husky note in his voice. 'Do you fancy making use of it now?

'How could I refuse an offer like that?' Holly poked him in the ribs playfully.

With that, they wandered back to Farringdon, Charlie's flat and a very warm bed.

* * *

The next morning, Holly, unaccustomed to the early-morning

city traffic, woke early. She smiled as she saw the curve of Charlie's back, turned towards her as he slept soundly. Stretching like
a cat, she smiled as she remembered what had happened after
they'd reached the flat, both of them suddenly high on the
novelty of being in London together and not having to be apart.
The sun was peering through the crack in the curtains, and for a
moment Holly just luxuriated in the warmth of the bed and the
sensations of waking up.

This wouldn't do for long, though; she had a train to catch
back to Willowbury and a shop to run. Swinging her legs over
the side of the bed, she stretched her arms above her head and
then swept down to touch her toes, feeling the muscles in her
back waking up as her spine extended. She stayed there for a
moment, breathing deeply, before straightening up and pushing
her arms out to the side, feeling the pull in her shoulder blades
as she breathed.

'Naked yoga? Is that something available in Willowbury,
too?' Charlie's sleepy but amused voice cut into her mind, which
she was trying to clear, and she smiled.

'It's not something I currently offer,' she replied, turning
unselfconsciously towards the bed, 'but if you think there might
be a market for it...'

'Don't you dare,' Charlie said, grabbing one of her hands and
pulling her back down to the bed. 'I'd like to think that worship-
ping that exquisite body of yours is something I can do in
private, thank you.'

'I'm sure that can be arranged,' Holly murmured as she flung
a thigh around him, straddling him. 'After all, this is as good a
workout as yoga.'

Charlie brought his hands to her hips as she guided him
inside her, and soon, the combination of his pleasurably persis-
tent fingertips and thrusting rhythms had her gasping and on
the edge.

'Do you have to go back to Willowbury today?' he asked

between thrusts, head thrown back and eyes half closed in ecstasy.

'Yup,' Holly replied, 'my shop won't run itself, and you've got a job to do, too, remember.'

'How could I forget?' Charlie's voice was getting breathier as he tried, and failed, to focus on her voice rather than her body. Holly felt another surge of heat as she saw how close he was to losing control. 'But I'll be... home... tonight.' He lost the battle.

As she toppled over the edge of her own precipice, throbbing and beating in time to Charlie's own rhythm, Holly felt that she, too, was finally coming home.

38

Charlie couldn't stop grinning as he finally made it to his desk just after 9 a.m. He wanted to start every morning that way, he thought. As he logged onto the Commons wi-fi and waited for his email to load, he considered sending Holly a quick text. She'd be on the train by now, probably as far as Reading; he hoped she'd managed to get a seat. They'd arranged to meet later that evening for another quiet dinner at The Travellers' Rest, and he planned to persuade her to come home with him after that. Although they lived so close together, he couldn't bear to be parted from her any longer than was necessary.

'You're in love, Charlie,' he said to himself as, finally, the email screen loaded. 'No sense trying to deny it. She's got right to you, and no mistake.'

Scanning through the title lines on the emails that had arrived overnight, his heart thumped as he saw one from the chair of the Health and Social Care Committee he'd observed the previous week. Perhaps he'd got himself noticed after all, he thought. Then, directly below it, there was another, more heart-thumping email from the Secretary of State for Health and

Social Care herself. Clicking on it immediately, when he read the contents, the coffee cup he'd been holding in his other hand froze on the way to his lips.

Charlie,
I note with interest your association with the campaign for CF drugs as part of NHS spending. Are you free to discuss further? Might I suggest meeting in my office at 2.30 p.m. tomorrow (Friday) to explore the current position and discuss a possible way forward?
Sincerely,
Cora Mellish,
Secretary of State for Health and Social Care.

Heart racing, Charlie didn't even waste time to think and sent an instant reply accepting the meeting.

This is it, he thought triumphantly. This, it seemed, was the first step into a bigger presence in the Department of Health and Social Care. And a step on the road to helping Harry and the other CF patients.

Of course, if he was now occupied in London until tomorrow afternoon, it meant he wouldn't get home to Willowbury that night, which meant no dinner with Holly.

With a pang of regret, he tried to call her, but reception was obviously not great while she was in transit to the West Country. He texted her quickly, not elaborating too much but letting her know that, as an upshot of his question, he had a meeting to attend at the Department of Health and Social Care. He'd fill her in on the details when he knew more after tomorrow. He hoped, by then, he'd finally be able to give her and Rachel the good news they'd been waiting for.

* * *

After a sleepless night on Thursday, and a restless morning in his office, Charlie headed over to the Department of Health and Social Care with a thumping heart. He was intrigued to know what the formidable Cora Mellish would have to say, and he hoped it would be worth the lost hours of sleep.

Cora met him in the foyer of the building and escorted him personally to her large office overlooking the Thames. She was a petite, blonde woman with a penchant for statement shoes, and her sharp blue eyes regarded Charlie keenly, seemingly assessing and weighing him up.

'Take a seat, Charlie,' she said in her broad Scottish brogue. 'Coffee?'

'Thanks,' Charlie replied, willing his hands not to shake as he picked up the bone-china cup and saucer. He refused the offer of a piece of shortbread for fear of choking on it out of nerves.

'Well, you certainly know how to get yourself noticed,' Cora said, once they'd both had a sip of their respective coffees. 'Only just taken over the Willowbury and Stavenham seat and already asking a question at PMQs. That takes bollocks.'

Charlie was surprised at the frankness of her language. 'I've always been a risk taker,' he replied, not entirely truthfully. In his experience, there were few things he considered taking risks for, except perhaps those he cared about. There was no doubt that Holly and her family fell into that category now.

'The Department of Health and Social Care isn't exactly a risk-friendly place, though,' Cora said meditatively. 'We prefer a rather more measured approach. Raising an emotive issue like drug funding for CF in the theatre of the Commons itself is rather too dramatic for our liking.'

Charlie felt his stomach turn over. Was this an official telling-off? If so, why summon him all the way over here? Cora could have just bollocked him by email. 'I apologise, Minister, if

I spoke out of turn. I do have a constituency interest in the outcome of the latest CF drug-funding discussions, though.'

'I'm well aware of your interest,' Cora replied smoothly. 'And perhaps, on this occasion, given your inexperience in matters of the House, your rashness in raising this issue while the committee is still in session could be forgiven, if you redirect your energies into something less controversial.'

'What are you saying, Minister?' Charlie's mind was whirling. Cora Mellish couldn't be warning him off this case, could she?

'I'm saying, Charlie, that getting yourself involved in something so complex at this early stage in your career could, by some, be considered a foolhardy move. One which might do your own standing more harm than good and also not accomplish a great deal in terms of moving the talks with the drug companies forward.' She finished her coffee and set the cup down on the saucer with a crisp chime, which echoed the tone of her voice.

'Are you telling me to drop this issue?' Charlie put his own cup and saucer down on the minister's desk with a clatter.

'I'm telling you that there is more at stake here than just the new CF drugs,' Cora replied. 'Even if we can come to an arrangement with the pharmaceutical company, that money, as I'm sure you're aware, has to come from somewhere. The NHS is not a bottomless pit of resources. Are you sure you want to be the one to have to balance the books, for this relatively small issue?'

'It might be small to you, Minister, but there are lives at stake here, every time we push the pause button on discussions. Lives that don't have the luxury of time, as I'm sure *you're* aware.' Charlie tried to keep his voice level, aware that antagonising Cora was not the best path to promotion within her department. He drew a deep breath. 'Is there a way forward?'

Cora smiled without warmth. 'There might be.' She paused,

her direct blue stare making the suggestion that she hadn't yet voiced.

'You want me to step back from the issue,' Charlie supplied, his heart sinking.

'Let the committee do its job, Charlie,' Cora's voice was suddenly lower, quieter. 'That's what it's there for. If these new drugs are cost-effective and worthwhile to fund on the NHS, they'll recommend it to government. If not, the money gets spent elsewhere, on equally important issues.'

'So, I just walk away, do I?' Charlie retorted. 'And how do you suggest I explain that to the members of my constituency that are directly affected by this situation? Who don't have the luxury of waiting years for an answer?'

'You're a politician,' Cora replied, brisk and efficient again. 'You'll find a way. Breaking bad news, as well as good, goes with the job description.'

Charlie looked down at his hands, clenched into fists on his knees. 'I know that,' he muttered.

'I know it's going to be hard, but you should have waited before jumping into the fire with this one. You might have raised the profile of the issue, but shouting in public will only get you so far. Work behind the scenes on other issues, by all means, but let this one take its course.'

'And then what?' Charlie said. 'What happens if I agree to stay quiet?'

There was another perceptible pause in the room. 'If you do your job, keep your nose clean and play the game... it will be looked upon favourably.'

Although it was unclear whether Cora was trying to warn him off the CF issue for his own good, or whether she did, in fact, have some other agenda, the message itself she was sending out was loud and clear. Charlie knew he was standing on a pillar in the middle of an abyss. Jump one way, keep pushing on the CF issue and Cora would make sure he never walked through those doors as a minister. Jump the other, win favour in Whitehall by leaving this issue alone and in a few years he might even have her job.

'I understand, Minister,' Charlie said quietly.

Standing quickly, he shook her hand, and, head spinning, tried to find his way back to his own office. This morning he'd been so excited to get back to Holly with good news; now, he didn't know how the hell he was going to face her.

39

Under normal circumstances, Charlie enjoyed the chance to unwind on the train home to Willowbury. On a Thursday evening, when he usually made the journey, he'd have to stand until Reading, but after that he'd more often than not get a seat and the chance to go through some non-confidential bits of work. Tonight, though, was different, and not just because it was Friday. With every mile that took him closer to home, and Holly, he felt the dread, like an illness, rising inside him.

He'd left the Department of Health reeling. The choice, although Cora hadn't put it into words, had been clear. Drop the CF issue, keep his head down and get promoted. Keep pushing it now, and get ignored for the rest of this Parliament, at least. With three and half years to go until the next general election, that was a long time in the political wilderness. The choice was his, but in reality there was no choice.

And, in the meantime, he had to look Holly in the eye and tell her his decision; be honest with her, either way. If he chose her and Harry, he'd be almost completely ineffective politically. If he chose to drop the issue, she, quite rightly, would drop him without a second thought. The argument they'd had in the car the night of the Stavenham Chamber of Commerce dinner at the Swanley Hotel came back to him. He'd told her that her small actions didn't make a difference; that he needed the donors and the political clout to make the real decisions. How stupidly naive he'd been to say that; it was clear, now, that he wielded precisely no influence over anything.

'Tickets from London Paddington and Reading, please!' The cheery voice of the train manager with its West Country burr broke into his brooding.

Charlie dug into his jacket pocket and handed over his season ticket to the attendant. Her name was Lydia, and she was a regular on this service. Always cheerful and a welcome reminder of home, she often shared a word or two with him on the way by.

'Good week?' she asked as she looked over his ticket.

'Not bad,' Charlie replied, although his heart wasn't in it. He forced a smile, remembering he was, to a certain extent, facing the public as much as she was.

'Thank you, sir; have a good weekend,' she replied.

'Thank you,' he said automatically. 'You too.'

Unable to focus on anything other than the whirling of his own thoughts, Charlie put his head back against the seat and tried to keep his gaze on the landscape passing the train's window. As it changed from the urban to the rural, the closer he came to his destination, he felt the sickness churning in his stomach. He still had absolutely no idea what he was going to say to Holly. How could he possibly explain? How could he unpick the complicated strands of a Westminster warning to an outsider without sounding like a callous bastard?

Far too soon, he was boarding the connecting train from Bristol Temple Meads to the branch line that served Willowbury. It took thirty-five minutes on a good day; Charlie needed every last second. Realising that the absolute last place he wanted to be was the pub when he broke the news to Holly, he disembarked the train and headed straight for her place.

Willowbury High Street held no dawdling charms for him this evening; he just wanted to get to Holly, to explain, calmly, what had happened. And then wait for the inevitable explosion she had every right to have.

As he approached ComIncense, he could see the lights were out and the shop sign was turned to 'Closed'. That wasn't surprising; it was just after six thirty in the evening, after all. How he wished he could just carry on as though nothing had happened; but that wasn't an option. Lying didn't come naturally, which, potentially, was a disadvantage in his job, but Charlie definitely preferred to play things straight.

Taking one last fortifying deep breath, he cut through the walkway that separated Holly's building from the other shop on one side of ComIncense and knocked at her wooden door.

'Hey,' Holly's face was so happy, she seemed so surprised and delighted to see him on her doorstep that Charlie's heart bled. 'I thought we were meeting at the pub.'

'I need to talk to you,' Charlie said. Not even stopping to kiss her, because he highly doubted that when he'd finished telling her about the meeting with the Secretary of State she'd want to be anywhere near him anyway, he wandered in through her door.

'Is everything OK?' Holly trailed behind him. Still in her jeans, a white T-shirt and a patchwork waistcoat, she'd clearly just finished cashing up in the shop and hadn't started getting ready for their date.

'Holly...' Charlie, who'd headed up the stairs to Holly's cosy living area, turned helplessly back around as she came into the room.

'Oh God, what's happened?' Immediately she was by his side, seeing the stricken look on his face. 'Are you OK? Have you had some bad news?'

'I think you'd better sit down.' He felt as though his own knees were going to give way but resolved to stand for as long as he could, otherwise he knew he'd collapse.

'What is it, Charlie? Please, you're freaking me out.'

Charlie shook his head and then realised he was going to lose the battle with his legs. He reached out and took Holly's hand, leading her gently to the sofa.

'I've come to tell you that I can't take Harry's case for the new medication any further,' he said softly. 'I won't be able to speak for him any more, for the moment at least.'

'Wh-what?' Holly looked as though she'd been slapped. All of the colour drained from her face, until a horrible red blush started to spread up her neck and into her cheeks as what Charlie had said began to sink in. 'What do you mean? You asked the question at PMQs. How can you say that's it?'

'Holly...' he swallowed hard, but the lump in his throat refused to budge. 'I got carpeted by the Secretary of State for Health and Social Care this afternoon. I thought she wanted to see me to discuss getting the case going again. She didn't. She told me to take a step back. Let the committee do its job. Stop poking my nose into things I didn't understand.'

'And you listened to her?' Holly's voice, formerly a whisper, rose suddenly. 'She told you to back off and so that's it? You're dumping Harry and the rest of the CF patients just like that?'

'There was nothing else I could do,' Charlie said wearily. 'If I don't agree to back off, she'll see to it that I never get anywhere near the Department of Health. All doors will be closed. I'll be stuck on the back benches for the rest of this Parliament and probably the one after that, if I'm fortunate enough to get re-elected. Powerless to do anything, for anyone.'

'No,' Holly replied. 'You told me that you were the one who could make a difference. That I could pick up all the carrier bags in the world and nothing would change. That you had the opportunity to make changes because of where you were, your job. Now you're telling me that's not true.' She began to cry, and Charlie ached to reach out to her, to comfort her, but he felt absolutely paralysed by indecision.

'Holly, believe me, if there was some other way, I would take it, but there isn't. I need to step away from this. And, perhaps, so do you.'

'How can I?' Holly raised her voice another notch. 'Harry is part of my life, Charlie. He's just a baby; he can't do it for himself. If people like us don't speak up for him, try to get him the drugs he needs just to live a normal life, what hope does he have? I thought you understood that. I thought you agreed with me.'

'I do,' Charlie could see the anguish on her face, and he desperately wanted to hold her and make it all go away, but he couldn't. How could he? 'Believe me, Holly, if there was another way of doing this, I'd do it. But I've been warned; make a fuss about this and everything else I need to do will be ignored. I'll have no career.'

'That's it, isn't it?' Suddenly, the penny dropped. Charlie could see it in Holly's eyes as they flashed in anger. 'She's told you that you won't have a ministerial career on her patch if you push this, hasn't she?'

'Not in so many words,' Charlie hedged. 'But she does wield a lot of influence. I have to play things carefully if I'm to make any progress.'

'This is not a game, Charlie!' Holly stood up and started pacing her lounge, wiping abortively at her eyes to rid them of tears as the anger took over. 'This is people's lives. Harry's life.' She stopped pacing and turned back towards him. 'Would you ever be able to forgive yourself if Harry becomes just another CF death statistic because this medication was held up and you could have done something about it? Made things happen for him?'

'I don't have that kind of power,' Charlie retorted. 'And if I keep pushing this now, I never will. Can't you see? It's the wrong time.'

'Try telling that to Harry, and to Rachel, and to all of the people who are relying on their government to make this happen.' Holly was suddenly very still.

'I'm sorry,' Charlie said quietly. 'I promised you I'd help, and now I have to go back on that promise. It's not good enough, I know.'

'You're just like every other politician,' Holly said, her voice now deceptively calm. 'On our side so long as it's convenient. So long as you can gain some kind of capital out of it. And as soon as the going gets a little bit tough, you renege on your promises and leave us all out in the cold.' She went to the door of her lounge and opened it. 'At least I know where I stand, now.'

'That's not true!' Charlie heard the frantic note in his own voice and hated himself almost as much for it as he did the decision to take Cora Mellish's advice. 'It wasn't as simple as that, I promise you. The NHS is not a bottomless pit of resources; decisions have to be made. The money for that drug could fund so many chemotherapy treatments for women with breast cancer; each course of treatment could fund five trainee nurses for a year. We can't ignore the finances here.'

'Don't bullshit me with that pseudo-political bollocks, Charlie!' Holly's voice was rising. 'It might wash with your so-called colleagues, but it doesn't work with me. You know Harry; you know the difference this could make to his life. And yet you still choose to do nothing. Well, I hope you're happy once you get to a plum job in the Department of Health.'

Charlie took a step back, as if she'd slapped him. 'Do you think I'd sell Harry out just for a job?' he said. 'Is that really what you think of me?'

'I thought you had principles,' Holly said. 'I thought, when you came to Willowbury, that you wanted to stand up for the people who live here. Harry might not be old enough to vote, but Rachel and I are. Why weren't you standing up for *us?*'

'Holly,' his voice was quiet. 'The maternity unit at the local hospital is under threat of closure. Can you imagine the pressure that's going to put on St Michael's in Bristol? On Musgrove Park in Taunton? In the grand scheme of things, we have to make choices. I have to choose to step away from this now, because I might be able to do something later, when I'm in a better position to help. It's not personal.'

'How can you say it's not personal?' Holly didn't care that she was shouting again now. 'After all the time you've spent with me and my family. All the time we've spent...'

And at that moment, Charlie knew she felt that he'd utterly betrayed her. He could still feel the way his knees went weak when he kissed her; the silk of her hair as he ran his fingers through it. It was all for nothing now; he'd done the unforgivable.

Charlie's face, stricken in the harsh light of Holly's halogen kitchen bulb, pleaded with her to understand, but how could she? After everything they'd been through, this was the situation he'd feared the most. He'd chosen his politics over his heart. He could dress it up to her any way he liked, but that, it seemed, was the bottom line. There was nothing more to say.

'I'm sorry, Holly,' he said one last time.

'Goodbye, Charlie,' Holly replied. He'd expected her to drop her gaze, but she looked him straight in the eye as she said it. He could feel his heart breaking.

As he walked out of the living room, down the stairs and out of her life, Charlie had never been more shattered.

40

'Right, sis, we're on our own again.' After a night of staring at the ceiling in her bedroom, forcing herself not to think about the fact that Charlie was probably doing the same a couple of streets away, Holly got back to business.

Rachel, who'd come in to help Holly do the Saturday lunchtime shift at ComIncense while Harry, back out of hospital and on the mend, had lunch with his grandparents, stopped floating the till and looked at her sister inquisitively. 'What do you mean?'

'Charlie's out. He's no longer going to be acting for Harry. So, it's back to the campaigning and the direct action if we want to get him the meds he needs.'

'What? How do you know? Are you sure?' Rachel sat down on the stool behind the shop counter with a thump.

'Absolutely sure,' Holly replied. 'He came to see me last night, straight from a meeting at the Department of Health and Social Care. He's been told to drop it.'

'And he's going to, just like that?'

Holly's eyes brimmed with tears at the note of anguish in her sister's voice, but she blinked them away impatiently. Now was not the time to give in to her own emotions; she had to be there for Rachel and Harry; she had to try to work out their next move. It was clear now that no one else was going to do that. She'd put her faith in Charlie, against her first judgement, and look where that had got her.

'He told me some bollocks about not being able to be influential on the back benches, that he needs to bide his time and push the issue from inside the department, but it sounds like he's chosen fast advancement over us. So, we're back to where we started.'

'I don't believe it,' Rachel whispered. 'After everything he said... he's going to leave us out in the cold again?'

Holly reached out a hand and pulled her sister into a hug. 'It's shit, I know,' she murmured, trying to push aside the feelings of hurt and anger at Charlie's betrayal and focus on Rachel and Harry right now. The sadness she felt at losing Charlie personally battled with her rage at his seeming ability to just walk away. 'But we'll get there, I promise you. I'll keep fighting for Harry, even if Charlie won't.'

'Thanks, sis.' Rachel hugged her back. 'I'm so proud I've got you on my side.'

'Always,' Holly said. 'Even if I have to sell this place to help fund this drug, I will do that for Harry.'

'Oh no you won't!' Rachel replied. 'This place is your security. You need it for your own future. But we'll find a way, I know we will.'

Despite the ache in her heart over Charlie's defection, Holly knew Rachel was right. It didn't take politicians to make the changes, that much she now knew. It would take courage, determination and a lot of shouting. The last one, especially, she was more than prepared to do. Charlie had better get his ear defenders on, she thought savagely, because she was about to make a lot of noise.

* * *

Holly immediately threw herself head first into boosting the campaign to get the CF drugs reassessed. This not only involved tweeting and social networking as much as possible, but since Isabella was working more regular shifts in ComIncense before tutorials for her Creative Writing degree started next term, Holly could attend the demonstrations that were being organised by friends and family of CF patients. A couple of them had been held in Bristol, but there was a bigger one, taking place over two days, planned for outside of the Houses of Parliament in the next few weeks. She'd also set up an online petition, which was gathering momentum. As was the convention in the UK, once the petition reached ten thousand signatures, it would get a written response from the government; if it reached a hundred thousand, it would be granted debating time in Parliament. Let Charlie sit in on that one, she thought, and let's see where his priorities lie. In the rare moments when she wasn't busy in the shop or masterminding the next steps for the campaign, she did catch herself missing Charlie; they'd been so good together, and had really been getting to know each other as people before he backed off. But he'd made his choice, and she'd made hers by throwing him out of her home. There was nothing else to be said.

Holly had already had her photo taken a fair few times in connection with the campaign and had even been interviewed on the early-evening regional news. She'd cut quite a figure with her long red hair bedecked with yellow ribbons, coltish legs encased in blue jeans and a figure-hugging tie-dyed T-shirt clinging to her curves. That she was also articulate and engaging on camera meant that she was now becoming the go-to person, a 'good talker', as it was known in the media business, for sound-bites about the campaign. It wasn't long before she had her own hashtag, #GreenGoddess, to go with the #JustBreathe #What-

PriceBreath and #CFDrugsNow ones that were doing the rounds on Twitter.

In truth, she found all this a bit embarrassing, but anything that drew attention to the campaign to get the drug on the NHS was worth it, she figured. Rachel had attended a few events by her side, but after Harry's recent hospital stay, she was trying to stay close to home, and so a trip to Westminster was out of the question.

So it was that, on a sunny Wednesday morning, Holly stepped off the train alone at London Paddington and headed to the Underground. Her base for the night would be an Air BnB just on the outskirts of Westminster, which enabled her to be present for as long as possible at the demonstration. A few stops later, hot from a train carriage crammed with commuters and a few tourists, she stepped off at Westminster and made ready to join what looked like hundreds of other protesters on Westminster Square.

As she approached the statue of Winston Churchill, around which most of the demonstrators were congregating, she was pounced upon by a news reporter who was covering the story.

'Cathy English, Channel 4 lunchtime news. Are you OK to have a word?'

'Sure,' Holly composed her features into a smile. 'Can you just give me a sec to sort my hair out?' Holly reached into her bag and pulled out several yellow ribbons attached to butterfly hair clips, shook her hair out and attached the ribbons in. She'd been practising a lot in the mirror at home, so they looked striking with very little effort. Yellow was the colour of the campaign, and the contrast with her red hair was powerful.

'You're Holly Renton, aren't you?' Cathy chatted as Holly ran her fingers through her hair to untangle it a little more. 'The Green Goddess?'

Holly grimaced. 'That seems to be my hashtag at the moment, yes.'

'OK, are you good to go? We'll record this for the twelve-thirty slot and it'll probably get a repeat on the evening news, too.'

'Yup, let's do this.' Holly pushed away the habitual butterflies that seemed to flutter in her stomach.

Cathy, calm, cool and confident, faced the camera person and did a brief intro before turning back to Holly. 'I'm standing here with Holly Renton, known on social media as the Green Goddess, who has a very personal reason for being at this demonstration today. Holly, why don't you tell us all about it?'

'My three-year-old nephew Harry has cystic fibrosis,' Holly began. 'And because of the hold-up in deciding whether or not a course of potentially life-extending drugs can be prescribed to patients on the National Health Service, he faces an uncertain future.'

'I understand you've had some support from MPs on this issue,' Cathy, nodding, replied.

Holly shook her head. 'Unfortunately, that support has also stalled, so more direct action is needed to move the campaign along. It's great to see so many people here today to support patients with CF, and I hope that this strength of feeling might be of some influence where the conventional routes to government have failed.'

'And how might viewers become more involved with this campaign, if they want to?'

'You can sign the petition at gov.uk, which will prompt a debate in Parliament, and, if you want to, you can contact your local Member of Parliament. I wouldn't hold out much hope that they'll respond, however.' For a moment, Holly's bitterness at the way Charlie had backed off both her and the campaign showed through.

'I take it you haven't had much luck through the parliamentary channels, then?' Cathy probed.

Holly paused, then smiled for the camera. 'On the contrary,

we have had some support from MPs, but, unfortunately, our current MP for Willowbury and Stavenham has chosen to distance himself from the issue, much like his predecessor did.' That would hurt, Holly thought, if Charlie saw the interview. He hated being compared to Hugo Fitzgerald.

'And do you have anything you'd like to say to him, while the camera's rolling?' Cathy gave her an encouraging smile.

'I'd rather just concentrate on moving the campaign forward, Cathy,' Holly said. The temptation to dump Charlie in it onscreen was nearly overwhelming, but Holly knew it would do more harm than good. Better just to focus on the demonstration and the cause itself.

Cathy continued. 'You've been hashtagged The Green Goddess online. How have you found being the face of the campaign?'

Holly laughed. 'I wouldn't call myself the face of it at all. It's better to focus on those who really need these new medications. I'm happy to speak up for CF patients though, since they can't form a physical group to campaign here themselves because of the risk of cross-infection.' Holly dug in her bag and found the blown-up photograph of Harry she kept with her for things like this. 'This is my nephew Harry and these new drugs could potentially extend his life. Isn't that worth taking a financial risk on?'

Cathy, who was professional enough to disguise her disappointment that she wasn't going to find out any of the finer details about Holly's reportedly more intimate dealings with her MP, smiled and thanked Holly, and then gestured to the camera person to stop filming. 'Just between us,' she said in an undertone, 'I fully support your campaign. Let me know if there's anything else I can help you to cover and I'll be there like a shot. My sister died two years ago after waiting too long for a lung transplant. Anything I can do to make other patients' lives more comfortable, I'm happy to support.'

'Thanks, Cathy,' Holly was touched by this admission. 'And thank you for continuing to show up at events like this. It's more support than we've had from some people not a million miles from here.'

Cathy's eyes twinkled. 'I'd love to hear about it, off the record sometime!'

Holly laughed. 'That's one story that I'm keeping under wraps for now. Sorry!'

'Fair enough.' Cathy moved on to talk to other demonstrators. 'Good luck, Holly,' she called as she left.

Inevitably, as a cause of the favourable media coverage, that lunchtime Holly once again found #GreenGoddess trending along with the regular hashtags. If it made a difference, Holly was more than happy to claim the title. She hoped that Charlie, probably sat in his office in Portcullis House a stone's throw away, was seeing what real political action looked like.

41

He'd behaved like a twat. There was no getting away from it. Charlie put down his iPad in exasperation as he realised he'd been staring at the same article in the online newspaper he subscribed to for the past twenty minutes. Twitter was a better source of news these days, anyway, he thought.

As the train to London Paddington ground and rumbled its way out of Reading, slowing almost to walking pace as it hit the London suburbs, Charlie didn't even care that he was going to be late again. What did it matter? His career was in jeopardy over the medication question and his love life was equally in tatters. He wasn't even sure why he was bothering to turn up to the House today; the Secretary of State for Health wouldn't be pleased to see him.

But there were other things to do, he reminded himself irritably. He was not the centre of the political universe, no matter how it sometimes felt that way when he was back in Willowbury. He'd glanced at the discussion papers for today before he'd eventually fallen asleep last night and he knew there was, as usual, plenty to be catching up on. Perhaps a day of parliamentary debate was exactly what he needed to take his mind off this whole mess.

As the train finally drew into Paddington, Charlie grabbed his wheeled suitcase from the luggage rack and headed down to the Tube station. At peak rush hour, the Tube was crammed, but at least it meant he didn't even have enough space to get his phone out. As the train started to clear out when it drew closer to the Westminster stop, he risked a look at it once more. Swiping through to the app and glancing at the trending topics, his knees started to tremble. With a no less shaky finger, he tapped the first of two hashtags that had inevitably drawn his attention. Collapsing back into the newly vacated seat behind him, he feverishly read the first few tweets.

How had he not known about this? Why had his constituency office not warned him? Two hashtags in combination were proving surprisingly popular, and both of them made Charlie's heart thud in his chest. #CFDrugsNow was there, but then it usually was, since the CF campaigners had mobilised. But the one that took his breath away was #GreenGoddess.

'No...' Charlie whispered, as image after image of Holly, decked out in the yellow ribbons that represented the cause, scrolled past on the feed for the hashtag. He was well aware of the #GreenGoddess hashtag, of course, but it was the fact that Holly was here in Westminster that shook him. In his head, he'd wanted to keep her in her Willowbury box, so that when he was in London, he didn't have to face the impact of his own decisions, politically and personally.

The two-day demo was in its second day today and, it seemed, they'd started early. How the hell was he going to slip past that unobserved?

The Tube train moved relentlessly towards Westminster, and Charlie felt a rising nausea, not at all caused by the permanent, sooty heat of the Underground. Taking several deep breaths to try to calm the dread that was rising in his mind and in his stomach, he put his phone away, unable to face more evidence of Holly's total commitment to her cause, and his contrasting lack of dedication to it. When he could trust his knees to hold him up, he stood and waited for the train to reach its destination.

As he stepped off the train, the short walk up to the daylight seemed interminable. Charlie felt himself propelled by the pace of the crowd into a speed that was half a walk, half a jog, and gave up trying to apologise to the people who he nudged with his suitcase. He reached the station's entrance and blinked in the daylight, bracing himself for whatever sight might greet him on College Green. He heard it before he saw it. Although he could easily have just turned left and headed into his office in Portcullis House, which was connected by an underground tunnel to the Palace of Westminster and meant he didn't have to go through the above-ground entrance into Parliament itself, he felt himself compelled by the crowds, and some deeper desire for information, to turn the other way, towards the sound and sight of the demonstration.

College Green, which was adjacent to the Houses of Parliament, was the hub for demonstrations about a whole range of political issues, and was home to various camps at any given time; some semi-permanent, and some more temporary. Charlie had become accustomed to the various banners, tents and flags that often filled the space, and became even more crowded when the various national media outlets flooded in to report on stories of note. Often, it was difficult to differentiate between the paraphernalia of the many different causes represented outside the House, but as Charlie drew closer, there was no mistaking the vibrant yellow ribbons and clothes, and the ringing chants of the CF campaigners. Standing out against the backdrop of historic Westminster, voices ringing in the morning air, they made an imposing group.

'NHS make CF drugs free! Let our children live and breathe! NHS make CF drugs free! Let our children live and breathe!'

The chant, and, even more heartbreakingly, the banners with pictures of young child CF patients on them, cut Charlie to the bone. And suddenly, inexplicably, he knew they were right. It didn't matter the cost, this had to be something that was voted through, for the sake of every child in the country with cystic fibrosis. He'd been wrong to question his instincts; he knew that now. He should have put Harry and his family first all along, and the thousands of other patients. But he still had no idea how to fix it.

'And if I'm not mistaken, here comes one of the figures at the centre of the debate about CF drugs, MP for Willowbury and Stavenham, Charlie Thorpe…' the reporter's voice cut into Charlie's thoughts, which, unseeingly, had guided his feet towards the eye of the storm. 'Mr Thorpe, have you any comment on the current stalemate between government and the pharmaceutical companies?'

Charlie's heart thumped as a microphone was thrust into his face by a blonde reporter, Ruth Middleton, for one of the morning television current affairs shows. When he'd started this job, he'd received some training about what to do when asked a question on the hop like this, but he'd been so preoccupied with the sight of the demonstration and thoughts of Holly that all of that useful advice had fled from his brain.

'Mr Thorpe, as the recent publicity for this cause shows, you and your constituents have a lot to gain if an agreement is reached. Do you have any comment on that?'

Charlie opened his mouth, but not for the first time in front of a microphone, didn't have the first clue how to respond. The chanting behind him grew in intensity, with one voice standing out above all others; a voice that split Charlie's heart the second he recognised it.

'I wouldn't bother asking him,' the voice taunted. 'He's not got any answers.'

Charlie glanced briefly away from the reporter's questioning gaze and his eyes locked with the speaker's. Eyes flashing with challenge, hair bedecked with yellow ribbons, Holly looked as formidable an opponent as he'd ever encountered across the benches inside the House. How awful it was to be on the opposite side to her. It felt wrong, all wrong.

The reporter caught his glance and turned towards Holly, motioning for the camera operator to do the same. 'Am I right in thinking that this is one of your constituents, Mr Thorpe?'

Charlie tore his gaze back to the reporter, uncomfortably aware that he still didn't quite know what he was going to say. 'That's correct, Ruth, yes. But at this present time I have no comment on the progress of the discussions. Regrettably, I have to step away from the issue.' Cursing how pathetically formal he sounded, reminding him of the very first on-camera interview he'd ever given, he also knew that his words would provoke nothing but derision from the assembled campaigners. He was just another politician going back on his word; saying one thing one day and then taking it back another.

'So, you are unable to give your support for an issue that you asked a question about recently at Prime Minister's Question Time?'

'I have no further comment,' Charlie said hopelessly, feeling his stomach sink at how incredibly lame that response sounded.

He glanced over the reporter's shoulder to see Holly had stopped chanting and had her gaze fixed firmly upon him. His face felt hot as he remembered the way they'd parted, back in Willowbury, and he found that he couldn't focus on what the reporter was now asking him.

'If you'll excuse me,' he said quietly. 'I have a job to get to.' Realising that this was not exactly the way he'd been taught in media training to end an interview, he forced a smile. 'I'm sure the issue will be resolved soon.'

Turning away as the reporter gave him the obligatory thank you, he chanced a glance back at Holly, who was still looking in his direction, eyes narrowed, face unreadable. For one aching, desperate moment, he wanted to throw caution to the wind and run to her, to gather her up in his arms and tell her it was all going to be all right, but he knew he couldn't; he couldn't risk discrediting her cause, and his career, any further.

Ducking his head to avoid more interrogations from the assorted media representatives, he hurried towards the Members' Entrance and through the gate, back inside the Westminster bubble and temporary safety.

42

Charlie did, inevitably, catch up with Holly's appearance on the Channel 4 news that evening. Still hiding out in his office, the thought of going back to his poky rented flat was too depressing to contemplate until security chucked him out. He wasn't even sure what time that would be. He replayed Cathy English's interview with Holly several times, hating himself more and more when he could see, repeatedly, the passion and fervour in Holly's eyes for the cause. Why hadn't he stood up to the Secretary of State when he'd had the chance? Why hadn't he pushed harder to lobby her when he'd had the perfect opportunity in the office that day?

He knew why; pragmatism had won out over passion. Cora Mellish hadn't been in touch since that meeting; she'd probably just filed it under minor irritations, scratched the itch and moved on. He, on the other hand, felt that his credibility had been eroded. Since Holly had told the media that he'd taken a step away from the campaign, he'd felt a chill wind blowing. Colleagues who'd previously bid him a cheery hello seemed to be avoiding him in the corridors, and he seemed to be becoming that thing all politicians were accused of: someone who valued his position more than his principles.

Gloomily, he slid the bar on the video back to the beginning of Holly's interview again, wanting to torture himself one more time with it. As he was about to lose himself in her voice for the umpteenth time, his brooding was interrupted by the shrill ring of his mobile. Heart lurching, still hoping that it might be Holly on the other end, he swiped without looking at the caller's ID.

'Hello, Mr Thorpe,' a voice on the other end said when he'd identified himself. 'This is Peter Eddington from the news website AllFeed here. Do you have any comment on the story that's about to break that you put pressure on a vulnerable constituent to sleep with you in exchange for political help?'

'Wh-what?' Charlie was instantly alert. 'Where has this come from?'

'I can't reveal my sources, as you well know by now,' Eddington replied. 'Just wanted to see if I could add your version of events to the story before it goes live on the site tonight.'

'No,' Charlie replied. 'No comment at all.'

Hand shaking, he pressed the end-call button on his phone and sat back in his chair, mind reeling. Where the hell had this come from? As if it wasn't bad enough that Holly thought he was an unprincipled shit, now his name was going to be linked to hers and splashed all over the internet. Hands still shaking, he dialled Tom Fielding's number.

'Tom? Sorry, I know it's late. Has anyone from the media been on to you?' Briefly he outlined his conversation with the reporter. Tom's advice was succinct and to the point. 'OK, no, I'll stick to the no-comment line. We'll meet when I get home tomorrow night... No, I haven't spoken to her... No, I don't think she's the one who's spoken to them. I know she's angry with me, but it's not her style. She's more concerned with getting publicity for the CF campaign and this won't help it at all.' He rubbed his free hand over his eyes. 'OK. Goodnight, Tom.'

Charlie was stumped. He and Holly were two freely consenting adults. There was no abuse of trust there at all. They both knew what they were doing, and until it had all gone sour, it had been the best thing in his life. Who the hell would have the credibility and standing to leak this story and be believed?

He thought about phoning Holly, just to see if she could shed any light on where the story might have come from, but hesitated. Perhaps it was better to try to see her in person. A masochistic yearning for details then made him navigate to Twitter to see if the story had been picked up in places other than AllFeed.

Holly, also known as #GreenGoddess had a fair few results; mostly of her decked out with ribbons and waving a placard about at that afternoon's demonstration. Slightly more worryingly, though, when he searched for his own name on the social media platform, a few, less complimentary hashtags were attached. Among the more embarrassing included #WestCountryCad and #WhatACharlie. He felt physically sick when he saw some of the comments, too. If the story was playing out the way Peter Eddington had suggested, he'd get a reputation as a calculating predator before the week was out.

Swiping the iPad's screen angrily, he packed away his things and headed for the flat. Another sleepless night, then another uncomfortable day beckoned before he could regroup with Tom and work out the best approach to this mess. At the moment, he just didn't know which way to jump, although throwing himself off Westminster Bridge seemed a decent prospect right now. Hurrying out of the building and heading for Farringdon on the Tube, he hoped he'd get home without being stopped.

* * *

The next morning, bleary-eyed from insomnia, Charlie virtually sleepwalked to the Tube. He'd finally put the iPad down at about

3 a.m., after reading pretty much every link on social media that might throw some light on when the story about him and Holly had broken. He was still none the wiser about who had leaked it. Swiping wearily to the AllFeed website as the Tube pulled out, there it was in all its glory in the sidebar of shame on the right-hand side of the page.

'She just wanted to help her nephew: what he asked for in return will blow your mind!'

Below it were a couple of blurred photographs of himself and Holly during their picnic on Willowbury Hill. The angle of the photos suggested things had been a lot more intimate in that moment than they actually had been, and Charlie couldn't help groaning when he saw them. An old lady sitting next to him shuffled away in surprise.

It was worse when he clicked the link. Several pictures, obviously snapped with a long lens at Willowfest, showed the two of them in various lovelorn poses. The copy was worse still.

Charlie Thorpe is believed to have seduced health and well-being shop owner and CF campaigner Holly Renton in return for promising her his support over the legislation of new drugs for the chronic condition, cystic fibrosis. Vulnerable Holly's tragic thee-year-old nephew Harry is a sufferer of the condition, which may dramatically shorten his life if he does not gain access to these life-altering medications. After initially pledging his support, Thorpe has since withdrawn from the campaign, according to sources close to Ms Renton, and seeks instead to pursue promotion in other areas, leaving lovelorn Holly and tragic Harry high and dry.

It was nothing more than hearsay and tittle-tattle, but damaging enough. Furiously, Charlie wondered who the hell the source was. Who would be looking to ruin not just his reputation, but Holly's as well? Immediately he discounted anyone who actually cared about them both, with this story painting Holly as a naive damsel in distress and himself as some self-serving predator who put pressure on women to get what he wanted. Neither could be further from the truth, and Holly would be furious if she knew she was being presented like that. A victim she most certainly was not. So, the question was, who had leaked this ridiculous story?

As he was thinking, his phone bleeped with a text. It was from Tom.

Done some digging overnight. Think I know who the source was. Get home as early as you can for crisis management planning tomorrow.

Charlie breathed out. Tom was handling it. All he had to do now was get through today and get home to Willowbury without incident. Suddenly, the day ahead seemed interminably long.

43

It had been a phenomenally shitty day, there was no getting away from it. As Charlie collapsed down into the seat on the train he'd managed to grab just outside Reading, having given up his seat for a heavily pregnant commuter at Paddington, he closed his eyes and tried to blot out the horror of the past few days. Being in London involved far more work than he could have imagined, taking him further away from constituency business than he'd ever wanted to be. Also, since the relentless hashtags on Twitter about his relationship with Holly, and the reasons she'd dumped him, had gone public, he'd had to run the gauntlet of alternate glances of sympathy, amusement and curiosity from his colleagues in the House wherever he went. Or at least, that's how it felt.

Perhaps lack of sleep was making him paranoid. It was true that he hadn't slept properly since his relationship with Holly had imploded so spectacularly, and the memory of her smile, her touch and her presence haunted his every waking moment. He'd failed utterly by choosing the wrong side of the argument; there was no way back. As another wave of despair washed over him, like the rain that was now lashing the windows of the carriage, he closed his eyes in utter defeat. Usually he'd try to keep his eyes open on the commute; it really wouldn't do to be photographed snoring and dribbling and then have those photographs plastered all over social media, but tonight he was past caring. What could be worse than the coverage he'd already had, anyway?

'All tickets from London Paddington and Reading, please!' Just as Charlie was dropping off, Train Manager Lydia's familiar cheery voice lurched him awake.

Fumbling around in his jacket pocket for his season ticket, Charlie felt a rising sense of panic. Surely he hadn't taken it out of his jacket since he'd been in London? A peak ticket from London to the west was well over a hundred quid if it had to be bought there and then, and he'd already forked out a king's ransom for the year's ticket. Groping in his outside pockets, even unzipping his bag to check abortively for it though he knew he always kept it on him, Charlie realised it was no use. With a sinking feeling, it dawned on him; he'd turned out his pockets to find his Westminster pass that morning, and in his state of exhaustion, he must have left his season ticket on the kitchen table of his flat. In fact, he could visualise it now, waiting there for when he returned on Sunday evening, or early Monday morning if he chose to spend another lonely Sunday in Willowbury, in the hope that Holly might have a change of heart and drop in.

'Tickets from London Paddington and Reading?' Lydia had reached his row of seats and was looking expectantly at him.

He immediately knew from the expression that flickered across her face before she composed it into a more neutrally friendly one that she was aware of that awful AllFeed story. His face grew hot as he tried to compose himself. His eyes pricked in frustration, and he cleared his throat.

'Have you got a ticket, my love?' Lydia asked him kindly. She was smiling down at him, her eyes full of world-weary been-there-seen-it-heard-it-all humour, and Charlie had the sudden, inexplicable urge to give in and cry.

Realising the game was up, he decided that honesty was the best policy. 'I'm so sorry,' he said quietly. 'It's confession time. I left my season ticket on the kitchen table before I went to work this morning.' Wearily he reached for his wallet. 'How much do I owe you?'

Lydia's smile broadened. 'Well, I feel like I should be wearing a dog collar tonight! You're the third person who's fessed up to not having the right ticket, or even a ticket at all. Must be getting close to the weekend.' She glanced behind her furtively. 'Look, I know this train was a few minutes late as the previous one was cancelled, which probably meant that you were inconvenienced, especially since you've had to stand since Paddington.' She glanced meaningfully at him. 'I saw you give up your seat for that lovely pregnant lady. Doesn't seem like the kind of thing someone with your apparent reputation would do, really.'

'You've seen that news story, then?'

'Yup.' Lydia smiled. 'Just remember that today's top story is tomorrow's clickbait, regardless of how true it is, or not. Interesting that that so-called source didn't give their name.'

'They very rarely do when they're making stuff up,' Charlie muttered.

'Your Holly doesn't seem the sort to be taken in by anyone, either,' Lydia continued. 'Knows her own mind, from what else I've seen across the media. Wouldn't want to be seen as some helpless girl.'

'She's not my Holly any more, if she ever was, but she definitely wouldn't want to be seen as that,' Charlie agreed. 'But I still don't know who stuck the boot in.'

'Oh, people will do anything to get what they want,' Lydia replied. 'I'm sure office politics are even worse, working where you do. Made any enemies lately?'

'You're asking a politician?' Charlie was surprised to hear his own laughter, albeit rather more brittle than it would usually be. 'I'll have to make a list.'

'But, anyway, what do I know?' Lydia smiled knowingly and looked down at her ticket machine. 'Now, onto this missing ticket. I know you're a regular on this service, and I've seen your season ticket a fair few times, so let's say no more about it. Show me your ticket next time. I'm sure you won't forget it again!'

Charlie swallowed hard and suddenly found he had immense trouble speaking. He looked down at his shoes, frightened to look up at her in case he disgraced himself and the stiff upper lip his father was so fond of failed him. *Dignity at all times, Charlie.* 'Thank you,' he said quietly. 'I appreciate it.'

'No problem,' Lydia replied. Glancing around again, to make sure there was nothing more urgent requiring her attention, she put a hand briefly on Charlie's shoulder. 'You can only do what you can do. Remember that, Charlie Thorpe.'

As she moved down the carriage to check the remaining tickets, Charlie felt his barely-there composure start to crumble. He hadn't realised how close to the edge he was until one person's kindness sent him hurtling over it. As he stared fixedly down at his shoes, hot, heavy tears, the first he'd shed in a long time, dripped warmly onto his clenched hands.

44

By the time he'd got on the connection to Willowbury, Charlie was feeling less distraught and more up to facing the hell of the news story. With Tom on the case, he was sure everything would be sorted out and the facts righted in no time. He was almost feeling optimistic by the time he'd agreed to meet Tom at the constituency office. Taking a bottle of whisky along might be a bit premature, but he had faith it would all turn out all right, once Tom told him who he suspected the source was.

One look at Tom's face as he pushed open the front door to the office was enough to make all hope flee, however. Charlie had never seen the man so angry.

'What the fuck were you thinking?' Tom shouted, before Charlie could open his mouth and say anything. 'Going on national television and publicly denouncing Holly and her case without even a thought for the bad publicity it would generate?'

'What? I didn't...' Charlie was befuddled.

'You might as well just have twirled a moustache and given an evil laugh, the way the media's painting you right now.'

'Ruth Middleton...' Charlie sighed, instantly seeing the reporter's cool stare in his mind's eye. 'She caught me on the hop. And I had no idea Holly was going to be smack in the middle of that demonstration until I got there. Seeing her, I just lost the thread of what I was saying.'

'Oh, so you decided to publicly step away from the campaign that you became the poster boy for after PMQs and not expect any fallout? Not only do you look like a total prat, now, but you look like an indecisive, heartless one, too. And add that to that fucking awful Charlie the Cad story on AllFeed, it's a wonder the selection committee aren't calling for your resignation.' Tom began to pace the threadbare carpet of the office. 'Didn't I tell you enough times that the first rule of politics is never to be doorstepped – talk to the press on your own terms. It seems Holly knows that better than you do.'

At the mention of her name, Charlie's heart lurched. 'Have you spoken to her?'

'No,' Tom replied. 'I thought it was best to keep some distance between her and this office for now, until I've worked out who the hell fed that pile of crap to AllFeed in the first place.'

'You said you had your suspicions?' Charlie said, relieved that the barrage he was facing seemed to be ending.

'I do indeed.' Tom stopped pacing and rummaged in his briefcase, open on the desk.

'Well?' Charlie suddenly felt very stressed and very, very tired. It had been a long week, and it wasn't over yet. He wished he could turn to Holly for comfort, but he'd be the last person she'd want to see.

'If I'm right, this all goes back to Miles Fairbrother.' Tom passed Charlie a piece of what looked like fax paper.

'What's this?' Charlie couldn't make any sense of the information.

'As you know, Miles was more than just put out when Holly bought the freehold to the building where she now runs her shop. He'd been gagging to expand the bakery for years and wanted any excuse to put the boot in once he realised that she'd bought one of the prime locations on the High Street outright, and with her grandfather's money, too.'

'She once told me that Miles and her grandfather had had some kind of falling out.' Charlie furrowed his brow. 'But why would Miles want to get me out of a job, too? He's been sucking up to me since I got into the seat.'

'Look at what I've just given you.' Tom paused, allowing Charlie to look again at the piece of paper in his hand.

Although it was blurred, being a fax transmission, he could just about make out a series of figures.

'These are payments that Miles made to your predecessor Hugo Fitzgerald when he was alive and in office,' Tom said. 'Don't ask me where I got hold of them; I can't tell you or someone in the Town Hall will lose their job. They show that Miles was paying Hugo off to give his blessing for planning permission for the bakery extension, even though that building was ineligible for a hot food licence. And still is.'

'So Miles was greasing Hugo's palm to get the licence approved, using his clout, in return for quite a substantial cut of the projected profits.'

'Exactly. Of course, all that went out the window when Holly came into her inheritance and gazumped Miles in the sale. She probably didn't even know she'd done it. She gets the building, and he ends up out of pocket, having paid off Hugo for nothing.'

'As a result, he's trying to discredit Holly, ruin her reputation and take me down because I'm connected to her and, thankfully unbribeable.' The irony of that statement, given his own career ambitions, was not lost on either of them.

'Exactly. Miles has been keeping tabs on you and Holly, the odd photo here, the odd exchange there. After you two split, it was easy for him to pretend to be a "concerned friend", feed the story about you taking advantage of a local business owner sexually to AllFeed, who, unlike a lot of the more reputable online news sites, don't tend to look too closely at what they publish, and make it look like you're a sleazebag and unfit for office. People already think most of Willowbury is absolutely insane; it wouldn't be so great a leap to paint Holly as a vulnerable, misguided woman.' Tom raised an eyebrow. 'Unless they'd actually met her, of course.'

'That bastard!' Charlie brought his fist down on the desk. 'I'll bloody kill him.'

'Wouldn't look good for your reputation, especially not at the moment,' Tom said. 'You've just publicly distanced yourself from Holly's campaign after supporting her a few weeks ago. It looks like you got the publicity you wanted, and then dumped her to pursue your own career interests, plain and simple. It really doesn't matter what story Miles fed to AllFeed; you've done enough to ruin your own reputation. And if there's one thing the voters round here won't stomach, it's a lack of integrity.'

Charlie walked over to the chair in front of his own desk and slumped in it, utterly defeated. 'You're right,' he said bleakly. 'I screwed it up myself. This thing with Miles is just the icing on the cake. If you'll pardon the pun.' He turned his gaze back to Tom. 'So, what do you suggest I do, Tom? How do we get out of this mess?'

'You have to learn something first,' Tom said.

'What's that?'

'This is an important job you've got, Charlie. Everything you say, everything you do, every time you speak to a constituent, make a statement to the media, speak in the House, it matters. You can't just go freestyling your way through it, especially not when you're dealing with emotive issues like the CF medication one.' Tom sighed. 'Ten years ago, before social media and people getting their news from the Twittersphere, it wouldn't have mattered so much, but now the traditional media outlets are often the last to pick up on a story. It's usually trending on Twitter before it's even a twinkle in a newspaper editor's eye. You're under scrutiny the whole time.'

'I know that, Tom, and I'm sorry,' Charlie muttered. He felt like he was standing in the head teacher's office from his old secondary school in Yorkshire, getting a massive bollocking. Which, in a sense, he figured, he was. Although he was the Member of Parliament and Tom was his agent, he now realised that the titles meant nothing; not when it came to toeing the party line and being seen to do the right thing.

'So, in summary, not only has the media made you look like you were using Holly and her family to boost your own profile, but now you've split up with her and gone against her campaign, you look like a callous, heartless bastard for choosing your career and selling them out. Add that to Miles trying to discredit your tenure here and you could not be in more shit if you'd fallen in the slurry pit of George Barker's dairy farm.'

'Governments make U-turns all the time,' Charlie muttered stubbornly.

'And get called out on it by the press and the voters,' Tom retorted. 'You're not going to just be able to walk away from this.'

'Again, Tom, I know that, and I'm sorry.' Charlie rubbed a hand over his eyes. 'The question is, how do I get myself back out of it?'

Tom slumped back down into the office chair. The man looked exhausted, and Charlie appreciated, not for the first time, just how hard Tom worked behind the scenes to keep the Charlie Thorpe show on the road. The hours of preparation that went into every event obviously took its toll on him, and managing the fallout from each one, too. His majority might be safe now, but that could very swiftly change. Especially in the light of a scandal or perceived poor decision. Constituents might be forgiving of certain things, but, as a more senior Member of Parliament said to him shortly after he'd been appointed, echoing Tom's warning, integrity was all.

'So, what do I do?' Charlie asked again. 'There's got to be a way out of this mess somehow.'

Tom glanced back up at Charlie. 'It depends what you're prepared to lose.'

Charlie's heart went through the floor. On the one hand, he could keep quiet, hope Cora Mellish remembered his sacrifice and aim for promotion. It would be the first rung on a ladder that he'd aspired to for most of his twenties. It would be a challenge to brazen this all out; to move on and forget Holly and the campaign. He'd have to wash his hands of them, and focus on climbing the greasy pole to greater ministerial responsibility, in the hope that, when he got there, he'd be able to wield more influence. On the other hand, there was Holly and her family. And Harry, whose time could be limited if he didn't get access to the life-altering CF drugs. He could throw himself wholeheartedly behind their campaign, go against the warning from Cora and put his job not just at risk, but also perhaps lose it all together. It was a politician's worst nightmare; head versus heart. Passion versus pragmatism.

'Honestly, Tom?' Charlie said, shaking his head. 'I don't know.'

'I can't help you make that decision, Charlie.' Tom spoke gruffly. Charlie knew he was a man unaccustomed to making spontaneous physical contact, so he was jolted when Tom put a hand on his shoulder. 'But I will help you, whichever way you decide to go. Just remember that this is more than just a game. There are people's lives at stake with every decision you and your colleagues make. The question is, how best can you do your part to help them? And that's up to you to decide.'

As Charlie left the office that night, he knew he had a lot of thinking to do, and not a lot of time to do it in. Never more had he ached for Holly.

45

Holly returned to Willowbury feeling more than a little bit confused. How could it be that, while her heart was still break-ing, she felt so elated by the coverage from the demonstration? Although the media attention had, at first, been unsettling, she saw it as shining a much-needed light on a very important issue, and she was pleased that, through the media, she'd been able to reach out to so many people. What Charlie had been unable to accomplish, perhaps she and the other campaigners, through more grass-roots action, could achieve.

As she let herself back into her flat that evening, she allowed herself another quick search of Twitter to see if there were any more developments on the case. Alongside the usual hashtags, and the cringe-inducing #GreenGoddess one, she noticed a couple of links to a story on one of the more sensationalist so-called news websites, AllFeed. With growing incredulity, she read the story, heart thumping faster and faster as she took in the full extent of it.

'What the hell...?' she murmured. She saw the same blurred photographs, obviously pinched from some tourist's Instagram feed, and felt a rising sense of horror and outrage. How dare they say those things about her and Charlie? Damsel in distress, indeed! The thought of selling herself to Charlie in exchange for his political help was sickening and would do absolutely no good for the CF medication campaign.

Re-reading it carefully, to be absolutely sure she wasn't misunderstanding anything, she wondered, finally, who the 'concerned source' had been. Could they even get away with printing something like this uncorroborated? Even in these days of so-called 'Fake News'?

She sat down in her armchair, head spinning, and not just because she hadn't eaten since lunchtime. What should her next move be? A small voice told her to call Charlie; they needed to talk about the full implications of a story like this, for both of them. But what, reasonably, could they do? A denial would just fan the flames, and they'd split up anyway, so it wouldn't bring them back together. But who else could she talk to? Rachel would just tell her to laugh it off, to forget about it; it was a non-news story. But it damaged her credibility, as a woman, a campaigner and a business owner. She *had* to find out who'd fed AllFeed the story and she needed to do something about it. But how could she?

While she was mulling all this over, her phone pinged with a message. Heart thumping, she swiped the screen. She'd deleted Charlie's number from her phone when they'd had their last face-to-face conversation, so for a moment she didn't realise the message was from him, but as she read it, there was no doubt.

I know I'm the last person you want to see right now, but I think we need to talk. Are you at home?

She sighed. He was right, of course, but that didn't make the prospect of it any easier. And after two full on days in London, she really couldn't face seeing him tonight. Should she reply, or just ignore the text? With some messaging apps, it was possible to see if someone had opened a message, but, thankfully, Charlie had sent her an old-fashioned text message so he had no way of knowing if she'd read it or not. That, at least, gave her a few minutes to think about how best to respond.

But what was the point? It wasn't as if they were going to go on record and respond to what was, essentially a Fake News story, fed to a scurrilous news website to discredit them both. Getting together to talk and agonise about that wouldn't make a scrap of difference. And, actually, seeing Charlie would be far too painful.

Before she could think twice about it, and to make sure that he didn't just rock up at her door, she sent him back a swift response.

Not much to say, really. Better to just ignore it and get on with things. Nothing we can do.

As she sent it, she knew she was avoiding another confrontation, but she also knew it was far better for her own mental health to put some distance between herself and Charlie. And it was definitely better for them both not to be seen together.

'Hey, gorgeous,' she called as Arthur came strolling through his cat flap and jumped onto her lap. 'I hope Isabella remembered to feed you before she shut up shop tonight.' Since he didn't seem to be complaining for his dinner, Holly assumed that was the case.

Leaning back in the armchair, she soon found herself becoming drowsy. As she drifted off, she was assailed by dreams of herself as a medieval maiden in a long, flowing yellow dress, and Charlie as some kind of Black Knight, flinging her over the rump of his horse and absconding with her. If the AllFeed news story hadn't been so offensive, the dream would almost have been funny.

* * *

The next morning, it was a relief to open the door to her shop and get back to being the retailer she was by trade. So much of her attention had been distracted by Charlie, and the CF campaign lately, that she was losing sight of the passion that had driven her to open ComIncense in the first place. This place, and her family, were all that mattered. It was about time she focused on them. Harry seemed to be doing fine and she was looking forward to catching up with him one evening this week.

The morning was beautifully quiet and sunny, so Holly busied herself in tidying up a few of the shelves, rearranging the altar candles into a more regular pattern, instead of the slightly random configuration that had grown organically as the range in one corner of the shop had expanded. She smiled sadly as she remembered selling the beeswax ones to the hesitant new Pagan, and Charlie's suggestively raised eyebrow as she'd wrapped them. She'd loved his slightly schoolboy sense of the naughty.

She had a look at the apothecary's jars behind the counter, too, and made a note of which ones needed reordering. The lavender needed a top-up, and, so did the heartsease. She wasn't sure what would ease her heart, though, no matter how busy she kept herself.

As she turned away to her notebook again to add it to the reorder list, she didn't notice someone coming through the front door of the shop. In fact, he made it all the way to the counter before she realised. Glancing up, she blinked in shock, then composed her face into a more welcoming smile.

'Oh hi,' she said quickly. 'You startled me. I was just sorting out some order notes.'

'Sorry,' Tom Fielding smiled tightly but apologetically. 'I wasn't sure I'd find you here today. Didn't know if the demonstration was still going on.'

'No, not until next month now,' Holly replied. 'And I do have a business to run.'

'Of course.' He paused. 'Have you spoken to our mutual friend?'

Holly felt her cheeks start to burn as she shook her head. 'I thought it would be better to put some distance between ourselves and that crappy news story. And, as far as anything else is concerned, there's not really a lot to say now, is there?'

'He really is very sorry, Holly,' Tom said quietly. 'He knows that, in your eyes, and the eyes of pretty much everyone else, he's acted reprehensibly. But you must understand that he had some quite significant pressure put on him from a higher power. He might have been a researcher for most of his career, but it didn't quite prepare him for the machinations of Westminster life as an MP.'

'So, someone put pressure on him. What about his principles, his beliefs? He told me he would help us.'

'I know that, but you must know that things change very quickly in this game. What seems right one day can cause all sorts of problems the next.'

'So that's all me and my family are to him now?' Holly could feel her temper rising, but, realising she'd be lashing out at the wrong person, she tried to quell it. 'Harry's just a problem, is he?'

'Of course not,' Tom replied. 'Charlie's very fond of Harry, and I know that he, well, as far as I can read it, he's a bit more than just fond of you.'

'Well, he's got a funny way of showing it,' Holly replied. 'I suppose he asked you to come here and speak to me, did he? Is he hiding out at home, or has he buggered off back to London?'

'No, he didn't,' Tom said. 'He doesn't know I'm here. And I didn't come here to defend him. I know it's difficult, Holly, but you're both adults and you'll work it out. I'm actually here about the source of that AllFeed story.'

Holly's head snapped up again from her order book. 'Do you know who it was?'

'I'm pretty sure it was Miles Fairbrother.'

Holly sighed. 'Well, I can't say I'm surprised. He's had it in for me since I bought this place.'

'There's a bit more to it than that,' Tom said and, glancing behind him, showed her the piece of paper he'd shown to Charlie the day before.

'I don't understand...'

As Tom explained, Holly's face drained of all colour.

'I had no idea he'd been paying off Hugo. No wonder he's pissed off. And you reckon he wants rid of Charlie because of his association with me. What a toxic bastard.'

'Of course, there's no way to prove it, but this is pretty strong circumstantial evidence,' Tom said. 'My advice to you is to let it lie, though. Issue a denial and the story'll keep running. Confront Miles and he'll just deny it anyway. You've nothing to gain.'

'Is this what it's always going to be like for Charlie?' Holly mused, half to herself. 'Having to watch his step all the time, be careful who he pisses off, careful who he... who he *loves*?'

'I'm afraid it goes with the territory,' Tom said. 'There'll always be someone who wants to either take him down or exploit him politically. He's a good man, though, Holly, even though you find that hard to believe at the moment. And he does still want to find a solution to all this. The problem is, he's learning all the time.' He sighed. 'I think it was one of the more recent Prime Ministers who said that you enter office at your least competent and get booted out when you're the most capable. He's not been in the job that long.'

'I know,' Holly said. 'But I'm just so angry with him. I put my faith in him to support us no matter what, and at the first sign of difficulty he's dropped us.'

'Give him time, Holly.'

'Harry doesn't have time,' Holly said bleakly. 'That's the one thing I just can't afford to do.'

Tom held her gaze for another moment and then shook his head and bade her goodbye. As she watched him leave, she ruminated on all he'd told her. She might have a few more of the puzzle pieces in her possession now, but she still had no idea how to put them together.

46

Charlie, unable to face a lonely weekend in Willowbury with no Holly to lighten his days, got back on the train to London on Friday morning. It was supposed to be his constituency surgery day, but he'd cried off, making his excuses to Helen, his office manager and case worker, that he had a cold. He was pretty sure she didn't believe him, but at that point he didn't care. He just had to get out.

He spent the day hiding out in his office, but when he couldn't face the four walls any longer, and still unable to endure being in the Farringdon flat alone, he headed to the bar. He wasn't a habitual visitor to the bar, needing to keep a clear head in his first few months in the job, and feeling like an interloper at times in this very well-established club. Tonight, however, he didn't want to go back to his poky flat and brood, yet again, on all that he had done, all that he had lost. So he figured he might as well do the brooding in the bar, instead.

Grabbing a double whisky, he seated himself in one corner, where he could observe the comings and goings without being too conspicuous himself. As he was checking AllFeed, once more on his phone, he didn't notice the shadow falling across his table until it was too late.

'Well, you've really fucked this one up, haven't you?' The voice of Cora Mellish, Secretary of State for Health, cut into his thoughts as Charlie put down his phone hurriedly. As Cora thudded down into the chair opposite him, a drink in her hand, he wished he had just buggered off back to the flat.

'Hello, Minister,' Charlie said wearily. 'To what do I owe the pleasure?'

Cora took a long sip of the gin and tonic she'd brought with her and seemed to be letting Charlie stew. Having nothing else to do but drink, he continued to do so. The Scotch was having a warming effect on his body, even if his bones felt perennially cold since all of this had started.

After making him sweat for a moment longer, finally, Cora put down her own drink. 'Indecisiveness is probably the worst trait a politician can have, you know,' she said conversationally. 'And public indecisiveness is even worse.'

'You saw that car crash of an interview with Ruth Middleton, then?'

'Couldn't miss it, really – connected as it is to the very current topic under discussion in the committee. What the hell were you thinking?'

'I don't think I was, actually,' Charlie muttered. 'I suppose that means I've burned my bridges already with you and your department.'

Cora let the silence hang between them, and Charlie felt the sweat trickling down his back. What was it about this place that made him feel as though he was back in school at every turn? Eventually, she spoke.

'Indecisiveness might be a politician's worst trait in the eyes of the public,' she said. 'But passion, and real emotion, can often be a vote winner. Despite making a mess of that interview with that meddling cow Ruth Middleton, your willingness to stand

up for a cause you believe in before that was impressive, particularly so early in your career.'

'I thought you didn't approve of my support for that particular cause,' Charlie said dryly. 'Certainly seemed that way when
I was in your office.'

Cora shrugged. 'I might have been a bit hasty. Initiative is a
good thing.'

Charlie put down his drink and looked her straight in the
eye. 'What am I missing here? You as good as told me to step
away from the CF issue. Why are you saying this now?'

Cora looked a fraction less composed. Obviously playing for
time, she took another sip of her gin and tonic. 'The PM's had a
word,' she said quietly.

'Really?' Charlie's heart leapt. 'About what?'

'Apparently our Prime Minister was impressed with the way
you managed to ask that question, and has asked me to keep an
eye on you.'

Charlie's head started to spin, and it wasn't just the whisky.
'Even after that interview?'

'Charlie,' Cora said, looking him straight in the eye. 'This is
the twenty-first century. What matters is how you connect with
people on a personal level, and how you conduct yourself on
social media. After you asked that question, you, and the CF
issue, were trending on Twitter for an hour. The public has got
hold of the story, and combined with your recent girlfriend's
campaigning, it's got a platform that a lot of other campaigners
would die for.'

'But you told me to leave it alone.' Charlie shook his head in
confusion.

'Things might seem slow-moving and traditionalist around
here, but they move faster than you think.' Cora eyed him spec-
ulatively. 'Perhaps I was a little hasty in warning you off the
issue.'

'How do I know we won't be having a different conversation

in another week's time?' Charlie said. 'I'm not sure I can keep up with the speed of change in this place.'

'Well, you'd better learn,' Cora said firmly, finishing her drink. 'No one wants to get left behind, especially if you're young and ambitious. Think about it.' She stood up and gave him a fleeting, not quite warm smile. 'Have a good weekend, Mr Thorpe.'

'You too, Minister,' Charlie replied.

As she left, he shook his head. More confused than ever, Charlie took his time finishing his own drink, and then decided against having another one. It was about time he headed home, anyway.

The conversation with Cora had thrown him off balance; he was so confused. As he walked through the cooling air back to Farringdon, he felt a restlessness that was at odds with his indecision. He just didn't know which way to jump.

Pulling out his mobile phone, on impulse he searched out a number, and then, heart pounding, waited for it to be answered.

'Hello?' The voice on the end of the phone sounded tired, and a long way away. 'Who is it?'

Charlie took a deep breath. 'It's me, Dad. I need to ask your advice about something.'

There was silence as his father, presumably, digested what Charlie had said.

'Been a long time since you've asked your father for any advice. What makes you ring me now?'

Charlie laughed hollowly. 'I know I've not been the best at keeping in touch since I moved south, but I'm in a bit of a pickle, Dad.'

'That's putting it mildly. That on-the-hop interview was a disaster.' His father was never one to mince his words.

'I know.'

'So, what are you going to do about it?'

'That's what I'm hoping you can tell me.'

There was a heavy sigh on the end of the line. 'When you first told us you were going into politics, can you remember what I said to you?'

'That line about anyone who wants to enter politics probably shouldn't enter politics?' Charlie said quietly.

'Well, not that bit, but the next bit, really.'

'Refresh my memory, Dad.' The scent in the air, soot mixed with low cloud, suggested rain, and Charlie upped his pace a little.

'That sooner or later you'd be faced with a political decision that you'd need to take with your head or your heart. That there would be consequences all round, and that you'd need to see the bigger picture as well as the details. Do you remember?'

Charlie's eyes blurred as he reacted to the sudden gentleness in his father's tone. 'I do,' he murmured.

'You need to decide what's more important, and act accordingly. There are so few conviction politicians left in this game. Are you going to be one of them? Or are you going to play at pragmatics for your career? The rewards for both could be different, but equally great, and really, son, the choice is yours.'

'Thanks, Dad,' Charlie said, rubbing his eyes wearily with his free hand.

'What for?' the old man barked, not unkindly. 'I probably haven't helped much. But I thought it was worth reminding you of the rules of the game. At least as I see them.'

'You've helped more than you know,' Charlie said. 'Bye, Dad.'

'Don't leave it so long between calls next time,' John Thorpe said, by way of parting. 'And come and see your mother soon. She misses you.'

'I will. I miss you both, too.'

Charlie pressed the end-call button and swiftly pocketed his phone before the rain started bucketing down. Turning up his jacket collar, he headed up the road to his flat. As he drew a deep breath to try to steady his thoughts, he was struck, like a bolt from the blue, of how precious every breath Harry Jamieson took was, not just to him, but to his family, who were campaigning so hard on his behalf. And in that moment, when the cool night air filled his lungs, he knew exactly what he needed to do. Checking the train times app on his phone, he looked to what time the earliest train back to Willowbury was in the morning.

47

'Thanks for stepping in at such short notice, Chelsea,' Holly said on Saturday morning as she checked over the things she'd packed into her backpack. She was about to go somewhere a bit unusual for a deep-vision meditation session and was feeling more than a little nervous about it. If she forgot to take anything with her now, she wouldn't just be able to nip back into the shop and get it, so she had to make sure she had enough supplies.

Although, really, since the session was to be held in the outdoors anyway, she actually needed fewer things, she figured. A few bottles of water for after the session, her phone in case anything came up urgently at ComIncense, or with Harry, and a towel for her hair, since the mist that had been descending all morning had finally turned into rain, and that was about it.

'No worries,' Chelsea replied. 'Rather you than me, up there on a day like this.' She peered out of the front window of the shop, where she'd been adjusting the display, and wrinkled her nose. 'I guess I'm what you might call a fair-weather meditator!'

'You don't know what you're missing,' Holly smiled. 'There's something immediate about deep vision in the rain. You should try it sometime.'

'I don't fancy trying to meditate when I'm soaked through to my underwear!' Chelsea shuddered. 'But don't worry, I'll hold the fort here while you and your mad punters do.'

'I'll see you a bit later,' Holly said. 'If anything comes up, call me.'

'I will.'

Holly threw her backpack into the passenger seat of her car and headed towards her destination. She didn't have time to walk there today, and the last time she had been up there the weather had been completely different and she'd had company. Shoving all thoughts of that particular company firmly out of her hopefully soon to be cleared mind, she focused on the techniques she was going to use in this deep-vision session.

In some ways, the rain amplified the thoughts and emotions, so it could be very helpful for pinpointing what might be holding her back. Although meditating in the sunshine was more physically comfortable, there was something about doing it in the rain that left you feeling cleansed.

She had a group of ten coming, including Rachel, who she'd invited along for some moral support, since it was the first time she'd led a session in this very special place. Also, if anyone needed escorting back early, Rachel could do it for her. They were all going back for a warming drink afterwards, anyway.

The sight never failed to awe her as she drove closer, its presence magisterial and powerful even in the mist, as it rose majestically from the green landscape all around. It was a beacon of spirituality and sent a shiver down her spine every time she saw it rising to the sky. She would never tire of living in its shadow. She pushed away the memory of the kisses she and Charlie had shared last time she was there and tried again to focus on the landscape.

As she parked the car, she could see a few people from her group had already arrived. She was pleased to see they'd all worn sensible footwear for the mildly strenuous walk up the hill.

'Morning!' she said cheerily. 'Sorry about the rain, but it'll make the meditation session a little different today.'

'No kidding,' one of the group laughed. 'I don't think I've ever done it in the rain before!'

'It'll be a whole new experience, especially with the mist rolling in around us,' Holly said, determined to put a positive spin on it for those who might still have doubts. She glanced around the group, and, as the last couple of people arrived, did a quick headcount. 'OK. I think we're all here. Are you ready?'

'As we'll ever be,' said Rachel.

'Best foot forward, then,' Holly said, feeling like a Scout leader.

Heading up the group, she drew a deep breath, preparing mentally to lead her first ever deep-vision meditation session on Willowbury Hill. The trouble was, the harder she tried to forget what it felt like to be here with Charlie, the more those memories stubbornly refused to go away.

48

A little time later on Saturday morning, hot off the train from London, the rain lashed down on Charlie's back as he panted upwards towards Willowbury Hill's summit. 'How the fuck does anyone meditate in this bloody weather?' he said to himself as he tracked further up. His heart had both leapt and sunk when Chelsea had, albeit reluctantly, revealed where Holly was heading. His white shirt, untucked and unkempt, was drenched already, but the humidity made him sweat as he put one foot in front of the other. He prided himself on being reasonably fit, so why was it, then, that he was struggling to breathe as he hoofed it up the hill? Why was it that his heart felt constricted and his stomach was turning somersaults?

The mist swirled all around the base of the hill, and it was as if the landscape itself was holding its breath, waiting to see what the outcome of this meeting would be.

Further, further, further up the hill he went, stomach fluttering more and more with nerves as he tried to think about what the hell he was going to say to Holly when he got to the top. *I love you; I was wrong; I'm a twat,* was the simplest way to put it, but how could nine words, any words, possibly sum up everything he'd put her through? From the unwanted media attention to the furore over his ill-advised indecision, he just didn't know where to start. Would *he* listen to *her* if the situation was reversed? Probably not, he conceded.

But he had to try. Had to drag himself up this bloody hillside in the warm, pouring rain and talk to her. If she didn't want to know after this, then fair enough; he was prepared to admit it was over. But if there was just one tiny chance that she would…

A harsh, guttural yell pierced the air as Charlie was about twenty yards from the top of the hill. From his position, he couldn't yet see the group that Holly was leading, but Charlie's heart nearly failed him at the sound. Just when he thought he couldn't feel any more nervous, more yells tore the humid air at the top of the hill apart. Panic gripped him at the sound as he imagined finding Holly in some sort of terrible state. Perhaps, distraught, she'd stumbled in the mist and rain and was now lying injured?

'Holly!' he shouted against the raindrops that were now splattering into his face.

No response. Then another yell.

Picking up speed, he dashed up and around the side of the hill, stumbling up the steps that were hewn into the earth as he neared the top, until he spotted several seated figures, legs crossed, facing outwards, looking over the view of Brent Knoll and Steep Holm, yelling their heads off into the rising wind and rain.

Charlie felt weak with relief, before a feeling of total embarrassment and stupidity took over. Slowing to a rather humiliated shuffle, he dropped his head, sweeping his rain-drenched hair out of his eyes as he did so, and then burying his suddenly shaking hands in his pockets.

'One more time,' Holly's raised voice entreated. 'Let all of that negative energy go; be filled by the positive energies of the hill and the forces that reside here.'

And yet again, guttural yells sounded across the vale.

'And relax.'

Charlie saw Holly's head drop to her chest, the graceful curve of her pale neck revealed as her sodden plait flopped over one equally white shoulder, drenched a deeper, almost blood red by the driving rain. Frozen there, transfixed by the vision of a soaking-wet Holly, it took him a moment to realise that he'd attracted the attention of her group, some of whom were now turning to look at him with either ill-disguised irritation or humour in their eyes.

'Are you here for the deep-vision meditation session?' a woman on the end of the row said, uncrossing her legs and turning towards him. 'You're a bit late – we've just finished.'

Charlie shook his head. 'No. I'm not here for that—' he paused, considering his next words carefully, 'sort of thing. It's your instructor I need to see.'

Holly was still facing away from him, her head bowed to the ground, the raindrops dripping from her plait and running down her back.

'Holly,' Charlie said gently. 'I really need to talk to you.'

Time seemed to stand still as Holly slowly turned her head to look at him. Even from ten yards away, he could see the mixture of emotions flickering in her green eyes. First irritation, then hurt, then, and he was sure he didn't imagine it, hope.

'I'm in the middle of something,' Holly said quietly.

'Um... I thought we'd finished,' the woman next to her said. 'I mean, not that it wasn't, er, therapeutic, but I'm soaked through to my knickers, sitting here. Isn't it time we went back down the hill?'

Holly turned and smiled briefly. 'Absolutely. If you want to head off home, that's fine, but if you're up to dropping back into the shop, there are towels, tea and cake down there.' As the rest of her class staggered to their feet, Holly remained sitting but turned to Rachel. 'Can you sort the drinks and cake out? Or tell Chelsea to do it? I'll be down in a minute.'

'Sure thing,' Rachel said. As she passed Charlie, she looked him straight in the eye. 'Fuck her up again, and I will remove your testicles,' she murmured, smiling sweetly as she did so. Charlie didn't want to know just how literally to take that threat.

Eventually, he and Holly were the only two left on the hill. Holly still hadn't stood up.

'May I join you?' Charlie asked, walking hesitantly over to where she sat, gazing out over the rain-soaked but nonetheless impressive vista.

'Well, you've already scared off my class, so feel free,' Holly said quietly. She looked, uncharacteristically, utterly defeated. Charlie's heart ached.

The pause between them seemed to stretch for an eternity. Not worrying about his suit trousers, that were probably ruined beyond all redemption anyway by the rain and the mud, he plonked himself down next to her, turning to look at the view, to see what she saw. Suddenly, all of the primeval yelling made sense. The rain was easing and the rolling mists were beginning to clear. There was something about that view, even about the wide-open space between himself and the still semi-shrouded land and seascapes beyond, that made him want to yell out too. The sound built up inside him, rising in his chest until he felt he couldn't contain it for a moment longer, and he released it, a long, loud, scream into the warm wind and what was left of the rain.

'Feeling better?' Holly's expression was unreadable, but Charlie was sure he'd seen the slightest of smiles lifting her mouth at the corners.

'Not much,' he admitted. 'But at least I've got rid of some of the frustrations.'

'Lucky you.'

An uncomfortable pause fell like the raindrops between them, made all the more so by a sudden gust of cold wind.

'Look, can we get off this bloody hill and talk?' Charlie made to stand up, but Holly's hand on his knee stopped him.

'No. You've come all the way up here, you might as well say what you have to say right here, right now, in the rain.'

She was drenched from head to foot, but Charlie thought he saw a tear slide out from under her lashes as she raised her eyes to look at him before she scrubbed impatiently at her face.

'OK.' Charlie drew a deep breath. 'You were right. You've been right this whole time, about my job, about the Department of Health, about the drugs campaign... and I'm hoping it's not too late to do something about that to show you how right you were.'

'What can you do? It's over,' Holly replied. 'At least as far as you're concerned. You made that clear when we last spoke, and in that ridiculous interview.'

'Well, not exactly,' Charlie replied. 'One of the good things about being a rookie at this job is that, if I make a mistake, people tend to be a bit more forgiving for a while. Provided it's not too serious, of course.'

'Like involving a duck house or a brothel?'

'Exactly.' Charlie struggled to his feet, sopping-wet trousers flapping in the breeze. 'So, from this moment on, I'm putting myself wholeheartedly behind the campaign to get these drugs on the NHS and to get them to Harry.' He reached out a hand to Holly, who, after a moment's pause, took it and stood up.

'Forgive me if I'm a little sceptical,' she said, 'but you said that to me and Rachel before. Why should we believe you now?'

Charlie took a risk and reached out a hand to brush the sodden hair from Holly's forehead, so he could see her eyes better. 'Because some things are more important than careers. And because you, and your family, are the most important things in the world.' He felt dizzy as he stared into her eyes. 'And one day, if you decide you'll have me, I wouldn't want to think that our children wouldn't be able to benefit from the most up-to-date drugs, should they need them.'

'I don't know, Charlie,' Holly said. 'These are great words, but you're a politician, that's what you do. I'm struggling to see how that translates into anything actually helpful.'

'I guess what I'm trying to say is that I was wrong to back away because of my career. And I hope it's not too late to do something about it. I want to put all of my weight, for what it's worth, behind this campaign. I'll talk to the committee, start making some proper noise in the House, anything it takes to help get this drug reassessed.'

'But without the backing of the Secretary of State, you're shouting in the wilderness,' Holly replied. 'You're just one voice, at the end of the day.'

'Wasn't it you who told me off for saying your plastic bags and litter picks achieved nothing?' Charlie replied, a note of frustration in his voice. 'Isn't it a start?'

'Harry doesn't have time for grand gestures,' Holly dropped her hand from Charlie's. 'If he gets access to this drug now, he could get another twenty-eight years of life. If he waits until he's twelve, it'll be twelve more. Can you see how important this is?'

'What do I have to do to convince you?' Charlie tried to touch her again, but Holly, agonisingly, stepped out of his reach. 'Jesus, Holly, I'll cross the floor if I have to.' Charlie was referring, of course, to the tradition of MPs who disagreed with the government, leaving their political party to sit on the opposition benches and act as independent candidates, which, at times of national crisis, seemed to happen with alarming regularity.

'Then you'd be out of office quicker than a mouse up your trouser leg,' Holly said. 'And absolutely no use to us at all. Politically, at least. You know how Stavenham is about its politicians. They've only voted one way in the past twenty-five years.'

'Then let me help. I know I messed up by backing off; my

father always moaned at me that I thought too much and did too little, but this time I want to act. I want to make things count. Please, Holly, put your faith in me one more time.'

'What do you propose to do?' There was just a flicker of hope in Holly's eyes, now, and Charlie seized on it, quickly.

Charlie smiled. 'What if I told you I was going to begin by tabling an Adjournment Debate on it? That your influence on me, and the media, might just be the thing that swings the drug company to lower the price and come back to the government with a deal?'

'Then I'd say you were probably lying. Again,' Holly snapped. 'Besides, government has been talking for months. What difference can it make?'

'Go with me for a second, please.' Charlie took a deep breath. 'If I can get some time, some real time, on the floor of the House, if I can get this debated, it might just be the step that we need to put those wheels in motion.'

'That sounds very noble and high-minded, Charlie, but am I right in thinking that, by making your first proper speech all about CF drug funding, you'll be trying to secure your future in the Ministry of Health, and that it's got nothing to do with Harry, or me, or anything other than your own bloody self-interest?'

Charlie jerked as if she'd hit him. 'You know how much I'm risking by going out on a limb with this. The Secretary of State's decidedly ambivalent about it. One week she's warning me off, and the next she's telling me I've got the PM's attention. As far as I can see, my career in the ministry will effectively be fucked either way.' He reached out and she finally allowed him to take one of her hands in his. Her hands were freezing cold, and he had to resist the urge to pull her into his arms before they both ended up with hypothermia.

'But it could all be for nothing,' Holly said. 'And then we're back where we started. And Harry...'

'At least we'll know we've tried everything we can to get this through.' Charlie wrapped his other hand over the top of the one of hers he held, shocked by just how cold she felt. 'That's what I'm trying to tell you. There are some things that are more important than politics. That supersede the bloody party line. This is one of them. You are one of them. And so is Harry. I will fight for you both until my last breath if I have to.'

Charlie mentally kicked himself at the irony of his ill-thought-out phrase. But when Holly raised her eyes to his, he saw hope there, and something that very much looked like love.

'Will you trust me now?' he asked quietly.

The pause seemed to stretch to the far edges of the vista that was slowly being revealed again as the mists of Avalon receded and the rain finally stopped. A dull, hazy sun struggled to cut through the higher cloud above and, standing on top of the hill, Charlie held his breath.

'I don't know,' Holly replied. 'But perhaps I'm willing to at least hope.'

'For the moment, that's good enough for me,' Charlie murmured. He ached to kiss her, but he sensed that now was definitely not the right time to risk anything more intimate than he had already. It was a step, that they were talking again. The next one, he hoped tentatively, they'd take together.

The ping of Holly's mobile phone in her backpack broke the tension, and she bent down to get it from the front pocket where she'd safely stowed it. 'Oh no,' she whispered as she read the message.

'What is it?' Charlie was immediately alert. 'Can I help?'

Holly, visibly struggling, turned to him. 'Rachel's had a text from Mum, who was looking after Harry while she helped me with this session. She's going to have to take Harry up to Bristol Royal Children's Hospital again. That chest infection that knocked him out is still sitting on his lungs. The GP's just phoned and they've found staphylococcus aureus, a bacterial infection, in his swab sample. It's likely he's going to need to be in for at least a week this time.' She shook her head. 'This bloody condition!' Putting her phone back quickly, she picked up her backpack. 'Come with me,' she said suddenly. 'Come and see what it's like to sit beside a child with CF during the bad spells.' The challenge was in her eyes, and Charlie knew this was a test as well as an invitation back into her life.

49

Stopping briefly to get a change of clothes, Holly and Charlie sped up the A38 to Bristol at a pace just within the legal limits. Rachel had told them not to rush, that she was settling Harry in and there was nothing they could do except provide moral support, but Holly felt drawn to the hospital, with Charlie by her side, so that he could understand the true implications of what it was like to have a child with CF and an infection. But more than that, she wanted to be there for her sister and nephew, to help chase away the loneliness and isolation that walked hand in hand with cystic fibrosis.

'We've been lucky so far,' Holly explained as Charlie drove, his BMW being more reliable than Holly's older Vauxhall Astra. 'Harry's had one stint in hospital, but the fresh air of Willowbury is great for him, and Rachel's very vigilant. She'll be blaming herself, unfairly, for this current hospital stay, but—'

'Short of keeping Harry in a bubble, though, there's nothing she can do,' Charlie finished Holly's obvious line of thought.

'True,' Holly replied, feeling, despite herself, comforted to have Charlie there by her side. 'Of course, this new generation of drugs could change all that.'

'I know,' Charlie said quietly.

They pulled into the nearest car park and headed swiftly down the hilly street towards the BRHC. It sat off to the side of the Bristol Royal Infirmary and was buzzing with activity, as always. Once through the doors, after a quick stop in the hospital's gift shop, they headed up to the Paediatric Respiratory Ward and navigated their way to Harry and Rachel. After checking in with the desk, Holly turned to Charlie.

'I'll go and see how they are.' She paused, looking up at him, searching his face, as if looking for an answer. 'I think you need to see him, too, but they probably won't let both of us in at once.' Before she could think better of it, she leaned upwards and placed a light kiss on his mouth. She felt him stiffen in surprise, but then return the kiss, very tentatively.

'Thanks for coming with me,' she murmured.

'I wanted to,' Charlie replied. 'Let me know when I can see them.'

Holly, on slightly shaky legs, headed down the hallway to the room where Harry and Rachel were. Because of the high risk of cross-infection, CF patients could not be put together on a general ward, so needed to be kept separate from each other. Looking through the window in the door, she saw Rachel sitting in the high-backed chair beside Harry's bed. The toddler was sitting up on the hospital bed, hooked up to an IV line that Holly presumed contained stronger antibiotics and wearing a nebuliser. Despite this, he looked chirpy, and she could see him smiling under the mask when she opened the door. For such a young child, he never failed to inspire her, handling everything that was thrown at him like it was normal when, in a lot of respects, his life was anything but.

'Hey,' she said gently. 'How are you doing, titch?'

Harry looked up and smiled. 'OK, Aunty Holly,' he said, his voice muffled by the mask.

Holly leaned in and gave him a kiss on the forehead, and

then passed him a fluffy rabbit she'd bought in the gift shop as they'd come in.

'How's he doing?' Holly asked Rachel as she gave her sister a hug.

'Not too badly,' Rachel replied. Holly's heart went out to her at how tired and anxious her sister looked. 'Just a bit fed up, as I am, at being back here for the second time this year. But they're great, as ever.'

'I've got someone with me,' Holly said. 'Are you happy to see him?'

Rachel's eyebrows raised. 'It depends. Were *you* happy to see him?'

Holly smiled briefly. 'To a point. He wants to lend us his full support.'

'Haven't we been here before?' Rachel said wearily. She suddenly looked very, very tired. 'What's changed? The direction of the wind?'

'I know he's been indecisive, but there's something different this time,' as Holly said the words, she realised she believed them. 'I think you should hear what he has to say.'

Rachel smiled. 'OK. But I don't want this one disturbed or upset – he might look better, but he's still fighting infection. Charlie can come and see him, but only for a minute.'

'I'll go and get him,' Holly offered, relieved that Rachel would, at least, listen to what Charlie had to say.

* * *

A couple of minutes later, Charlie poked his head around the door of the room.

'Hey, Harry,' Charlie said as he closed the door behind him, leaving Holly waiting in the corridor outside. 'How are you doing?'

'OK,' Harry replied, beaming. The little boy liked having

visitors, and he'd taken a shine to Charlie over the time he'd known him.

'Hey,' Rachel said. 'Holly said you wanted to speak to me.'

Charlie looked from Harry, who seemed incredibly little, propped up on the brilliant-white sheets of the hospital bed, to his mother, who, though calm, looked tired. This was the reality of a hospital stay with a CF patient, he realised; long hours waiting for medications to take effect, constant monitoring, and in between, trying to fill the time for a young child. No wonder Rachel was tired. He felt his throat constrict as he glanced back at Harry, who, aside from being a little bit pale, seemed in good spirits, possibly to do with the huge pile of sweets on the top of the cupboard next to him. Tearing his gaze back to Rachel, he took a deep breath.

'I want to help properly this time,' Charlie said, keeping his voice low, respectful of the fact that Harry, like all children, had ears on elastic. 'I made a mistake by stepping away from your campaign. This time, I'll do things right.'

Rachel shook her head. 'When Hugo Fitzgerald was the MP, I was frustrated because he wouldn't speak up for us, but at least I knew where we stood. It became a fight from the grass roots, with people who truly understood what it was like to be in our situation.' She paused, and Charlie swallowed hard. Her clarity and grace under pressure was inspiring; he wished he'd had half her composure when he'd been caught on the hop during that ill-fated interview. 'When you stepped up and asked that question at PMQs, I actually dared to hope that finally we'd have some support for getting this new medication funded. For a little while, Holly, me and all of the other families affected hoped things would start to change. But then you stepped back, for whatever reason.' Rachel held up a hand as Charlie opened his mouth to interrupt. 'I don't expect you to explain or justify yourself to me, Charlie. I'm sure you've been through all that with Holly, and she's made you go through it until you're blue in the face as it is. The fact is that it happened, and suddenly we were back on our own again.'

'I'm sorry—' Charlie said, but Rachel cut him off.

'I know you are.' She smiled gently. 'But being sorry doesn't make Harry get better any faster. We need action, and we need it now, Charlie.' She reached over and squeezed Harry's little hand, and he promptly stuck his tongue out under the mask. 'If you truly do mean to help us, then make it count. Otherwise it's all just hot air and wasted breath. And this little one, and all of the other patients out there, they don't have the breath to waste.'

'I will do everything I can,' Charlie replied. 'From here, I'm going straight home and Holly's going to help me work on my opening speech for the Adjournment Debate I'm going to table.'

'That's a good start,' Rachel said. 'I know the big things move slowly in the political world, but time is important here, not just for Harry but for all of the CF patients.'

'You'd be surprised how time seems to operate in Westminster,' Charlie said, a wry note entering his low voice. 'Sometimes it grinds so slowly, nothing ever seems to change, and then you blink and something's been passed. Let's hope the CF medication is one of those things.'

Their attention was drawn quickly to the bed as Harry had a sudden fit of coughing. Rachel sat him up a little bit straighter and tapped him sharply on the back, starting a routine of physio that would help to keep the mucus from settling on his lungs. Charlie was struck, yet again, by the delicate balance Harry had to sustain in order to stay healthy and how easily this could be disrupted. He felt his resolve renewing to do something.

'I promise you that by the time you two come home, I'll have written my speech and be more than ready to give it,' he said firmly. 'And I'm going to speak to the Health and Social Care Committee, find out what's holding up the decision. I will do everything I can, Rachel.'

'I know,' Rachel said, as Harry's coughing subsided. 'I trust you.'

To a politician, that was a great endorsement, and to a man who had grown so attached to this family, it was an indication of much more. He leaned forward and kissed Rachel on the cheek. 'I'm grateful for that.'

As he walked out of the hospital room and rejoined Holly in the corridor, she glanced up from the book she'd been reading on her phone, obviously trying to distract herself from whatever conversation was being held between Charlie and Rachel.

'OK?' she asked softly.

'Yes,' Charlie replied. 'Apart from the fact that I've now got to break the news to someone that they're going to be spending their spare time this weekend helping me to compose a killer speech.'

'Oh yes?' Holly said, a little behind the curve for once. 'Tom's going to love that.'

'Tom's on holiday until tomorrow,' Charlie replied, grinning. 'It was you I was thinking about.'

'I have got a business to run, you know!' Holly said, trying not to give him an inch, but the light in her eyes gave her away. 'You'll have to use the kitchen table at my place if you want my help.'

'Is that an offer?' Charlie asked carefully. 'Does that mean you can actually bear to be in the same room as me again?'

'We'll see how it goes,' Holly said noncommittally, but she did draw closer to Charlie as she stood. 'You've got a lot of ground to make up. And you can't have any distractions.'

'You won't even know I'm there,' Charlie said.

'It's a deal,' Holly replied. She hesitated as though she was going to take his hand as they left the hospital, but held back at the last moment. In a not entirely companionable silence, they headed back to the Trenchard Street car park.

50

'So, the way this works is that I need to apply to the Speaker on Wednesday if I'm going to get a chance to head up an Adjournment Debate over the next week. Effectively, we've got four days to research, time and then put the finishing touches on this speech, should it get picked by the Speaker or in the ballot,' Charlie said as, after collecting up as many of his research materials as he could lay his hands on from his constituency office, he set up a temporary space at Holly's kitchen table on Saturday evening. They'd also collected a takeaway from the Chinese restaurant at the top of Willowbury High Street but decided against a bottle of wine; they needed clear heads. Rachel would be dropping in briefly when she got back from the hospital later, as Vivian Renton was doing a shift at the BRHC, giving her a bit of respite, and a chance to come home and collect more things.

'So, there's still no guarantee it'll be picked?' Holly asked.

'Well, no,' Charlie conceded. 'But thanks to you and the other campaigners giving the campaign a huge media boost, I'd be surprised if it didn't get at least a fleeting moment of the Speaker's attention. He's quite fond of political drama, and he's not been unknown to choose an Adjournment Debate because he knows it'll get decent media coverage.'

'So we'd effectively be using the media for good this time?' Holly said wryly. 'Instead of being plastered all over it for all the wrong reasons. But what about doing it right before recess? Is that a good time?' Holly's brow creased with a frown. 'Doesn't that make all you lot extra demob-happy, just like it used to at school?'

'Well, possibly,' Charlie said. 'But it also means the Health and Social Care Committee can schedule a meeting with the drug companies over the summer, get negotiations going and hopefully have a decision by the first sitting in back in the autumn.'

'I hope you're right,' Holly said. She had to resist the urge, as she was standing next to him where he was seated at her large, round table, to run her hand through his hair and caress the back of his neck. Old habits were hard to break, especially as she still felt such a powerful pull of attraction to him, in spite of all that had happened. 'So, er, what's the best approach to take for this speech?' she coughed nervously.

'Oh, you know, rhetoric, statistics, emotion and cold hard numbers, followed by a punch to the gut to finish,' Charlie said wryly. 'All that stuff we learned about how to write a decent speech for GCSE English isn't that far off the mark, really. I've been putting my old English teacher's advice into practice ever since!'

'I'm sure he or she would be very proud,' Holly replied dryly.

Charlie flipped the screen on his laptop and called up a new document. 'Let's do this.'

Later on, when she looked back at the hours they spent working on the speech, Holly felt it would all have been covered in some cheesy montage scene in a film; Charlie certainly made a decent-looking leading man, and no mistake. She was amazed at his focus, once he got going, and his organisational skills. The political animal under his skin was in full flow, statistics at his fingertips, pithy and passionate turns of phrase interwoven with the clear, unadulterated facts of the case.

He kept muttering parts of what he'd written, testing the cadences, feeling the rhythms of the words to see if they sounded correct, would engage the House as well as being informative. Holly, who was going through the piles of research materials, kept getting distracted by his voice, which, although not in full public-speaking mode, was still low and authoritative, prompting her to listen. She suddenly had a vision of him as a teenager again, when she'd seen him on the platform at the youth conference, gestures slightly more mechanical, self-consciously intended to imitate the open-handed poses of the politicians of the day, voice mostly commanding but with a tremor of nerves that he, thankfully, seemed to have banished in later years.

Back in the moment, when the thirty-something Charlie rolled up his sleeves to expose his wonderful wrists and forearms, she swallowed back a sudden surge of lust. Power, she thought wryly, even that of a backbench MP, was a decent aphrodisiac when that MP was as good a speaker as Charlie was. But now was not the time for thoughts like that.

It amazed her how much material Charlie would need for a ten-minute speech in the debate. Even accounting for interruptions to allow debate to be free-flowing, he'd have to be prepared. As he wove in statistics with real-life examples from Harry's life, and those of other CF patients, the speech started to take shape.

'Tom's just emailed me to let me know he'll be back late tomorrow afternoon, but he wants to see a version of the speech as soon as we've got something to share.' Charlie, back obviously sore after hours of hunching over his laptop, leaned back in the wooden chair and raised his arms above his head. 'I wish you and I were on better terms right now,' he said, half to himself but looking at Holly. 'I'd ask for one of those amazing massages.'

Holly's breath caught in her throat and she laughed nervously to cover up the sudden surge of desire that his words, and his slightly dishevelled appearance, provoked in her. 'Mind on the job, Mr Thorpe. Tom's not going to want to see a subpar version of this speech that's supposed to change everything.'

Charlie looked troubled for a moment, and he stood up from the table. Holly felt frozen to the spot as he moved towards her. She caught the warm scent of his body and the cologne he habitually wore and saw the trace of five-o'clock shadow on his jawline. His eyes, darker away from the lamp at the side of the table where he'd been working, seemed to read into her soul.

'You know we can only do our best, don't you?' he said softly as he approached her. 'All I can do is present the issue to the House as powerfully as I can. It's up to the pharmaceutical company and the Department of Health to come to a decision after that.'

'I know,' Holly replied, her own voice low in the warm light of her living room. 'But you said to me that real change is effected by politicians; perhaps this is an issue where politics and public opinion together really can make a difference; have an influence.'

'I hope so,' Charlie said. 'And I want you to know that I am going to put everything I have into this debate. I will not walk away from this again, Holly.' He drew closer to her and she breathed in his scent, so intoxicating that she could feel a warmth spreading through her, and her own breath shortening. As if he didn't realise what he was doing, he reached out a slightly trembling hand and ran the back of his fingertips down the side of her cheek.

'Charlie...' she murmured, head swimming at his closeness.

'I know,' he replied. 'It's not a good idea. But I just need... I just want...' With the softness of an exhaled breath, he brought his mouth to hers in a kiss that was as sweet and tentative as that first one they'd shared back in London all those years ago.

As if it had a mind of its own, Holly's hand found its way to Charlie's hair, fingers tangling in his dark, wavy locks and pulling his mouth closer, for a deeper, more intense kiss. He tasted of coffee and sweetness, and her senses reeled as she realised just how much she'd missed him in the time they'd been apart.

'We can't,' Holly gasped when they pulled apart. 'We shouldn't...'

'I know,' Charlie whispered, 'but right now, I think we need to.' He slid an arm around her waist and pressed closer to her, until she had her back against the wall of her living room.

Holly could feel his arousal, and she pressed back against him, one thigh wrapping around his as her senses reeled at his closeness.

'I think you're right,' Holly murmured into the kiss. 'I've missed you.'

'You have no idea how much I've missed you, too,' Charlie's voice trembled as he pulled back, just for a moment, to look into Holly's eyes. 'Every minute I haven't been able to call you, to see you, to share my life with you, has been bloody awful.'

Holly pulled him closer to her again, feeling the frantic beating of his heart that matched her own. 'It's late,' she said softly. 'Do you want to stay?'

'No pressure,' Charlie replied. 'We don't have to do... anything. I just need to be close to you.'

Holly's eyes sparkled. 'That's very sweet, Charlie, but I have enough trouble keeping my hands off you as it is!'

Charlie laughed, breaking the palpable tension. 'Well, if you insist, I'm not going to argue.'

Hand in hand, both weak with relief that, for the moment at least, they could acknowledge what still existed between them, they headed off to bed.

51

It was only on Sunday morning that Holly remembered Rachel
had been going to pop over on Saturday night after she'd got
back from the hospital. Grabbing her phone from the bedside
table, she swiped guiltily, wondering if she'd been so caught up
in kissing Charlie, and what had happened after the kisses, that
she hadn't heard her sister knocking at the door.

As it was, Rachel had sent an apologetic text at around ten
o'clock the previous night saying that she'd got home after their
mother had relieved her at the hospital, had a bath and then
crashed out. Holly texted back a quick reply, then turned to
where Charlie was still dozing in the bed next to her.

'Come on, sleepyhead! Some of us have jobs to go to.' She
ran a hand down Charlie's bicep, tangling his fingers in her own
and placing a kiss on his shoulder. Last night had been magical:
exactly what they both needed. She tried not to let the worries
and doubts creep in again as the daylight was creeping through
the gap in the curtains.

Charlie groaned. 'Do we have to move just yet?'

'I do, I'm afraid – the shop won't open itself, and besides, I
only open for a couple of hours on a Sunday. You can have a lie-

in if you want.' Holly gasped as Charlie rolled onto his back and pulled her on top of him. She was left in no doubt as to what he intended to spend his lie-in doing, if she could be convinced to stay in bed with him. 'Later,' she said playfully, kissing him and then breaking free. 'I've been playing hooky from ComIncense enough lately.' She wriggled out of bed and headed for the shower, even though other parts of her were definitely wanting to stay in bed, wrapped around Charlie. 'And you've got a speech to finish, remember?' She looked playfully over her shoulder at him and grinned. 'If you get up now, you can share a shower with me.'

'That's an offer I can't refuse!' Charlie said, jumping out of bed and following in Holly's wake.

* * *

Holly had a busy morning at the shop, and was pleased to note that the continuing warm weather meant more tourist footfall, despite the lack of progress on the motorway junction. Lots of people now seemed to visit by train, so perhaps the road building wouldn't become necessary in the longer term, after all. Charlie popped down from time to time, to try out various excerpts of the speech on her, and she was honest in the feedback she gave him. He was a good speaker but occasionally had the tendency to overdo the mannered hand gestures that a lot of current politicians favoured.

'Just put your left hand in your pocket, or something,' she chided as he repeated the hands open, palms outwards gesture once again. 'You look as though you're going to break into song.'

Charlie swatted her playfully with the notes he'd brought down with him. 'Remember that in the chamber, it's a bit like being onstage in the round – people see you as much as hear you, so I do have to make the body language count as well.'

'That's all well and good, but you're making me dizzy with all the perfect posturing!' She leaned up on tiptoe and kissed him briefly. 'Go and practice in front of the mirror, or something.'

As she came back down to her feet, she suddenly became aware of a presence other than herself and Charlie in the shop, and it was one, instinctively, she didn't like.

'How cosy,' Miles Fairbother's voice cut through their good mood like a knife through lard.

Holly was instinctively on her guard and drew breath to retort, but Charlie, who was still holding her hand, squeezed it gently, as if in warning.

'Hello, Miles,' he said softly. 'What can we do for you?'

'Your office said I could find you here,' Miles said. 'I've been trying to reach you to let you know something. I assume you don't mind if *she* listens in, too?' He gestured to Holly dismissively, who tried not to bristle.

'And what would that be?' Charlie still had hold of Holly's hand, but he stepped a little closer to her protectively at the perceived dismissal.

'As of the next parliamentary session, Fairbrothers will be withdrawing their support for your office and any future election campaigns,' Miles announced, evidently taking great satisfaction in breaking the news. 'I feel that your... associations with certain other *interests* in the constituency are not in line with the values we at Fairbrothers support.'

'And what would those be, Miles?' Charlie's voice was calm, although Holly winced as he squeezed her hand a little more tightly.

'Oh, I'm sure you know,' Miles replied, a deceptively light tone in his voice. 'While you and your, er, friend, might be more progressive in your attitudes to showing yourself canoodling on social media, and playing the politics of emotion rather than economics, I feel that our aims are, at best, incompatible.'

Charlie shook his head. 'You surprise me, Miles. From what I understand, you're not above a bit of behaviour unbecoming to the party yourself, at least if the saga over the premises you're standing in is anything to go by. Don't you think it's about time you called it quits and crawled back to the rock you live under?'

'I beg your pardon?' Miles' eyes began to protrude at Charlie's forthright tone. 'Have you forgotten I was one of the local party's biggest donors? You need me.'

'Really?' Charlie said innocently. 'You see, I rather think that you just told me you were withdrawing support for me and my office. So, actually, if I was to tell you to shove your overpriced gluten-free bread rolls up your arse, there would be very little you could do about it.'

Miles' jaw dropped. 'Well, I think we know where we both stand, then.' He looked from Charlie to Holly. 'Your predecessor was a much better MP, you know. Was far more aligned with tradition, and the importance of it. I'm surprised you can call yourself a party member with the way you've been making decisions since you got in. Mark my words, you'd better enjoy it while you can, because you'll soon lose that cosy majority without me and my like behind you.'

'Frankly, Miles, I'd rather not have you behind me, if you're planning on stabbing me in the back.' Charlie's tone hardened. 'And you couldn't get much more offensive than that non-story you leaked to AllFeed, could you?'

'You can't prove anything,' Miles said, his tone unconcerned. 'That could have come from anyone.'

'True, but it's rather a coincidence that you're withdrawing funding now, having allegedly tried to discredit me personally and politically, isn't it? And all because I wasn't prepared to be in your pocket like Hugo Fitzgerald was.'

'More lies and slander,' Miles retorted, but there was an edge of steel to his voice.

'Maybe not, but I think we all know where we stand.' Charlie's said, staring evenly at Miles. 'And if that's all you have to say,

I suggest you stop harassing Holly in, what I'm sure you don't need me to remind you, is actually *her* shop.'

Miles paused, staring in undisguised anger at Holly and Charlie, for a moment longer, before nodding briskly and exiting the shop.

'Christ,' Charlie muttered.

Holly looked up at him and her heart flipped in concern. His face had drained of all colour, and, still clasped in hers, his hand had begun to shake. 'Are you OK?' she said gently. She moved closer to him, to hold him in her arms. 'I can't quite believe what you just said to that idiot.'

Charlie buried his head in her shoulder and his voice was muffled. 'Just between us, neither can I.' He began to laugh shakily. 'The constituency accountant's going to string me up when she finds out I didn't try to talk Miles back into funding us. He wasn't joking when he said he was basically financing the local party, you know.'

'Then it's about time you found a new generation of donors,' Holly said stoutly. 'I'm sure there are plenty of people out there who'll cough up if you ask them nicely enough.'

'Says the confirmed Green Party voter!' Charlie laughed a little more strongly.

'I think I can lend my support in other ways,' Holly replied. 'Now, get back to the table and finish that speech – you said you'd send a draft to Tom, today, remember, before you see him tomorrow.'

'Absolutely,' Charlie replied but stopped to kiss her. 'Screw Miles,' he said as they parted. 'I've worked out what's most important, and he definitely doesn't come close. Not even with that party donation.'

Holly smiled. Charlie's idealistic streak was something she was beginning to love about him; she just prayed that his inner pragmatist was right on this one, too.

52

A nail-biting few days were to follow. Charlie knew that the Speaker wouldn't be announcing debates until Wednesday, which would give him, at worst, twenty-four hours to put the finishing touches on his opening speech, should his Adjournment Debate be the first to be timetabled, literally for the next day. With ten days left until the summer recess, time was unnervingly short. If he wasn't successful this time around, it would have to wait until September when the House sat again. Charlie wasn't sure he could take a summer of suspense, and all the time he was aware that, for Harry, literally every day without a decision was a ticking time bomb.

Charlie, who'd decided to spend the time until Wednesday in Willowbury, rather than shooting back to London as he usually did on a Sunday night or Monday morning, had, with Holly's tacit blessing, virtually moved into her flat while they waited for a decision on the Adjournment Debate. He had a lot of constituency casework to catch up on, and when he wasn't using Holly's place as a base, he'd been out and about on constituency visits, which managed to take his mind off the agonising wait for Wednesday's news, as had spending his spare time with Holly. He'd even managed to catch up, informally, with Mrs Garner, she of the noisy neighbours, and was relieved to discover that the council had acted swiftly and that the situation had been resolved amicably on all sides. He allowed himself a small glow of satisfaction for that particular case. It wouldn't change the world, but it had made a pretty significant difference to Mrs Garner's life.

Nevertheless, Charlie was still climbing the walls by the time Wednesday afternoon rolled around. The refresh button on his webmail had been pushed so many times, he was surprised he hadn't single-handedly crashed the system. Holly kept popping up from the shop floor when she could to offer a word of encouragement or reassurance, but even she was feeling the strain. Tom, knowing the decision was imminent, had brought some work from the office and was also using Holly's kitchen table as a de-facto hot desk.

Eventually, the much-longed-for email came through, and Charlie's heart, as well as his stomach, fell through the floor. 'Oh Christ,' he breathed.

'What is it?' Tom, lost in a world of paperwork of his own, was, nevertheless, instantly alert.

'You're not going to believe this, but it's scheduled for tomorrow.'

'Christ, indeed,' Tom replied. 'You'd better start looking up trains.'

'Am I going to be ready?' Charlie looked down at the speech and it seemed to swim before his eyes.

'Well, that's the question,' Tom said. He let the pause hang in the air as Charlie and Holly, who'd dashed up between customers, mindful of the time, and that there could be an email any minute, looked expectantly at him.

'And?' Charlie leaned forward eagerly in his seat, like a schoolboy expecting praise.

Tom let the pause linger a little longer while he took a long pull of his coffee. 'You're a lover of rhetoric, that's clear. And your turns of phrase definitely veer to the wrong side of melodramatic from time to time.' Tom took another sip, clearly enjoying watching Charlie squirm. 'However...' he smiled. 'You manage, just, to walk the fine line between the emotional and the informative. You've scattered just the right amount of statistics throughout to counteract the utter frustration and heartbreak of your – and I hesitate, with respect, to use this phrase, Holly, knowing your links to Harry – but your case studies. I think it'll go down very well.'

'If he remembers not to flap his hands around too much,' Holly quipped.

'Ah, the curse of the modern politician,' Tom sighed. 'You wouldn't have seen Douglas Hurd or John Smith using those tactics.'

'Got to play to the crowd,' Charlie said but made a note to tone it down a little, if he could. Although at this stage, he was more preoccupied with remembering the words of the speech; the hand gestures might just have to remain.

'And, of course, you'd better do your best to keep your eye on the benches, too. There's bound to be at least one of your colleagues who'll want to interject on such an emotive issue, and probably quite a few on the other side who'll use it as an excuse to castigate the Department of Health for not acting quickly enough up to now.'

'Which will undoubtedly piss off Cora Mellish and her team,' Charlie reflected ruefully.

'Well, yes, but since she's been playing fast and loose with you over this whole issue, I wouldn't worry too much about that. I suspect the PM has had a quiet word and reminded her about bringing on talent rather than alienating it.'

'You think so?' Charlie's heart leapt for a different reason.

'You know what Westminster's like,' Tom said. 'They're talent-spotting constantly, and you know the PM was impressed when you stood up the first time. This is your chance to really make an impression.'

Charlie shook his head. 'That's what I thought I wanted, Tom, but, to be honest, I just want to do right by Harry and his family, and the rest of the CF patients in the country. As best as I can, anyway.'

'Careful,' Holly quipped, although her voice trembled a little. 'You're beginning to sound like a human being, rather than a politician.'

'Thanks,' Charlie said dryly. He stood up from the kitchen table and wandered over to where Holly was leaning against the door frame of her living room, so she could hear if the shop bell signalled a customer. 'What's wrong?' he asked softly, seeing the conflicted look on her face.

Holly smiled. 'I know you've worked really hard to get to this point, but I'm still so afraid that all of it could be for nothing. We could still be in a stalemate in another year's time.'

Charlie slipped a hand around her waist and drew her a little closer. 'It won't be,' he said softly. He reached out with his other hand and squeezed one of hers. 'I said I'd do everything I can, and I meant it. This is my defining issue now, just as it's been yours since Harry was diagnosed. I will not let you down this time.'

In the ensuing silence, Tom coughed. 'Well, now we know, I'd best get back to Claudia, since it's nearly time to get home, anyway. She sends her regards, Holly, by the way, and hopes she might see you again at another one of "those bloody boring dinners" soon. She quite liked having someone new, and younger to talk to.'

Holly laughed. 'I'm not sure Charlie would share Claudia's enthusiasm to have me back, after the last time.'

'Well, you livened up the evening in a lot of ways,' Tom said. 'Even if a certain local baker doesn't think so!'

'I shouldn't have gone off at Miles,' Holly said. 'Not on Charlie's night, anyway. My sister reckons I should just hex him next time!'

'I thought you didn't go in for that sort of thing,' Charlie replied. 'Because if you did, there are a few people in the House of Commons I'd get you to try it on!'

'I don't,' Holly said firmly. 'Or I'd have hexed Miles years ago. You should only send out what you want to get back, no matter how much someone hurts you or pisses you off.'

'So I can't blame you for the dodgy stomach I had for a week after we split up, then?' Charlie teased.

'Nope,' Holly said. 'Blame that on your liking for ropey London takeaway food!'

As they all laughed, Tom glanced at his watch. 'I'll leave you to it.' He turned to Charlie. 'And don't you forget you need to be back in Westminster tomorrow morning. No staying up all night perfecting your speech... or whatever.'

'OK, Dad!' Charlie teased. 'I promise an early night and an even earlier train is the order of the day.' He turned back to Holly, 'Much as I hate to have to tear myself away from you.'

'Love's young dream,' Tom said wryly. 'But, seriously, don't miss that bloody train tomorrow or all of this hard work will be for nothing.'

'Five thirty a.m., Willowbury station. I'll be there.' The two men shook hands. 'Thanks, Tom,' Charlie said quietly, 'for everything. I know I've put you through a lot in the time I've been in office here, but I certainly wouldn't have got this far without you.'

'Don't thank me until you're out of that chamber tomorrow,' Tom said gruffly, to hide how touched he was. 'And make sure you smash it.'

'I'll give it my best shot,' Charlie replied.

Tom bade goodnight to Holly, repeating his warnings not to stay up too late, and once more they were alone, barring Arthur, who strolled through, demanding his bedtime treats.

'Right,' Holly said. 'You heard your agent. You'd best get back home, since you don't have any spare suits here, and I'm certainly not going to iron you a shirt.'

'Yes, Ma'am!' Lingering at the door to Holly's flat, Charlie kissed her, long and deep.

'Break a leg,' Holly murmured as they broke apart. 'And see you when you come home.'

'I'm counting on it,' Charlie pulled her close in a tight hug before wandering out to her doorstep. 'I do love you, you know.'

'I know.' Watching Charlie leave, Holly was filled with a mixture of hope and heartbreak. This was a massive step for the campaign, and having Charlie back on board was a huge bonus, but as he left, all she could thing about was tiny little Harry, who had come home from hospital yesterday morning, much better but still fighting the disease that wanted to steal his lungs. 'Please God, make this happen,' she was shocked to hear herself saying out loud, to the moon and the waking stars. She'd never been a churchgoer, but just for a moment she wanted to believe that someone out there was watching over Harry, and keeping him safe.

Charlie didn't think he'd ever felt so nervous in the chamber as he did when he took his seat at eleven o'clock the next morning for the debate. He'd thought asking a question at PMQs had been bad, but this, with the renewed weight of expectation on his shoulders from Harry, and by proxy, all of the CF patients who were depending on him to convince the House that the drugs needed re-evaluating, felt almost as though it would crush him. He'd made rookie mistakes on his way to this moment, but now he had a real chance to put his case forward. He just hoped he was up to the job. As he looked around the chamber, he was gratified to see the Opposition MP Stephen Brabham sitting on the other side, and reassured when Stephen gave him a brief smile, mouthing *good luck* across the floor. Charlie grinned nervously back, before mouthing *thanks*. Then, as the Speaker took his place in the front and centre of the chamber, it was time for the off.

* * *

Back in Willowbury, Holly had brought her iPad down to the

shop counter and had set it up to live-stream the debate through Parliament TV. Usually it was a channel only watched by the most hardened politics junkies, but, news that their very own Member of Parliament was introducing an Adjournment Debate on an issue so close to the constituency's hearts had spread through Willowbury and Holly wasn't surprised, half an hour before the debate, when Rachel came barrelling through the door of the shop to tell her that the landlord of The Travellers' Rest had set up a big screen in the bar and was intending on serving drinks at half price for the duration of the debate.

'Can't you shut up shop and come over?' Rachel asked. 'I took Harry back to nursery this morning now the hospital's cleared him, and he's there until one o'clock, so I should be able to catch most of it. Why don't you see if Isabella's free to cover this place?' Harry, once out of hospital, had bounced back enough to spend the morning at nursery and he'd been over-joyed to see his friends again.

'I'll call her,' Holly replied. She had enormous butterflies flapping in her stomach, and wasn't actually sure whether she was emotionally prepared to watch Charlie in action surrounded by loads of other people.

Rachel paused, as if she was debating whether or not to continue.

'What is it, sis?' Holly asked, instantly alert.

'I know this is a big moment,' Rachel said carefully, 'but I also know that it won't just be about this debate. The NHS still has to agree a price with the drug companies, even if Parliament puts pressure on both sides. What if, even after all this, it doesn't work? What if we're still sat here in twelve months' time, and Harry's lost another year's lung function? I just feel... flat.'

Holly came out from behind her counter and put her arms around her sister. 'I know it's just another step on a very long road,' she said softly. 'But this issue has enough support among MPs of all parties now that, if nothing else, the weight of public opinion will put pressure on everyone involved. I don't know what the outcome of today will be, but Charlie and I will be by your side, fighting for Harry.'

Rachel hugged her sister back, and, shaking her head, gave a smile. 'I know. And I appreciate everything you and Charlie have done so far. I'm just so used to having my hopes raised and then dashed.'

'Then you'd better sit next to me at the pub,' Holly replied. 'And we can celebrate together when Charlie smashes it. Or commiserate if he massively cocks it up.'

'Sounds like a deal,' Rachel offered a tentative smile.

* * *

Once Holly had secured Isabella for a shift, she headed over to The Travellers' Rest just in time to grab a drink before the debate started. She felt even more nervous when the camera panned around the chamber, and she caught sight of Charlie, looking paler than usual but carefully composed, sitting close to the Speaker's chair at the front of the hall.

'There's our boy,' Mike Sullivan, jovial landlord of the pub commented, and a cheer went up from the assembled Willow-bury residents who had managed to shut up shop and get away to witness the debate. 'Looks a bit nervy, though.'

'Wouldn't you be?' Holly said as she picked up the coffees she'd ordered for herself and Rachel. 'Apart from that question at PMQs, he's not spoken in the chamber since, and this is a big debate that he's responsible for bringing.'

'Absolutely,' Mike agreed. 'You look a bit peaky yourself,' he murmured. 'Have a couple of giant chocolate cookies on the house.'

'Thanks, Mike,' Holly smiled. 'I'll eat them if I can manage to uncross my fingers!' She surmised that her nerves were telling on her face, too.

Grabbing a seat off to the left of the big screen at one of the bar tables, she passed Rachel's coffee to her, and drummed her fingers nervously on the tabletop.

'Calm down,' Rachel said. 'He's a professional, remember? And you've rehearsed that speech with him so many times that he knows it backwards. Even if he only gets to use half of it in the actual debate, it's enough.'

'I know,' Holly sipped her coffee, willing the bitter liquid to take the edge off her nerves but knowing it would, most likely, do the opposite. 'I just wish I was there with him.' She kept thinking that she should be the one reassuring Rachel, not the other way round, given that Harry was Rachel's son, but she couldn't help it; she was just so nervous, both for Charlie and for Harry.

'Careful, sis,' Rachel's eyes twinkled. 'That almost sounded soppy.'

'Whatever,' Holly muttered, but smiled a little. 'It's only because I don't trust him not to cock it up.'

'Yeah, right.'

The tones familiar to any regular watcher or listener of parliamentary debates broke into their conversation as the Speaker's cry of 'Order, Order!' came over the pub's sound system.

Holly sat up a little straighter in her chair. There was no way of knowing how long this debate would take, but she was determined to pay attention to all of it.

The camera switched focus from the Speaker to a long shot of the Commons Chamber, and Holly again caught sight of Charlie, who had sat up in his place on the green government benches and was looking attentively at the Speaker.

'I give the floor to the Honourable Member for Willowbury and Stavenham.' Holly's hands started to shake, and she felt clammy all over. Would Charlie be up to the job? He'd only been in post a few months, after all. Hugo Fitzgerald had had a long career of this, although Hugo hadn't even made a ripple in the political pond in all his years as the local MP, being content to sit in his very comfortable seat and do virtually nothing to keep it. She watched intently as the camera switched from the long shot of the whole chamber to focusing on Charlie himself, who, looking pale but composed, had risen from his seat.

'Thank you, Mr Speaker,' he began. 'Today we're here to discuss the provision of next generation drugs for the degenerative condition cystic fibrosis on the National Health Service. It gives me no pleasure to be here, leading this debate, in the knowledge that so much time has been wasted already in making arrangements with the pharmaceutical companies to allow this to happen. Mr Speaker, I am the close friend of a constituent whose three-year-old nephew Harry has this debilitating and isolating condition...'

'*Close friend!*' snorted Rachel. 'Well, I suppose he couldn't really say lover, sweetheart, cuddle buddy...'

'Ssh!' Holly chided, taking her eyes off the screen briefly to shoot Rachel a warning glance. 'Tease me later.'

Charlie was holding his notes in one hand, so thankfully his tendency to gesticulate was curtailed by half. As he continued with his speech, Holly felt a frisson of excitement; he was an articulate and confident speaker, and although she felt as though she knew the speech backwards, having heard Charlie practising it for days, there was something electrifying about hearing him actually speak at length in this most venerable of auditoriums. She could almost smell the aromas of wood polish and leather that she remembered so well from when she'd visited the Commons for Prime Minister's Questions.

'He's good,' Rachel said as she, too, seemed glued to the screen.

The custom was for other members of the house to interject, and for the keynote speaker to 'give way', and, sure enough, a few minutes into his speech, Charlie did just that for others to offer their perspectives and opinions. Charlie remained on his feet during these, and Holly found herself examining his expressions closely, watching every blink and frown as colleagues from both sides of the House spoke. Sometimes it was a brief, supportive point that was made, but sometimes they were more involved and intricate, and Holly began to realise that there was a real skill in both remembering your own arguments and responding coherently to others' points on the floor, all under the twin gazes of the television cameras and the Speaker himself, who, Holly thought, seemed like the head teacher of a particularly rowdy school, and who had to keep order among the students.

As another of his colleagues gave way, Charlie continued with his speech. Holly knew he was roughly two thirds of the way through, and she found herself muttering along with him, willing him to the finish line. Just as he was nearing the closing paragraphs, a member from the opposite bench, seated a couple of rows behind Charlie, rose to his feet.

'Will you give way?' the Speaker asked.

Charlie glanced behind him in the direction of the new potential speaker, and for a moment there was a look in indecision on his face. 'I will,' he said, eventually, after a pause.

'I am grateful to my *honourable* colleague for giving way.' The voice, obsequious in tone, rang around the chamber with just a little undertone of sarcasm. 'I would ask, at this point, if the Honourable Member for Willowbury and Stavenham is at all concerned that the adverse publicity generated by his own actions in this case might affect the government's willingness to push forward with negotiations with the drug companies. After all, as a result of adverse media coverage of his *very close association* with one of the key figures in the campaign, it was very nearly derailed. Does he not feel as though his very presence in this debate will do more harm than good?'

There was a collective intake of breath from the Willowbury pub crowd, before a boo went up from the back of the bar.

'Below the belt,' Mike muttered as he topped up a pint of Guinness for a regular.

Charlie took a moment to compose himself. 'I am surprised by the Honourable Member's point, to be honest,' he began. 'Given that the issue we are discussing is of such importance and any adverse news reporting is entirely peripheral. As I was saying...' And he picked back up with the last quarter of his speech.

'Well played,' came a call from the back of the pub.

Holly breathed out again. As Charlie finished his speech and, at last, seated himself back on the green bench, Holly saw a tissue being thrust into her hand. It was only then she realised she was crying.

54

It was around six thirty by the time Charlie stepped off the train at Willowbury. All the way back from London, he'd been reliving the two hours of the debate, which had been the most exhilarating and terrifying two hours of his life. The sheer adrenaline rush of presenting the information, and then thinking on his feet, had kept him buzzing long after he exited the chamber, picked up his paperwork and decided, on impulse, to head back to Willowbury for the night. It would mean an early train back in the morning, but he didn't care; he wasn't sure he'd end up sleeping, anyway, he was so wired. And, in truth, there was only one place he wanted to be tonight, and one person he wanted to see.

As he approached the High Street, the sound of revelry from The Travellers' Rest was drifting on the early-evening air, which was humid, although admittedly fresher than London. Drawing closer, he saw Jack Winter sitting out on one of the picnic benches in the front of the pub, who waved at him and then raised his glass with his other hand.

'Ah,' he said, when Charlie was in speaking distance 'here's the man of the hour. Well done.'

Charlie grinned, still high on adrenaline. 'Thanks. I did my best.'

'Virtually the whole town watched it in the pub,' Jack continued. 'And it seemed only right to carry on the party after you'd finished.'

Charlie glanced inside the open door of the pub and saw that the bar was still pretty packed. 'Is, er, Holly in there?' he asked.

Jack grinned. 'Somewhere.'

Feeling a most unaccustomed flutter of butterflies in his stomach, which, he considered, was ridiculous after leading the Adjournment Debate today, Charlie took a deep breath and headed into the pub.

A cheer went up as he crossed the threshold, and a pint of Carter's Gold was thrust into his hand in moments. He took a sip quickly, as his mouth had gone suddenly dry as he caught sight of Holly standing with Rachel at the bar. She was waiting for another drink, her long red hair distinctive in the crowd of punters that thronged around the pub. Negotiating his way carefully towards her, pint in hand, his knees started to tremble more violently than they had in the chamber. Winning Holly's stamp of approval was even more important now than ever before.

As he drew nearer, she turned in his direction, and, visibly surprised he should appear so swiftly in the pub, having only been on screen a few hours ago, she put her glass back down on the bar.

'Hey,' she said softly as he drew a little closer to her. The crowd parted slightly to let him through, and Charlie noticed quite a few glances in their direction.

'Hey,' he replied. The pause, the long list of things not yet spoken, hung in the air between them. It was as if both were just trying to reconnect to the reality of being in the same room after an emotionally charged day.

'Oh, for heaven's sake!' Rachel, relaxed after a few glasses of wine, butted in between them and gave Charlie a huge hug. 'She's obviously incapable of speech, or starstruck or something, but I'm not. Well done. You did brilliantly.'

'Thank you,' Charlie said, glancing from Holly, who was still quiet, to Rachel. 'That means a lot to me from you, of all people. I hope I've done something that will, actually, help this time.'

'Whatever happens over the next few weeks, you can be sure you've done your best,' Rachel replied. She glanced at her watch. 'I'd better get going, now you've come to walk my sister home – Mum and Dad picked up Harry from nursery so I could stay a bit longer and celebrate, but much as I've enjoyed it, I wouldn't wish Harry's bedtime routine on them.'

'Is it complicated?' Charlie asked, imagining a rigmarole of drugs and inhalers.

Rachel laughed. 'The medications are the least of my worries! It's wrestling him into bed that's the problem – he gets a second wind at about six thirty.'

Charlie joined in the laughter. 'I'll have to come and help out sometime.'

'I think he'd like that.' Rachel turned to Holly, 'I'm just going to pop to the loo. Can you keep an eye on my bag?'

'Sure,' Holly replied as Rachel wandered off.

Turning his attention back to Holly, Charlie's heart flipped again. 'Was it OK?' he asked, feeling like a teenager seeking approval.

Holly shook her head. 'No. It wasn't.'

'Wh-what?' Charlie's stomach turned. He thought he'd done the very best he could; seemingly, that wasn't good enough. Then, as Holly smiled and put her arms around him, his knees went weak.

'It was bloody brilliant,' she whispered. 'I know you couldn't have done any better. And there's no one else I'd rather have speaking for Harry.'

Charlie tightened his embrace and buried his head momentarily in Holly's shoulder, feeling again like he was going to lose the battle against tears. 'Thank you,' he murmured gruffly. Holding Holly in his arms, knowing he had her seal of approval, was worth all the votes in his majority.

They were both distracted a moment later by the ping of the email notification on his phone.

'Excuse me a minute?' he said, releasing Holly. 'I think I have to look at this.'

'Probably the PM offering personal congratulations!' Holly teased. 'And a Cabinet job?'

Charlie shook his head. 'That stuff tends to happen by letter, still, I'm afraid.' He swiped his phone, and, a moment later, he felt his knees going weak again. 'Oh my God...' he murmured. Blinking, he reread the text on the screen.

'What is it?' Holly's face, so recently euphoric, paled. 'Is something wrong?'

'No, not at all,' Charlie said guardedly. He read it again. 'In fact, I don't think it could be better if we tried.'

'Tell me!' Holly grabbed his arm.

Charlie looked up from the screen, and he could feel the schoolboyish, beyond-happy grin that Holly had so often evoked in him spreading across his face.

'Cora Mellish, the Secretary of State for Health and Social Care has just emailed me. As a result of the Adjournment Debate, and the passion of the campaigners on College Green over the past few weeks, the pharmaceutical company has been in contact with a better, more viable counter-offer for the pricing of the CF drugs.' He paused, unsure if the middle of the pub was the best place to announce such news, since it wouldn't be going public for a week or two.

'And?' Holly prompted him. 'Is the offer an acceptable one?'

Charlie exhaled. 'Cora seems to think so. They're going to get around the table next Wednesday and hammer out a contract.'

'Wow...' Holly put a hand to her mouth, and then she turned back to Rachel, who'd come to collect her bag before heading off. 'We did it, sis. The three of us. We did it.' Quickly she filled Rachel in on the details of the text from Cora Mellish.

Rachel, clearly unable to speak, nodded. As she did so, the tears fell. Charlie, who'd had such a tense day himself, felt near to the edge as well. He watched as Holly turned and enveloped her sister in a warm, tearful hug.

'I can't believe it,' Rachel said once Holly had released her. 'This is the best, best news.'

'Cora also says that, subject to contract, it's going to be rushed through over the summer recess, if she can swing it, which means the first tranche of medications should reach patients by September.'

Rachel shook her head. 'That's amazing. It's going to make such a difference, Charlie. I can't think you enough.' She started. 'Can I tell Mum and Dad?'

'Of course, but try not to put it on Twitter until it's officially public.'

'Thank you,' Rachel said. 'I'd better go.'

Charlie smiled a little shakily. 'I'm so glad I could help.' Then, he was nearly knocked sideways as Holly careered into him, wrapping her arms around him again so tightly he gasped for a breath he wasn't sure he could draw without breaking down and crying himself. When she released him, she drew back so she could look into his eyes.

'You once told me that in order to make a difference, you had to have the support and backup of the donors and those with the economic power. That whatever I did was fine, but it didn't really make a difference.' She paused, and he felt as though she was looking into his soul with her unnerving, direct gaze. 'Do you still believe that?'

Charlie brushed a teardrop from Holly's lower lashes. 'We did this together,' he said softly. 'And that's the way I always want to do things.' He glanced around him at the punters in the pub, who, drawn by the drama unfolding in front of them, were all gazing in their direction, holding their drinks. Suddenly, he knew exactly what he wanted to do. There was a small voice telling him that it was too soon, that there was no way Holly would respond in the way he wanted, but a far bigger one was shouting at him to seize the day. If getting to know Holly, Rachel and Harry had taught him anything over the past couple of months, it was that he needed to seize the day: to make each one count.

'*You* once told *me* you could never imagine being a politician's wife,' he said carefully. 'That it would be too much, having to hold your tongue and toe the party line.'

'Yes, I remember saying that,' Holly replied wryly. 'But then I say a lot of things.'

'So, if I asked you, now, in front of all of these good people of Willowbury, to reconsider that opinion, and instead of holding your tongue, to give me your uncensored opinion on all things, do you think you might see your way to becoming a politician's wife after all?'

'Well,' Holly replied, a teasing note in her voice. 'That depends...'

'On what?' Charlie's heart thumped.

'I'm not really that keen on the name tag,' she said. 'So instead of me being a politician's wife, perhaps you could see fit to be a shopkeeper's husband instead. What do you say?'

Charlie laughed in relief. 'I would say yes, yes and all things yes.' He dipped his head and kissed her. 'So long as the wedding ceremony is right here in Willowbury. I wouldn't want to be accused of taking you away from your roots and principles.'

Holly cocked an eyebrow. 'Are you sure? Weddings in Willowbury tend to be a little... alternative.'

'I wouldn't want it any other way,' Charlie said. And the deal was sealed with a long, sweet kiss, and a cheer from the residents of the weirdest and wackiest town in Somerset.

EPILOGUE

MIDSUMMER'S DAY – A YEAR LATER

The day could not have been planned any more perfectly, Holly reflected as she smoothed down the skirt of her ivory lace dress. The flower wreath in her hair, created for her by the florist on the High Street, was, for the moment, sitting nicely in her freshly curled dark red tresses. Eschewing any thoughts of a veil, the only other adornment to the dress was a long string of pearls, which trailed down the deep V of the dress's back and were casually knotted to carry the weight. Despite her mother's slight stiffening of her lip when she'd tried the dress on, one delicate wing of Holly's shoulder tattoo peeked out as usual.

'Are you ready?' Rachel called from the other bedroom. 'We'll have to go in a minute.'

'Yup, just finishing off,' Holly replied, adjusting the stem of one of the early roses that sat in the wreath on top of her head.

Rachel appeared at the door of the bedroom, slightly flushed from having to wrestle the now four-year-old Harry into his shirt and trousers. An increasing bundle of energy as he grew older, in part due to the course of new medication that had made a huge difference to his life, he was turning out to be as wilful as his aunt Holly, and had expressed his opinion loudly on the choice and colour of his clothes.

'You look amazing,' Rachel sighed as she caught full sight of Holly.

'It's incredible what you can find second-hand on Gumtree!' Holly quipped. 'And you look pretty cool, too, Harry.'

Harry, who was still to be convinced over the bright purple trousers and white shirt he was wearing, giggled. 'Mummy says I can put my shorts on after the wedding.'

'Of course you can,' Holly replied. 'As long as you don't forget to give me back my flower bouquet at the end of the ceremony.' Holly hadn't chosen any bridesmaids, so Harry was going to be official holder of flowers while the service was carried out.

At that moment, her phone pinged. Swiping the screen, she smiled. 'Charlie's arrived at the Priory.'

'You'd better get going, then.' Rachel hugged her sister but carefully enough so as not to dislodge the flowers in their hair.

They stepped out onto Willowbury High Street and were greeted by the sight of rows and rows of fabric bunting, which stretched from one shop front to the next, all the way to the Priory. With, Holly noted wryly, Fairbrothers Bakery being the dishonourable exception. Miles had shut up shop, claiming that he was off on holiday for the week. Holly didn't believe in coincidence, but she let it lie. She'd found a far better baker for her wedding cake anyway.

'I'm glad you insisted on sensible wedding shoes,' Rachel said as she took her sister's arm and began to wander up the street. As they passed the shop fronts, waves went up from those who were staying open during the wedding and joining them in the Priory gardens later. Holly's parents were also meeting them at the ruins, and as they reached the Priory, Holly could see her father, looking as pleased as punch to be accompanying his daughter on her wedding day.

'Are you ready?' he asked softly as she reached his side.

'Absolutely,' Holly replied. She took his arm, and Rachel followed behind as they took a stroll towards the ruined nave, where their guests were waiting for them. At the end of the nave stood Charlie, conventional in a morning suit but wearing a substantial buttonhole of spring flowers.

'This may not be legally binding, but it certainly feels special,' Holly murmured to him as she reached the nave. She drew a quick breath as she saw up close just how gorgeous Charlie looked in his morning suit, the purple waistcoat a vibrant splash of colour, and a perfect match for Harry's trousers. They'd had a quieter ceremony in the chapel at Westminster last week, with just their parents in attendance. This blessing in the grounds of the Priory was less formal, but meant just as much to them both, taking place, as it was, in the heart of the town they'd both come to love. As Holly handed her small bouquet of freesias to Harry, who scuttled off back to the chair Rachel had saved for him next to her and his grandmother, Holly once again marvelled at the change in the little boy. His 'off' days were substantially fewer since he'd been on the new medication, and the hope that he could now live a longer, more healthy life filled her with gratitude and joy every time she looked at him.

Mariad O'Flaherty, the reader and cleaner of auras, also doubled as a priestess in her downtime, and, resplendent in the robes of her Pagan office, she drew Holly and Charlie closer together on the bridge of the Priory nave. 'I bring you together in the grounds of this sacred space, sacred not just to Christians but to all faiths and followers, to bless your marriage and sanctify it in the eyes of those you love and care for.' Mariad smiled around at the assembled guests, and then took Holly and Charlie's left hands. Binding them together with a long, silken scarf, she whispered, 'Your turn.'

Charlie looked down at Holly, and she was breathtaken by the love and intensity in his eyes. 'When I first met you, Holly

Renton, you were a sensible, quiet, shy student who jumped at her own shadow and had far too old a head on your shoulders.' He grinned as Holly felt herself shaking her head, but smiling; she allowed him to continue. 'Fifteen years passed between our first and our second meeting, and although it took us both a while to realise we'd met before, once we had, to me it felt as though I'd known you always.' Charlie squeezed the hand that was bound with Holly's. 'And that's how I want us to be, always. I know we might not always agree politically—' he paused again as laughter rippled its way around the assembled guests, 'but I know that we will manage, because if there's one thing you've taught me, it's that love, and passion, will win over everything else in the end.'

A ripple of applause went round the guests, and Holly waited a moment for it to subside.

'Charlie Thorpe,' she began, staring up into his happy, open face. 'When I first met you, you were a geeky, earnest, slightly pompous teenager with ambitions. Fifteen years passed before we met again, and...' she paused mischievously, 'when we did, I still thought you were pompous and ambitious.'

Charlie laughed. 'Fair enough,' he murmured.

'But then I realised that, underneath all of that burning ideology, was a heart that also burned for love, and for justice, and with a genuine desire to be good, and do good. And that I loved you for it. And I will love you, for always.' She paused again, and smiled mischievously. 'And you're great in bed,' she murmured, so that only he could hear.

Mariad, who, thankfully, hadn't heard the last part, or at least if she had, she didn't appear in the least shocked, lifted their hands as they turned to the guests. 'I bless this union, and join with you, their friends and loved ones, to wish them happy, healthy and long lives. Blessed be!'

A cheer went up from the guests as Charlie and Holly turned back to one another and kissed. As their lips met, a shaft of sunlight bathed them warmly, and the ley lines seemed to quiver under their feet.

'Welcome home to Willowbury, Mr Thorpe,' Holly smiled as they parted.

'Thank you, Mrs Thorpe,' Charlie replied. 'I wouldn't want to ever be anywhere else.'

AUTHOR'S NOTE

This novel was, in part, inspired by real-life events. At the time of writing, National Health England is still in stalemate with a major drug company over the provision of next generation drugs for cystic fibrosis patients. Because the issue is far more complicated than can be covered in a work of fiction like this, I have intentionally simplified the processes by which these drugs become available through the NHS, suggesting that Parliament is the body to make these decisions, and I have not covered the complex and involved job of the National Institute for Clinical Excellence and NHS England in real-life decisions of this nature, and the important role of the pharmaceutical companies themselves. I have mentioned, fleetingly, the role of the Health and Social Care Committee, as testimony by various witnesses to this committee on the CF treatment issue was both incredibly moving and very informative. These decisions were made purely for reasons of narrative and drama.

In no way are my creative choices intended to diminish the importance of the issue, or the processes involved in coming to a decision of this nature. Having read the Hansard reports of the debates about CF drug funding, I owe a debt of gratitude to the real-life politicians who have been debating the issue both before and after the public petition to move the discussion on towards a satisfactory resolution. The 'Orkambi and Cystic Fibrosis' debate of 19 March 2018 made fascinating reading, as did the Adjournment Debate of the same name of 4 February 2019, and I am grateful to all of those who took part in that for the insight it gave me into the language and form of a parliamentary debate, and the complexity of the specific issues involved here. I hope that, in doing a small amount to raise awareness of this issue, I can be forgiven for playing a little fast and loose with parliamentary procedure in the name of a good story.

I have also drawn on the real-life campaigning of the families and friends of CF patients and learned a great deal from the accounts of patients and relatives about the day-to-day implications and complications of this condition, as well as the learning processes and rewards. Although I have, again for reasons of narrative and drama, adapted these, the events in the story are based broadly on the truth of this condition and the experiences of the patients and their families. I am so grateful to those who gave up their time, and gave me such an insight. These campaigners continue to fight for the very lives of CF patients in the UK and worldwide.

Fay Keenan, July 2019

ACKNOWLEDGMENTS

There are so many people, as always, to thank for their invaluable help with this book. Firstly, huge thanks, as ever, to the professionals who believe in me and my stories. Sara Keane, agent extraordinaire, for help, support and an incredible eye for detail. In addition, Sarah Ritherdon, my brilliant editor, whose guiding hand curbs my more florid turns of phrase and so much more, and all the team at the brilliant Boldwood Publishing for allowing me to bring this story to readers.

To Claire Wilson I give heartfelt thanks for being such a knowledgeable CF adviser and supermum. I'm in awe, constantly, of what you do and how you do it, the fights you fight to give Rufus the best chances for a long life. I'm still crossing my fingers for you and the other CF families, that things will change. I couldn't have written a lot of this book without you and your help – thanks so much for fact checking the draft and answering a lot of questions.

I made quite a few jokes about having politicians in the chair for this novel, but in all seriousness, I owe huge thanks to Liam Fox, John Penrose and James Heappey, all Members of Parliament for the West Country, who were so generous with their time and candid in their answers to my wide ranging and slightly odd questions. Your insights into the pleasure and pain of your job, and your openness in talking about them have been so incredibly useful – thank you so much. Additional thanks to James for being such a brilliant and informative tour guide for my day at Westminster. In a similar vein, huge thanks to Ione Douglas, Marc Aplin, Zainab Hussain and Melissa French for facilitating these meetings, and extra thanks to Melissa for talking me through the role of an MP's caseworker, being a mine of useful information and showing me the office setup of a constituency MP. Final thanks on the political side to Sarah Axton, who again gave such a good insight into the role of the constituency office in an MP's life and work.

As ever, I have a great network of people who support me during the writing of my novels, and friends and family have been patient, tolerant and brilliant listeners throughout. I genuinely couldn't do all this without you, and I'm so glad to have each and every one of you in my life. Thank you for reading, listening, providing wine and coffee and getting me away from the desk from time to time.

Finally, thanks to you, the readers, for embarking on this new adventure with me.

MORE FROM FAY KEENAN

We hope you enjoyed reading *A Place To Call Home*. If you did, please leave a review.

If you'd like to gift a copy, this book is also available as an ebook, digital audio download and audiobook CD.

Sign up to Fay Keenan's mailing list for news, competitions and updates on future books.

http://bit.ly/FayKeenanNewsletter

Snowflakes Over Bay Tree Terrace, another heartwarming story from Fay Keenan, is available to order now.

ABOUT THE AUTHOR

Fay Keenan is the author of the bestselling *Little Somerby* series of novels. She has led writing workshops with Bristol University and has been a visiting speaker in schools. She is a full-time teacher and lives in Somerset.

Visit Fay's website: https://faykeenan.com/

Follow Fay on social media:

facebook.com/faykeenanauthor

twitter.com/faykeenan

instagram.com/faykeenan

bookbub.com/authors/fay-keenan

ABOUT BOLDWOOD BOOKS

Boldwood Books is a fiction publishing company seeking out the best stories from around the world.

Find out more at www.boldwoodbooks.com

Sign up to the Book and Tonic newsletter for news, offers and competitions from Boldwood Books!

http://www.bit.ly/bookandtonic

We'd love to hear from you, follow us on social media:

 facebook.com/BookandTonic

twitter.com/BoldwoodBooks

instagram.com/BookandTonic